DUDLEY PUBLIC LIBRARIES

The loan of this book may be renewed if not required by other readers, by contacting the library from which it was borrowed.

X ∅

1 1 JUN 2019

1 2 JUN 2019

D0532464

000003009051

Also by Nicole Helm

Wyoming Cowboy Marine
Wyoming Cowboy Sniper
Wyoming Cowboy Justice
Wyoming Cowboy Protection
Wyoming Christmas Ransom
Stone Cold Texas Ranger
Stone Cold Undercover Agent
Stone Cold Christmas Ranger
All I Have
All I Am

Also by Janice Kay Johnson

Hide the Child
Trusting the Sheriff
From This Day On
One Frosty Night
More Than Neighbors
Because of a Girl
A Mother's Claim

Discover more at millsandboon.co.uk

WYOMING COWBOY RANGER

NICOLE HELM

WITHIN RANGE

JANICE KAY JOHNSON

This book is produced from independently certified FSC™ paper to ensure responsible forest management.

For more information visit: www.harpercollins.co.uk/green

Printed and bound in Spain
by CPI, Barcelona

MILLS & BOON

All rights reserved including the right of reproduction in whole or in part in any form. This edition is published by arrangement with Harlequin Books S.A.

This is a work of fiction. Names, characters, places, locations and incidents are purely fictional and bear no relationship to any real life individuals, living or dead, or to any actual places, business establishments, locations, events or incidents. Any resemblance is entirely coincidental.

This book is sold subject to the condition that it shall not, by way of trade or otherwise, be lent, resold, hired out or otherwise circulated without the prior consent of the publisher in any form of binding or cover other than that in which it is published and without a similar condition including this condition being imposed on the subsequent purchaser.

® and ™ are trademarks owned and used by the trademark owner and/ or its licensee. Trademarks marked with ® are registered with the United Kingdom Patent Office and/or the Office for Harmonisation in the Internal Market and in other countries.

First Published in Great Britain 2019
by Mills & Boon, an imprint of HarperCollins*Publishers*
1 London Bridge Street, London, SE1 9GF

Wyoming Cowboy Ranger © 2019 Nicole Helm
Within Range © 2019 Janice Kay Johnson

ISBN: 978-0-263-27421-9

0619

MIX
Paper from
responsible sources
FSC® C007454

DUDLEY LIBRARIES	
000003009051	
Askews & Holts	13-May-2019
AF ROM	£5.99
2DU	

WYOMING COWBOY RANGER

NICOLE HELM

For anyone who found the courage to go home again, and those who had the bravery to stay.

Chapter One

Jen Delaney loved Bent, Wyoming, the town she'd been born in, grown up in. She was a respected member of the community, in part because she ran the only store that sold groceries and other essentials within a twenty-mile radius of town.

From her position crouched on the linoleum while she stocked shelves, she looked around the small town store she'd taken over at the ripe age of eighteen. For the past ten years it had been her baby with its narrow aisles and hodgepodge of necessities.

She'd always known she'd spend the entirety of her life happily ensconced in Bent and her store, no matter what happened around her.

The reappearance of Ty Carson didn't change that knowledge so much as make it...annoying. No, annoying would have been just his being in town again. The fact their families had somehow intermingled in the last year was...a catastrophe.

Her sister, Laurel, marrying Ty's cousin Grady had been a shock, very close to a betrayal, though it was hard to hold it against Laurel when Grady was so head over heels for her it was comical. They both glowed with love and happiness and impending parenthood.

Jen tried not to hate them for it.

She could forgive Cam, her oldest brother, for his serious relationship with Hilly. Hilly was biologically a Carson, but she'd only just found that out. Besides, Hilly wasn't like other Carsons. She was so sweet and earnest.

But Dylan and Vanessa… Her business-minded, sophisticated older brother *impregnating* and marrying snarky bad girl Vanessa Carson… *That* was a nightmare.

And none of it was fair. Jen was now, out of nowhere, surrounded by Carsons and Delaneys intermingling—which went against everything Bent had ever stood for. Carsons and Delaneys hated each other. They didn't fall in love and get married and have *babies*.

And still, she could have handled all that in a certain amount of stride if it weren't for *Ty* Carson. Everywhere she turned he seemed to be right there, his stoic gaze always locked on *her*, reminding her of a past she'd spent a lot of time trying to bury and forget.

When she'd been seventeen and the stupidest girl alive, she would have done anything for Ty Carson. Risked the Delaney-Carson curse that, even with all these Carson-Delaney marriages, Bent still had their heart set on. She would have risked her father's wrath over daring to connect herself with a *Carson*. She would have given up anything and everything for Ty.

Instead he'd made promises to love her forever, then disappeared to join the army—which she'd found out only a good month after the fact. He hadn't just broken her heart—he'd crushed it to bits.

But Ty was a blip of her past she'd been able to forget about, mostly, for the past ten years. She'd accepted his choices and moved on with her life. For a decade she had grown into the adult who didn't care at all about Ty Carson.

Then Ty had come home for good, and all she'd convinced herself of faded away.

She was half convinced he'd returned simply to make her miserable.

"You look angry. Must be thinking about me."

Her head whipped up, the jolt of surprise having nothing on the white-hot flash of fury. "I never think about you, Tyler." She definitely wasn't about to admit she *had* been.

His cocksure grin faded somewhat. He hated his full first name with a passion she'd certainly never understood, but it was one of the few tools in her arsenal she had to get under his unflappable demeanor.

He wasn't the only person who made her want to lash out, but considering what he'd done to her, she didn't make an effort to curb that impulse like she did with everyone else.

She slowly rose from where she'd been crouched, dusting her hands off by slapping them together. "Don't you have anything better to do than stalk me?" she asked haughtily, sailing past him in the narrow aisle with as much grace as she could muster.

"Don't flatter yourself, babe."

Babe. Oh, she'd like to knock his teeth out. Instead she scooted behind the checkout counter and smiled sweetly at him. "Then might I kindly suggest you make your purchases."

"You really think I'd be talking to you if I didn't have to be? I've got ample time to corner you if I wanted to at a family gathering with all the recent Carson-Delaney insanity going around."

She narrowed her eyes at him. He'd always been tall, rangy, dangerous. Age only enhanced all of those things. It was hardly fair he looked even better now than he had then. Certainly unfair he was talking to her as if *she'd* been the one to disappear in the middle of the night a decade ago.

"So what is it you want?" she demanded, but the fact he had a point had fear sneaking past her Ty-defenses. "There's not more trouble, is there?" Bent had been a beacon for it lately.

Laurel and Dylan and even Vanessa dang Carson might be going around town yapping they didn't believe in curses or love solved curses or *whatever*, but trouble after trouble didn't lie. Jen was convinced there had to be *something* to the old curse that said a Carson and Delaney falling in love only spelled trouble.

"No trouble," Ty said casually. "Just a concern. We'll call it a gut feeling."

Develop those off army rangering, did you? She bit her tongue so the words wouldn't escape and reveal how many scraps of information she'd collected about him over the years.

"How can *I* help?" *Mr. Army Ranger should take care of his gut feelings himself, shouldn't he?*

"I just need you to give me a heads-up if you get any new people in the store. You can even send the info through Hilly or Addie, if you'd rather."

Jen raised her chin. It'd be a cold day in hell before she gave this heartless, careless jerk any clue she still had feelings for him. "I don't need to go through anyone, but surely you don't need to know every single stranger I get in here."

"And just how many strangers do you typically get in here?" Ty asked drily.

"Enough."

He didn't respond right away, though she could tell by the tiniest firming of his mouth that he was irritated with her. It nearly made her smile. Ty was not an easy man to irritate—at least not visibly.

"This isn't about us," he said in low, heavy tones.

Any twitch of a smile died. *Us.* They did not acknowledge *us*, and hadn't since his return. There'd been no mention that they'd ever sworn their love for each other. They'd been stupid teenagers, yes, but she'd so believed those words.

"We've had enough trouble lately," Ty said, and she hated that she could see the stiffness in his posture. Anyone else wouldn't have noticed the change, but she knew him too well even all these years later to miss that slight tightening in the way he held himself. "If there's going to be more, I want to head it off at the pass. You run the most visited place in Bent. All I'm asking is for you to—"

"Yes, I understand what you're asking," she replied primly. "Consider it done. Now, feel free to leave." Because she hated him here. Hated breathing the same air as him. Hated looking into those blue eyes she knew too well, because his build could change, the skin around his eyes could crinkle with the years, but the sharp blue of tropical ocean would always be the exact same.

And it would always hurt, no matter how much she tried to exorcise that pain.

He rapped his knuckles against her counter lightly, his lips curved into something like a wry smile. "See you around, Jen."

Not if I can help it.

TY COULDN'T EXPLAIN the feeling that needled along his spine. It had nothing to do with the heavy weight that settled in his stomach. The needling was his gut feeling, honed as an army ranger, that told him the strange, threatening letters he'd been receiving weren't a prank or a joke.

The hard ball of weight was all Jen. Regrets. Guilt. Things he'd never, ever expected to feel, but adulthood had changed him. The army and army rangers had changed him. All the regrets he swore to himself at eighteen to never, ever entertain swamped him every time he saw her.

He tried not to see her, but his family was making it even harder than this small town.

All that was emotional crap he could at least pretend to ignore or will away. Which was exactly what he could not do with the latest letter that had been mixed in with the other mail to Rightful Claim, the bar his cousin owned and where Ty worked.

Vague. Ominous. Unsigned. And addressed to him. He had his share of enemies in Bent. Being a Carson in this town lent itself toward Delaney enemies everywhere he went. But though he'd love to pin it on a Delaney or a crony of theirs, it wasn't.

This was something outside, which meant it likely connected to his time in the army. Yeah, he'd made a few enemies there, too. He wasn't a guy who went looking for trouble. In fact, he could get along with just about anyone.

Until he couldn't.

He blew out a breath as he crossed Main. Away from the prim and tidy Delaney side of the street, to the right side. The rough-and-tumble Carson side with Rightful

Claim at the end—with its bright neon signs and assurance that nothing in this town would ever be truly civilized like the Delaneys over there wanted.

Except the lines weren't so clear anymore, were they?

Dylan Delaney was standing in the garage opening to Carson Cars & Bikes. Vanessa and her swell of a baby bump stood next to him, grinning happily up at the man she used to hate.

What was *wrong* with his cousins? He could give a pass to his brother. Noah's wife was barely a Delaney. Oh, somewhere along the line, but Addie hadn't grown up here. Dylan and Laurel? Born and bred rule-abiding proper Delaney citizens, and somehow Vanessa and Grady were head over heels in dumb.

Ty should know, shouldn't he? He'd been there first. He'd just had the good sense to get the hell out of that mess while he could.

But that only conjured images of Jen, who hadn't had the decency to change in his near decade away. Once upon a time he'd been stupid enough to count the freckles on her nose and commit that number to memory.

It wasn't the first time he wished he could medically remove the part of his brain still so in tune to that long past time, and it probably wouldn't be the last.

He didn't nod or greet Dylan as he passed and felt only moderately guilty for being rude. Until Vanessa's voice cut through the air.

"Hey, jerkoff."

He heaved out a sigh and slowly turned to face her. Her baby bump was so incongruous to the sharp rest of her. "Yes, Mrs. Delaney," he replied.

She didn't even flinch, just slid her arm around Dylan's waist. As though a Carson and a Delaney—

opposites in every possible way—could be the kind of lifetime partners real marriages were made out of.

If he could erase four years of his adolescent life, it would have been funny. He would have had a heck of a time making fun of all of the fallen Carsons. But since he'd given all *that* up once upon a time, and no one had any clue, all this wedded bliss and the popping out of babies was hard to swallow.

"You coming to the baby shower?" Vanessa demanded. Marriage and pregnancy hadn't softened her any. At least there was that.

"Do I look like the kind of man who goes to baby showers?"

"Oh, don't be a wuss. It's coed."

"It's co-no."

"Noah's coming."

Hell.

"You're way more of a baby shower guy than Noah."

"I take offense to that."

She grinned. "Good. I'll count you down for a yes."

"I don't think—"

"Give him a break, Van," Dylan said, his arm resting across her shoulders, as if just a few months ago they hadn't hated each other's guts. "It's only because Jen's going to be there."

Ty stiffened, fixing Dylan with an icy look. "What's Jen got to do with anything?"

Vanessa's smile went sly, but she nodded agreeably to her husband's words. "It's no secret you two *hate* each other." She enunciated the word *hate* as if it didn't mean what it ought.

But it darn well had to. "I can't stand the whole lot of you, but I've suffered through a few weddings now—a lot better than the two of you did on that first one," he replied, nodding toward Vanessa's expanding stomach.

Vanessa rubbed her belly. "That was fate."

"That was alcohol. Now, I have things to do."

"One o'clock tomorrow. Don't be late."

He grunted. He could disappear for the night, easily enough. Even his brother wouldn't be able to find him. But Noah would be disappointed if he baled. Worse, Noah's wife, Addie, would be disappointed in him. She'd give him that wounded deer look.

Damn Delaney females.

Ty stalked down the street, edgy and snarling and with nothing to take it out on. He pushed into Rightful Claim knowing he had to rein in his temper lest Grady poke at it. Though Grady owned Rightful Claim, Ty lived above it and worked most nights as a bartender.

He'd been toying around with the idea of convincing Grady to let him buy in as partner. He just wasn't 100 percent sure he wanted to be home for good. He was done with the army rangers, that much was for sure, but that didn't mean he was ready to water the roots that tied him to Bent.

Didn't mean he wasn't. The problem was he wasn't sure. Until he was, he was going to focus on taking it one day at a time.

Grady looked up from his place behind the bar where he was filling the cash register to get it ready for the three o'clock opening. "You got a letter in the mail," Grady offered lightly, nodding toward a pile of envelopes and glossy postcards. "No postage. Odd."

Ty shrugged and snatched up the letter with his name on it. "Women never leave you secret admirer notes, Grady?"

"No, women used to leave me themselves," Grady said with a sharp grin.

"Used to," Ty replied with a snort. "Old married man."

"Ain't half-bad with the right marriage, in my experience."

"Sage advice from the married-for-less-than-a-year. You come talk to me when you've got a few decades under your belt."

"Won't change anything," Grady replied with a certainty that didn't make any sense to Ty. How could anyone possibly be sure? Especially Grady? His mother had been married more times than Ty could count. At least Ty's dad had had the good sense to stop after Mom had died. Focused his making people miserable on his kids instead of on a new woman.

"You okay?" Grady asked casually enough.

"Why wouldn't I be okay?"

"You seem…"

Ty looked up at his cousin and raised an eyebrow.

"Edgy," Grady finished, heeding none of Ty's nonverbal warnings.

"I'm always edgy," Ty said, trying to flash the kind of grin he always flashed. It fell flat, and he knew it.

"No. You're always a little sharp, a little hard, but you're not usually *edgy*."

Ty shrugged. "Just waiting for the curse to hit us trifold. Or is it quadruple-fold? Can't keep up with you all."

"If you believe in town curses, it's out-of-your-mind-fold." Grady still stood behind the cash register even though he'd finished his work. "If you've got trouble, you only need to share it, cousin. Mine, cow or woman?"

Ty wanted to smile at the old code they'd developed as kids. But the problem was he didn't know *what* kind of trouble he'd brought home. Whatever trouble it was, though, it was his problem. They'd had enough around here lately, and with Van and Laurel pregnant, Ty wasn't going to make a deal about things.

He was going to handle it. He always handled it.

"Be down for opening," Ty grumbled, dreading the Saturday night crowd. He moved through the bar to the back room, not looking down at the letter clutched in his fist. He walked up the stairs, forcing himself not to break into a jog. When he stepped into his apartment, he ripped open the envelope, trying not to focus on the lack of postage.

He pulled out a small, white piece of paper, eyes hurrying over the neatly printed words.

It must be nice to be home with the people you love—family, sure, but first loves most of all.

It won't be so nice to lose. One or the other.

Ty crumpled the note as his hand curled into a fist. He reared his arm back, ready to hurl it into the trash, but he stopped himself.

He smoothed the note out on the counter and studied it. Whoever was threatening him anonymously would have to be stopped.

Which meant he had to figure out who wanted to hurt him and was close enough to drop an unstamped letter in his mailbox.

The people you love.

Not on his watch.

JEN DELANEY WAS as pretty as he'd been told. It gave him a little thrill. As did watching her while she hadn't a clue anyone was watching. She stocked shelves, waited on the occasional customer, all while he watched from the viewfinder of his camera.

He'd had to take a break when Ty Carson had sauntered up, but that had given him time to leave the note.

Ty Carson.

Feeling the black anger bubble in his gut, he lowered the camera. He took deep calming breaths, and counted backward from ten just like Dr. Michaels always told him to.

He found his calm. He found his purpose. He slid into the car he'd parked in the little church parking lot. He exchanged his camera for his binoculars.

He could just barely make Jen out through the storefront of Delaney General. She was the perfect target. In every way.

And when he targeted her, he'd make Ty fear. He'd make Ty hurt. He'd ruin his life, step by step.

Just like Ty had ruined his.

On one last breath, he smiled at himself in the rearview mirror. Calm and happy, because he had his plan in place.

Step one: charm Jen Delaney.

It shouldn't be hard. He knew everything about her. Thanks to Ty.

Chapter Two

Saturday evenings at Delaney General were always fairly busy. During the week Jen's crowd was minimal and usually the browsing kind. Weekends were more frantic—trips to grab what had been forgotten over the week. A twelve-pack of beer, sauce for spaghetti already on the stove and, in the case of one nervous young gentleman, a box of condoms.

She'd made one joke about telling his mother. He'd scurried away, beet red. There was *some* joy in living in a small town. Jim Bufford hefted a twenty-four-pack of her cheapest beer onto the checkout counter and grinned at her, flashing his missing bottom tooth. "Care to drink dinner with me, darling?"

"Hmm," she replied, pulling the case over the scanner. Jim had been making this particular offer since she'd turned twenty. Since he made it to just about every female who'd ever worked in Delaney General, she didn't take it personally. "Some other night, Jim. Got my nose to the grindstone here."

He handed over a wad of wrinkled bills and tutted while she made change. "Young pretty thing shouldn't work so hard."

"And a nice man like you shouldn't drink his dinner." She handed him his change and he hefted the case off the counter.

"Yeah, yeah," he grumbled, offering a half-hearted goodbye as he pushed open the door and stepped out. Just a few seconds later the bell on the door tinkled again and someone stepped inside.

She didn't recognize this customer. He wore his cowboy hat low, obscuring most of his face. Still, she could usually recognize her regulars by size, clothes, posture and so on. This was a stranger.

She remembered Ty's words from earlier and an icy dread skittered up her spine, but she smiled. "Good evening."

"Evening," the man returned, a pleasant smile of his own. She couldn't see his eyes, but his smile wasn't off-putting. He was wearing what appeared to be hiking gear and had a fancy-looking camera hanging from his neck. "I don't suppose you carry film?" He lifted the camera and his smile turned sheepish.

"Afraid not."

He sighed. "Didn't expect to use so much. You've got a fascinating town here, ma'am."

"We like to think so." She kept her smile in place. The man was perfectly polite. No different from any other stranger who walked into her store looking for provisions of any kind.

Her palms were sweaty, though, and her heart beat too hard. It was only her and him in the store right now, and Ty had warned her about strangers.

And you're going to trust Ty Carson on anything? No. No, she wasn't, but… Well, there'd been too much trouble lately not to heed his warning. So, she'd be smart. Do what her deputy sister would do in this situation: pay attention to details. The man was tall, maybe around her brother Cam's height. But not broad. He had narrow shoulders, though the way he walked exuded a kind of strength. Like a runner, she supposed. Slim, but athletic. She couldn't determine the exact shade of his hair because of the way the hat was positioned and the way he was angled away from her, but it wasn't dark hair.

"I don't have film, but I've got food and drinks or anything else you might need." She smiled at him, but he still didn't look her way. He examined the store.

"Actually I stopped because I was wondering if you'd mind if I took a few pictures of your store."

"I thought you were out of film."

"I am, which is a shame. But I use my phone for pictures, too. I was using film out here because the ambiance seemed to call for it. I was over at the saloon. I hear the swinging doors are original."

"So they claim," Jen muttered, irritably thinking of Ty.

"Amazing." He meandered over to a row of candy, studied the offerings. "I took way too many pictures. And the boardwalks. The signs. It's like stepping back in time. I've been mostly sticking to ghost towns but the mix of past and present here… It's irresistible."

"So you were out at Cain, then?" she asked, referencing a popular ghost town destination for photographers and adventurers.

He nodded, still keeping his head tilted away from her. "That's what brought me out this way."

"From where?"

He chuckled. "You ask every stranger where they're from?"

She had to work to keep the pleasant smile on her

face. She couldn't blow this. "Tend to. We don't get many outsiders."

"Ah. Outsiders. Must be nice to live in a community that protects itself against outsiders. You'd feel…safe. Protected and cared for."

She hadn't felt particularly safe after the craziness of the past year, but she decided to agree anyway. "Very."

He swayed on his feet, trying to brace himself on the shelf and upending some candy before he fell backward onto the floor.

Stunned, Jen rushed forward, but he was already struggling to sit up.

"I'm all right," he said, holding out a hand to keep her back. "Just haven't eaten since breakfast. Got caught up, and I suppose the lack of food caught up with me. I'll be all right."

She grabbed one of the candy bars that had fallen to the ground and ripped it open before she handed it to him. She didn't think he'd gotten caught up. She was starting to think he didn't have any money. She almost felt sorry for him. "Here. Don't worry about paying for it. Just eat."

He took the candy, and then a bite. "You're too kind." He looked up for a second.

Blue eyes. A vibrant blue. Blond hair, wispy and nearly white really. Not with age, just a very, very light shade of blond. His nose was crooked. To the left.

"Didn't expect to run across someone so young and pretty in a tiny little Wyoming town."

"Uh—"

"Sorry." He looked back down at the candy bar, the brim of his hat hiding everything again. "That's awkward and uncomfortable. Let's blame it on the lack of food. Do you think I could trouble you for a small sip of water?"

Jen jumped to her feet and hurried for the cooler that boasted rows of water bottles. She grabbed one of the larger ones and twisted it open. "Here," she said, returning to his side. "You just take this."

He took a sip and then nodded, using the back of his arm to wipe the water droplets off his mouth. He kept his head down.

Was it purposeful? Was he trying to make sure she couldn't identify him? Was he planning something awful? But she'd seen his eyes and the color of his hair—she only had to remember the details.

He took another bite of the candy bar, then a drink of the water. She racked her brain trying to figure out what to do. How to defend herself if he lunged at her. This could all be an act. A ploy. Weaken her defenses, catch her off guard.

Carefully, Jen leaned slightly away and got to her feet, keeping her eyes on him and her body tense and ready to react.

"Thank you for the kindness," he said, sounding exhausted. But it *could* be acting. "I should be out of your way." He struggled to his feet, swayed again, but righted himself.

He seemed so genuinely thankful and feeble. The man was a mess, and maybe he *was* Ty's threatening stranger, but he wasn't doing anything to put her in danger at the moment.

And why would he? He was probably just after Ty. How could she blame anyone on that front?

"Can I get you anything else? Maybe a sandwich? A bag of chips?" His clear weakness ate at her. A man shouldn't go hungry. Though, she supposed, he could sell that nice camera if he was really that bad off.

"No. No, I'll be fine." He kept his head tilted away, but the corner of his smile was soft and kind as he lifted the water bottle in salute. "I appreciate it, ma'am. Your kindness won't be forgotten." And with that, he walked out of the store. No trouble. No danger.

Leaving Jen unsure about what to do.

TY DIDN'T OFTEN find himself uncomfortable. He'd learned early to roll with whatever punches life threw at him. There'd been quite a few.

But nothing could have prepared him for a baby shower. A Carson-Delaney baby shower. Laurel and Vanessa were laughing over their baby bumps, pastel pink and blue decorations everywhere, and Carsons and Delaneys mingled like there'd never been a feud.

Jen was in a corner talking to Addie and Noah, Addie's toddler trying to crawl up Noah and laughing hysterically when he fell. Noah watched with the patience of a happy man.

Ty had never particularly understood his brother, though he loved him with a fierceness that meant he'd lay down his life for the man. What he did know about Noah was that having Addie and Seth in his life and on his ranch made him happy, and that was all Ty really cared about.

"Delaney Delirium getting to you?"

Ty gave Grady a cool look. "Just trying to understand all this baby business," he said, nodding toward Noah and the way he held Seth easily on his hip.

Grady patted him on the back. Hard. "Sure, buddy."

"You really want to be a dad after the way we grew

up?" Ty asked, unable to stop himself. He didn't get it. The way Noah had taken to Addie's nephew that she was guardian and mother to, as if it were easy to step into the role of guardian and father. The way Vanessa and Grady seemed calm and even happy about their impending parenthood.

The Carson generation before theirs had not been a particular parental one. More fists and threats than nurturing happiness.

"Figure I got a pretty good example of what *not* to do," Grady said with a shrug. "And a woman to knock some sense into me when I make mistakes. Besides, we turned out okay in spite of it all."

"And Delaney senior ain't got a problem with his grandchild being raised by a cop and saloon owner?"

"Laurel's father doesn't get a say."

Ty knew it was different for Grady. Ty had been eighteen when Mr. Delaney had flexed his parental and town muscles to make sure Ty got the hell away from his daughter. Grady wasn't a dumb teenager, and neither was Laurel. They could refuse a parent's interference.

Couldn't you have?

He shook his head. Ancient history. No amount of Carson and Delaney comingling was reason to go back there.

Laurel called Grady over and he left Ty in the middle of all this goodwill and pastel baby nonsense. He was somewhere in no-man's land. He almost wished a sniper would take him out.

There were toasts and cake and presents of tiny clothes and board books. No matter that their families had been enemies for over a century, no matter that people in town still whispered about curses and the inevitable terrible ends they would all meet, Carsons and Delaneys sat together celebrating new lives.

Some unknown ache spread through him. He couldn't name it, and he couldn't seem to force it away. It sat in his gut, throbbing out to all his limbs.

Faking his best smile, he went to Vanessa and Grady and made his half-hearted excuses to leave early. No one stopped him, but his family sure watched him slip out the front door. He could feel their eyes, their questions. And worst of all, their pity.

As if being alone was the worst fate a person could face. He'd seen a lot worse. This was fine. And good. Right for him. Alone suited—

"Ty."

There was something his gut did when she said his name. No matter the years, he couldn't seem to control that intrinsic physical reaction to his name forming on her lips. A softening. A longing.

He took a minute to brace himself before he turned around. Jen stood on the porch of Grady and Laurel's cabin. She looked like cotton candy in some lacy, frothy pink thing.

And all too viscerally he could remember what she looked like completely *unclothed*. No matter that he assured himself time changed things—bodies, minds, hearts. It was hard to remember as she approached him with a face that wasn't shooting daggers at him for the first time since he'd arrived home.

"Listen." She looked back at the open door, then took a few more steps toward him on the walk. "I wanted to let you know I had a stranger come in the store last night."

"What?" he demanded, fury easily taking over the

ache inside him. *Last night?* "Why didn't you call me? I told you—"

She lifted her chin, her eyes cold as ice. "You told me to let you know. Here I am, letting you know. I don't think he's whatever you're looking for. He was perfectly nice. He just asked to take pictures of the store, and then he—"

"What time did he come in?"

"Well, seven but—"

"He was going to take pictures when it was pitch-black?"

She frowned at that, a line forming between her brows that once upon a time he'd loved tracing with his thumb. Where had *that* memory come from?

"He was hungry. He *fainted*. He was out of it. Confused maybe. And totally polite and harmless."

"Damn it, Jen. I told you to call me. I could have—"

"He didn't *do* anything. I know you're paranoid, but—"

"I am *not* paranoid. You think a man who gets a letter with no postage delivered to where he lives and works is paranoid?"

She tilted her head, studying him, and he realized with a start he'd said too much.

He never said too much.

"What was in the letter?" she asked, her voice calm and her eyes on him.

It was hell, this. Still wanting her. Missing that old tiny slice of his life where she'd been his. He didn't want this, but he couldn't seem to get rid of it. It ate at him, had him dreaming about doing things he couldn't possibly allow himself to do. Every once in a while he'd think…what would just one touch do?

But he knew the answer to that.

She audibly swallowed and looked away, a faint blush staining her cheeks. She felt it, too, and yet…

"It doesn't matter," he grumbled, trying to find his usual center of calm. His normal, everyday clear-eyed view of the world and of this problem he had. "What did he look like? Better yet—I want to see your security tape."

Her eyes flashed anger and frustration. "You are *not* looking at my security tape."

"Why not?"

"It's an invasion of my customers' privacy."

He snorted. "I don't care that Mary Lynn Jones bought a pack of Marlboros even though her husband thinks she quit or that little Adam Teller was buying condoms because he talked his way into Lizzie Granger's pants."

Jen's mouth twitched, but then she firmed it into a scowl. "How do you know all that?"

"I pay attention, babe."

Her scowl deepened and she folded her arms across her chest. "Blond hair, blue eyes. About the same height as Cam. I'm not sure what that'd be in feet and inches, but I imagine you would. Skinny, but strong, like a marathon runner. He wore hiking clothes and boots, all in tan, and a big, fancy camera around his neck. Topped it off with a Stetson. Said he was taking pictures of ghost towns and happened upon Bent."

It was more to go on than he thought he'd get out of her, but still not enough to ring any bells. "Tattoos? Scars? Something off about him?"

She shook her head. "Not that I could see."

"I want the tape, Jen. If someone is…" He didn't

want to tell her. Didn't trust her to keep it a secret and let him handle it, but he needed to see the man himself. Needed to identify him so he could neutralize this threat. "I'm getting letters. They're not threatening exactly, but they're not...not. I know you don't care about me, but your family is all tangled up with mine now." He gestured at the whole irritating lot of them. "Don't you want to protect what's yours?"

"Of course I do."

That sharp chin of hers came up, defiant and angry. Her temper used to amuse him. Now it just made that ache center in his heart.

But that wasn't the problem at hand. "Then let me see the tape. If I recognize him, I'll know what to do. If I don't, then maybe you're right and it's harmless coincidence." He didn't believe that, but he'd let her think he did.

She was quiet and stiff for humming seconds, then finally she sighed. "Oh, fine. I suppose you want to go now?"

He only raised an eyebrow.

She rolled her eyes. "Let me get my purse and say my goodbyes." She stalked back inside, grumbling about irritating, stubborn males the whole way up.

All Ty could do was pray he'd recognize whoever was on that tape and everything would be over.

JEN STEPPED OUT of her tiny little sedan, dressed all in pink, her dark hair in pretty waves around her shoulders.

Sweet. Just like Ty had said. She'd been wary of him last night when he'd first walked into the store. He'd seen it in her eyes, but the feigned hunger and stumble had softened her. She'd given him food and water. Good-hearted, she was indeed.

He smiled, watching as Jen stood there in front of her store. When a motorcycle roared into view, his smile died.

Even before the man took off his helmet, he knew who it was. He watched Jen. She didn't seem *happy* to see Ty, but nor did she seem surprised or *un*happy.

He scowled, watching as Ty strode over to Jen. They exchanged a few words and then Jen unlocked the store and stepped inside, Ty right behind her.

She didn't flip the sign from Closed to Open.

He narrowed his eyes. The rage that slammed into him was sudden and violent, but he'd learned a thing or two about how to handle it. Hone it.

Ty would get his. He *would*.

So, patience would be the name of the game. And another letter.

This time in blood.

Chapter Three

Jen set her purse down on her desk in the back room of the store and tried not to sigh. Why was she getting involved in this?

Don't you want to protect what's yours?

It grated all over again. That he could even ask her that. She would have protected *him*, sacrificed for *him*, and he'd left her alone and confused and so broken-hearted she'd…

She booted up her computer, stabbing at the buttons in irritation. She'd eradicate the past if she could, but since she couldn't she had to find a better way of managing her reaction to it in Ty's presence.

Looming over her like some hulking specter. She flicked a glance over her shoulder and up. "Do you mind?"

His eyes were hard and his mouth was harder. He was taking this so seriously, and that irritated her. Ty was never serious. Oh, deep down he was, but he usually masked it with lazy smiles and sarcastic remarks.

But whatever this was had him giving no pretense of humor.

She focused on the computer and brought up the security footage. She ignored the flutter of panic in her throat, dismissed it as foolish. Whatever was going on was Ty's problem, and once she showed him the footage he'd realize that and leave her alone.

She fast-forwarded through the day, moving the cursor to around seven when the man had come in. She zipped through her conversation with Jim and his case of beer, then hit Play when the door opened after Jim's exit.

They both watched in silence, heads nearly together as they studied the video.

"You can't see him," Ty said flatly, his breath making the hair at her ear dance. She ignored the shiver of reaction and made sure her voice was even before she spoke.

"Give it a second."

They continued to watch, and Jen could only hope Ty was so focused on the video he didn't notice the goose bumps on her arm or the way her breathing wasn't exactly even.

She had to fight viciously against the memories that wanted to worm their way into her consciousness. Memories of them together. Close like this. Not at *all* clothed like this.

But it was silence around them, heavy, pregnant silence, and she didn't dare look to see if Ty was keeping his eyes on the computer. Of course he was. That's what they were here for.

"You can't see his face," Ty repeated.

Jen peered at the form on the screen. She saw herself, watching the man's entrance. And everywhere the man moved, his hat obscured his face from the camera.

"He did it on purpose."

"How would he have known where the camera is?" Jen returned. It was so natural, the way the stranger on the video kept his head down. She wanted to believe Ty was overreacting, but an uncomfortable feeling itched along her spine.

"He did it on purpose," Ty said in that same flat tone.

"Keep watching. We'll get a glimpse when he falls."

But as the man on the screen pitched forward into the candy, and then staggered back before falling to the ground, his face remained completely hidden by the hat.

Jen frowned at that. But surely a man who fell over didn't *purposefully* shield himself from a security camera. It was just coincidence.

"Rewind it," Ty ordered.

She opened her mouth to tell him not to order her around, but then huffed out a breath. Why bother arguing with a brick wall? She moved the cursor back to the man's entrance, then slowed down the time.

Nothing changed. You couldn't see the guy's face. But she let Ty watch. She turned to study him. He was so close her nose all but brushed his cheek. If he noticed, he didn't show it. His gaze was flat and blank, seeing nothing but the computer screen.

His profile could be so hard. *He* could be so hard, but there'd been softness and kindness underneath that mask all those years ago. Did it still exist? Or had military life sucked it out of him? Were any of the parts of him that she loved still in there, or were they all gone?

Horrified with that thought, she blinked at the stinging in her eyes. Stupid. It didn't matter one way or the other. Yes, he'd broken her heart years ago, but she'd gotten over it. She'd moved on. And he definitely had.

So, her brain needed to stop taking detours to the past.

"He faked that fall," Ty said, as if it was fact, not just his insane opinion on the matter.

"You're being paranoid."

He turned his head so fast she startled back. His eyes were blazing blue, and no matter how tightly he held his jaw, his mouth was soft. She knew exactly what it would feel like on hers.

What the hell was wrong with her? She closed her eyes against the heated wave of embarrassment.

"I am not being paranoid," he said, his voice low and controlled. "I'm being rational. I'm putting all the dots together. That man didn't fall because he was starving. Did you see that fancy camera? He can afford to eat."

She opened her eyes, irritation exceeding embarrassment and old stupid feelings. "That doesn't mean—"

"And furthermore," Ty said, getting in her face no matter how she leaned away in her chair, "even if he *did* fall, he kept his face away from that camera for a reason. I *know* it. Now, you want to prove it, you watch hours of your own security tape and see if that happens with any other person."

He held her gaze, though after a while some of that furious, righteous anger softened into something else. Something… *Something* as his blue eyes roamed her face, settled on her mouth.

Jen shot out of the chair, ignoring the fact she bumped into him, and then scrambled away. "I…have to open the store," she stuttered. "Everyone's expecting me to open at three." She was being foolish, but her heart was hammering in her throat and she had to get out of this tiny room where Ty loomed far too large.

He stood, blocking the door, still as a rock, eyeing her carefully. "You have to be careful, Jen."

She fisted her hands on her hips. "He isn't after me. Now let me out."

"He came in here. He talked to you. There's something purposeful in that."

"What do *I* have to do with your threatening letters?"

He heaved out a breath. "Look." He shook his head, crossed his arms over his chest. He looked at the ceiling, then dropped his arms and shoved his hands in his pockets.

She raised her eyebrows. Nerves? No, not exactly, but definitely discomfort. She wasn't sure she'd ever seen Ty something like unsure.

"I have a feeling this ties to someone I was in the military with," he said, sounding disgusted with himself.

"Again, what does that have to do with me?"

"If it's someone I knew? Someone I bunked with? They would have listened to me talk about home, about my family, about…" He nodded in her direction.

She could only blink at him. He'd talked about *her*? After leaving her like she was garbage you dumped on the side of the road? It didn't make any sense.

"I can't tell anything from that tape, but I've got threatening letters and a strange man in your store, so I've got to think of the obvious conclusion here. You could be in danger."

"That's absurd," she responded. It had to be.

He stepped forward, and before she could sidestep him, he took her by the chin. Her whole body zoomed off into some other dimension she hadn't been to in a very long time. She could only stare at him, while his big, rough hand held her face in place.

"I need you to be careful." He was so solemn, so serious.

Her throat constricted and her heart beat so hard

she was sure her whole body vibrated from the violence of it.

His grip on her chin softened, his fingertip moving along the line of her jaw. She wanted to melt into a puddle, but she wasn't seventeen anymore, and with that fission of delight she was reminded she *hated* Ty Carson.

She slapped his hand away, raising her chin at him, trying for regal instead of panicked. "Don't manhandle me."

He only raised an eyebrow.

"I don't know what you want from me," she said, with more feeling than she should have shown him.

"I want you to be aware. Take precautions. Keep yourself safe and protected, and if that man comes in your store again, I want you to call me immediately." He moved out of the way of the door and her exit. "It's that simple."

Simple? Sure. As if anything to do with Ty Carson was *simple*.

TY WALKED OUT of the general store knowing he'd overplayed his hand. Disgusted with himself for getting wrapped up in old feelings and memories and not focusing on the task at hand, he stalked to his motorcycle.

But he couldn't eradicate the look of Jen's brown eyes, wide on his, her mouth open in shock as he'd held her face. The flutter of pulse. It felt as though in that moment a million memories had arced between them.

He tried to shake it off. They weren't the same people. He had regrets, sure. He should have handled everything with her father differently. But he hadn't and there was no reason to beat himself up over it. You couldn't change the past.

And he couldn't change the fact being a soldier and away from home for nearly a decade with only sporadic visits when on leave had altered him. He wasn't the same teenager who'd run off when the right pressure was applied. Even though Jen had stayed in Bent, she wasn't the same girl.

They were different people, and if there was still a physical attraction it would be best if they both ignored it.

But even more important than that, he had to protect her from whatever was going on. He wasn't sure how to do that yet, but he knew he had to figure it out.

He almost ran right into someone, so lost in his own irritable thoughts. He opened his mouth to apologize, until he recognized the middle-aged man before him.

Mr. Delaney's eyes went from the store, to Ty, and then went hard and flat. "I hope you know what you're doing, Carson."

Funny how time didn't change the utter authority in this man's voice. Jen's father thought he owned the *world*, and Ty was sick with regret for ever being a part of that certainty.

"Know what I'm doing? Hmm." Ty smiled. "I suppose I always do."

"You'll watch your step where my daughter is concerned."

Ty raised an eyebrow and looked back at the store himself. Then he let his smile widen into a wolfish grin.

"I got rid of you once, Tyler. I don't know why I couldn't do it again."

Ty didn't let the violent fury show. He wouldn't give this man the satisfaction. He kept the smile in place, made sure his voice was lazy, but with enough edge to carry a threat. "I seem to recall you fooling around with a married woman, Delaney. I wonder what other dirty skeletons are rattling around in your closet. More torrid connections to other Carsons? Or are your kids taking care of that these days?"

It irritated Ty that not even a flicker of that blow hitting showed on Delaney's face, though he knew it was at least a little knock to the man's pride. That it had come out he'd had an affair with a woman who'd been married to someone else. And not just that, a woman who was blood related to Ty himself.

"Your cousins have made my children very happy," Delaney said, surprising the hell out of Ty. "Maybe you shouldn't have run away all those years ago." He smiled pleasantly. "But you did. The kind of running away that isn't so easy to forgive."

Ty kept his smile in place by sheer force of will. He'd faced down his father's fists. He had no trouble facing down Delaney's barbs. "Funny thing about coming back home again." He glanced at the store. "Some things never change, and some people are more forgiving than others."

Finally he got a reaction out of Delaney, though it was only a tightening of his jaw. Still, it was better than nothing. "Impending grandparenthood looks good on you, Delaney. Have a nice day." He patted the man's shoulder, gratified when Delaney jerked away and stalked into the store.

To Jen. Ty sighed. The simple truth was he had more to worry about than Jen or her father. He had to worry about the messages he was receiving, the uncomfortable gut feeling he had that Jen was in danger. Because of him.

The most important thing was keeping her safe. Not because he still had feelings for her, but because it was the right thing to do. The timing of the letter, the mention of first loves and this stranger's appearance in the store were too close to be coincidental or for him to believe Jen wasn't a target.

If this connected to his military days—which were the only days he'd spent away from Bent—and Jen was a target, it would have to be from early in his career. Before the rangers.

He racked his brain for someone he'd wronged, someone he'd had friction with. A few superiors, but nothing personal. Just normal army stuff, and he'd hardly been the only soldier who'd occasionally mouthed off and gotten punished for it. There'd been the man he'd ratted out, but the man on the tape wasn't Oscar. Not even close. Besides, Oscar had to have known his time in the army was limited when he couldn't keep himself out of the booze or drugs.

Ty brought to mind the figure from Jen's security tape. Not even a tingle of recognition. It ate at him, the faceless man manipulating Jen in her own store. It damn near burned him alive to think she'd be a target of something she had nothing to do with.

Target or not, her cooperation or not, he'd keep her safe. He just had to figure out how.

HE DIDN'T MIND cutting himself. He rather liked it. Watching the blood well up, drip down. He'd always liked blood. Dr. Michaels said he had to be careful, not to get too caught up in it.

She was right. He only had so much time. Ty would stay at the store for only so long, and it would take time to sneak into Rightful Claim. He had to craft his message quickly, then deliver it with just as much precision and speed.

The paper hadn't worked, so he'd torn off a piece of his T-shirt and concentrated carefully as he used his bloody fingertip to spell out the message.

He admired his work. He supposed blood might tell, giving away his identity, but he wasn't so worried about that. He liked the message of blood too much to worry about the connections.

Besides, by the time blood told, he'd have his revenge.

Chapter Four

Jen had done a lot of pretending in her life. All through high school she'd pretended she wasn't involved with Ty Carson, then after he'd left she'd pretended she wasn't heartbroken. She did her best to pretend Laurel's marriage to Grady and Dylan's marriage to Vanessa didn't bother her. For most of her life, she'd fooled those she loved the most.

She didn't think she'd fooled anyone tonight as she'd pretended to cheerfully spend her evening making dinner for her family at the Delaney Ranch. She'd chattered happily through dinner, then cleaned up diligently, refusing help and earning looks.

Pity looks.

Even though Ty's whole *thing* was giving her the constant creeps and a feeling of being watched, she went home to her apartment above the store after tidying up at Delaney Ranch. She'd rather face off with someone who might be "targeting" her than withstand her family's pity—most especially the in-law Carson portion of her "family."

Jen always passed the storefront on Main before pulling into the alley where stairs led up to her apartment behind the store. No matter what time of day, she always scanned the front to make sure everything was as it should be.

Her heart slammed painfully against her chest at the shadowy figure looming under the awning of the store's front door, highlighted by the faint security lights inside. She whipped her gaze from the door to the road, jerking the wheel to miss the sidewalk she'd been about to careen onto.

Heart pounding, palms sweating, Jen kept driving, taking her normal turn onto the alley. What should she do? Who was lurking outside her store?

It could be anyone. Jim wanted a six-pack. Someone taking an evening stroll. It could be nothing. But it felt like something.

She fished her phone out of her purse, debating whether she should park or keep driving. The person had to have seen her erratic driving. Would whomever it was know who she was? Would the individual walk back here? Threaten her?

"Oh, damn you, Ty Carson." She pushed the car into Park, watching the alley in case anyone appeared. She started to dial Ty, then cursed herself for it. A smart woman didn't call the idiotic, paranoid man who was causing her panic in the first place. A smart woman called the cops.

And lucky for her, her sister was the cops.

Except Laurel was a detective. And pregnant. *Don't you want to protect what's yours?* She cursed Ty all over again, staring at her phone with indecision. Laurel or Ty? Bent County Sheriff's Department or handle this herself?

She looked back up at the alley entrance. There was no sign of anyone. Surely someone nefarious would have run away upon being spotted. She wouldn't be foolish when everyone already pitied her. No.

Quickly and decisively, she got out of her car and hurried to the back door of the store. She watched the alley, fumbling with her keys as she worked to get the door open. Once inside she quickly shut it and locked it behind her, taking a deep breath and trying to steady her shaky limbs.

"You're being ridiculous," she muttered into the empty room. Still, her heartbeat didn't calm and her nerves continued to fray as she moved from the back of the store to the front. At first she didn't see anything, then a shadow moved and she barely held back the impulse to scream.

It was the man who'd fainted in her store.

Despite all the assurances she'd given Ty that the stranger was no one and completely nonthreatening, *this* felt very threatening.

She backed away from the door, pulling her phone out of her purse. Quickly, she dialed the dispatch number for the sheriff's department. When a woman answered, she explained as calmly and concisely as she could that someone was outside her store, and she didn't consider him dangerous but she did have some concerns.

"I'll have a deputy out your way as soon as possible, ma'am."

"Thank you." Jen hit End and then steeled herself to turn around. He was still there, which had her breath coming in quick puffs. He wasn't pounding on the door or the storefront glass. He was simply standing there, same as he had been.

Except, she realized, he was holding something

against the window of the door. Unsteady, Jen inched toward the door, realizing it was a piece of paper. He was holding something like a sign against the glass.

In careful print, it read: *I only wanted to thank you for the other day.*

Though the soft security lights from inside the store lit up the boardwalk enough to illuminate him, he had his cowboy hat pulled low. He smiled sheepishly and it sent a tickle of panic through her that his mouth was the only part of him she could make out.

"I called the police," she shouted, wondering if the sound would carry through the glass.

His sheepish smile didn't fade, but he did nod. He pulled a pen out of his pocket and began to write on the paper again. When he flipped it around, she had to squint and step a little closer to read it.

Didn't mean to frighten you. I'll be on my way. See you soon, Jen.

Jen.

He'd written her name, clear as day. Why did he know her name?

He could have overheard it. He could have asked around. Neither made her feel comforted.

She noticed the flash of red and blue lights. She craned her head to see the cruiser's progress with some relief easing away the panic.

But when she looked back at the door the man was gone, and dread pooled inside her stomach.

None of it was threatening, and yet she felt threatened. Chilled to the bone. She hugged herself as she waited for the deputy to get out of his cruiser and walk up to the door.

She forced herself to smile at him when she opened

the door to him. Thanks to her sister's position with the sheriff's department, she knew most of the deputies. Thomas better than most. "Thomas, thanks for coming, but I feel a little silly. He went away without any fuss."

"It's no problem, Jen. Better safe than sorry, and you know your sister would have my butt if I didn't check it out. Now, why don't you tell me everything that happened."

She sighed, knowing it would all get back to Laurel, and she'd have to answer a thousand questions. Knowing Laurel would tell Grady, who'd undoubtedly mention it to Ty. She'd have to tell Ty herself in that case.

She faced that with about as much dread as she had the stranger at her door.

Ty YAWNED, FEELING unaccountably tired for an early Sunday night. Rightful Claim closed down at midnight rather than two, and he should have felt revved.

Instead, the lack of sleep over the past few days was getting to him. Was he getting old? He shook his head, pushing his apartment door open.

Something fluttered at his feet and he knew immediately it would be another note. He bent down to pick it up, but the odd shape and color of the letters stopped him midcrouch. Icy cold settled in his gut and spread through his limbs.

It was blood. Even as he warned himself it could be fake, he knew. It was blood. A message written in blood.

It wasn't hard to access the part of his brain he'd spent a decade honing in the army and the army rangers. It clicked into place like a machine switched on.

He stood to his full height, taking a careful step backward. The less he disturbed the scene, the better chance he had of nipping this all in the bud before anyone got hurt.

Jen. He pulled the phone out of his pocket and dialed her number. He refused to put her as a contact in his phone, but he knew the number nevertheless. All it had taken was Laurel insisting her wedding party had each other's phone numbers to have it lodged in his brain like a tumor.

It rang, ending on her voice mail message. She was probably asleep, but it didn't assuage his fear. He left a terse message. "Call me. ASAP."

He clicked End and pushed away that jangle of worry. Once he took care of this, he'd make sure she was fast asleep. He'd make sure, wherever she was and whatever she was doing, she was safe and sound.

Safe.

Ty looked at his phone and couldn't believe what he was about to do. He was a Carson and Carsons handled their own stuff, but with Jen involved for whatever reason, he couldn't take that chance.

Because Jen *was* involved, he knew that. Even without reading this new message. He knew the man trying to frighten him would use Jen to do it.

So, he called the Bent County Sheriff's Department. He explained the situation and was assured someone would be over shortly.

Then he called Jen again, cursing her refusal to answer. *She's asleep and has her phone on silent.*

"Screw it," he muttered, moving out of his apartment and back down the stairs. If he walked around to the front of the saloon, he'd be able to see her store. He knew he should wait for the cops, but if her security lights were on, if he jogged over and checked to make sure her car was in the back lot…

Of course, she might have spent the night at the Delaney Ranch. Jen didn't keep a regular schedule, which was going to be a problem if he was going to keep her safe. Not that he could force her to change anything. She'd only get more erratic if he warned her to stay in one place.

Hardheaded woman.

He stepped outside and his heart all but stopped. The flashing lights of a police cruiser were across the road and down the street, right in front of Delaney General.

Without thinking it through, he was ready to run down the street, bust in and save her from whatever was wrong.

But his name broke through the haze.

"Carson?"

Ty whirled to face the cop walking toward him. Younger guy. Ty didn't like cops, period, but if he had to deal with one he would have preferred Hart. Ty was pretty sure this was the one who'd nearly bungled Addie's kidnapping last year.

"What?" Ty barked. "What's going on over there?"

"Nothing serious. Just a suspicious figure. But you put in a call, too. Something about a note?"

Ty looked at the car down by Delaney General, and then at the too-young deputy trying to be tough.

Ty felt his age for a moment, not in years, but in the decade he'd spent in the military. He remembered what it was like to be young and eager. Foolishly sure of his role in helping people. No doubt this moron had the same conviction, and someday it would be beaten out of him.

Ty tried to keep his voice from being a harsh demand. "So, everyone's okay down there?"

"Looks like it was innocent and harmless. Spooked Ms. Delaney some, but no real threat. We've canvassed the area for a while now, with no evidence of anyone. We were just finishing up when we got your call on the radio. Now, why don't you show me the note."

"Who's with her?"

"Hart."

Ty nodded. That was good. That was fine. Let the police take care of Jen. *Suspicious figure.* Ty looked around Main Street, mostly pitch-black except for the occasional glow from nearby businesses' security lights.

Someone was out there. A suspicious figure.

"Carson?"

"Right. Upstairs. You got stuff to collect it or whatever? I'm pretty sure it's written in blood."

The deputy's eyebrows rose, but he nodded. "I've got everything I need to handle it." He patted his utility belt and then followed Ty around the bar and into the back entrance.

Ty led him to the letter, and the deputy crouched and pulled on rubber gloves as he examined it. "Is this the first letter you've received like this?"

"It's the first one in blood, but it isn't the first one."

The deputy spared him a look. One that said *and you're just now calling the police?* It was only his worry over Jen and her suspicious figure that kept him from kicking the cop out and telling him he'd handle it faster and better.

The deputy picked it up and slid it into what looked like a ziplock bag.

"What's it say?" Ty demanded.

The deputy stood and raised his eyebrows. "You didn't read it?"

"I didn't want to touch it. Blood or fingerprints… You'll be able to get something off it?"

"Should be. Blood could be animal, but there might be something here. Though it'll take some time to send that off for analysis."

"But you will?"

"I'll be recommending it," the deputy returned with a nod. "This is a serious threat." He held up the bag and read through it. "I'd warn you to watch your back, but it won't be your back I'm after."

Jen. He didn't know why this person was fixating on Jen, but he was sure of it. "We need to know who that is."

"You don't have any clues?"

"None. Someone from my army days, maybe? But I'm in the dark. If we can get DNA off that—"

"What about the other letters? Where are they?"

Struggling between his need to do this on his own and his understanding he needed the cops in on this if Jen was going to stay safe, Ty stalked over to the kitchen drawer he'd shoved the other letters in. He grabbed them and held them out to the deputy.

The deputy took them, then nodded toward the door as footfalls sounded on the stairs. "That'll be Hart. We'll want to consider the connection angle on this. A note to you, a threatening figure at Ms. Delaney's store. Same time frame."

It was indeed Hart, but Ty frowned at Jen walking into the room behind him.

"What's going on?" Jen demanded. "Was he here, too?"

Hart turned to Jen, placed a gentle hand on her shoulder. Gentle enough that Ty's eyes narrowed.

"Jen," Hart said quietly. "Maybe you should calm—"

"Don't you dare tell me to calm down, Thomas." Jen shrugged off his hand and glared at him, then Ty. "Ty seems to think this man is connected—the one sending him threatening notes, and the stranger at my store. And you told me he got another one. Well, it's not okay, and I'm somehow involved. I want to know why."

"We don't know it's the same person," the deputy with the letters said to Hart and Jen. "We only know it's suspicious timing. Do you have an idea of when the letter was dropped off?"

Ty sighed. "I've been bartending since four. Didn't come up till after midnight. I don't know how someone would have broken in without me noticing anything, but it could have happened anytime."

Hart jotted something down on a notepad while the other deputy read through the notes Ty had handed him.

"Excuse us a moment," Hart said, nodding to the other deputy into the hallway. They stood there, conferring in low tones.

Ty studied Jen. She looked calm and collected, pretty as a picture considering it was the middle of the night and she'd called the police over a suspicious figure.

"You and Hart got a thing?" Ty asked, harsher than he'd intended, and if he'd been thinking at all he wouldn't have asked. But the way Hart had touched her raked along his skin like nails on a chalkboard. He didn't like it.

She blinked, looked up at him as though he'd lost his mind. "A thing?"

Ty probably *had* lost his mind, but he wasn't going to let her see that. So he shrugged lazily. "You're the

only one I've ever heard call him Thomas. I was starting to think his first name *was* Hart."

"Oh. Well."

"So, you have a thing." He didn't ask it. He stated it.
Because of course they did. Delaneys loved their law
and order.

Any embarrassment or discomfort she'd had on her
face morphed into full-on bristle. "It's none of your
business, is it?"

Ty shrugged, forcing the move to be negligent even
though his shoulders felt like iron. "It is if he's got a
vested interest in keeping you safe. Make it easier for
me to trust him anyhow."

"You don't need to worry about me, Tyler."

He tried not to scowl, since she was clearly trying
to irritate him, but his name was one of the few things
that irritated him no matter how hard he tried to let it
go. "If something I did brought you danger, I'll worry
about you as much as I want."

She softened at that some. "Ty—"

He didn't want her softening. "You need to stay with
your family until this is sorted. The cops might look
into it, but they're useless. With the exception of maybe
your boyfriend there. This is escalating, and you need
to be protected."

"Because heaven forbid I protect myself?"

"Honey, you're Bambi in the woods full of wolves.
Stay at that mansion of yours where your brothers can
keep an eye on you."

"My *brothers*. Right. Because only men can protect."

"They've got some military experience. That isn't
sexism. It's reality."

"The reality is Laurel's a police officer, and I know how to handle myself."

"Laurel's pregnant," Ty responded simply. "You really want her keeping your butt out of trouble?"

"My *butt* is in trouble because of *you*, somehow. You leave without a peep, disappear into thin air, leaving me…" She sucked in a breath and closed her eyes. "You know what? Ancient history doesn't matter. You got me into this mess, and I expect *you* to get me out. Not my brothers, not the police—you."

He looked down at her grimly, then forced himself to smile. "You sure you want that, babe?"

She scowled at him, shaking her hair back like a woman ready to kick some butt. "And why wouldn't I?"

Hart stepped back in, eyeing them both with something like consideration. "We'll take this back to the station, see what kind of analysis we can get. I'd caution you both to be careful, and call me or Deputy McCarthy if you think of anything that might help us figure out the identity of either the suspicious figure or the person writing the notes."

Ty nodded and Jen sent Hart a sweet smile.

"Of course."

"Do you want me to escort you back to your store, Jen?" Hart asked.

Jen sent Ty a killing look, then beamed at Hart. "Thank you, Thomas. I'd appreciate that." She strode over to him, and they walked out of Ty's apartment chatting in low tones.

Deputy McCarthy tipped his hat at Ty. "Call if you think of anything, and we'll be in touch."

Ty only grunted, paying more attention to Hart's and Jen's retreating backs than McCarthy's words.

If she had Hart wrapped around her finger, she'd be fine. Safe. Watched after by more than just her cop sister who was busy growing a human being inside her. He should stop worrying. Jen was a Delaney and would be protected at all costs, regardless of what Ty did.

But no matter how hard he tried to convince himself of that, the worry didn't go away.

HE LIKED WATCHING the police lights flash red and blue. He liked knowing he'd caused a few scenes, and there was a hot lick of thrill at the idea everyone was thinking about him, trying to figure out who he was and what he wanted.

He slunk through the shadows, evading the stupid, useless cops with ease. Watching, always watching.

He'd had a moment of rage when Jen had hurried toward Ty's place with the cop. She'd looked worried.

The cop had touched her.

Now they were walking back out of Ty's. They smiled at each other. The other cop exited shortly thereafter, but the first cop stayed by Jen's side as they walked back to her store.

He followed, melting into the shadows, watching. Jen touched the cop's arm, and he could all but read her lips.

Thank you.

No. This wouldn't do. Jen was his now. His quarry and his to do with whatever he wanted. Part revenge, yes. Hurt Ty. His first objective was always to hurt Ty.

But Jen was pretty and sweet. She had a nice smile. He didn't want her just to hurt Ty anymore, he wanted her. She would be his prize when he tipped the scales back. When he had revenge, he'd have Jen, too.

This cop wouldn't do. Not at all.

Chapter Five

Jen was exhausted when her alarm went off the next morning. Exhausted and then irritated when she knew, without even getting up, that someone was in her apartment.

She might have been scared if she didn't know her family so well, or if she didn't smell what she assumed was Laurel's "famous" omelet—i.e., the only thing she ever bothered to cook.

Jen grabbed her fluffy pink robe that so often brought her comfort and slipped it on as she got out of bed. Summer was beginning to fade, and mornings were colder every day.

Jen moved from her bedroom to the small cramped space of living room and kitchen. "This better be a bad dream," she said, glaring at her sister.

Laurel raised an eyebrow at her as she flipped the omelet in the skillet. "You're telling me."

"Thomas shouldn't have called you." She'd known he would, but he *shouldn't* have. It was at least a small part of the reason the few dates she'd been on with him hadn't worked out. He all but idolized her sister as a police officer, and whether it was petty or not, Jen had never been completely comfortable with it.

"Hart knew better than to keep it from me. I'd have heard about it when I got into the station later, if not before." Laurel turned her attention back to the eggs, and her tone was purposefully mild. "I thought it didn't work out between you two."

Laurel was only ten months older than her, and they'd grown up not just as sisters, but also as friends. Still, ever since high school there'd been this Ty-sized distance between them. Because Jen hadn't told *anyone* about Ty, even her sister. Jen had always known Laurel felt it, and yet she'd never been able to cross that distance. She'd been too embarrassed.

Jen moved into the kitchen, hating the way all this ancient history swirled around her no matter what she did. "It didn't work out with Thomas."

"Then why do you still call him Thomas?"

"Because I wanted it to." Jen sank into her kitchen chair, giving up on sending her sister home. She raked her hands through her hair. "Can't you tell your husband to send his cousin back to wherever he came from and stop ruining my life?"

"So, it didn't work out with Hart because of Ty?"

"No, that isn't what I'm saying." Frowning at Laurel's back, Jen worked through that. "What would Ty have to do with me dating Thomas?"

Laurel shrugged. "I always suspected… Well, something." Laurel moved the omelet onto a plate before turning to face Jen and sliding it in front of her. "Why don't you tell me the truth?"

Jen should. Ty was old news, and it didn't matter now. He'd left. She'd gotten over it. Why not tell her sister? What she'd done in her teens shouldn't be embarrassing in her late twenties. "It's ancient history."

History she hated to rehash so much she just couldn't bring herself to.

"Is it?"

"Yes." Jen pushed the plate back at Laurel. "Eat some of this, preggo."

Laurel grimaced and placed a hand to her stomach. "No. Eggs are an emphatic no right now."

Touched Laurel had made them for her even though she was feeling off about them, Jen gave in. All these twisting emotions were silly. "Ty and I had a secret thing back in high school. But that was forever ago." She wanted to say it had hardly mattered, but she knew she'd never make that lie sound like the truth.

"It seems like there's still—"

"No." Maybe things were still complicated, and maybe the *real* reason things hadn't worked out with Thomas was that because no matter how good-looking or funny or kind he was, he'd never made her feel the way Ty had—still did. But that didn't mean…

She didn't know what anything meant anymore.

"Do they know who wrote Ty those letters?" Because she could tell herself she didn't care, and that it was his problem, but the fact Ty Carson had called the police last night made her worry for him. It was so out of character he must be beyond concerned.

"No, and that's why I'm here. Jen, the last letter is in blood, and every letter points at someone who doesn't want to hurt Ty, but hurt the people he loves."

Though a cold chill had spread through her at the idea of a note written in blood, Jen attempted to keep her demeanor calm and unmoved. "He doesn't love me."

"Are you so sure about that?"

"Positive. He left. He made sure it was a clean break,

and we're both different people now. Whatever feelings are between us are those weird old ones born out of nostalgia, not love. Of that I'm sure." She wanted to be sure.

"Okay, so maybe he doesn't still love you. But maybe whoever is threatening Ty thinks he does. From what Hart told me, Ty thinks it's someone from his army days, which points to someone who knew him when he still had a closer connection to you. It doesn't have to make sense to us, if we're dealing with someone who's deranged. And this stranger sniffing around your store is too much of a coincidence. You need to be careful until the police clear everything up."

Jen frowned. "Ty told me to stay at the ranch. I don't want to."

"As much as I'd usually support a contrary refusal to do anything a Carson ordered—"

Jen jumped to her feet and began to pace. "I'm not being contrary. I'm trying to be *sane*. If this man is really after Ty, and for some reason I'm his target, couldn't someone just tell him I don't mean anything to Ty? Wouldn't it be obvious?"

"So he can turn his attention to someone else? Grady? Vanessa? Noah and Addie and Seth?"

Jen closed her eyes against the wave of fear. "Laurel."

"I know it isn't fair, but the fact of the matter is, what we have to do is find out who this individual is and let the law handle them. Not try to shift his focus, much as I'd love it not to be on you."

Overwhelmed and feeling just a pinch sorry for herself, Jen sank back into the chair. "Why do bad things keep happening here?"

Laurel placed her hand over her slightly rounding stomach. "Maybe bad things need to happen to exorcise old feud demons. Maybe it's just bad luck of the draw, but at the end of every one of these 'bad things,' something really good has come out of it."

"I hope that's pregnancy brain talking because when I think of how badly you all have been hurt over the course of the past year—how many hospital visits I've made, how scared I've been—it isn't worth it."

Laurel reached over and squeezed her arm, still rubbing her stomach with her other hand. "It's been worth it to me. And we're all still here. You will be, too, but I want you to be careful, Jen. I want you to take some precautions. Whoever is behind this has left a lot of clues, has been careless, really. I'm hopeful it's all nipped in the bud before anything bad happens, but that means you watching your step and letting some people protect you until this person is caught."

Jen had worked very hard to never feel inferior to her siblings. They'd all always known exactly what they wanted to be, and had sacrificed to become it. Cam and his exemplary military service, and Laurel and her dedication to the law. Dylan and what they'd all thought was his education, but had turned out to be a secret military service of his own.

Jen had only ever wanted to run the store, and then once upon a time she'd wanted to risk everything for Ty Carson.

But it had never come to fruition and her life had been simple and exactly how she liked it. For ten years she'd had exactly what she'd wanted.

Except Ty.

"Why can't I protect myself every now and then?" Jen asked, not daring to meet her sister's gaze. "Why am I always the one who needs to be sheltered?"

"Because the people who love you are all licensed and trained to carry weapons. Because if there's anything the past year should teach us it's that working together and protecting each other is far better than trying to do it all alone. We're not asking you to hide in a corner while we fight your battles for you, Jen. We're asking you to let your family work *with* you to keep you safe during a dangerous time."

"I hate staying at the ranch."

"Join the club. Look, you can come stay with Grady and me, but…"

Jen wrinkled her nose. "He's asking Ty to come stay with you, isn't he?"

Laurel shrugged. "If it's all old news…"

"I'll stay at the ranch, but I'm still running my store. All my normal hours."

"Of course you are. We'll just want someone here with you while you do."

"Laurel."

Laurel pushed to her feet. "We'll come up with a schedule. You don't need to worry about that. Just be vigilant and don't go anywhere alone. That's all."

"That's all," Jen grumbled. "I enjoy being alone, Laurel."

"Well, for a little while you'll enjoy being safe instead." Laurel pulled Jen into a rare hug since she was not the touchy-feely type. "I have to get ready for work. Cam and Hilly are on Jen duty today. They'll just hang around your store being adorably in love. Give them a hard time about when they're going to get married. You'll have fun."

Jen grunted. "So what you meant by 'we'll figure out a schedule' is you already have."

Laurel ignored that statement and pointed to the eggs. "Eat that." She walked to the front door, all policewoman certainty.

"I wish I could be more like you," Jen muttered, not meaning for Laurel to catch it.

But she clearly did. She stopped in the doorway and turned to face Jen, her forehead lined with concern. "No you don't," she said forcefully. "You're exactly who you should be." Then she flashed a grin. "Besides, if you were more like me, you'd be married to a Carson, and no one wants that."

She left on a laugh, and Jen joined in, feeling somehow a little better for it.

"OVER MY DEAD BODY."

Grady rolled his eyes as he wiped down the scarred bar of Rightful Claim. "You're putting my bar in danger, cousin."

Ty didn't bother to roll his eyes right back. It was such bull he couldn't even pretend to get worked up about it. "I can handle myself, Grady. Lest you forget, I was an army ranger." Methodically, he kept pulling chairs off the tables and placing them on the floor.

"Lest you forget, two Carsons against a nut job are better than one."

"You've got a pregnant wife. Noah's got a wife and a kid at the ranch. I don't buy you're worried about your bar more than you're worried about that. Living here is the best place for me. Besides, it's all nothing."

Grady shook his head, clearly taking his irritation out on the bar. "My wife's a cop and she—"

"Yeah, funny, that."

Grady didn't rise to that bait. "Laurel's worried,

which means I'm worried. You shouldn't be sleeping in that apartment alone."

Ty flashed a grin. "I'll see what I can do."

"Yeah, I'll believe that once you're able to look away from Jen Delaney long enough to hook up with someone."

"Jen Delaney." Ty made a dismissive noise, though his shoulders tensed against his will. "Sure."

Grady clapped him on the back. "Lie to yourself all you want, Ty, but you aren't fooling anyone. Probably including Jen. You're coming home with me tonight, and that's that."

"You're not my type."

Grady just flashed him a grin. "Your type's just changed, pal. Jen's going to stay at the Delaney Ranch, against her will, and you're going to be under Carson and cop surveillance against yours. Laurel thinks they'll catch this guy in a few days. You can survive a few days in the presence of marital bliss."

Ty knew Grady's humorous tone wasn't to be believed. His moves were jerky, and though he wore that easy grin, there was an edge to his gaze Ty knew better than to challenge.

At least until he found the *right* challenge.

Because he wasn't about to put Grady and Laurel in danger. Or Noah and Addie and Seth for that matter. It was good Jen would be staying out at the Delaney Ranch. Cam lived in the cabin on the property, and Dylan was currently residing in the house. Much as Ty didn't trust a Delaney as far as he could throw one, both men had been in the military and would protect their own.

Ty couldn't help thinking he'd do a better job of it,

and all without bringing any innocent bystanders in. Not that Delaneys were ever really innocent, were they?

Jen is.

Hell. He worked with Grady in silence the rest of their opening routine. He manned the bar while Grady waited tables. The afternoon crowd was sparse, but it slowly got busier and busier as evening inched closer. Even a Monday night could have business booming, especially on a pretty day like today.

Autumn was threatening, and in Wyoming people knew to enjoy the last dregs of summer while they could.

Ty scanned the crowd, that old familiar *bad gut* feeling whispering over his skin. He recognized most of the patrons, but because of the historical atmosphere of the bar they often got strangers in from surrounding towns. It was unusual for him to know *everyone*.

But every stranger's face made him wonder, and every stranger's casual smile made him fear. He thought of all the real danger he'd faced as an army ranger and had never been jittery. Concerned on occasion, but never *nervous*. Determination and right and the mission before him had always given him a center of calm, of certainty.

But Jen had never been unwittingly tied to all those missions, and as much as he detested himself for being that weak, he knew it was the reason. Fear for *her*.

He had a terrible feeling whoever was doing this knew that, too.

His gaze landed on a stranger in a dark corner. All he could make out was a cowboy hat, pulled low.

Like the man on Jen's tape.

Ty forced himself to keep his gaze moving, keep his

moves casual. He took the order of a usual customer, pulled the lever on the beer and glanced again at the man in the corner.

A flash of eye contact, and while he still felt no recognition to this man, he saw the *hate* in that gaze, and more damning, the flash of white-blond hair as Jen had described.

Fighting to keep his cool, and think clearly, he turned to give the beer to the person at the bar. When he quickly turned back to the stranger in the corner—he was gone, and the saloon doors were swinging.

Ty didn't think. Everything around him blanked except getting to that man. If he caught him, this would all be over.

He jumped the bar and ran, ignoring shouts of outrage over spilled beers and Grady's own concerned calling after him. Outside, Ty caught the flash of the man disappearing across the street.

Jen. Her store.

Ty ran as fast as he could, ignoring all else except catching the man who *had* to be responsible for all this. The stranger disappeared behind the buildings on Main, but since Ty had a feeling he knew where the man was running to, he kept his track on the boardwalk.

Once he got to the alley before Delaney General, he took a sharp turn and all but leaped into the back parking lot. Ty came to a stop, breathing hard, scanning the area around him, but there was nothing.

Nothing. With quick, efficient moves, Ty checked the back door. Locked and he hadn't heard a sound, so it was unlikely the man had beat him here and broken in.

He scanned the dark around him, but there was nothing, not even that gut feeling that warned him someone

must be watching. He'd had to have run somewhere
else. Ty could search but there were too many options.
He could have even stashed a vehicle behind another
business on Main and taken the back road out of town.

Ty cursed himself and he cursed the whole situation,
but he also came to a conclusion.

He was going to have to do something even more
drastic than getting the cops involved. Something no
one would approve of, and something that could get
him in quite a bit of trouble.

But Ty knew it was the only answer.

JEN HAD GOTTEN SURVEILLANCE. Bitterness ate through
him like acid at the memory. How dare she protect herself against him and not Ty. She'd let that piece of trash
into the back room of her store. Let him talk to her. She
hadn't called the cops on Ty.

Red clouded his vision, and he had to be careful or
the blood pounding in his ears would get too loud. Too
insistent.

He concentrated on the steering wheel underneath
his palms as he drove in a deliberate circle around Bent.
He thought about Ty chasing after him and losing.

That made him smile. Yes, yes indeed. Ty wasn't
nearly as fast as him, was he? Ty wasn't nearly as smart
and strong and brave as he thought, was he?

The comfort at that thought lasted only a moment
as he thought about earlier in the day. Jen and her surveillance. Anger came back, swift and addicting. He
liked the way rage licked through his system, revved
his mind.

Dr. Michaels said it was bad, but he didn't think
so. He liked it too much for it to be bad. Didn't he de-

serve some of what he liked after everything he'd been through?

The man who'd been in Jen's store all day was clearly military, and he carried. He also touched Jen with far too much familiarity. The man guarding her would have to go on the list under the cop.

Yes, that would be good. Ty, the cop, the man in the store. Targets were good. The rage was good, but it had to have targets. Purpose. That's what Dr. Michaels didn't understand.

Maybe she'd go on the list, too. But not yet. Not now. First, he'd deal with the problems in Bent, Wyoming.

He drove down the back road behind the businesses on Main. He looked at the brick of Delaney General, the heavy steel door that would be tough to break into.

He'd have to make his move soon. He preferred to wait. Draw out the anticipation. Level out some of his rage lest he make a mistake.

But they weren't letting him, were they? And they'd be the ones who paid for his mistakes...so why not make a few?

Chapter Six

Jen had never felt particularly at home at the Delaney Ranch, though it was where she'd grown up. Unlike her brothers, she'd never been interested in the ranch work. She'd found the vast landscape unnerving rather than calming.

When she turned eighteen and moved into the apartment above the store, she'd been happier. She felt more herself there, like the building had simply been waiting for her. She liked to think it was the connection to her ancestors who'd run this store rather than raise cattle or protect the town with badge and honor. Like Laurel had always wanted to be a cop, Jen had always wanted her store.

So, waking up on the Delaney Ranch grated. But she did what she always did when she had to be here and didn't want to be—she made herself useful. It was the one thing that softened her feelings toward the place. Making meals or cleaning up. Laurel used to make fun of her "überdomesticity" but Jen found comfort in the tangible things she could do.

Surprisingly, Vanessa was the first person to enter the kitchen. Well, *stumble* was a better term for it. She was bleary-eyed, with messy hair, and she spoke only one word. "Coffee."

"Decaf?" Jen asked sweetly.

"Don't make me hurt you this early in the morning. I am allowed one cup of coffee per day and I will darn well take it."

Jen hid a smile and pulled down a mug. Though she knew Vanessa would just as soon do everything for herself, Jen didn't have any issue waiting on people. Especially pregnant people. "Sit," she ordered, pouring the coffee herself.

Vanessa lowered herself into a chair at the table and grasped the mug carefully when Jen set it in front of her. "Thanks. I don't suppose you're taking breakfast orders?"

"Only for pregnant women. The men around here get cold cereal as far as I'm concerned."

"Turns out I like you, Jen Delaney. I'm starving and the sound of everything makes my stomach turn."

Jen chatted with Vanessa over some possibilities until they came to something Vanessa thought she could stomach. Jen poured coffee for Dylan and then Dad when they arrived, but they both hurried out over some early meeting at the bank.

Dylan, of course, gave Jen a stern warning not to head to the store until Cam came over to escort her. She rolled her eyes at him, but then he kissed Vanessa's cheek and rested his hand on her belly and everything in Jen softened.

And sharp Vanessa Carson-Delaney softened, too.

"He'll be such a good dad," Jen said, more to herself than Vanessa.

"I'm counting on it. I don't have much in the way

of good role models on the whole parenting thing." She shrugged philosophically. "Though I guess Dylan doesn't either."

Jen slid into the seat across from Vanessa with her own breakfast. "Doesn't it bother you, living here?"

"It's nice digs," Vanessa replied before taking a tentative bite of the oatmeal Jen had put together. "Apparently pregnancy has put your dad on his best behavior around me. Not much to complain about."

"Well, I'm glad, then."

"Gee, I think you mean that. Carsons and Delaneys might start holding hands and singing 'Kumbaya' before you know it."

Jen laughed. Even though it was ridiculous, the idea they were finding some common ground between their two families warmed her.

As long as she didn't think about Ty.

They ate breakfast companionably before Vanessa made her excuses to go take a shower and get ready for work. "Don't worry," Vanessa offered on her way out of the kitchen. "I won't leave till Cam gets here."

Jen huffed out a breath. She hated this babysitting. The stranger going after Ty, or her because of Ty, was hardly going to bust into the house and take her away. If he really was the stranger in her store, he'd already had ample opportunity to do that.

She cleaned up breakfast, glancing at her phone when it trilled. She frowned at the fact the text was from Ty of all people. Her frown turned into a scowl when she saw what he'd texted.

High Noon

It was their old code. Back in the days before they'd had cell phones, he'd simply leave a little note somewhere she'd see it, and that's all it would say for her to know to sneak out the back of the house and meet him at *their* tree.

She shoved the phone back on the counter. She was *not* responding to that. Not at all.

She focused on cleaning, and if occasionally she happened to crane her head toward the window, she stopped herself before she took a look toward the old gnarled tree in the backyard.

If Ty had something to say to her, he could come to the front door.

Her phone trilled again.

Come on, Jen. I need to talk to you.

Baloney. She wiped her hands off on a dish towel, then typed a response. Then talk.

I chased him last night.

She blinked down at those words, then swore. Oh, that man. Was he a moron? Did he have any sense of keeping *himself* safe? Chased him! And what him? Were they sure the note leaver and the man at her store were even the same person?

She shoved her phone into her pocket, then stalked to the front door. She yanked on boots, muttering the whole way. She marched out the front and around the back, a far cry from the teenager who would have snuck around, doing anything to avoid being seen by her family or the ranch hands.

She didn't care who saw her now, because she was about to give Ty Carson a piece of her mind.

She stalked back to that old tree, determined to hold on to her anger and frustration, but the sight of him turned it to dust. His motorcycle was parked exactly where he always used to park it. Older and more lethal, he still looked windswept and she felt her heart do that long slow roll it had always done because Ty Carson was waiting for her.

Her.

She had to swallow at the lump that formed in her throat, embarrassed enough by the emotion to be irritated all over again. "We aren't in high school," she spat, terrified he'd read the rustiness in her voice as old longing.

If he did, he didn't comment on it. "No, we aren't, but I thought it'd get your attention."

She lifted her chin, wanting to feel lofty and above him. "It didn't."

"But me chasing after the guy did." He patted the motorcycle parked in the grass. "Hop on now. I need to talk to you about what happened. Privately."

"Is this yard not private enough?"

He tossed the helmet at her. She caught it out of reflex.

"Nope." He grinned. "Come on, Jen. You know you want to."

She did, God help her. She'd loved riding on the back of Ty's motorcycle in the middle of the night back in high school. It had been the most thrilling thing she'd ever done, aside from share herself with him. Ten years later and her life was staid. Boring. *Just the way you like it. You love your life.*

"Just up to the Carson cabin right quick, then I'll bring you back."

The fact he was so calm confused her. The fact she was tempted upset her. "They'll wonder where I am. They're worried enough."

"So tell them," he said, nodding toward the phone in her pocket. "This isn't cloak-and-dagger."

"Then why do we have to go somewhere else?"

Ty gave her a bland look. "You should really try to be more difficult, Jen. This back-and-forth is so much fun."

"I'm not getting on your motorcycle."

"All right. We can take your car."

She wanted to punch him, but it'd do about as much good as arguing with him. His body was as thick as his skull. "Fine. Just fine." She pulled her phone out and texted Cam and Vanessa that she was with Ty, and she'd let them know the minute she was back. Then she jerked the helmet onto her head and glared at him as she fastened it. "Let's get this over with."

She caught the boyish grin on his face, hated her body's shivering, *lustful* reaction to it. He swung his leg over the bike, waited for her to take her spot.

Your rightful spot.

She was making a mistake. She *knew* she was making a mistake, and yet she clambered onto the motorcycle just like she used to. She wrapped her arms around his waist just like she used to, and he walked the bike a ways down the hill until they were far enough away from the house for the roar of the engine not to reach anyone.

And *oh* the motorcycle roared and the wind whipped through her hair. She wanted to press her cheek to the leather at his back. She wanted to cry. It still felt like flying. It still felt *wonderful*. But she was old enough to understand it was having her arms around Ty, not the machine between her legs.

It was like traveling back in time, visiting with someone who'd died, knowing you'd have to go back to the living all too soon. She was too desperate for that feeling to let it go, even knowing pain awaited her on the other side.

He drove too fast, took turns too sharply, and through it all she held on to him, biting her lip to keep from laughing into the wind.

When he reached the Carson cabin and cut the engine, it took her a moment to pull herself together and release him, then swing herself off the motorcycle. Took her far too many moments to wipe the grin off her face.

She sighed at the tiny clearing and the ramshackle cabin no one lived in but the Carson family used off and on. So many firsts in that cabin, though it had clearly had some repairs over the years. Uneasily, she remembered that last year Noah and Addie had fought off mobsters from Addie's past at this very place.

"Isn't it awful to be back here?"

Ty shrugged. "I don't care to remember Noah being shot, but he's all right now. Lots of shady crap happened here over the years. Such is life as a Carson. Besides, Addie's fixed it all up and they come up here. I figure they can take it, so can I."

She pulled off her helmet and hung it on the handle of the parked bike. "So, what did you want to talk about?"

His gaze was on the cabin, his expression...haunted. Was it what had happened to Noah here or was it that ride that felt like going back in time?

She didn't want to know.

"Let's go inside."

"Ty—"

He walked up to the door, pulling a key out of his pocket and ignoring all her protests.

She could ignore his demands. She could be petulant and wait outside and refuse to do any number of things.

But with a sigh, she followed him inside.

STEP ONE HAD been easy enough. Ty was a little surprised. Oh, he figured he still knew Jen well enough to press the right buttons, but it had all been so easy.

Now came the hard part. He had to get her phone off her. Once he had that, it'd be easy enough to keep her here. Safe and sound and under his supervision. There was the potential that someone would figure out where he'd taken her, but he had to hope they realized what he was doing was for Jen's safety.

And if they had to move elsewhere, well, he'd figure that out, too.

She'd probably consider it "kidnapping." He preferred to think of it as "safekeeping." She'd thank him eventually. Well, probably not ever to his face, but philosophically she might realize he did what was right.

Maybe.

Regardless, he *was* right. So, he had to go about getting her phone off her. "Why don't you have a seat."

Eyebrows furrowed, she looked around the room. Addie's redecorating had made it look family friendly and inviting instead of what it used to be—a place to hide from the law or trouble.

Now it looked like a cozy cottage instead of an outlaw hideout. Ty couldn't say he liked the change, but with Noah and Grady all domesticated now, who was he to complain? They'd bring their kids up here and teach them to hunt, or have sleepovers with their cousins or second cousins. Make a nice little Carson-Delaney future on old Carson land. On old Delaney land.

Ty glanced at Jen, who'd taken a seat on the sky blue couch Addie had gotten to brighten up the living room. But Jen was the real thing that brightened the room. Her long, wispy brown hair and her pixie face, tawny brown eyes with flecks of green. She had a dainty, fairy-like quality to her and he felt like an oaf.

She looked so right there it hurt, like someone had shoved a knife right in his heart. He was halfway surprised to look down and see nothing there except his jacket.

Shoving his hands in his pockets, he ordered himself to focus. Get her phone away from her, and then keep her safe until the cops caught this lunatic. It'd be a few days, tops, he was almost sure of it.

If it was more, well, they'd reevaluate then.

He crossed to the couch, sat next to her. She raised an eyebrow at him, but he needed the proximity to get to her phone. So, he only smiled blandly in response.

Clearly irritated with him, Jen crossed her arms over her chest. "So, you have something to tell me that just had to be done in private?"

"Yes. The stranger that was in your store, he was at Rightful Claim last night."

Immediate concern softened her features, and he was momentarily distracted by all those things that had made him, of all people, fall for a Delaney in the first place.

Jen had been the softest, sweetest place he'd ever had the pleasure of landing. Growing up with an abu-

sive father, she'd been like a balm. It hadn't mattered
that she was a Delaney because she was kind. No matter how Grady or Noah had believed in the feud at the
time—and wasn't that a laugh now?—Ty hadn't cared,
because someone had loved him with a gentleness he'd
never, ever had in his life.

Jen blinked, looked away as a soft blush stained her
cheeks. Like she could read his thoughts, or had a few
memories of her own.

"Jen—" But whatever ridiculous soft words had bubbled up inside him, desperate to be free, were cut off
by the way she looked at him.

Coolly. Detached, she returned his gaze. "You chased
him. That's what your text said."

Business. All business. Good thing, too. Best decision he'd ever made had been to get the hell out of Jen
Delaney's life. No use playing back over what might
have been, or even what still lurked between them.
"Yeah. I thought he was heading for your store, but I
lost him."

"I stayed out at the ranch last night, so it wouldn't
have mattered."

"It matters." In a casual move, he rested his hand on
the cushion between them—close enough his finger
could gently nudge the phone farther out of her pocket.

She frowned down at his hand, but he kept it there as
her gaze returned. He didn't say anything because he
was intent on inching his finger close enough to touch
the phone that just barely peeked out of the pocket of
her jeans.

"Why did you bring me here, Ty? What's going on?"

He used his index finger to nudge the corner of her
phone out of her pocket. If he could move it enough, get

it at the right angle, it'd fall out once she stood up. Then he'd just have to hope she didn't feel it or notice it for how long it would take him to secret it away.

So, he nudged and spoke. "The cops are on this whole thing, but I'm worried. I don't like that this guy was hanging around your place and Rightful Claim. It feels off."

"Laurel said he's sloppy and they'll get him in no time." But no matter how brave she tried to sound, she chewed on her bottom lip. She shifted slightly, as if she'd felt the move of her phone.

Ty grabbed her hand before she could pat her pocket down. He'd done it out of desperation, but the sizzle of connection shocked him into forgetting all about the phone.

How did her hand fit with his, like a key to a lock? Even now that simple touch was all it took to make him forget his real purpose and remember her. The feel of her. The rightness of her. And how he'd been the one to mishandle it all, ruin it all.

She blinked once, as if coming out of the same dream, and then jerked her hand away. "What is this?" she demanded. She popped to her feet and he was relieved the phone fell right out, and she didn't even notice. She paced as he scooted over and gently nudged the phone deep into the cushions.

Finally she whirled, as if she'd come to some grand determination. "It's time to take me home."

He smiled lazily, knowing it would make her narrow her eyes and curl her hands into fists. "About that."

"Tyler," she warned through clenched teeth.

It amazed him that he couldn't control his negative reaction to his full name when he'd spent a lifetime controlling any and all negative reactions he didn't want to broadcast. But he nearly flinched every time she leveled him with that haughty *Tyler*.

"We're not going anywhere. Not for a while."

She made a sound of outrage, then did exactly what he'd hoped. She stormed for the door.

He took the moment to fish her phone out of the couch and click off the sound before sliding it into the drawer of the coffee table. Even as she wrenched the front door open and stomped outside, he closed and locked the drawer before sauntering after her.

She stalked right over to his motorcycle and then kicked it over. She gave him a defiant look, but he refused to rise to the bait. Barely. No one, *no one* hurt his bike. But he'd give her a pass since he was…well, not kidnapping her.

Exactly.

"Very mature, Jen."

She flipped him off, which did give him enough of a jolt to laugh. He'd forgotten how much he enjoyed her rare flashes of temper.

"I'm calling Laurel. Do you really think—" She stopped as her hands patted every pocket of her jeans. Once, twice, before shoving her hands into each pocket.

She looked up at him with shock in her gaze. It quickly turned to murder as she let out a primal scream and lunged at him.

Chapter Seven

Jen couldn't ever remember being so angry. She wanted to take a chunk out of Ty. She wanted to bloody his nose or knee him in the crotch, and if she'd been able to see anything more than the red haze of anger, she might have been strategic enough to do any of those things. Maybe.

But she was too mad, stupid with it, and she launched herself at him, only to be caught and corralled. She landed precisely one punch to his rock-hard chest before he had his arms wrapped around her tight enough she couldn't wriggle her arms free.

She kicked, but he only lifted her off the ground, angling her so her kicks did nothing.

"I hate you," she spat, right in his face.

He only grinned. "Now, now, darling, your hellcat is showing."

She wriggled on an outraged growl, but he only clamped his arms around her tighter so she could barely move at all as he marched her back inside. So she was pressed against the hard wall of muscle that was the love of her life.

He'd brought her up here, stolen her phone and was thwarting all her attempts to unleash her anger.

"This is ridiculous. Insane. You've lost your mind. Do you really think my family won't come up here and—"

"No, I don't think they will," he replied, equitably, as he all too easily moved her to the living room.

She kept wriggling, but it was no use. He was very, *very* strong, and she refused to acknowledge the hot lick of heat that centered itself in her core.

He dumped her on the couch and when she popped to her feet, he nudged her back down, looming over her.

"Stay put."

"Or what?" she demanded, outrage at his behavior and her body's response boiling together into nothing but pure fury. "Going to stalk me? Leave me some threatening letters in blood? You're no better than—"

He all but shoved his face into hers, cutting off not just her words but also her breath. His eyes shone with that fierce battle light that had thrilled her once upon a time, and maybe it still did, though she didn't much feel like being honest with herself right now. She'd rather pretend the shaky feeling in her limbs was fear, not that old desire to soothe the outlaw in him. To love him until he softened.

"Don't compare me to the man doing this, Jen. Not now. Not ever. You may not like my methods, but I'm doing what I have to do to keep *you* safe."

Her heart jittered, and that pulsing heat she remembered so well spread through her belly like a sip of straight whiskey. But she forced herself to be calm, to be disdainful. "I'm only in danger because of you."

He pushed away from the couch then, but not before she caught the flash of hurt in his eyes. Why did it still hurt *her* to cause him pain? Why couldn't she be completely and utterly unaffected by him, his emotions, his muscles or that past they'd shared?

"Yeah, that's true, which is why it's my duty to protect you."

"I have a family full of dutiful protectors. I don't need you."

His back was to her, so she couldn't read how that statement might have affected him. He was silent for the longest time.

She should speak. Demand her phone back and demand to be taken home. Threaten and yell until she got her way.

But she knew how useless that was. A Carson had an idea in his head and she'd never be able to get through that thick skull. She'd have to be sneakier than that. More devious.

Sneaky and devious weren't exactly natural for her like they were for Ty, but hadn't she loved him and watched him for years? Didn't she know how to retreat, circumnavigate and end up with what she wanted?

And if she didn't know how to do that, she'd figure it out. He wasn't going to lock her up here in the Carson cabin like some sort of helpless princess.

Which meant she had to be calm and reasonable in response to his…his…idiocy.

"Ty," she began, her voice like that of a teacher instructing a student. "Be reasonable. You can't take my phone away from me, lock the doors and expect me to stay put. It isn't sensible, and I'm surprised at you. It isn't like you to act without thinking."

He turned to face her, appearing detached and vaguely, disdainfully amused. A trick of his she'd always envied.

"I've thought it through, darling. I know exactly what I'm doing. I was also quite aware you wouldn't like it."

Bristling, Jen curled her fingers into fists, trying to center her frustration there instead of at him. "Laurel won't—"

"Laurel will. Because you'll be safe and out of harm's way, won't you?"

"Like Addie and Noah were?" she returned, knowing it would hit him where it hurt. No matter that she hated to hurt him, she was very aware she needed to.

"This guy isn't the mob," Ty replied, referring to the men who had hurt Noah and Addie here, but Ty had that blank look on his face that belied the emotion hidden underneath.

"You don't know who he is," Jen returned, gentling her tone without realizing it.

He was so *still*. The stillness that had once prompted her to soothe, to love. Because Ty's stillness wasn't the actual reaction. His stillness hid all the myriad reactions inside him. Ever since he'd been a boy she knew he'd developed that skill, a response to an abusive father, and she'd always seen his stillness for that little boy's hurt. She'd always ached over it.

God, she wished she no longer did, but it was there. Deep and painful. It was against every instinct she had to clamp her mouth shut and keep the soothing words inside.

"I can't figure out who he is when you're in danger. I can't *think* when I'm worried about you."

"I'm not your concern."

He scoffed audibly. "Oh, please."

"I haven't been for ten years. You didn't concern yourself with me when you disappeared without a goodbye. You didn't concern yourself with me for ten full years after you just…" It was bubbling up inside her, all the betrayal and the hurt she'd been hiding from him.

"You want to have that out now?" he asked, so cool and stoic it was like being stabbed.

Jen closed her eyes and pressed fingers to her temple. She had to find some semblance of control when it came to him. "No, I don't. It's ancient history."

"Maybe, but ancient history can fester and rot."

She opened her eyes, worked up her steeliest, most determined look. "Mine hasn't."

"Yeah. You and *Thomas* make a real cute couple."

Jen angled her chin. If he thought that, well, she'd use it. She'd use it to protect her heart. "We're very happy."

But his mouth quirked. "You haven't slept together."

Outraged, she stood. "You don't know that."

"Oh, I know it." He took a step toward her, but she would not back down.

She refused to be affected by the large man looming over her. He was not some romantic hero sweeping her off her feet. He was a thick-skulled caveman thinking he knew better than her and casting aspersions on her made-up relationship with a perfectly decent man.

However, she knew Ty well enough to know that arrogant grin meant he wanted a fight. She wouldn't give him one.

"I guess we'll have to agree to disagree," she said coolly. "Now, I'd appreciate my phone back. You can rest assured if my family agrees, I'll stay put."

"Because you're so good at doing what your family says?"

She smiled, trying to match his arrogance, though she was afraid it only read brittle. "I only made one very regrettable mistake in that regard. I learned never to make it again." She'd been hurt too deeply by the way he'd left her to ever, ever go back to a place where she'd give her whole heart so completely to someone.

She'd been stupid with youth and innocence, but she was older and wiser and she'd *learned*.

"Touché," he returned wryly.

"Now, perhaps we can have an adult conversation."

"I wouldn't count on it, darling."

She wouldn't let him get to her. He wanted to irritate her. He enjoyed it. So, she wouldn't give him the satisfaction. "Just what exactly is your plan? Surely you're aware you'll have to contact my family."

"Surely."

"As much sway as you have over Grady, it's highly unlikely he'll side with you over Laurel."

"Highly unlikely indeed," he returned, clearly mocking her.

Do not snap. Do not snap at this hardheaded moron. "So. What's the plan?"

"The plan is I tell your family we decided to get out of Dodge for a while, so to speak."

"They won't believe that."

He raised an eyebrow. "You came with me willingly, if you recall. What's not to believe?"

"That I didn't discuss it with them first."

Ty grinned at that. "Yeah, they'll have a real hard time believing we went off and did something without getting approval."

She waved a hand. "It's not like they know about us."

Ty blinked at that, some piece of that sentence piercing his impenetrable shell enough to show surprise. "What do you mean?"

"I mean no one knows what happened between us back then. Well, Laurel and I discussed it briefly the other day, but mostly no Delaney knows that there was ever an us, or that I ever did something without approval. They'd be shocked." She forced herself to laugh. "Can you imagine my father's reaction if he knew I'd been seeing you?"

Ty was too still, and not that stillness that covered up an emotional reaction. No, this was something more like a stillness born of horror. It didn't make any sense, and it made her heart pound too hard in her chest.

"Ty…"

He blinked and turned away. "I should call Grady. He'll believe me. We'll hide out here a few days, and if they still haven't caught the guy, we'll reevaluate."

"Ty—"

"I think Hilly will be able to run the store for you well enough. If not, your father will come up with someone. Consider it a vacation. Relax. Enjoy yourself. Take a bath or whatever it is women do."

"Ty," she snapped, vibrating now with unknown emotions, like a premonition. There was too much happening here and his evasion wasn't nearly as tidy as he'd clearly wanted it to be. Dread weighted her limbs, but she had to understand this. Even when her heart shied away from knowing. "Who knew?"

"Knew what? That I'd bring you he—"

"Tyler." She didn't snap this time. It was little more than a whisper, because she had this horrible, horrible weight in her gut she couldn't unload. "Who knew about us before?"

"It's a small town, Jen. I'm sure any number of—"

She stepped forward. While thoughts of violence

whirled in her head, she merely placed her hand over his heart with a gentleness she didn't understand. It was hardly the first time her mind and heart were at odds when it came to Ty. "Tell me the truth."

He didn't look at her. He kept his gaze on the wall and his jaw clamped tight. She thought he was refusing to answer her, but as her hand fell from his chest, his throat moved.

"Jen, you said it was ancient history." But his voice was too soft, too gentle. Two things Ty almost never was—now or then.

But she had to know. She had to... There was too much she didn't know or understand and she needed this whole thing to make sense. If it made sense maybe she could lock all these feelings back in the past where they belonged. "And you said ancient history could fester and rot."

He looked down at her then, and it was like looking at the boy she'd loved. Strong and defiant in everything, but in the depth of those blue eyes she could see his storms and his hurts and his desperation to make things *right*.

It was what she'd always loved about him. Then. Now? Her brain knew a person didn't still love someone after a ten-year absence, after the betrayal of leaving without a goodbye, and yet her heart...

"Your father knew."

It was a blow. It didn't matter and yet it felt like someone had plowed something into her stomach.

"He threatened you," Jen surmised, a light-headed queasiness replacing the pain. "That's why you left."

Ty laughed bitterly. "Sure, I was scared of the big bad Delaney. Get a grip, Jen. I left because I left."

She knew better, and it occurred to her now the reason she hadn't been able to get over Ty and her love for him was that she knew he hadn't abandoned her without a reason. He had a reason—one he didn't want her to know about.

It was ancient history, and she wanted to forget. But after he'd disappeared, she'd experienced grief as if he'd died, not just left.

Still, she didn't think he was lying, exactly. Ty had never been intimidated by her father. He'd never been scared of his reaction like she had been. She'd wanted to please her father, and she'd wanted to love Ty. She'd known both couldn't exist, so she'd kept them separate.

Or thought she had. Her father had known. Ty had left because her father had known and—Oh, *God.* "He threatened me," she realized, aloud. "You left because he threatened *me.*"

"I would have joined the army no matter what." So still. So blank, and yet in his blankness she knew he felt a million things. In his blankness he confirmed her realization. He'd left only because of something Dad had done to threaten her life.

Ty hadn't left to save his own skin, or even simply because he'd wanted to. He'd left to protect her in some way. She wanted it to ease or heal something inside her, but it didn't. "You could have said goodbye."

"I have to call Grady. I have to—"

"What are you afraid of, Ty? That the truth from a decade ago will change something? I'm not so sure it will. The why of what you did doesn't change what you did, but maybe the truth would give us both some peace."

"Fine. You want truth and peace and moving on?"

Temper sizzled, but he kept his hands jammed into his pockets. "Yeah, he threatened you. Said he'd sell the store if I didn't get the hell out and away from you. So, I did. You got your store, and I got the army, and life went the hell on." He jerked his shoulders in a violent shrug. "I figured he would have told you all that at some point."

Her store. Dad had threatened to sell her store. Jen sank onto the couch behind her. No, her father had never told her that. He wouldn't have, for one simple reason. "He wouldn't have sold the store. It was a bluff."

Ty raised a pitying eyebrow. "Sure, darling."

She wouldn't fall apart in front of Ty. Not when he was being so dismissive. Not when it proved what she'd always felt but tried to talk herself out of.

He hadn't left out of malice, or even to save his own skin. He'd left the way he had out of love. It changed nothing in the here and now, but somehow it changed her. Something deep inside her.

She didn't understand the shift, the feeling, but she figured with enough time she would. She glanced up at Ty, who looked like a storm encased in skin.

Time. They needed more time. So, she'd stay until the threat against her—against *them*—was gone. Then…

Well, then she'd figure out the next step.

THEY'D DISAPPEARED. A morning skulking around town and he hadn't seen hide nor hair. They'd tried to escape him.

It was nearly impossible to swim out of the black, bubbling anger threatening to drown him. But he couldn't let it win, because then he wouldn't succeed in his mission. In his revenge.

Using the prepaid phone he'd picked up at a gas station in Fremont, he dialed the old familiar number, trying to focus on the help he would find.

When the perky secretary answered, he tightened his grip on the phone. Some old memory was whispering something to him, but he couldn't understand it with the fury swamping him.

"I need to speak with Dr. Michaels."

There was a pause on the other end, and he snarled. He narrowly resisted bashing the phone against his steering wheel.

"I'm so sorry," the secretary said soothingly. It did nothing to soothe. "I thought we'd contacted all of her patients. Dr. Michaels will be off for quite a bit. We have a temporary—"

"I need to speak with Dr. Michaels. Now." He closed his eyes against the pain in his skull. It smelled like blood, and for a moment he remembered the singing joy of knocking the life out of that uppity doctor.

Hadn't that only been a dream?

Yes, just a dream, sneaking into her house and waiting for her to get home. Just a dream, standing in her closet and waiting for her to open it to hang up her coat.

Stab. Stab. Stab.

A dream.

The secretary was lying, that was all. Covering for her boss who was off *vacationing*. He'd put them both on the list.

On an oath, he hit End on the phone and threw it against the windshield. It thudded but didn't crack the glass like he'd hoped.

He needed to hurt something. Someone. Now.

But he wanted Ty. Jen. So maybe he'd just save up all the anger.

When he found them, they'd pay.

Chapter Eight

Ty didn't care for the tightness in his chest, but he wasn't about to let the woman sitting quietly at the small kitchen table see that. She'd already seen too much, disarming him with the gentle way she'd touched his heart and asked him to explain.

Who cared? So old man Delaney had told him he'd sell Jen's dream out from under her if Ty didn't disappear. So, Ty had listened. Didn't make him good or right. It was simply what had happened.

Why'd Jen have to bring it up? How had she not… known for all these years?

"You know, we have bigger fish to fry than our past," he snapped into the edgy silence they'd lapsed into while he'd put together some food for dinner.

"Yes, we do," she agreed easily. Too easily.

He shouldn't look at her. He knew what he'd see and what he'd feel, but he was helpless to resist a glance. Her expression was placid, reasonable even, but her hands were clasped tightly on the table and there was misery in her eyes.

He'd always known he'd bring her misery. He just hadn't known it would last so long.

"I'm going to call Grady. Tell him we're lying low for a few days."

She didn't look at him as she nodded. "Yes. All right."

She wasn't listening to him. She was lost in a past that didn't—couldn't—matter anymore.

He pulled his phone out of his pocket and dialed Grady's number as he walked into a bedroom. He stepped inside, closed the door and let the pained breath whoosh out of him.

What the hell did he think he was doing? Saving her? It wasn't his job or place. Maybe she was in danger because of him, but that didn't mean…

"You know Laurel's going to kill you, right?"

Ty might have laughed at his cousin's greeting if he didn't feel like he'd swallowed glass. "She should probably hear me out first."

"Good luck with that."

"Which is why I called you, not her," Ty said, keeping his voice steady and certain. "We're just going to lie low for a few days. Let the cops find the guy. Sensible plan if you ask me."

"Since when does a Carson do the sensible thing and leave it to the cops?"

Ty wanted to be amused, but he was all raw edges and, if he was totally honest with himself, gaping wounds.

But wounds could heal. Would. Once this was all over.

"Your wife seems to have a handle on finding this guy," Ty explained. "Plus, a Delaney is in the line of fire, not me. Let Laurel and her little deputies figure out who this guy is and—"

"Who this guy is that's targeting *you*, Ty. Why aren't you trying to figure out who it is?"

The blow landed, and Ty refused to acknowledge it. "The cops have his DNA now. What am I supposed to do about it?"

"You've got the brain in your head, which I used to think was quite sharp. Now I'm wondering."

It hurt, and Ty would blame it on already being raw. "I don't know who it is. Not sure how I'm supposed to magically figure it out. I'm not a cop. Look. Jen and I will stay out of sight for a few days. Let the law work, much as it pains me. Safest bet all the way around."

"Then what?"

"What do you mean, then what? Then things go back the way they were and everyone's safe."

Grady was silent for too many humming moments. "You can't run away every time you don't know what to do, or how to face what you have to do."

Shocked, knocked back as if the words had been a physical blow, Ty did everything he could to keep his voice low. "Are you calling me a coward?"

"No, Ty, I'm noticing a pattern. One you're better than." He sighed into the phone.

Ty searched for something nasty or dismissive to say, but Grady's words had hooks, barbs that took hold and tore him open.

"Stay out of town and keep Jen safe if that's what you have to do," Grady said, with enough doubt to have Ty bristling. "I'll convince my wife it isn't such a bad idea. I'll do that for you because I love you, but I think you're better than this. Maybe someday you'll figure that out."

Ty didn't have any earthly idea what to say to that, and he was someone who always knew what to say—

even if it was a pithy comment designed to piss someone off.

In the end, he didn't have to say anything. Grady cut the connection and Ty was left in the small bedroom he'd snuck Jen off to for very different reasons their junior year of high school.

Grady didn't understand. He hadn't gotten out of Bent like Ty had. He didn't understand the world out there was different from their isolated little community in Wyoming. He didn't understand that sometimes a man had to get out and let someone else handle the aftermath.

Grady could think it was cowardice, but Ty knew it took a bigger man to do the right thing without concerning himself over his ego. Carsons ran on ego, and Ty had learned not to.

He'd keep Jen safe, and Grady might never understand, but Ty had never needed anyone's understanding. Ever.

Temper vibrated and he ruthlessly controlled it as he stepped back into the cabin's living area.

Jen sat in the same exact place at the kitchen table, looking at the same spot on the wall, fingers still laced together on the glossy wood Addie always kept clean. She'd barely eaten any of the canned chili he'd fixed earlier. She looked like a statue, regal and frozen and far too beautiful to touch without getting his dirty fingerprints all over her.

He shook that thought away. The days of loving her and feeling inferior to her were over. All that was left was keeping her safe from trouble he'd unwittingly brought to her door, and if he had to wade through some past ugly waters to do it, well, he'd survive.

"Grady'll handle Laurel."

Jen's all-too-pulled-together demeanor changed. She looked over her shoulder at him and rolled her eyes. "Handle. You don't have a clue."

"So she's got him wrapped up in her. Doesn't mean he can't handle her."

"Do you pay attention at all? They work because they talk. They don't agree on everything, they don't handle each other, they *communicate*. And sometimes they still don't agree, but they love each other anyway because if you actually try to understand someone else's point of view, even if you don't share it, you're both a lot better off."

"Is that some kind of lecture?"

She snorted. "God, you're such a piece of work."

He flashed his easy grin and didn't understand why everything seemed to curdle in his stomach. "That's what they all say, darling."

She stood carefully, brushing imaginary wrinkles out of her shirt. "I want my phone back."

"Afraid not."

"I've agreed to stay with you. There's no reason for you to keep my property from me."

She'd never used that Delaney disdain on him. Not back then, and not even in the time since he'd been back now. Snarky sometimes, yes. Irritated, always. But not that cold, haughty voice as if she was a master talking to a servant.

He'd deal with a lot to keep her safe, to keep his own wounded emotions safe and locked away, but there was no way in hell he was putting up with that.

So he kept walking toward her, grinning the grin that made his soul feel black and shriveled. "Make me, darling."

JEN KNEW OF absolutely no one else who made her consider bodily harm on a person more than Ty. Being stuck in this cabin with him for even a few hours was already torture, and she'd shown admirable restraint if she did say so herself.

She would not lower herself to try to physically best him again. There was no point in a shouting match or demanding her phone back. So, she'd take a page out of her father's notebook and play the better-than-thou Delaney.

She didn't *feel* better than anyone, but she supposed that didn't really matter.

"Fine, if you want to play your childish games, keep my phone." She shrugged as if it was of no consequence. "We're not going to sit around here like lumps on logs," she decided. "We're going to do our own detective work. We'll start with a list of people who would have reason to threaten you, and me through you. You'll need to get a piece of paper and a pen so we can write it all down."

"You're not very good at the lady of the manor crap. You'll have to practice."

She raised an eyebrow at him and knew her face didn't betray a flicker of irritation or hurt. "Lucky for me, I have all the time in the world to do so."

He held her gaze for a long time. Too long to win the staring match. Still, she thought the move to get situated on the couch in the most dismissive manner she could manage was a good enough substitute to staring him down.

Then she simply waited, fixing him with a bland stare of expectation. His jaw worked before he finally gave in and walked over to the kitchen silently. He jerked open a few drawers before pulling out a pad of paper and a pen.

"Thank my sister-in-law for these homey little touches." He returned, dropping the paper and pen on the coffee table in front of her.

"I like Addie," Jen returned.

"She's a Delaney, so I don't know why you wouldn't."

"She makes Noah happy," Jen persisted, wanting *something* to get through that hard shell of his. "She and Seth make Noah as happy as I've ever seen him."

"Your point?"

"Maybe *you* should thank Addie for the homey touches without being so derisive."

He held her gaze, but nothing changed in his expression. "You wanted to make a list?" he said, just the tiniest hint of irritation edging his tone.

She picked up the paper and the pen, because she did want to do this and there was no need to belabor points about love and happiness in this little hell she found herself in. She poised pen on paper and ignored the way her heart hitched. "I suppose my father would be on the list."

Ty heaved out a sigh. "It ain't your father."

"No, it seems unlikely," Jen agreed, doing everything to sound calm and polite. "But we're starting from nothing, which means no stone left unturned. My father dislikes you. He's threatened me to get to you before apparently. He fits."

"He's not the man who's been skulking around your store or my saloon."

"No. He isn't. But that man could be working for my father. It's not out of the realm of possibility."

Ty didn't argue with that, but he paced the small

living room area. "I don't recognize him. If he was someone I'd known, someone who knew *me* personally, wouldn't I recognize him? In your tape. In Rightful Claim. There'd be *some* recognition."

She could see the fact he didn't know the man bothered him on a deeper level than she'd originally thought. The fact there was even the smallest ounce of helplessness inside him softened her. She wanted to reach out and touch his hand, something gentle and friendly and reassuring. She even lifted her hand, but then she let it drop back onto her thigh.

"It's not unheard of for someone to pay someone else to enact some sort of revenge or whatever this is."

Ty shook his head. "I saw him, Jen. There in Rightful Claim. He hated me. I saw it on his face. He *hated* me. But I don't know who he is."

She stayed quiet for a few humming seconds, reminding herself it wasn't her job to comfort him. She was angry with him and she would give him no solace in this, no matter how impotent he felt—not something a man like Ty Carson was used to.

Not her problem, and *not* something she was going to care about. "You don't recognize him, but he hates you. So, who hates you? If you just start naming people it might dislodge a memory. It's also possible this man is connected to someone on the list. Sitting here waiting for Laurel to figure it out—"

"I'd settle for any half-brained cop to figure it out, or a lab to get DNA on that blood."

"I'm sure they'd settle for that, too," Jen replied primly. She wanted to defend Laurel, considering her older sister was the strongest, smartest, most dedicated person Jen knew, but it would land against that hard head like a peaceful breeze and fall on deaf ears. "For now, we write a list." She smiled sweetly over at him. "Even if the police figure it out first, you'll have a handy reference for the next time someone tries to…" She trailed off and frowned.

This person wasn't trying to hurt Ty—not physically. The person who wrote the notes, if he was the same person stalking her store, wanted to cause fear. Worry—not for Ty's own welfare, but for hers.

"They don't want to hurt you—they want to cause you pain," Jen muttered, working through the problem aloud.

"I think that's the same thing, darling."

"No. No, it isn't. If they hated you, they'd want to hurt you."

"He *does* hate me, that's what I'm saying."

She waved him away, trying to think and connect the dots she was so close to connecting. "This person you don't recognize hates *you*, but wants to hurt someone he thinks you l-love." She tripped over that l-word a bit, but she hurried past it and didn't look at him. "So, it would make sense that you didn't hurt this individual. You hurt someone *he* loved."

"You really want a list of all the women I've hurt, Jen?"

"It doesn't have to be a woman, Ty. There are lots of different kinds of love. But yes, if you hurt someone enough that they hated you—that someone who loved them might have hated you—then we should put it on the list. Again, my father qualifies."

"It's not your father."

Jen couldn't see it either, but it fascinated her that Ty was so insistent. Ty, who'd always hated her father, and surely still did. But he refused to consider her father might be behind this.

So, she kept poking at it. "Then who is it?"

Ty shook his head, but in his next breath he started naming names, and Jen went to work to write them down.

WITH THE POLICE SCANNER, the cops were easy to thwart. They only had three on duty in the area at any given time, so he always knew where they were or where they were headed.

The detective was a little bit harder to track, but knowing she was sister to Jen and married to one of Ty's relatives gave him some intel.

He'd followed the detective around a bit in the afternoon on foot. She'd been in her patrol car, but the town was small, and with his radio she was easy to find.

To watch.

To wait.

She looked like Jen. She might do as a substitute. He'd hurt her just a little. Just a little. It'd take the edge off.

He considered it as he got back in his car when he realized her shift was over. He followed, taking a few turns out of her line of sight so she didn't suspect anything. When she turned off the highway, he parked his car along the shoulder. He slapped one of the abandoned-vehicle tags he'd stolen weeks ago on the back window so no one would think twice about his car being there.

Then he walked up the lane, and to the gleaming-new-looking cabin in a little cove of rock and trees. She was pulling things out of the trunk of her police car.

He could do it. Hurt her. Kill her. Spill blood. Right here, right now. She wore a gun, but what were the chances she'd have the reflexes to hurt him first?

Keep your focus. Keep your focus.

Dr. Michaels told him he did better with a goal. And his goal was causing as much emotional and *then* physical harm to Ty Carson as possible. The cop would be a distraction.

But he ached with the need to kill, and Jen's sister was ripe for the killing.

A loud engine sound cut through the quiet, and the cop shouldered her bag and shaded her eyes against the setting sun. A man roared up on a motorcycle. Not Ty as he'd hoped, but the other one. Not the brother, but a cousin, maybe.

People who mattered to Ty. It would be Ty's fault if they were harmed or killed. Ty would have all that guilt, and his would be gone.

He could pick them off in quick succession—bam, bam—and they'd fall to the ground. He wanted it. Needed it. His hand even reached for his side, but he remembered when he came up with nothing that he'd purposefully left his pistol in his car.

"Ty's the target," he whispered, reminding himself this was premature. Have a goal, Dr. Michaels had always told him. He ignored the tears of rage and disappointment streaming down his cheeks.

The goal was Ty, not these people. Jen was the best target. A decision he hadn't made lightly.

He'd do everything he wanted to do to Jen and more, maybe in front of Ty himself. Yes, Ty had secreted her away, but he'd find them.

He'd find them and they would know true pain, and Ty would know true guilt.

And him? He'd finally be at peace.

Chapter Nine

The world was black and she couldn't breathe. Jen tried to thrash, but her body wouldn't move. She saw blood, smelled it even. But it wasn't her blood. It bathed the floor around her, but she wasn't hurt. So who was?

She sat bolt upright, eyes flying wide, her sister's name on her lips.

But Laurel wasn't in this unfamiliar room with her. There was no blood. Only slabs of wood, bathed gold in the faint light of a lamp on the bedside table.

Jen wasn't alone, though. No Laurel, no blood. She was in a comfortable bed, heart beating so loud she couldn't hear the horrible sound of her ragged breathing. "Ty?"

Still not fully awake, she reached for him, found his hand warm and strong. Something inside her eased, the sharp claws of panic slowly receding with the contact. Ty was holding her hand and she was safe.

"You were dreaming." His voice was flat, but he was there. When they'd decided to call it a night, he'd gone into one bedroom and she'd gone into another. But just now she'd been in the middle of a horrible nightmare she couldn't seem to fully shake, and he was here in this room with her.

Holding her hand.

"Breathe," he ordered, but there was no snap to his tone. A tinge of desperation, but nothing harsh.

So, she sucked in a breath and let it out. She squeezed his hand because it was her anchor. "It was Laurel. She was hurt."

"Laurel is fine."

"I know. It was just a dream." She fisted her free hand to her heart. "It just felt real. So horribly real. I could smell it."

"Just keep breathing."

So she did. She looked around the room, trying to orient herself. The Carson cabin. It looked so different from when they'd been in high school and snuck up here to…

Well, it wouldn't do to think of that, or how good it would feel to curl up into Ty's strong, comforting body and—

Yeah, no. She focused on the room. It was different from how it had been. New furniture, new curtains. Definitely new linens on the bed, and a pretty area rug that softened the harsh wood walls that had stood for over a century.

It smelled the same, though. The slight must of old not-often-used house and laundry detergent. She blinked owlishly at the lamplight, then at Ty.

He was rumpled, and still. So very still, perched on the edge of that bed like she might bite. But his hand held hers.

It would have amused her, if it didn't make her unbearably sad.

"Good?" he asked abruptly.

She nodded and he withdrew his hand and got to his

feet. He shoved his hands into the pockets of his sweat-pants and refused to meet her gaze. "Need anything?"

She did, but she didn't know what exactly. Surely not whatever he was offering, or rather, hoping she wouldn't take him up on.

She rubbed her hand over her chest. She'd calmed her breathing and her mind, but she felt clammy and shaken. There'd been so much blood, and it had been real enough to smell it, to feel it.

It was worse, worrying for someone you loved. So much worse than being concerned over your own safety. But it had been only a dream. Laurel was safe and sound at home, with Grady. Jen hadn't had any silly danger dreams last year when Laurel had been facing down *real* danger, so it was foolish to believe her dreams were suddenly premonitions.

"Jen. Do you need anything?"

She shook her head, trying to focus. "No. No, I'm all right." Which wasn't true. At all.

Ty moved swiftly for the door, and that made all the ways she wasn't all right twine together into panic.

"No, that's a lie. I'm not all right. I'm afraid."

He paused at the door. He didn't turn, but he stopped. "Fear's natural," he said quietly, surprising her.

She rarely told anyone in her family when she was afraid. She'd learned at a young age Delaneys weren't supposed to be afraid. They were supposed to *endure.* And if not, she was the weak one to be protected.

Hadn't that been the appeal of Ty Carson? He hadn't treated her like a fragile little girl, or like she was a little beneath him. He'd been curt with her, rough at times, and she'd known, deep down, he'd thought she was a little better than him.

It wasn't true, but she'd known he'd felt that way, and part of her had relished that. A painful thing to realize, to admit to herself. But she'd been a teenager. Didn't she get to cut herself some slack?

Shouldn't she cut *him* some? "You're not going to tell me not to worry about it, that you'll handle it and I'm just fine?"

"No."

She picked at the coverlet over her legs. She knew he didn't want to have this conversation, to listen to her insecurities, but she also knew he would. And she'd feel better for it. "Everyone else does."

"Everyone else… Listen…" He turned to face her, hands still shoved deep in his pockets and a scowl on his face. He looked like he was preparing for a brawl, but she knew that was always how he looked when faced with a conversation he felt like he needed to have even though he didn't want to. "I've been in a lot of real dangerous situations, and a lot that only *felt* dangerous. Nothing I did could erase the fear whether the danger was real or perceived. You learn to hone it. You should be afraid. What's going on is scary."

She wrapped her arms around herself, trying to hold those words to her heart. "As pep talks go, that was surprisingly effective."

"It isn't always the fear that gets us, it's the idea we can't or shouldn't be afraid. Fear is natural. To fear is to be human."

Human. Such a complex idea she never really considered. In her memories of Ty he was either that perfect paragon of nostalgic first love, or he was the symbol of the way he'd left her. The way she'd thought about him since he'd been back had been one-dimensional.

It had been about *her* feelings, and nothing to do with him as a human being.

It wasn't wrong, exactly. It was just more complicated than that. He was human. She was human. Fears, confusions, mistakes.

Whoever was trying to hurt them was human, too, underneath whatever warped thing made a person want to hurt someone. Human and hurting and doing terrible things to alleviate the hurt.

She didn't want that to be her. She'd done no terrible things, but she'd shoved herself farther and farther into a box without ever dealing with the here and now. The feelings that hurt and diminished all that she was.

It was time to stop. "I don't really want to be alone." She didn't admit things like that. She'd never had to. She'd never had to ask for what she wanted or needed—she either got it easily or she kept that want locked away until she forgot about it or learned to live without it.

She'd thought that was being adaptable, learning to live without what life refused to give her. But sitting here in this bed that wasn't hers, a man who wasn't hers lurking by the door, fear and confusion and hurt lying heavy on her heart, she had to wonder.

Was never asking for the things she wanted holding her back? Is that what had kept her comparing every man she'd ever dated with the man of her high school dreams? A fear of asking for more—for what she wanted—for anything.

"Could you stay?" They might have been the scariest words she'd ever voiced. They opened up every fear of rejection she'd ever harbored without fully realizing it.

But if she could live without the thing when she didn't ask, why not be able to live with it when she did?

It was the same. Living without was all the same. If she asked, though, she might get something.

Ty eased himself onto the corner of the bed, still keeping a large distance between them. Because he didn't want to be here. He didn't want to stay with her, but she'd asked.

She'd asked, and he stayed.

WHEN TY WOKE up to the ringing of his phone, he was stiff and disoriented. A mix of familiar and unfamiliar assaulting his senses. The smell of the cabin, mixed with something fruity. The familiar warmth of the sunlight on his face that always snuck through the crack in the curtains, the unfamiliar warmth of a body next to him.

The phone stopped, and groggily he tried to figure out why he should care. Jen shifted next to him, and when he looked down on her—a completely ill-advised move—her eyes blinked open.

A deep brown with flecks of green that reminded him of the woods they used to sneak off into. That reminded him of the plans he'd let die because he'd been young and stupid. Because for all his ego and bluster, he'd believed, deep down, he wasn't fit to touch her.

As she held his gaze, sleepy but probing, he wasn't sure if he still believed that. Fear was human, he'd said last night. And people were human. No better or worse for their name or their mistakes. Just…human.

Maybe there was something here to…

"Thank you."

Thank God for those two words. It broke the spell. *Thank you* disgusted him enough to swing off the bed. "For what?" he grumbled, already heading for the door.

He wanted her gratitude as much as he wanted another hole in the head.

"For staying," she replied simply.

His eyes were on the door, on exit and escape, but the vision of that dark forest that had been theirs haunted him, that little seed of a thought that things could be different now. As adults. "You were scared, and it was my fault," he said disgustedly.

"Yes. Of course. It could have only been done out of guilt."

Surprised, he turned on her. "What other reason would I have?"

She held his gaze, but then shook her head and yawned. She slid out of bed, shuffling toward the door. "I need coffee for this."

Remembering how annoyingly chipper she got after her first cup in her, he lied. "We never have any coffee at the cabin."

She whirled on him so fast, so violently, he actually moved back a step, afraid she was going to punch him.

He held up his hands in surrender, amused in spite of himself. "That was a joke, darling."

Her eyes narrowed, those dainty fingers curling into fists. "Not. Funny." Then she whirled back around and sailed out of the room.

"It was a little funny," he murmured to himself. He made a move to follow her, since he could use a jolt of caffeine himself. Before he managed to move, his phone rang again.

Frowning, he crossed the room and grabbed it off the nightstand. He didn't recognize the number, so he answered it cautiously.

"Yeah?"

"Would it kill you to answer your phone on the first call?" He recognized Laurel's irritated voice immediately. She must have been calling from the police station.

He sneered a little at that. "What do you want, Deputy?"

"I want to talk to my sister, but first I need to talk to both of you. Speaker on."

Ty strolled into the living room. "I ain't one of your deputies you get to boss around, Laurel."

"No, but I am your cousin-in-law, the detective in charge of this investigation and the woman who could charge you with kidnapping if you don't do what I say."

"I—"

"But beyond all that, Carson. I've got a name for your guy. So, why don't you cooperate so we can actually talk this out."

He wanted to find a comeback for that. A way to defend that kidnapping charge and pretend the rest didn't matter. But a name mattered. "Fine," he ground out, hitting Speaker on his phone and slapping it against the kitchen table.

"Jen? You're all right?"

"Yes," Jen replied, leaning closer to the phone. "I didn't realize Ty was talking to you, but I suppose I should have with all the bickering. How on earth do you and Grady get along?" Jen wondered, looking longingly at the slow-dripping coffee machine. "Your natural bossiness and his natural Carson-ness."

"Somehow it works," Laurel replied. She was in *all*-cop mode right now—even over the phone—and didn't rise to Jen's sisterly teasing bait. "I've got a missing person who matches the description of the man that was in

Rightful Claim and what we could see of the customer who fainted on Jen's store tape."

"The blood?" Ty demanded.

"Still waiting on the results, but we have a name to confirm against, so that's a step. The next step—"

"What's the name?"

"The next step will be—"

"I want his name."

Jen placed her hand on his forearm, and it was only then he realized his entire body had hardened, and that he was all but ready to punch a phone. Worse, that her simple touch did ease some of the tension inside him.

"Laurel. Ty just wants to know if he recognizes the name. Let's start with that, then go through all the steps."

"His name is Braxton Lynn. It's not a perfect match since we don't have a clear picture of him, but it's close enough to wonder."

All the tenseness inside Ty leaked out fully, and futility swept in heavily and depressingly in its wake. "I don't know that name." A dead end. No matter how he went through his memory, the name Braxton *or* Lynn didn't ring any bells whatsoever. Someone was after him, ready to hurt the people he…cared for, and he didn't know the face *or* the name.

"Apparently he's from Phoenix, Arizona," Laurel continued. "I've got some calls in with a couple PDs in the area to get more information on him, maybe get a more positive ID. Criminal record on the Braxton name appears clear from what I've been able to search, but he's been missing for three months. Adult, twenty-six, no family looking for him. A foster sister reported the missing person, but it doesn't seem like anyone's too eager or worried to find him."

"I don't know that name," Ty repeated irritably.

"But we discussed something last night that I think is pertinent," Jen interrupted, sounding so equitable he wanted to growl. "Whoever is here might be threatening Ty or me because of a perceived hurt on a loved one. This Braxton might have a family member or friend who *does* have a connection to Ty."

"It's a solid theory," Laurel said, considering it. But then she barreled on, pure cop. "Like I said, I've got calls in trying to get some more background. Since this is all desk work, I'll handle trying to track down more of a profile and I'll keep you both updated. What about Phoenix?"

"What about it?" Ty retorted, repeating the name in his head like an incantation. *Braxton Lynn. Braxton Lynn.* Why didn't he know that name?

"You don't know the name," Laurel said as if it wasn't a failure on his part. "But what about anyone from the area? If it's a connection we're looking for, maybe it's Phoenix."

Ty stomped away from the phone on the table and paced, raking his hands through his hair. Phoenix? Not that he could think of, but Arizona…maybe. Maybe?

He moved back to the table, leaned close enough to talk into the speaker. "I had a buddy back in the army, before I became a ranger." One who'd had reason to hate him, but how could a kid from Phoenix be connected to a soldier from a small town? "Oscar Villanueva. I can't see as how there'd be any connection, but he was from Arizona. Not Phoenix, though. Some place I'd never heard of and can't remember now."

"Okay. You got any contact information for Oscar?"

Just another failure. "No," Ty managed to say, still sounding pissed instead of broken. "No. We lost touch when I got into the rangers." He didn't mention why Oscar might hate him. It wasn't pertinent until they found a connection.

"Okay. I'll dig into that angle. If you think of the name of the town, you let me know. I find any more connections or the blood results come in, I'll give you a call."

"Yeah," Ty returned, gut churning with emotions that would get in the way of clearheaded thinking. He needed all this...stuff inside him out of the way. He needed to compartmentalize like he had back in the army.

Tie it up. Set it aside. Act on fact and order over feelings.

"Take care of my sister, Carson, or you'll have a lot more than me to answer to."

Ty scowled at his phone. "She'll take care of herself." He hit End without waiting to hear what Laurel had to say about that.

Jen sighed. "Ty. You shouldn't have said that."

"Why not?" he returned. "You can and do take care of yourself."

He wanted to pace, to expend the frustrated energy inside him, but pacing was wasted. Maybe he'd go lock himself in the bedroom and do as many push-ups and sit-ups as it took to clear his mind.

"Yes, but you know how Laurel worries. How my family worries. You just added to it by—"

"They should get a new hobby, and so should you for that matter. It isn't your job to placate them."

She didn't bristle like he'd thought she would. She moved to the coffeemaker, unerringly finding the right cupboard for the coffee mugs. "It's been a rough year," she said, and though she sounded unshakable, there was a sadness to those words.

But she hardly had the monopoly on hard years. The Carsons had been through their fair share of what the Delaneys had gone through—though a few more Delaneys had landed themselves in the hospital. Carsons, too, though, so… "For mine, too, darling."

"I don't want to fight with you, Ty." She took a sip of coffee, winced, presumably at the heat. "I want to figure this out so I can go home to my store and live my life."

"Funny, I thought we could do that *and* bicker."

Her mouth almost curved, but the sadness remained. "We can, but I don't want to." She held out a hand. "Truce?"

He didn't want to touch her. There'd been too much already, and his brain had taken a few more detours than he cared for. But the less she knew about all that, the better. "Fine. Truce." He shook her hand.

The chill that skittered up his spine had nothing to do with the handshake. He frowned, looking at the door. He wasn't sure what the feeling was, the foreboding signal that something was off.

"I feel it, too," Jen whispered. "What is it?"

"It's your gut," Ty replied, eyeing every possible entrance in the cabin. Not too many windows, but enough. The door would be impossible to penetrate. The secret passageway had been bolted shut after Addie'd had to use it last year.

"My gut says we should get a gun," Jen said, still holding his hand in hers.

"Yeah, your gut ain't half-bad."

IT HAD BEEN easy to track the motorcycle marks once he'd found them. It had taken him longer than he'd wanted to finally discover the trail, but the Delaney Ranch was rather hard to breach even with all its stretching fields and nooks and crannies.

Good security there, plus a parcel of ranch hands always roaming about and a passel of vigilante residents. He'd nearly gotten himself caught three times.

But now, *now* he was following the heavy divot in the grass clearly made when a motorcycle had irresponsibly driven up the east side of the property, and then driven off again on dirt roads.

Irresponsible Ty. Always making mistakes. Including driving up the unpaved road, rather than turning back to the highway.

He could track the land—especially since the sun had seemed to bake the tracks in good, different from the truck tires that also marred the dirt.

He clucked his tongue at Ty's idiocy. Such a shame Ty would make it so easy for him. The laugh bubbled into his throat, escaped and echoed through the trees. He rather liked the sound of it, but he should be more careful. He wouldn't make a stupid mistake like Ty had.

No. Mistakes wouldn't bring him peace or closure. Mistakes weren't his goal. So, he climbed, following the motorcycle track up and up and up.

He was starting to get winded as morning began to dawn in earnest. Mist that had filtered through the trees began to burn off.

The higher he got, the more the trees thickened, but the road remained. Ty's careless tire tracks guiding him. What utter stupidity.

Jen was better off with him, not Ty. She'd see that

eventually. She'd be his prize. Oh, he'd have to hurt her to hurt Ty, but she'd understand. Once she knew the whole story, she'd understand. They could build a life together. Because he'd have peace then. Peace and closure.

Hurt Jen. Kill Ty. Live happily ever after?

It wasn't the plan. Dr. Michaels told him he did better with a plan. With a goal. But couldn't plans and goals change? Didn't he deserve a prize? Jen didn't deserve to die.

But she'd run away from him. She'd called the cops on him. She was *with* Ty. Clearly, she needed to be punished. Like Dr. Michaels, who hadn't listened—not close enough.

So, perhaps it would be up to Jen herself. Defend Ty? Die. Let Ty touch her? Die more painfully. He could envision it. The glint of the knife. The smell of the blood. Just like the uppity doctor.

No, no, that had been only a dream. Maybe he'd dream about Jen, too. Dream about her begging for Ty to save her, but he wouldn't. Ty wouldn't be able to. Ty would have to watch her die. Slowly.

He could see it and he needed it. Now. He needed the kill now. Murder sang its siren song. It flowed through his blood. He could *feel* it there, boiling inside him. It needed release. Knife to throat.

He had his knife out in his hand. Maybe he'd use it on himself. Just a little bit. Just to take the edge off.

Then he saw the cabin.

Chapter Ten

Jen watched Ty sweep the cabin with military precision. It didn't seem to matter that they hadn't heard anything, that it had been only this cold chill of a feeling that had gone through both of them. Ty was behaving like they were in imminent danger.

Surely it was just coincidence or…something. It unnerved her more than the feeling itself that he'd felt it, too, and that he took it seriously.

People didn't just *feel* things. If they did, her dream last night about Laurel was a lot more ominous. But Laurel had called this morning with a lead and everything had been fine.

Everything *was* fine, because Ty found nothing. He was now perched in what appeared to be an uncomfortable position, looking through the slight gap in the curtain at the front of the cabin.

"Ty, this is silly. There's nothing out there. We're both wired and worried."

"We both felt something," Ty returned, as if that was just a normal thing people experienced. As if a shared feeling of discomfort or unease magically meant someone was out there.

"But that doesn't make any sense, Ty. It can't be possible."

He shrugged, his gaze never leaving the small patch of yard. "In the rangers you learn to roll with the things that don't make sense. It's not like *we* ever made any sense."

"Why not?" she asked before she remembered that this constant mix-up of them and this situation was only going to cause more heartache. She'd had her epiphany last night about asking for what she wanted, but what about things she didn't know if she wanted?

Part of her wanted Ty, but she didn't think it was a very intelligent part of herself.

Ty scoffed at her question. "Aside from the fact we're opposite in just about every way—a Carson and a Delaney. Ring any cursed bells?"

"That's not holding much weight these days."

"That's these days. Besides, we're still opposites."

"And opposites attract."

Ty shook his head, but his gaze was outside and his demeanor was completely unreadable. "There's got to be some common ground for all those differences to rest on. Attraction is easy."

She didn't know why she felt the need to argue with him, only that she did. It made what they'd had before seem…doomed. An unimportant castoff.

It wasn't that. She wouldn't *let* it be that to him. "Then how do you explain Laurel and Grady?"

"Aside from the fact they both love and would protect the people they love with their life, they love Bent. They believe in it. Honestly, deep down, Laurel and Grady have more alike things than different."

Even knowing it was true, even having said the same

to her brother Dylan in defending Grady and Laurel—back before he himself had been felled by a Carson—it irked her that Ty of all people recognized it.

"All right. Explain Dylan and Vanessa."

"Again, they might antagonize each other, but it's only because they're so alike deep down. They want the world to see the persona they put forth, not who they actually are."

It had taken her *years* to understand that about Dylan, and Ty said it like it was common knowledge.

But there was one truth he was refusing to acknowledge, and since he was irritating her with his truths, she'd irritate him with hers. "We're the same deep down, too."

He snorted. "I don't think so, darling."

"You don't have to. I know so. You've only ever tried to harden yourself against that gaping need for someone to love and cherish you and let you protect them, and I've hidden myself against the very same thing."

She watched those words land—that stillness, then the slight rotation of shoulders as if he was willing the words to roll off his back.

But truths weren't easy to shrug away. That she knew.

Then everything in him stiffened, and he brought the binoculars he held in one hand to his eyes.

"Don't pretend you see something just to get out of—"

"There. He's out there."

She rolled her eyes and fisted her hands on her hips. She was not this stupid, and it was insulting he thought she was. "You are not going to change the subject by—"

He thrust the binoculars at her. "He's out there."

Frowning at the binoculars, Jen took them hesitantly. "How do you know it's him?"

"Movement."

"It could be an animal," she replied, studying the binoculars in her hands. She didn't want to look out the window. Didn't want to be fooled into thinking something was out there, and what's more, didn't want something—or someone—to actually be out there.

"I know what I saw."

She looked back to find him checking a pistol. She'd had no doubt there were guns hidden throughout the Carson cabin, but it was a bit of a jolt to see him efficiently working with the weapon.

He was serious, though. This was no dramatic attempt at changing the subject. His movements were too economical. His jaw was too tight. In his eyes that fierce protector light she'd always loved.

She swallowed at the mix of fear and love and turned back to the window. Lifting the binoculars with no small amount of trepidation, she studied the small part of the tree line she could make out through the natural gap in the curtain.

"I don't—" But then she did. First it was just a flash, the sun glinting off something metal. Then she could make out the faint movements of something that blended into the trees but was clearly human.

Human. Her breath caught in her throat, and for a full second or two, she was completely frozen in fear, watching the movement of someone.

"See him?"

Jen had to force herself to swallow, and then embarrassingly had to clear her throat in order to speak. "Yes," she managed, but it was little more than a croak. Fear was paralyzing her and it was demoralizing, but she couldn't seem to control it. "What do we do?"

"You stay put. I go out there and shoot him."

"You can't..." She trailed off. If this man was here to harm them, shouldn't Ty shoot him? She watched the figure, then the glint of light. What was the sun reflecting off?

"I'm not going to kill him. I want to know why the hell he's trying to torture you and me. But I'm not going to give him a chance to hurt you either. Stay put."

"I should call Laurel." But she didn't drop the binoculars. She kept thinking she could figure something out if she could only see his face.

Then she did.

And she screamed.

Jen's scream echoed through the cabin almost in time with a crash against the window, but the minute her scream had pierced the air, Ty had lunged.

The window glass shattered above them, pieces raining down on his back. He thought he'd protected Jen from the brunt of it, thanks to the help of the curtain that kept most of the glass contained.

"Are you okay?" he asked, panicked that maybe something had shot through and reached her before he had.

"I'm fine," she said, her voice muffled underneath him. "What was it? A bullet?"

Ty looked at the curtain. There was a slight rip. He checked around the trajectory of the shot and frowned at what he saw.

An arrow piercing the thick area rug. Not just a flimsy Boy Scout arrow, though. This was a three-blade steel broadhead, the kind used for hunting. Which explained its impact on the window.

The window. Ty rolled off Jen, crouched and waited for someone to try to come through the window. When nothing happened, he looked down at Jen.

She was sitting now but looked dazed. "An arrow," she muttered. "That's...weird."

"A stupid, pointless stunt," Ty muttered. Oh, it was an arrow that could do some damage, but he didn't think that had been kill-shot aim. It was more scare tactics.

Ty got to his feet, done with these childish games. He flicked the safety off his pistol and strode for the door.

"Wait. Wait, Ty, there's a note." Jen crawled over to the arrow and cocked her head to read the piece of paper affixed to the back of the arrow.

Ty said something crude about what he could do with the note, but Jen crouched down to read aloud.

"Why don't you come and find me?"

She wrinkled her nose, but Ty barely heard what she'd read aloud. Rage spread through him like a wildfire. He was nothing but heat and hate. She was bleeding. Just a little trickle from a spot on her cheek, but he'd make someone pay for that.

"I'll find him," he said, low and lethal. He reached the door, ready to jerk it open and start shooting. "I'll—"

"Ty." Jen's gentle admonition did nothing to soothe the riot of fury and worry inside him, but it did stop his forward movement. "He wants you to."

"Yeah, well, I'll give him the fight he wants." His hand was on the knob, but Jen kept talking.

"He doesn't want a fight. He could have had that back in Bent."

"He doesn't want to hurt me, then, or he could have done that, too."

"He wants to hurt you, but he's playing a game. I don't understand it, but it's a game. Come and find me—he wouldn't want you angrily going after him if he didn't have a plan to take you down."

Ty flicked the lock. "Let him try."

"Use your brain," Jen snapped with surprising force as she stalked over from where the arrow stuck out of the rug. She flicked the lock back in place and glared up at him. "He's trying to mess with you, and has been this whole time. Not only does he know we're alone up here, but he knows *us*. We don't know a darn thing about him. You don't even recognize his name. We can't underestimate him."

She'd never have any idea of how those words hurt. He knew, intellectually, she wasn't blaming him for not knowing the name, for not recognizing the man, but he felt the blame anyway.

Who had he let down? Who had he hurt? How had he lured Braxton Lynn to Bent, Wyoming, and Jen Delaney?

"You can't leave me here without my phone. I need to call Laurel," she said, sounding calm and efficient. "And you need to do something about the window. Maybe duct-tape the curtains to the wall? I know it doesn't keep him out, but it seals us in better."

"That could have hit you," he said because he didn't understand her calm. Didn't understand how she could talk about calling the police and duct-taping curtains of all things.

He needed to eliminate the threat now, and she wanted to do housekeeping.

"I know it could have." She rubbed her palm over her heart. "Or you." Her gaze met his. He'd convinced himself that ache in his heart was nostalgia or even remorse. It was sweet memories but had no bearing on the present.

Except looking at her now, knowing she could have been—and still could be hurt by all this—there was nothing *past* about it. He still loved her, deep into his bones. The kind of love time didn't dull or erase. Something all but meant to be, stitched together in whatever ruled this crazy world.

She felt it, too, in the knowledge he could have been hurt. In the realization, if she hadn't beat him to it already, that what they'd had once upon a time lived and breathed in the here and now—no matter how little either of them wanted it.

Or could have it.

He pointed to his phone on the table. "Call Laurel. I have to go out there."

"Ty—"

"Call Laurel." Then he stalked outside, ready to fight.

HE HUMMED TO HIMSELF. The shattering crash of arrow against window had been satisfying enough to put a little levity in his step.

He didn't think he'd hit anyone—surely he'd have heard a scream of pain or someone would have run out. But the fear…there had to be fear now. He looked up as he heard something. The door opening.

So, Ty had taken the bait to come after him.

He tsked under his breath. What a foolish man Ty Carson turned out to be.

Bending down, he pulled another trap out of his

backpack. Antique bear trap. All steel and menace. He'd brought them lovingly back from rusty relics to shining pieces of beauty.

He hadn't been sure how or where to use them, but he'd hauled them around just the same. Now he set the three he had hefted up the hill at three separate points around the cabin.

The police would be coming soon. Surely they'd called. Gently, reverently, he pulled the trap open and set it. He watched the ragged edges glint in the light of the sun filtering through the trees.

Like a parent caressing a baby's cheek, he drifted his finger down the sharp edge. "You'll do good work for me, won't you?"

Footsteps sounded, faint but getting closer.

He had to melt away now. Luckily he was excellent at disappearing.

And reappearing when the people who deserved pain least expected it.

Chapter Eleven

Jen hated the fact she was pacing and wringing her hands like some helpless creature. The princess in the tower again. Waiting for Ty to return or the police to show up.

What kind of coward was she?

She fisted her hands on her hips. She was *choosing* the coward's way out because she was used to fading into the background and letting everyone else handle the tough stuff. The scary stuff.

Being used to something wasn't an excuse, though. She wouldn't be stupid. Leave fighting the bad guys to the people with guns they were trained and licensed to carry. It didn't mean she couldn't do *something*.

Protection. She didn't think Ty was going to find anything stomping around out there. If he did, he'd probably get hurt. At first, she shied away from that possibility, but then she stopped herself. No. She had to face facts.

He'd gone off half-cocked after a taunt from an unstable maniac. He'd put himself in danger. Luckily, Laurel was sending deputies up. They would handle whatever mess Ty had gotten himself into.

In the meantime, she needed to handle *her* mess.

She was in a cabin all by herself with an unstable maniac on the loose. The man she shouldn't love, but apparently did, was off *proving* something or other. And the police were on their way.

What would they all need?

Coffee for the police. Possibly first aid for Ty. And then, she needed to protect herself.

No. Reverse all that. For once she would put herself first. Find a weapon, or ten. Then the coffee. And the dope gallivanting around the woods with a pistol could fend for himself. She'd do the first aid last.

Or so she told herself. In the end, love won out. It irritated her, but she couldn't have lived with herself if he'd staggered in bleeding like she'd imagined too many times to count already and she didn't have *something*.

Maybe it wasn't so wrong, she decided, placing the first aid kit on the table before going on a gun hunt. Maybe it wasn't about always putting others first or always putting yourself first. Not always about asking for what you wanted, but choosing the when and knowing the why.

Maybe, it was all about *balance*.

Everything with Ty was complicated, but the feeling she had for him was simple. She pawed through a closet, turning that over in head. Maybe in the midst of this…weirdness, she would focus on the simple.

As if on cue, she found a hunting rifle in the back corner of the closet. The chamber was empty, but she'd seen some boxes of ammunition in the tiny cabinet above the refrigerator when she'd been looking for a first aid kit.

She was no fan of guns, but her father had forced

her to go hunting when she'd been a kid. All Delaneys needed to know how to hunt.

She'd hated every second of it, which had made her just another anomaly in the great Delaney clan. The rest of them might not love it, but they were good with guns, good with hunting. Jen had never had the patience or the aptitude.

She sighed heavily, grabbing the box of ammunition. Who knew being vaguely threatened by a stranger would have her rehashing so many of her childhood emotional issues?

Still, it allowed her to load the gun efficiently so she'd gotten something out of it.

She felt safer with the gun in her hand, felt calmer with the first aid kit within reach. But she was still just *waiting*.

Before she could decide what to do about that, something at the door clicked and the door opened. She knew it would be Ty since he obviously had the key, but still she lifted the rifle.

You never knew, after all.

He stepped inside, closing and locking the door behind him before he glanced at her in the kitchen. When she didn't lower the gun, he quirked an eyebrow.

"Gonna shoot me, darling?"

Since she didn't care for his blasé tone, she used one of her own. "Considering it."

"Well, I came back unscathed, so apparently your theory about that note trying to draw me out was incorrect."

"That's what you think," Jen muttered, finally lowering the rifle. Mostly because she heard the distinct sound of a car engine, which she figured had to be the police.

Ty lifted the curtain and looked out the broken glass. He nodded. "Police. You stay here."

"Because?"

"Because."

"No. Let them come to the door. Where we'll all discuss what happened together. Rather than you taking over."

"I wasn't—"

"You were going to go out there and tell them what's what—from your perspective, and that wouldn't be a problem, except I'm the one who actually saw him shoot the arrow. You searched the woods and all, but *I* saw the whole thing happen. They'll come to the door and we'll talk to them together."

She could tell she'd surprised him. He wasn't used to her giving orders. Well, everyone was going to start getting used to it.

A knock sounded and Ty considered it. "Well, I guess you got your way."

"It's not *my* way, Ty. It's the right way." She reached past him and opened the door. She was a little disappointed Hart wasn't the deputy on the other side of the door, but he was currently working nights so it made sense. "Come in, Deputy." She gestured him inside.

"Ms. Delaney."

"I've left the arrow where it landed, and I'm sure you can see where it made impact with the window." She could feel Ty watch her as she took the deputy through the sequence of events. Still, he didn't interrupt. He didn't try to take over. He simply watched while Jen answered questions and the deputy wrote notes down in his little notebook.

"And you saw all of this, Mr. Carson?"

Ty shook his head. "No. Once I handed the binoculars over to Jen I went to get my pistol."

"The one you're wearing now?"

"Yes." He flashed the man his cocky Carson grin. "Not going to ask me if it's registered, are you?"

The deputy only grunted. Clearly he'd had enough run-ins with Carsons not to press the issue. "So you're getting the pistol—then what?"

Ty walked him through heading for the door, jumping on Jen when he heard the crash. Then her reading the letter aloud and his heading outside.

"And once you were outside, you searched for the man?"

"No. Not searched. I didn't go into the woods or look for tracks, I went to the stables."

Jen frowned. News to her. He'd let her think he was going after whoever had shot the arrow, to hurt him. But he'd gone to the stables?

"There's a hayloft up there," Ty continued. "It's rickety, but if you know where to step you can get up and get a decent view of the surrounding area. I'll admit, I'd planned to go after him, but the stables caught my eye first. I knew I'd be able to see him if he was anywhere close. But I looked all around and I didn't see anyone. There could be tracks, but I didn't want to risk it alone."

Also news to her. The jerk. She'd been worried for no reason. Maybe she should have given him more credit, but he'd been so angry when he'd huffed off. Was she really supposed to just *expect* him to make smart decisions?

Maybe the answer was yes, but she wasn't about to admit her mistake to him.

"We'll search the woods and see what we can find."

"He isn't there," Ty said flatly.

"No, but he might have left a clue behind. You let us investigate Mr. Carson and we'll—"

Ty said something crude and Jen sighed, stepping forward to smile at the deputy. "Excuse him. He's so grumpy when he hasn't had his nap. Like a toddler." She smiled at the officer, enjoying Ty's disgusted grunt. "Would you like some coffee?"

"No, ma'am, thank you. I'll join Burns out there and we'll see what we can find. If I have any more questions I'll be in touch, and we'll let you know if we find anything. And everything we find gets turned over to your sister and Deputy Hart."

"Why Hart?" Ty demanded.

The deputy eyed Ty with some disdain. "Hart is taking over as detective now that Laurel's on desk duty. He'll handle all investigations with her until she's on maternity leave, then on his own."

Ty grunted irritably. "I'll search with you."

The deputy shook his head and Jen thought Ty would bite it off if he could. So, she moved easily between law and wannabe outlaw and started ushering the police officer to the door.

"Don't worry, I'll keep him occupied while you do your *jobs*." She gave Ty a pointed look at the word, but he only stared back at her, clearly furious. But he let the deputy exit the cabin while he stayed put.

He narrowed his eyes at her once the door was shut.

"What?" she demanded loftily.

"So, you finally decided to use it."

"Use what?"

"That backbone you've been trying to ignore for almost thirty years."

HE EXPECTED HER to be pissed. That was the point after all. Undermine all this annoying confidence and take charge thing she had going on, and make her angry.

But she didn't so much as flinch. She considered.

It was beautiful to watch. This was the woman he'd always known she could be. More like her sister, but still herself. Because she'd only ever needed to stop trying to *please* everyone, including him.

She wasn't trying to please him like she had when they'd been together, and it gave him a perverse thrill. It was always the Jen he'd wanted, because he didn't deserve the girl who'd bent over backward to give everything to him. He'd never deserve her.

"I suppose that is what I decided while you let me believe you were off chasing down a madman, not looking for him from a safe vantage point."

"If I'd seen him, I'd have gone after him."

"But you didn't search the woods. You looked for him from a safe vantage point and then you came back."

Why her repetition of his very intelligent choices irritated him, he didn't know. So he shrugged. "Your point?"

"My point is you want me to believe you're this one thing—you've always wanted me to believe certain things about you, but they're very rarely true." She frowned a little, as if thinking that over. "Even leaving without a goodbye. You came home ten years later, let me believe you were just a careless jerk—even though

I'd known you weren't, but the truth was you'd done it to protect me."

"Like you said earlier. I still could have said good-bye." But he couldn't have. Not and actually done it. He hadn't been strong enough then to tell her he was leaving, to be callous and nasty and cut all ties. So, he'd taken the coward's way out.

He'd like to believe as an adult, he would have made different choices, but sometimes, when he looked into her eyes, he figured he'd always take the coward's way out when it came to hurting her.

He wanted to cross to her. Hold her. Tell her all the ways he hadn't been able to face her. Beg her to forgive him.

It unmanned him, all that swirling emotion inside. Worse, the hideous thought she might be able to see it.

"We should—" Jen was cut off by a knock on the door, thank God. "Maybe they found something," she muttered. Ty was closer, so he answered it. But it wasn't one of the deputies. It was Zach Simmons.

Ty had found out about Zach's existence only a few months ago when his aunt, who'd run away long before he'd been born, had come back to town. Zach was technically Ty's cousin, but he hadn't quite warmed to the man. Zach might be a Carson by blood, but he'd been FBI and his dad had been ATF and everything about him screamed *Delaney* to Ty—even if there weren't any Delaney ties.

So he flat out didn't trust the man. "Zach," he greeted coolly.

"Ty. Jen. Laurel called me. Sounded like you two need some security, so I hitched a ride up with a deputy," Zach said, his eyes taking in his surroundings, reminding Ty of a soldier. He wore a big black backpack and was carrying a weapon openly on his hip, and he had eyes that reminded Ty way too much of the father he'd hated. Eyes he saw in the mirror.

"We don't need security." The only reason Ty didn't slam the door in his face was the whole blood-tie thing. It wasn't Zach's fault he had the old bastard's eyes. And he'd been nothing but pleasant enough since he'd moved to Bent to work with Cam Delaney at his new security business.

But Ty didn't trust him.

"I'm pretty sure security is exactly what you need. You might not want it, but you need it," Zach returned evenly. "Laurel insisted. More, my sister insisted. You try saying no to Hilly."

It was that evenness Ty couldn't quite work out. There was a blankness to Zach, a way he kept all personality locked under a very bland shell. But he was a Carson. Even if he'd grown up away from Bent with an ATF agent father, there was Carson blood in there. A man *had* to feel it.

"Ignore him," Jen interrupted, smiling at Zach in a way that had Ty grinding his teeth together. She even took his arm and pulled him into the living room. "There's plenty of room, and I think an extra set of eyes is a good idea."

"Laurel thought so, too. She wants me to move you—"

"No," Ty said, trying for some of Zach's evenness. It came out like a barked order. "We stay where I know the turf."

Zach looked at Jen as if he was expecting her to

argue. That was what Ty didn't trust about Zach. He didn't know when to stick with his own.

"I think Ty's right," Jen said, surprising him. "Clearly this man is going to track us wherever we go, and we can hardly be on the run forever. It's best to stay in a familiar place, and protect ourselves." She smiled winsomely at Zach. "Especially with a security expert around."

"I want to set up some cameras then. Nothing invasive. Just your typical security measures for dangerous lunatics lurking in the woods." He pulled the pack off his back and gave it a little pat.

"How much is that going to cost me?" Ty demanded.

Zach arched an eyebrow at him. "I suppose I'd have to give you a family discount. It'll be borrowed equipment—we can take it all down once this is over. Consider the labor my charitable donation to a good cause."

Ty wanted to tell him they didn't need the security again, but that was knee-jerk and stupid. The more footage they had of this Braxton Lynn, the better chance they had of figuring out why he was after Ty.

"I know Laurel's investigating," Zach continued. "And I respect your sister and her work ethic. She'll work on this till she's keeling over, but she's going to investigate like a detective."

"Is there another way?" Jen asked.

"Sure. There's the FBI way, which I'm rather familiar with. There's also the bend-the-rules-so-we-can-get-our-man way. I'm a bit fond of that one." He pulled a laptop out of his backpack and placed it on the table. "Now that I'm not FBI, I'm not beholden to their rules, and I know a lot of ways to get around the bureaucratic red tape."

Ty considered the computer, then the man. He grinned. "Now you're sounding like a Carson. Let's cut some red tape, cousin."

HE GAVE IT a full twenty-four hours before he returned to the cabin. He could tell the cops had sniffed around some, but none had come close to his traps.

He was mildly disappointed, he could admit. It was for the best for his plan that no one had stumbled into one, but finding a bloody corpse or someone whose life was spilling out painfully would have lifted his spirits just a tad.

He looked up from the trap he lovingly caressed. He couldn't see the cabin from here, but he knew where it was.

Jen was probably letting Ty touch her in there. No, no. She was too pure for that. Jen Delaney seemed so kind, so good. No, Ty was probably forcing himself upon her. She was a victim, and it was his duty to save her.

He rubbed at the headache that began to drum. No, that was all wrong. Ty needed to pay, but he could do that only through Jen. Ty had irreparably damaged Oscar.

Ty had broken his brother when they'd been in the army. It was the only explanation, and once he'd gotten through to Oscar, Oscar had agreed it was all Ty's fault. Other people were always to blame for Oscar's shortcomings, but he'd come up with a way to fix that. To get Oscar on his side again.

He would break Ty's woman, for Oscar. It was only fair. Sometimes innocents were hurt because bad men roamed the world. Bad men needed to be hurt. They needed to suffer.

Once Ty did, his own suffering would go away.

He looked down at his shaking hands. He was getting too far out of control. The plan was hazy and he wasn't focused on the goal. The goal.

It was all this waiting. All this planning. Vengeance needed to wait and be planned, but a hero acted. A hero did what he came here to do.

He would be Oscar's hero. *Now.*

Chapter Twelve

The next morning, Jen was happy to make breakfast for
the two men she was temporarily sharing a cabin with.
She might have discovered her backbone yesterday, or
trusted it enough to use it, but she'd long ago decided
she'd rather make the meals her way than be waited on.

Zach had spent most of yesterday tapping away on
his computer conferring with Ty in low tones about
what little they knew about Braxton Lynn, going over
the layout of the cabin and where they could feasibly
install cameras.

They had a plan for the cameras now, but Zach hadn't
been able to find much about the man.

Frustrated, they'd called it a night, and now today
was a fresh day. Zach was going to install his surveillance equipment, then try his hand at some hacking.

Jen had felt superfluous. At best. Last night and now,
but she didn't know how to set up cameras or hack into
government records, or anything about Braxton or Ty's
military past, so she'd had to accept it. This wasn't her
time.

But she'd listened, and she'd come up with her own
conclusions. She'd always been good at observing people and reading them. If you were going to contort your-

self to be what someone else wanted, or try, you had to understand them on some level.

The man after Ty didn't want something as simple as just to hurt him. He wanted to *torture* Ty, terrorize him, using whatever means—family or past lovers—to do it. The question was, why didn't he focus on Ty's family, the most important thing to him?

There was the most obvious reason, one that made Jen's gut burn with shame. She was the easy target. Carsons were rough and tough and harder to threaten. She was weak and easy pickings.

Well, no thank you.

She let Ty and Zach settle into breakfast as she sipped her coffee and watched them eat and discuss. Like she wasn't even there.

No thank you to that, too.

"You're going about this the wrong way," she announced casually, so irritated with them and herself that it didn't even bother her when they both gave her the same patently Carson questioning look. Eyebrow raised, mouth quirked, with just enough disbelief in their gaze to make a person feel stupid.

She refused.

"You're thinking about this like he's after *me*, when we know he's trying to hurt Ty."

"No. He's trying to hurt *you* because of me."

She rolled her eyes. "Let's try to step outside of macho egomaniac land for one second. Yes, he wants to hurt you. But how? Emotionally, not physically."

"So?"

"So? Everything you're planning is physical. And factual. He's not interested in either thing. He doesn't want to physically hurt you. He wants to terrorize you via someone you care about. Even when you're trying to figure out his connection to you, it's only so you know his identity, so you can identify and isolate his threat. But what you need to be doing is trying to understand him."

"How can we understand him if we don't know who he is?" Zach asked reasonably.

"But we do know. We know his name. We know his foster sister reported him missing, but no one's really looking for him. So, what does that tell you?"

"Not a whole lot."

Ty shook his head. "She's right," he said, with no small amount of irritation. "He's alone in the world. No one really cares about him. Which means you can make the reasonable connection that whoever he's looking to avenge *did* care about him, or he thought they did."

"Exactly. And if he's blaming Ty, out to terrorize Ty, he blames Ty for losing this mystery person. Maybe they died, or maybe they left him. Maybe there's something else, but he wants Ty to hurt the way *he* hurts. The key isn't Braxton or me, it's the link."

Both men stared at her, with no small amount of doubt in their expressions. And they were so quiet and military still, Jen fidgeted with her coffee mug. She didn't let herself blurt out the apologies or *at least that's what I think* that filled her brain.

She knew, *knew*, whether they agreed or not, her theory had more merit than the way they were currently going about things.

"I can't discount it," Zach returned, still frowning as if considering and finding her lacking.

No, not *her*. Her theory. She needed to be better about acknowledging that difference.

"But I can't wrap my head around it either. It doesn't make sense why anyone would get it all so mixed up in their head."

"You're trying to reason it out," Ty interrupted. "I think what Jen's saying is it's not the kind of reason that's going to make sense to, well, reasonable people."

"Exactly," Jen said, emboldened by Ty's understanding. "You can't think about facts and reason, you have to think about the emotion. Revenge is led by emotion."

"You have to consider both," Zach countered. "You've got a good point. His motivation isn't one we're necessarily going to understand because clearly he's not well. But if we know who *he* is, identity-wise, we have a better idea of how to deal with his emotion *and* a better shot at finding the missing link. Facts and emotion need a balance."

Jen considered that. "I suppose you're right. Fact informs the emotion side of things, even if it's not a straight line."

Zach grinned at her. "Can you say that again? 'I suppose you're right.' I've never heard any Carson or Delaney or Simmons for that matter say anything remotely admitting I'm right. I think you're the most reasonable person in the whole dang bunch."

Jen flushed with pleasure.

"Maybe you'd like me to leave you two alone," Ty grumbled.

Jen rolled her eyes at him and got to her feet, clearing the breakfast dishes, but Zach was taking them out of her hand before she could make it to the sink.

"I should do that. You made breakfast. I'll clean up."

It was her first instinct to argue, to insist she did the work she knew she could do. But she wasn't here because she could cook or clean. She wasn't here to take care of everyone while they did the important work.

No.

She was here because she'd been put in danger. Maybe Zach and Ty were here to protect her, but that didn't mean she had to take care of everything.

Wow. It was a lightning bolt of a thought. That she didn't have to be the one to clean up all the messes to earn her place here. That she didn't have to bend over backward to do whatever was asked of her simply because everyone else was more qualified to handle the threat against them.

Because the threat was against her, too.

So, she beamed at Zach and let him take the dishes. "Thank you. I'm going to go call Hilly and see how the store is faring." And she was going to spend some time thinking about how when this was all over, she was going to make sure her life changed.

"Sure is a pretty little thing. Good cook, too."

Ty looked at where Zach was cheerfully washing the breakfast dishes. He was so shocked by the casual commentary all he could seem to manage was, "Excuse me?"

Zach shrugged. "Best breakfast I've had in a while."

When Ty only stared, Zach kept yammering on.

"Certainly the prettiest scenery I've had for breakfast in a *long* while. Maybe ever. Something about sweet—"

"That'll be enough," Ty interrupted, pushing away from the table.

"What? Am I breaking some Carson code? Not supposed to admit a Delaney is pretty as a picture and nice to have around? Figured that nonsense was on the way out with the way everyone's pairing off. Carsons and Delaneys seem destined to end up saying 'I do' in this particular point in history." Zach stopped drying a plate, an overly thoughtful expression on his face. "She's a Delaney. Technically I'm a Carson. I suppose—"

"I said, that'll be enough."

Zach surprised him by laughing and turned back to finishing the dishes. "You've got it *bad*."

Ty blinked. "I don't—"

"I don't see much point in denying everything. Everyone seems to know you two had something way back when, and it doesn't take my former FBI training to figure out it's still simmering under the surface." He shrugged negligently as he put away the last plate. "Why don't you do something about it instead of stomping around snarling like a lion with a thorn in its paw?"

It was horrifying to be seen through so easily by someone he barely knew, so he went for derision. "Yeah, let's just forget the unstable maniac shooting arrows at us."

"Haven't seen an arrow yet today. Even unstable maniacs have to rest, and the fact of the matter is, your brain's going to be a lot clearer if you do something other than brood."

"I don't brood."

"You do an excellent imitation of it, then."

"What business is that of yours?" Ty demanded sharply.

Zach raised an eyebrow with enough condescension in his expression to remind Ty irritably of Grady.

"Absolutely none," Zach replied, pleasantly enough. He wiped his hands on a dish towel and nodded toward the door. "I'm going to set up the cameras like we talked about."

How that made Ty feel guilty was beyond him. He had nothing to feel guilty about. Zach might technically be his cousin, but it wasn't like they'd grown up together. He hadn't even known Zach existed until a couple of months ago. Why would he take advice or ribbing from a virtual stranger?

But as Zach stepped outside, his pack with all its surveillance equipment and computer nonsense on his back, Ty felt *awash* in familial guilt—the kind he hadn't entertained for a very long time. He shook his head and walked to the room he'd given over to Zach last night to just have a second of privacy to…something.

But he had to pass by the open door to the room Jen was in, where she was happily making the bed— whistling. Her cheerfulness scraped across every last raw nerve.

He scowled at her back. "Hart. Zach. You really go for the law-and-order type."

She straightened, leveling him with a look he didn't recognize. "I suppose it's better than the idiot, pea-brained jealous-for-no-reason type." She smiled at him, a surprisingly vicious edge to it.

There had to be something a little screwy in him that even as irritation simmered in his gut, he liked the idea of Jen getting a little vicious. "I am not jealous." Which he knew, very well, was the thing someone said when that was exactly the ugly thing worming around in the person's gut.

Zach calling her pretty, even if it was just to mess with him—it made him feral. It made him want to stake some claim he had no business claiming.

"No, not jealous," Jen said with a dismissive edge. "You just have to be snotty anytime another man even acknowledges I exist. Even though *you* don't acknowledge I exist half the time. Wouldn't, if I wasn't being threatened because of something *you* did."

"Is that some kind of complaint? Pretty sure you've been avoiding me as skillfully as I've been avoiding you since I've been home."

"So you admit it, then?"

"Admit what?"

"That you've avoided me."

He couldn't figure her out, or why there was now a headache drumming at his temples and all he really wanted to do was scoop her up and make good use of that freshly made bed. "Why's that an admission? We were both doing it."

She stepped closer, poked him in the chest. "Yeah, we both were. We both were. I thought it was because you didn't care, but what an idiot I was. It was because you felt the same way I did."

He crossed his arms over his chest, trying to look disdainful instead of whatever uncomfortable thing fluttered in his chest, squeezing his lungs. "And what way's that?"

"Hurt. You were hurting just as I was." She searched his face, so he did everything he could to keep it impassable.

Hurt had always been the enemy. You showed you were hurt, you got knocked around a little extra hard. Literal or metaphorical in his experience with life.

But here she was, calling it what it was, saying they'd both been walking around with it deep inside them. She was cracking away at something inside him, letting something loose he wouldn't name. Couldn't.

"You know what? I wish I *did* go for the 'law and order' type. I wish Hart or Zach were exactly what I wanted out of life. They're both polite. Kind. Good men who want to do the right thing and aren't afraid to admit it. In other words, the antithesis of *you*. But I…" She took a deep breath and squared her shoulders. She looked like she was getting ready to do battle, and he was…

Scared. That thing she was pulling out of him, that feeling a strong, immovable Carson was never supposed to feel over some *woman*. It stole over him, shamed him deeply that he was bone-deep scared of what this slip of a woman was going to say to him.

He allowed himself to recognize the fear, acknowledge it. Even accepted the fact it was worse than any fear he'd had in the army, because death hadn't seemed so bad. At least it would have been a noble one.

There was nothing noble or impressive about being scared of the woman who held your heart. No. So he would not be a coward no matter how he felt like one. He squared, too, and prepared for the blow.

"I love you," she said, and she certainly knew every one of those words was an unerring bullet against his heart. "Yeah, I love you, you big, overbearing moron. I have always loved you and I always will. And I want to punch you. And I'm still mad at the way you left, but understanding it means I can forgive, and I *do*."

"Don't." He choked it out, rough and telling. But the emotion that clogged his throat, that made his heart feel too big and beating in his chest, was winning against all control. It was this, right here, that had been his reason for leaving her without saying goodbye.

He wouldn't have ever been able to look at her and hide all those things he felt. He wasn't strong enough to hurt her, even for her own good. Not to her face anyway. He'd never be strong enough for that.

"It'd be awful for you, wouldn't it?" she asked, tears swimming and making her eyes look luminous. "If I didn't hold a grudge. If I just forgave you. Because then you'd have to forgive yourself, and that's the one thing you've never been any good at."

"I said stop."

"No, no. I'm done stopping for someone else's comfort." She stepped so close he could smell her, that light feminine scent that always seemed to float around her. He could feel the warmth of her—not just generic body warmth, but that piece of her soul that had drawn him long before he'd been willing to admit souls even existed.

Was he willing to admit that now? He didn't know.

When she touched him, her palm to his heart, he winced. The look she shot him was triumphant. Determined. And so damn strong he thought she might bring him to his knees.

"I love you," she said, her eyes never leaving his. "I *want* you."

He tried to move away, but so much of him was suddenly made out of lead and her hand fisted in his shirt, keeping him right where he was. In this nightmare where she said things he wanted and shouldn't have.

Couldn't. The word is couldn't.

"And what scares you, what horrifies you, is that you love and want me, too," she continued, hammering every last nail in the coffin that was his self-control. His belief that he could control his life, his emotions, his choices.

"But you know you'd have to forgive yourself for that love. You'd have to look back at seventeen-year-old Ty and think he actually did the best he could in the situation he was given. You'd have to look back at little ten-year-old Ty and forgive him for letting his dad knock him and his brother around, forgive yourself for not killing him when he started knocking Vanessa around, too. There's so much you'd have to stop blaming yourself for to admit you love me, that we deserve each other—then and now."

If there were words to be salvaged out of this nightmare, he didn't have them. She must have taken them all, because they kept pouring out of her.

"I should have said all that to you when you got back into town, because I knew it then even when I didn't know why you left. I've always known it. But I was too afraid to tell you what I knew, what I saw. I wanted to make you comfortable instead of making us...well, what would have endured. But I was seventeen, too. Young and scarred in my own ways, because we *always* are, Ty. All of us. Scarred and scared and uncertain. We're all doing the best we can with what we have."

He closed his eyes, but her other hand came to his cheek. He didn't want to believe her. She had to hate him for what he'd done—because he hated himself for the way he'd left. For the way he'd come back. He couldn't blame the latter on a young man with few choices. He'd been an adult, and he'd continued to act like she didn't matter.

Still, she touched him like forgiveness wasn't just

possible. It was done. A given. Something she wouldn't take back.

"Open your eyes, Ty."

He did, because he seemed to have no power here. She was in control. She gave the orders, and he obeyed, excellent soldier that he was.

But it was more than that. No matter how much he didn't want to believe he could have her, no matter how much he knew he didn't deserve her, his heart still wanted.

"I love you," she said, and it didn't hurt so much the second time. "And you love me. That's where we'll start."

So much of his scars and his past fought to win, to deny. But she was touching him, staring at him. Drowning in her eyes, he lost the battle with himself.

"No. This is where we start," he replied, covering her mouth with his.

THEY DIDN'T KNOW they were being watched.

Chapter Thirteen

It was home. Ty's kiss had always been exactly where Jen belonged, and somehow she had made it happen again.

So she threw herself into it, into him, wrapping herself around him with what she might have called desperation just days ago.

But she wasn't desperate. No. She was determined. She had finally figured out what she wanted, what she was willing to fight for, and it didn't matter if they were hiding out from danger or if they went home to Bent right now.

He was hers.

His hands streaked over her, rough and possessive. She returned the favor. He scraped his teeth across her bottom lip, so she dug her fingernails into his shoulders. Her knees buckled, but he held her up hard against his chest.

And then it all softened, as if all the tension simply leaked out of him. As if he was giving in to more than just the driving attraction that had always been between them. His mouth softened, his hands gentled. He held her as if she was spun glass and kissed her as if she were the center of his universe.

He was giving in to love.

She'd chosen it years ago, but she hadn't been mature enough to understand that. She'd called it fate or divine intervention, but it had been her. Her wanting him, and his wanting her. She'd been afraid of the consequences, but that had only made it more exciting.

Ten years later the excitement wasn't in thwarting her family's expectation, it was in the choice. In the knowledge of all that time, in the changes she'd made inside herself and the changes she hadn't made, he was still where she belonged.

The dull ring of a phone pierced the fog in her brain, but with her body humming and desperate for more of Ty, she didn't really acknowledge it. It couldn't be all that important, could it? Not as important as this.

Except, of course, it might be. Because they were not just realizing and deciding all these big, life-changing things in the midst of a normal day.

She managed to move her mouth away from his, though she kept her arms tight around him, and couldn't resist pressing a kiss to his jaw. "Phone."

"Nah." His hands slid up under her shirt, over the cotton of her bra. Hot and rough, he dragged his fingertips across the peaks of her nipples.

"It could, uh…" What was she talking about? It was hard to remember with need curling low in her stomach. But the phone kept jangling and somewhere in the fog of desperate lust she understood… "It could be important."

"Why would it—" He managed to lift his head, his expression as dazed as she felt. But he narrowed his eyes. "I guess it could be." But the sound died and they looked at each other, still holding on, still not close enough.

He lowered his mouth. "We'll just forget—"

But it immediately started ringing again and they both sighed. Ty let her go, and she had to sink onto the bed. Her legs simply wouldn't hold her.

He pulled the phone out of his pocket, frowned at the screen, then handed it to her. "Your sister. Why don't you answer it."

Jen cocked her head at the screen as she swiped to answer. "We can talk about why my sister is in your phone as Deputy PITA later." She lifted the receiver to her ear and answered, trying to sound breezy and light.

She was pretty sure she sounded deranged.

"Is everything okay?" Laurel asked without preamble, worry enhancing the demand in her tone. "Are you safe?"

"Safe? Of course. Everything is great. Everything is... Yes."

There was a long, contemplative silence over the phone and Jen had to squeeze her eyes shut and try to get a hold of herself.

But what she really wanted was a hold of Ty and to banish this ache that felt as though it had been growing inside her for a decade.

"You were commandeered to the Carson cabin by your ex—who left you without explanation ten years ago. You're in danger because someone who wants to hurt him thinks hurting you will do the trick. But you're great?"

Though Jen had gotten her breathing somewhat closer to being in control, she couldn't look at Ty or she'd never be able to have a coherent conversation. So, she stared at her lap and focused on the fact Laurel was calling them.

"I'm just making the best out of a bad situation," she offered brightly.

"Is that best in Ty Carson's pants?"

"Laurel!" Jen managed through strangled laughter. It was a little too apt.

"Well, you're panting like you're running away from a bad guy or…"

"Did you call for a reason?" Jen asked primly, wondering just how red her cheeks were and just what Ty would read into her embarrassment over her sister's seeing right through her even over the phone.

"Yes. Actually. I want to talk to both of you on Speaker, and Zach if he's there. I think I'm hoping he's not there or things would be weird."

"He's out putting up some of his surveillance equipment," Jen grumbled.

"Okay, that's fine. You can fill him in. Put me on Speaker. Unless Ty's naked. I don't want to talk to Ty on Speaker if he's naked."

"He's not…" Fumbling with his phone, Jen managed to switch on Speaker. She avoided Ty's steady gaze even though she felt it boring into her. She cleared her throat. "Laurel has some news."

"The DNA on your notes matches Braxton Lynn," Laurel announced. "And here's where things get interesting. We looked into the name you gave us, Ty. Oscar Villanueva of Minnow, Arizona. Turns out he and Braxton Lynn lived in the same group home for four years."

"He's connected to Oscar," Ty said dully.

Jen reached out and gave his hand a squeeze. Though she didn't know why it should hit him hard, she could tell from that voice devoid of all emotion it *did* hit him.

"Yes. I'm still working on information, but Braxton's behavior became erratic after Oscar left for the army. Bounced around different foster situations, and I wouldn't be surprised if he had some criminal issues, but I don't have any access to juvenile records. Which is why I want you to pass that along to Zach."

"You're telling me you, Ms. Law and Order, know full well Zach is hacking into closed files?" Ty asked incredulously.

"Don't sound so surprised. I *am* married to Grady. Something had to rub off. Besides, I'm not asking him to. I just know he can and probably is. So, give him the name and if he finds anything, I want to know. My men searched the woods. A few footprints, but nothing concrete enough to figure out where he disappeared to, so I want you two to stay put for the time being. Now that we're sure that it's him, we should be able to round him up soon enough."

"Where's Oscar?" Ty asked.

There was no answer, only the slight buzz of a phone connection. Jen looked up, her heart twisting at that blank expression on his face.

"Laurel." Ty's voice was quiet and calm, but Jen could see the tension in him underneath that stoic mask.

"It seems as if Oscar's been in a lot of trouble since he got out of the army," Laurel said gently, and vaguely Jen noted. "Since he was *kicked* out of the army I should say, but you knew that, didn't you?"

"Yeah, I knew."

"Is it possible that has something to do with Braxton's fixation on you? Oscar, his foster brother, was booted out, and you went into the rangers?"

Jen watched Ty rake his hands through his hair. And there it was—all that guilt he heaped upon himself.

"Yeah. Not possible. Probable. I reported Oscar's dependence on drugs and alcohol to our superiors. It directly resulted in Oscar's discharge."

"You didn't think to tell me that a little sooner?" Laurel demanded.

"No, I didn't. I didn't think they could be connected. Or maybe I didn't want them to be. I'll apologize for that, but it doesn't change anything."

"We should focus on Braxton," Jen said. She tried to reach for Ty's hand again, but he moved away from her. Out of reach. "Obviously he blames Ty for something, but Oscar having some trouble with the law—"

"He's in prison."

Jen closed her eyes. She didn't know the man, and yet her heart ached for what this would all do to Ty.

"I have to go," Laurel said, sounding understandably tired. No doubt she was putting in too many hours on top of pregnancy. "Fill Zach in. Keep yourselves safe. Got it?"

"Yeah. Thanks, Laurel," Jen managed. "Keep us updated."

"I will. Stay safe."

The call ended and Jen looked at Ty. He had his back to her, so rigid. Everything about him radiated *do not touch* energy. Her first instinct was to give him space, even as her heart ached to touch him. To soothe.

Her heart had been leading her today, not her instincts. So, she'd be brave enough to follow her heart again. She crossed the room to him, wrapped her arms around him from behind and leaned her cheek against his back.

TY DIDN'T WANT her comfort. That was what he told himself. He didn't want soft arms or sweet words. It was better, so much better, when you learned to do without. Because you could forget. You could convince yourself you didn't need it.

God, he needed her. Even something as simple as this hug kept that heavy blackness of guilt from consuming him completely.

But it slithered along the edges. The connection to Oscar made so much sense. He'd thought about Oscar on and off over the years. Ty had always felt bad for the way things had shaken out, but he'd known Oscar was a liability to everyone around him. He thought getting him booted home might be some kind of a favor.

Instead it had been a life sentence. Prison.

How could it not be his fault? His action had directly led to Oscar's discharge. Maybe bad things would have happened to Oscar either way, but it was hard to hold on to that when he could only think of all the ways he could have done it differently.

"Don't," Jen murmured.

He stiffened. "Don't what?" he asked, knowing exactly what she'd say.

She moved to his front and reached up to brush her fingers over his close-cropped hair. "You know what. Don't blame yourself for someone else's actions. We're too old for that now."

He could have shrugged her off. He could have ignored it all and focused on the task at hand: Braxton Lynn and his fixation on Jen. Instead, faced with her sympathetic brown eyes and her kiss and "I love yous" drifting through his mind, only the truth could spill out.

"I ratted him out, Jen. Now he's in prison. How am I not supposed to draw some conclusions on my guilt?"

"You informed your superiors of a problem because he was a potential threat—not just to others, but to himself."

"How did you…" But he realized she didn't *know* it. She just figured it out. She was always good at that—working out why people felt the way they did, thought the way they did, acted the way they did.

"So, say it."

He didn't want to. Partially because he couldn't believe it and partially because of that same emotion that had jolted him earlier. Fear. But again, he wouldn't let fear win. "It wasn't my fault," he intoned, even though it was a lie.

"Now, work on believing it." She smiled and then lifted on her toes to brush her mouth against his.

She kissed him like she believed he was worthy of it or her. She always had, and he'd figured it for a lack in judgment. A lack he took advantage of because he couldn't help himself.

But her judgment was just fine, and she understood him all too well. Still she loved him. Over years and distance, she loved him and was willing to forgive him. Forgive *him*.

"What are we going to do about this?" he asked, and he didn't have to specify which *this*. She clearly knew.

She smiled. "Embrace it."

HE WATCHED THE MAN. He still hadn't figured out who this third wheel was, and he didn't like it.

He didn't like anything right now. Through the night he'd managed to drill a hole in the room he'd figured to be a bedroom based on one of the few windows and cheerful curtains.

All while cops had tramped around in the night, loud and stupid, he had worked. It had been so easy to stand in the shadow against the cabin and quietly and carefully drill his hole. Everyone said his old-fashioned tools were pointless. But they were quiet. They were gruesomely effective.

He'd gotten a perfect hole to insert the tiny camera. Modern technology had its place, too. He appreciated the old and the antique of a simpler, better time, but Oscar had taught him how to use the modern, too. He'd taught him to drive when no one in that house had cared about him.

Oscar had been his big brother. They didn't need blood to have a bond.

But then Oscar had left. Tempted away by the army and their lies about bravery and courage and meaning something.

He would have followed. Had planned on it. But then Oscar had gotten thrown out.

Ty's fault.

Oscar had started getting into trouble. Oscar hadn't wanted him around anymore.

Ty's fault.

All of it, all the bad before he'd finally gotten his brother back was Ty's fault.

Maybe he'd been a little grateful for Oscar's prison time, because Oscar didn't have a choice anymore. If Oscar wanted a visit from the outside, it was from him. He didn't tell Oscar that, though. Instead, he told Oscar he would make everything right. Balance the scales so they were brothers again.

Oscar had liked the idea. Liked the idea of hurting anyone who'd harmed him.

First it was the girl in Phoenix. She'd led Oscar on, and then Oscar had had no choice but to hurt her. But Oscar had landed in jail, and the girl had gotten off scot-free.

He'd fixed that, and Oscar had been very appreciative. Oscar had even called him *brother* again.

He had to close his eyes to rid them of the tears that clouded his vision. They'd been brothers again.

And once he paid back Ty for all the ways he'd hurt Oscar, they'd be a real family. For good. No matter what.

He narrowed his eyes at the man walking out of the stables. This stranger was putting up surveillance equipment.

That wouldn't do.

He knelt and pulled the pack off his back and surveyed his weapon options. He wanted to save the bear traps for Ty, though anyone who wandered across them would be fine, but he wouldn't lure this stranger to one. The arrows were for Jen. She needed some comeuppance for the way she'd let Ty touch her.

The gun would probably be too loud. He pulled the pistol out, aimed it, pretended to fire. Then chuckled to himself. He was nothing if not resourceful. Why take out the stranger now when he could get two for the price of one?

And then Jen would be his.

She would need to be punished.

He was starting to ache for that. For her screams. For her blood.

She isn't your focus. She's only a tool to get to Ty.

But if she was only a tool, that meant whatever was left over could be his. Screams, blood and all.

Chapter Fourteen

Jen managed only a few bites of her canned chili dinner. Zach had hacked into the juvenile records system, and his expression was grim as he got ready to tell them what he'd found. It made her stomach churn.

"Unfortunately, this isn't the kind of record I'd want to see knowing said person is out there haunting the woods."

"That bad?"

"It looks like it started small. He's got some vague notes in his foster files about erratic behavior, threats of violence. A few assault charges he was given some leeway on since he was so young and bounced around. Things kind of level off, then spike up again right around the time Oscar would have left for the army. Stalking, assault—mostly against women. It looks like he had mandatory counseling as he got closer to eighteen."

"Clearly it solved all his problems," Ty returned drily.

"Record-wise? It seems to have helped. He doesn't have anything as an adult. Not so much as a speeding ticket. He left the group home as soon as he could. Had trouble keeping a job, but other than that…"

"Mostly against women," Jen murmured, turning that small piece of information over in her mind. It had to be relevant, and possibly the key. "And yet, his anger is directed at Ty, but he's chosen me as a target."

"He views you as weaker. A safer target," Zach offered.

"Yes. His behavior now… He has to know he's going to get in trouble—after years of not getting into any."

"Just because there's no record of it doesn't mean he didn't do anything wrong. It just means he wasn't caught," Ty pointed out.

"It's more likely," Zach agreed. "The lengths to which he's willing to go now doesn't point to an emotionally stable soul, or a man who was rehabilitated, then snapped back."

"If his violence is typically against women, then that's our answer." It explained the lack of action. She was stuck in a cabin with a former army ranger and a former FBI agent, so that would be threatening to Braxton. If they were going to draw him out, end this, it needed to be with someone he didn't find threatening. It just made sense. But then Ty laughed.

Not a real laugh—a harsh, sarcastic sound that had her bristling. "No," he said simply, as if she'd outlined her plan out loud, as if his word was final.

"You don't know what I was going to say."

"Of course I know what you were going to say. You're a Delaney, aren't you?" He pushed out of his chair and began to pace.

She was surprised enough by the angry strides to be quiet for a few seconds. He wasn't even trying to hide his irritation. It simmered around him plain as day, with every footstep one way and every whirl to pace in the opposite direction. Which wasn't like Ty at all.

"I don't know what being a Delaney has to do with the fact that a woman won't be threatening to him, and we need to draw him out."

"Addie did the same thing, didn't she?" Ty demanded, eyes blazing. "She tried to use herself as bait. And what happened?"

Jen frowned. She hated to think back to the way Addie had been kidnapped and hurt. Terrorized really, but she'd survived. And the man who'd hurt her couldn't anymore. "This isn't the same as the *mob*, Ty. I believe you pointed that out to me just a few days ago when I reminded you that Noah bringing Addie here hadn't exactly worked out for them back then."

"You're not going to be the lure, darling, so get it out of your head."

"Oh, well, you've told me," she replied, letting the sarcasm drip from her tone without trying to soften it any. She pretended to salute him. "Yes, sir. Et cetera."

Zach cleared his throat. "Maybe I could be the tiebreaker?"

They both glared at him with such venom he cleared his throat again. "And maybe I'll leave you two to argue it out. I'll go to my room and, er, watch the surveillance tape."

Jen didn't even watch him go. She turned her glare back to Ty. He was scowling at her.

"Do you think I'm weak?" she demanded.

He didn't even flinch, or hesitate. "No."

She had to admit it soothed her irritation a little bit. Until he kept talking.

"But I think this is my fight. And you know what?

Ten years in the military, yeah, I think I've got a little better handle on a psychopath who hates women than you do."

"That's doesn't mean—"

"Yes, it does. You will stay put. You will do as I say."

"Do as you…" Rage tinged her vision red. "You think you can order me around simply because I love you? Well, think again, Mister."

"Are you really going to keep saying that?"

"Yes, I am. I love you a million times over, but you will not boss me around like I'm still seventeen and need a keeper. What we have now is an adult relationship, Ty, and we're going to treat each other like adults."

He stared at her. All that irritable energy that had been pumping off him was gone, somehow wrapped up and shoved beneath this impenetrable veneer.

Then he softened. Not so much visibly—he was still all rigid military muscle, but that fighter's light in his eyes dimmed and he stepped toward her.

"I can't stand the thought of it, Jen," he said, his voice rough as he laid his hands on her shoulders. "You getting hurt in all this."

She didn't smile, though she wanted to. It was almost as if her whole life had been building to this moment—danger mixed with love, hope mixed with fear. "Tell me why," she murmured, leaning into him. "Besides your incessant need to heap guilt upon yourself."

For a hair of a second he went stiff, and honestly it soothed her as well as the gradual softening, the way his arms came around her. It wasn't *easy* for him to love her. She'd always known that. It was the fact he'd do it anyway that had always meant the world to her.

Love meant facing down all his fears and guilt, and he did so. For her.

It made the forgiveness for all that had come before easier and easier. It watered the seeds of determination until fear didn't have room to grow.

They'd come through this because they'd come so far. They'd find a way to work together to get home because now they got to go home together.

"I can't stand the thought of you getting hurt because I love you. Which you said you already knew," he grumbled.

"Doesn't hurt to hear." She sighed. "We're a team. I'm not a person you're protecting," she muttered into his chest. "It's not fair to use love against me to try to keep me safe and locked away."

He kissed her hair. "Who said I was going to be fair?"

"We have to do something. We can't stay shut up here forever. I have to get back to my store. I have to— we have to—get back to our lives. I don't want to wait around for the next note. I want to go home."

He pulled her back, though he held on to her shoulders. He looked into her eyes.

"I'll get you home. I promise you that."

"I don't need you to. I need you to work with me. For the three of us to work as a team so we can *all* go home. I want you to promise me we're in this together, not that you'll get me home."

He pulled a face, but he didn't let her go, didn't move away. So she traced her fingers along his scruffy jaw.

"I need that promise from you, Ty. As much as I need your love. Love might exist without teamwork and communication, but I think we both learned it doesn't *work* without it."

He sighed heavily, clearly struggling to agree, even though there was no way he could disagree. It was their simple truth, whether either of them liked it or not.

"I can't promise not to act instinctively to protect you. I can't promise to let you get hurt if I see a way around it, even if it hurts me. I can't promise you that."

"So, what are you going to promise me?"

"Just how demanding is new Jen going to be?"

She grinned at him, because she liked the idea. New Jen and more *demanding.* No, she'd never demanded things for herself. But now she would. Because life didn't protect the good girls who bent over backward to make other people happy, any more than it protected women who did the opposite. Life was undiscerning, and there was no cosmic reward of safety.

"Yeah, I think new Jen is demanding, but fair."

He swept his hand over the crown of her head. "New Jen's not so bad."

"Uh-huh. So, where's my promise?"

He grunted, but he held on to her shoulders, kept her gaze. "I promise that the three of us work together to get home safely. No secrets, no sacrificial plans. We're going to be smart. And we're going to work together."

Jen rose to her toes and pressed her mouth to his. "That's a fine promise."

HE WASN'T HAPPY about the promise. In fact, it sat heavy in his gut like a weight through the rest of the evening. Just like the knowledge Oscar was in prison. Just like the knowledge Jen was right.

They couldn't stand around waiting for the guy to make a move. Eventually they had to go home.

It was a surprise to him that Jen had flipped it all on its head. He wanted to go home. He wanted to live that life they'd planned, but with this new version of themselves—strong and smarter and capable of facing down the world. Facing Bent and her father and the incessant ribbing they'd surely get from their siblings and cousins.

He welcomed that.

He'd been a coward. He could admit that now, in the dark on this uncomfortable couch. Grady had been right. He ran away, not from dangerous situations, but from emotions. From love and hope and the things his childhood had taught him were traps.

But his brother, his cousins and Jen had all proved that wrong for him, and it was time to stop being ruled by his past. By the guilt of the abused.

He looked over at the door to the room Jen was in. He'd given Zach the other bedroom since the guy had all sorts of equipment. Besides, didn't he deserve to be the one on the couch since this was all his fault?

But Jen didn't blame him. Not for any of it. She loved him, forgave him and thought they could embrace a future together.

It had only taken a threat against her for him to see it, believe it might be possible. There was guilt there, too, and he knew it would be easy to stay on this uncomfortable couch and drown in it. He'd always let himself drown in it, considered his guilt so brave.

But Jen had called it childish, and as much as he wanted to tell himself—and her—that she didn't know what she was talking about, of course she did. She'd always known what she was talking about more than he did.

He rolled off the couch, surprised to find himself as shaky as he'd ever been facing down a dangerous mission.

This wasn't dangerous, but it was daunting. This wasn't life or death, but it was Jen's heart and for that he'd face life or death. He walked to the door to her room. He paused, breathing through the unfamiliar nerves.

If he went into this room, he was making promises he couldn't take back. He was accepting everything Jen had said. He was forgiving himself for a past he'd always blamed himself for.

Can you really do that?

He never thought the answer to that question would be yes, but it was. Because Jen had forgiven him, and she was the best person he knew. She had to be right in her forgiveness, so he'd believe in her, and forgiveness of self would follow.

He turned the knob, slipped into the dark room.

"Oh, Zach, is that you?" she murmured sleepily.

She was lucky he knew better. "You're a real laugh a minute."

She chuckled, so pleased with herself he couldn't help but find himself smiling in the dark. She'd always been his joy in the dark.

"What took you so long?" she demanded.

"I guess I had some things to work out." Even with no light, he knew exactly how many steps to the bed, what side she'd be sleeping on. He toed off his boots and then lowered himself onto the mattress.

She rolled into him, pulling the covers over him.

No hesitation. She'd made her decision, and it wouldn't waver. He couldn't either.

He pulled her close, his decision made, no matter where it took them. "I don't take it lightly."

She snuggled in. "I know. I don't either." She pressed a kiss to his jaw. "Make love to me, Ty."

"I figured a rousing game of gin rummy would be more my speed."

"Hmm." She kissed his temple, his cheek, his neck. "Are you sure about that?" she murmured, her hand drifting under his T-shirt.

He rolled her underneath him. "On second thought."

She laughed, tugging at his shirt. "Oh, hurry. It's been too long."

Far too long, so he did exactly what she asked. He hurried. They tugged off each other's clothes with more desperation than nimble fingers. He couldn't get enough of her, worse than the kiss earlier today because she was naked underneath him. His. Always.

They came together on a sigh, and it didn't matter his skin had scars and her curves had changed. They were the same here. Soul to soul. So he held her there, connected completely. So completely it didn't even bother him to feel the wetness of her tears on his shoulder. This was so big, so important, tears seemed vital.

"I love you," she whispered.

He said it back, for the first time without even an ounce of a twinge of guilt or regret, because she'd washed them away, with her love and forgiveness. All that was left in their wake was determination and surety.

So he moved, with slow, sure strokes, drawing her pleasure out with lazy patience. She chanted his name, rained kisses over his face, begged him for more, and still he kept a brutally easy pace.

Then she arched against him, scraping the lobe of his ear between her teeth. "All of you," she said, fingers digging into his arms. "I want all of you."

It unlocked that last piece of himself, and he gave her exactly what she asked for. All of him, every ounce of himself to her. Always and forever her.

They fell over that bright pulsing edge together, entwined tightly in each other. So tightly he was sure it took hours to unwind themselves from each other. Eternity to move off her, though he pulled her to him.

They lay there, breath slowing to normal, hearts eventually calming. And for the very first time in a very long time, he felt something like peace.

But they weren't ready for peace yet. Something evil still lurked out there, and they had to vanquish it before they could have their peace.

"I won't let anything happen to you, and you can get all prickly over that and go on about teamwork, but it doesn't change the simple truth I won't *let* anything happen to you."

She was quiet for a long moment, drawing gentle patterns across his chest. In the end, she didn't respond to that at all. She simply sighed. "I've missed you, Ty."

"I missed you, too, Jen." Never again would he let anything keep them apart that way. Not himself, and certainly not some maniac bent on terror.

JEN WILL DIE.

He wanted to carve those words into his skin, but he settled for the tree trunk. It was dark, a blackness that suited everything about his mood. Clouds had rolled in and not even the moon shone.

He couldn't see where he carved, but he carved the words anyway.

Jen will die.

Jen will die.

She'd let Ty touch her, and so she would die.

His hands cramped, and still he carved. Carved and carved trying to get rid of the need to carve the words into his own skin.

It would be her soon enough. The wait would have to be over.

At sunrise, his plan would begin.

Jen will die.

And Ty would watch.

Chapter Fifteen

Jen awoke the next morning with a contentment completely incongruous to the situation she found herself in.

She *knew* she should be worried and focused on the trouble at hand, but Ty's warm body next to her was everything she wanted, and the worry wouldn't win.

If there was anything she'd learned from the past year of troubles and fear for her family, it was that love endured. Hers and Ty's had endured all this time apart, and it would endure whatever danger the universe indiscriminately threw at them.

A few threatening notes and one arrow through a window were hardly going to take away this satisfied contentment, and that was that.

Her stomach growled, more than a little empty after she'd only picked at her dinner last night. She figured the numerous times they'd turned to each other in the night had burned off quite a few calories.

She looked at Ty's face in the dim glow of dawn filtering through the curtains. So strong and stern, even in sleep. It made her smile. It made her want to press her mouth to his. But her stomach was insistent and she figured Ty could use some extra sleep.

She slid out of bed and moved as quietly as possible for the door. The wind was rattling the cabin walls and it seemed to muffle the sound of her footsteps. She opened the door and peeked back at him. He didn't wake up, so she closed the door quietly behind her and went for the kitchen.

There was some bacon in the freezer she could defrost, along with some frozen hash browns she could fry up. She was in the mood for a deliciously filling, greasy breakfast and would be happy to putter about the kitchen for a bit. It would keep her mind occupied and her nerves settled.

She moved quietly around the kitchen, even let herself daydream about once this was all over. Would they spend the night at his place or hers? She couldn't imagine living above Rightful Claim, and not just because it would give her father a heart attack…but so would the alternative.

A Carson tramping around the apartment above the Delaney General Store. The thought made her smile.

A door creaked and she looked up, trying to hide her disappointment when it was Zach coming out of his bedroom door rather than Ty coming out of theirs.

He peered over at what she was doing. "You know you're an angel, right?"

She smiled at him. "An angel of fat."

"I'll take it. First I'm going to head out. One of the cameras is down. Could have been some animal interference, but I want to get it back up and running."

She frowned at Zach as he unlocked the door. "Don't you think you should wait? You shouldn't go out there alone."

"It's a typical malfunction." He held up his phone and tapped the screen. "I've got all the cameras tied in here, so I can look in all directions. I'll know if someone's out there before they know I am. Plus I'm carrying." He patted the gun at his hip. "You can watch me on the video on my computer in my room if you're nervous—I've got everything set up, you just have to walk in. Where's Ty?"

"Uh." He was still in her bed, fast asleep. Even though she wasn't embarrassed of being with Ty per se, it was a little awkward considering they were sharing a cabin with Zach. "He's, uh…" Her bedroom door opened and Ty stepped out, sleep rumpled and shirtless. "There."

"Ah." But Zach didn't say anything else. Just nodded his head and opened the door.

"Where are you going?"

"Jen'll fill you in." With that, he left and closed the door behind him.

Ty frowned, flipping the lock before turning to her. "He leaving us to our own devices?"

"A camera is down. He's going to check it out. Apparently he can see all the feeds on his phone and we shouldn't worry about it, but I don't like it."

"Me neither. I'll get dressed and head out there."

"I don't like that either," Jen muttered, but not loud enough for him to hear. She had no better ideas. Only dread creeping across all those places that had been happy and hopeful just a few moments before.

Ty returned, dressed in jeans and a T-shirt, boots on and laced. He'd fastened on his old Wild West–style holster that seemed more ominous than just part of his personal Carson style today.

"He said we can watch him on his computer. It's all

set up. Maybe we should just do that? Zach was an FBI agent. I feel like we should trust him a little."

"Shows what you know. FBI agents are a bunch of pencil pushers," Ty grumbled, but he strode for Zach's room instead of the door. Jen focused on breakfast prep as Ty returned with a laptop. He placed it on the kitchen table so she could see it out of the corner of her eye and he could sit at the table and watch.

On the screen were six boxes. Five of them showed areas around the cabin, but one was completely black.

"That must be the broken one," Ty murmured, sliding into a seat and watching the screen intently.

Then they were quiet, the only sounds Jen cooking up the hash browns and then the bacon. She plated breakfast, all daydreams lost to reality. When she slid into the seat next to Ty, they ate in continued silence, watching the screen of Zach's laptop. Occasionally Zach would appear in one box, then disappear.

The black screen popped back to life, showing a swath of trees moving with the wind.

"That's the view from the back of the cabin, right?" Jen asked. Though she'd lost her appetite to nerves, and now had a vague headache threatening at the base of her head, she forced herself to eat. She didn't want to admit that she was keeping her strength up in case they had to fight or run, but that was exactly the thought that prompted her to eat.

"Yeah, that's the one he fixed up on the roof. West corner." Ty chewed bacon thoughtfully. "I guess it could be as simple as the wind knocking it off. It's been blowing hard half the night."

"Zach said maybe animal interference."

Ty nodded. "That, too."

"It seems…far-fetched it'd be something that simple. That unthreatening."

Ty shrugged. "That's only because we're being threatened. Wind. Animals. Those things happen regardless of human threat."

She studied his profile. On the surface he seemed calm, but there was something about the way he ate. Mechanically, his eyes never drifting from the computer screen. "You're worried."

He flicked her a glance. "I'll worry about everything until this is over."

Yes, they both would. She turned her attention to the computer screen as well, and watched as Zach appeared and then disappeared again. "Maybe we should go out and tell him he fixed it."

"I think he knows. He's just checking the others."

The video flickered and all six sections of the screen went black for a moment before coming back.

Ty narrowed his eyes, moved closer to study the screen. "That look different to you?"

It didn't, but the cold feeling seeping into her skin definitely didn't help matters. "Something isn't right."

"Yeah. You keep watching, I'll go out and check."

"Ty—"

But he held up a hand and pulled a key out of his pocket. He walked over to the couch, stuck the key in the small end table's drawer, and then pulled out her phone. "You keep watch and call or text me if you see anything on the screen I should watch out for."

"But if someone is out there, the ringer—"

He pulled out his phone. "I'll set it to vibrate."

"He could still hear—"

"Do you have a better idea?" Ty asked, and it wasn't

laced with heat or derision. It was an honest question. "With Zach out there and something not right? I'm all ears, Jen, but I don't think we have time."

"Go. Be careful. Please."

He brushed a kiss over her cheek as he headed determinedly for the door. Jen didn't beg him to stay, though she wanted to. But she would be strong and she would be smart. She gripped her phone and watched all six boxes on the computer screen.

She was like the control tower. Much as it might feel like she was separate and doing nothing, she had an important function here.

So, she watched, waiting for Zach or Ty to appear. She frowned at the way the wind outside shrieked and made the entire house groan, then looked back at Zach's computer screen. Nothing moved. Not a tree, not a leaf, not a blade of grass.

Oh God. She jumped to her feet. Something was all wrong. She swiped open her phone and punched in Ty's number as she strode for the door.

It didn't ring. Nothing happened. She looked down at the screen. It was black. She hit the home button and tapped the screen, but nothing.

Her phone had died.

And Ty and Zach were out there and the cameras had been tampered with.

SOMETHING WAS OFF. The knowledge crept along Ty's skin as if he were walking through spider webs. But even when he checked his phone, there was no message from Jen so everything must be all right.

At least where the cameras were. There were spots

the cameras didn't reach, so there could still be something wrong. Someone could be lurking, watching.

He walked carefully along the perimeter of the cabin, one hand on his phone and one on the handle of his gun in its holster. He watched the woods and saw nothing but the trees swinging wildly in the tempestuous wind.

Ty realized now, seeing the actual scene before him, that the video had been frozen. No wind. No movement. Which meant Jen wouldn't be able to warn him if anything bad was coming because there was no real-time video feed going to her.

He pulled the gun out of its holster, flicked off the safety and watched. By the time he'd made a full path around the cabin and stables, Zach was nowhere to be found.

Dread pooled, but Ty didn't let worry grow out of it. He'd figure this out, with skills honed from the army and the rangers. He could take on one unbalanced lunatic, and would. Because people's lives were in danger, and it was…

He couldn't allow the guilt anymore. Not with Jen's words and I love yous in his head, but he could say this was his *responsibility*. His purpose was to keep Jen safe. And to find Zach.

Ty might not have felt a particular affinity for Zach, but he wasn't about to let anyone, especially a blood relation, be hurt over something that had to do with him. Besides, maybe Zach was busy kicking butt on his own. Ty would only be backup.

He could hope.

He texted Jen first, tried not to consider how irritated she'd be.

Trouble. Stay put. Call Laurel.

He shoved his phone in his pocket. Jen wouldn't be able to see anything to help him unless the video unfroze, and he didn't consider that likely, but it was still a better shot than having her come out here. Inside the cabin she was safe.

Ty walked the perimeter again, this time making his circle bigger. He searched the trees, paused to listen and wished he'd brought his binoculars.

At one pause before he made it back to the front door again, he heard a rustle. He moved toward it carefully, pretended to veer off in the wrong direction. He did it a few more times, always keeping the location of the first rustle in his mind as he made a very circular path toward it.

He caught sight of something black and ducked behind a tree, but the color didn't move. Carefully, inching forward by avoiding as many dry leaves and twigs as he could, Ty moved toward the color.

The closer he got, the surer he was the figure was human. Zach. Seated on the ground, which wasn't right at all. Ty took another step closer and could see he wasn't just sitting there whiling away the time, he was tied to the tree, his head lolled down, blood dripping from a wound to his temple.

The spurt of fear and need to help had him speeding forward but halfway through the step his military training kicked in. It could be a trick. It could be—

The pain was so quick, so sharp, so absolutely blinding he could only fall with a strangled breath. He landed hard on the unforgiving ground, writhing in pain and trying to stop his body's natural reaction because he had to think.

But it hurt so damn bad thoughts wouldn't form. Knives in his foot, clawing through him. Searing, tearing pain.

But the image of Zach tied to the tree, bloody, flashed into his brain and he bore down to focus. He moved himself into a sitting position and looked down at his foot.

He was caught in a trap of some kind. He focused on his breathing over the panic. He had to keep his head, and he concentrated on the in and out of breathing, and helping Zach, as he eyed the metal clawed onto his foot.

If there was a bright side, and it was a pretty dim one, it was that he'd tripped it so quickly that his thick work boots had taken some of the trauma. Though the blade had sliced through flesh and potentially bone, he wasn't likely to bleed out like he might have if the trap had gotten more of his leg.

Then he heard more than a rustle. Footfall and twigs snapping. He realized he'd dropped his gun in the fall, but that didn't mean he was weaponless. He just had to move for a knife and—

"Tsk. Tsk." The man from Rightful Claim and Jen's store stepped forward, gun trained not on Ty—but on Zach. "And to think you were an army ranger. What an embarrassment."

Ty swallowed down the pain, the fear, and focused on the mission. Eliminating the threat. So, he flashed a grin. "Well, hi there, Braxton. It's about time."

ALL THAT WAS missing from this joyous scene was a chorus of angels. Everything—everything—had worked out. He almost wanted to cry, but instead he surveyed the man who had caused all his problems.

"Have you been waiting long?" he asked of Ty. Ty's stoic response did nothing to irritate him. Oscar was also very good at appearing unmoved. It was a military thing.

Inside, Braxton *knew*, Ty was scared. In pain.

He studied the bear trap. It hadn't taken quite the chunk out of Ty he might have hoped, but Ty was stuck, and in pain. He wished it was more, but Ty's casual greeting couldn't hide the pale pallor to his face, or the grimace of pain.

It was better that Ty was only marginally hurt, and thus would not just live but stay conscious through what he had planned.

Yes, everything was better this way. He looked at the other man, still unconscious. Alive, but bleeding.

Braxton smiled. This was good. So good. In fact, he realized in this moment that Dr. Michaels had been wrong. So wrong she deserved the beating and stabbing he'd given her. Yes, he remembered it now. Every beautiful plunge into her fragile skin and hard bone.

He hadn't killed her, but he'd done irreparable damage.

It had been right all along. That violence. That payback.

He didn't need what Dr. Michaels had told him. Not focus. Not a *goal*.

He needed only blood.

So, without another word, Braxton walked away, whistling.

The next part of his plan was more blood, and it was already in place.

Chapter Sixteen

Jen had all the weapons she could find piled on the tabletop. Ignoring the way her arms shook, the way her head ached, she tried to figure different ways to carry as many guns and knives as possible on her person.

She refused to think about her dead phone, the dead landline she'd tried. She passed off the wave of dizziness that caught her as cowardly nerves and *refused* to give in to it.

She'd used Zach's computer to send an urgent email to Laurel, Cam, Grady and even the general email for the Bent County Sheriff's Department, but Zach's computer was so foreign to her she didn't have time to try to find an instant messaging service. She needed to protect herself, and she needed a plan.

A plan to protect the men out there trying to protect her.

Zach should be back by now, that was for sure, and the fact Ty wasn't caused her to worry, but she wouldn't worry uselessly. She would act.

Once it was loaded, she shoved a smaller gun into the waistband of her jeans. She fixed a sheathed knife into the side of her boot. One rifle had a strap, so she set it aside, ready and loaded.

She had to steady herself on the table. The dizziness wouldn't go away and the painful throbbing in her head wouldn't stop. For a moment, she thought she'd be sick.

She took a deep breath to center herself. Ty was a former army ranger and Zach was a former FBI agent. There was no way she was going to have to go out there and save their butts. They were either perfectly fine, or taking care of everything.

She could stay where she was. Maybe she was really sick or something.

She shook that ridiculous thought away. She was letting emotional nerves turn into physical responses, and she wouldn't be that weak or cowardly.

She would take precautions, go outside and search for Zach and Ty, armed to the teeth, and hope to God Laurel read her email and sent someone to help them.

Even though she was probably overreacting. If she found them out there, fine and in charge, she'd scold them both for scaring her to death.

And if they weren't, she'd fight for them the way they would fight for her. Maybe she wasn't as skilled, but she knew how to use a gun and she knew how to use her brain. Cowering inside wasn't acceptable. Not now.

Slowly, feeling sluggish and worse with every step, she hid the guns and knives she'd collected that she couldn't carry. But this time when she hid them, she put them places she would know where to get them. Places she might be able to reach if she needed to. Under couch cushions and under the sink in the bathroom.

More and more, she couldn't seem to think past the painful throbbing in her head. It was a heck of a time for her first migraine, but she wouldn't give in. Because Ty and Zach still weren't back and they should be.

They should be. So, even if things were fine, she had every right to be worried. To act. She gripped the table for a second, righting herself and breathing through the pain. She glanced at the computer screen, the six frozen boxes.

Except they weren't frozen anymore. Trees moved, grass swayed, and on one of the blocks, she saw two figures.

She swayed on her feet, nearly passed out, but it was Ty. Ty, caught in something. He couldn't seem to move his foot as he reached forward, fiddling with something around his foot. Zach was limp and clearly tied up. Since the feed was in black and white, she could only hope the smudge on his face was…anything except the blood it looked like it could be. Had to be if he was tied up.

No one showed up on any of the other screens, and Braxton or whoever had hurt them was nowhere to be seen. But they were hurt, and that made her decision.

She had to get to them. Save them. There was *no* choice. She slung the rifle over her shoulder and sprinted to the door. She fell forward, somehow grabbing onto the knob and keeping herself upright. She twisted, fought against the fog and the dizziness, then remembered she had to unlock the door.

It took too long to manage it. Why was fear making her so sluggish? Why couldn't she be strong and brave? She *had* to be. Zach and Ty were hurt and they needed her. She had to be brave.

She managed to twist the knob and push the door open.

To a man.

She screamed. Or thought she did. But the next thing

she knew she was on the floor, looking up into Braxton Lynn's face. He looked the same as he had in her store, but it reminded her more of when he'd held the note up to her door than when he'd thanked her for the candy bar.

Something was missing in his eyes, something human. His pleasant smile was all wrong. She was on the floor. She had to reach for her gun, but her limbs were so heavy. So heavy. They didn't move.

"Oopsie," Braxton said cheerfully, nudging her legs out of the way of the door with his boot before he closed the door and flipped the lock. "Looks like someone has themselves a little carbon monoxide poisoning. Isn't that a shame?"

Poison. God, it all made sense now, even as the black crept through her mind and she lost her tenuous grasp on consciousness.

TY GRITTED HIS teeth against the pain, against the dull edge of shock trying to win. It couldn't. Zach was bleeding and Jen was on her own. Vulnerable and no doubt that madman was heading right toward her.

The way Braxton had simply studied the trap on Ty's foot, peered at Zach's limp body, then walked away, whistling, was all Ty needed to know to understand he was going for Jen now. That he didn't expect Ty or Zach to die. No, he wanted them alive for whatever was next.

Ty had to stop it. He had to escape this.

He'd tried to use whatever he could reach to pry the jaws of the trap open, but everything had broken off. He'd tried to pull the chain holding the trap down, but that had sent such a jolt of pain through him he'd almost passed out.

There had to be a way out of this. Had to be. He simply refused any scenario where he didn't free his foot and go save Jen.

Maybe she'd save herself. She was armed, and clearly stronger than Braxton gave her credit for if he thought the only thing that had kept her safe thus far had been him and Zach. Ty would believe Jen could handle herself, but he'd work like hell to get out of this and make sure she could.

He was about ready to test the give of the chain again when he heard a low sound. He wouldn't have thought it human, but Zach also moved a little, his head lolling, eyelids fluttering.

"Zach," Ty called. "Wake up. Now." They weren't too far apart, but Ty couldn't reach him. Could only watch as he still wavered somewhere just out of reach.

Ty wasn't about to give up on him. He kept talking, kept repeating Zach's name. "Zach. Come on, man. We need you now."

"Hurts," he mumbled. "Can't move."

"You're tied up to a tree. Some kind of head injury. Braxton's got us stuck here and Jen's alone in the cabin. He's going to hurt her if we don't do something. You need to come out of it."

"Can't see. Black."

"Open your eyes," Ty commanded, trying to sound like an officer, not a desperate man shouting at an injured one.

It took another few minutes of talking him through it, repeating the situation over and over again, until Zach's eyes opened and stayed open. Finally, after what felt like eons, he seemed close to himself.

"We have to get out of this," Zach said, looking

around the wooded area they'd found themselves in. "I want to believe Jen can take care of herself, but he took us both out."

"It's our own stupid faults. He wouldn't have if we'd stayed inside." Ty leaned forward, trying to reach the chain of the trap to tug at with his hands. If he could reach it, he could pull it off whatever it was attached to and maybe walk with the damn thing on his foot.

"No, he would have gotten us. I've dealt with enough criminals and unbalanced individuals to know he's determined, and he won't stop until he gets what he wants, or someone stops him."

"I'll stop him," Ty said, a swear, a promise.

"And me." Zach rolled his shoulders. "The knots aren't great and he didn't tie my legs. I can get out of it. I just…" Zach swore, twisting his body one way and then the other. Ty might have been impressed if steel claws weren't digging into his foot. "I can get out of it," Zach said more firmly this time. He maneuvered his body this way and that, grimacing and wincing, but never losing consciousness again.

"How long had I been out?" he asked, then hissed in pain.

"Too damn long."

"I don't remember how it happened."

Ty recognized the disgust of failure and guilt in Zach's tone and knew it wouldn't serve them any. "Well, since I currently have my foot caught in what appears to be a bear trap, I can't cast stones. He's gone after Jen. We've got to—"

Zach stood, the ropes falling to the ground.

"How the hell'd you do that, Houdini?"

"I told you the knots sucked. Now let's see what

we've got here." He crouched in front of Ty's leg, squeezed his eyes shut for a second and swore a few more times. "Little bastard gave me a concussion."

"Let's give him a lot worse. Get me out of this thing."

It took too long, that much Ty knew. Like Ty, Zach used a variety of natural objects to try to pry the trap open.

"You should go."

Zach raised an eyebrow at Ty. "You want me to leave you here stuck in a nineteenth-century bear trap?"

"I've gotta believe Jen can ward off this guy, but I also believe two is better than one. Go. Help her and—"

Something clicked and the bear trap opened. It was almost as painful as the going in had been. His vision dimmed, but he focused on the hard ground beneath him and Zach's hand on his shoulder.

"Found the release mechanism. Can you walk?"

"Hell if I know. Let's find out." He took Zach's outstretched hand and got to his feet, putting pressure only on the good one. He had to have broken bones on top of the puncture wounds that were currently oozing blood.

"I could carry you."

Ty snorted. "You and what army? You've got a concussion and I'm not exactly a lightweight. Just give me an arm."

Zach did so, winding his arm around Ty, and Ty did the same. He took a tentative step with it, not putting full weight on. His good leg nearly buckled, but Zach kept him upright.

It would have to do. They moved slowly, and Ty swore, repeatedly, with every step of his injured foot, but kept stepping forward with Zach's help. "Toward the cabin," he said with gritted teeth.

"You aren't going to be much help."

Ty pointed to the gun that had fallen when the trap had gotten him. "The hell I'm not."

Zach bent to pick it up as Ty balanced on one foot. Ty took it from him and shoved it in its holster. "You got your phone on you?"

"No. He's got it. You?"

Ty paused. Much as it galled him to waste time, he pulled his phone out of his pocket and hit Laurel's number. He motioned Zach for them to keep walking as he used his free hand to hold the phone to his ear.

"T—"

He didn't even let her get his name out. "Get as many deputies up here as you can. Plus Grady and Noah." Cursing his bad luck, he added, "And Dylan and Cam. Everybody. Anybody."

"They're already on their way. We got an email from Jen. I tried to call but her phone goes straight to voice mail and the cabin phone line is dead. We've got some car trouble, but we're working on it. Someone should be there in ten minutes. You don't sound so good."

"Minor injuries. Have an ambulance ready, but don't send it up here yet."

"Is Jen okay?" Laurel demanded. Since Ty didn't know how to answer that, he didn't. "Gotta focus." He hit End and shoved his phone in his pocket. "Cavalry's coming," he said through gritted teeth.

"Good. I've got a bad feeling we're going to need it. We've still got a ways to go."

Too much of a ways. "Go ahead."

"How are you going to—"

He leaned against a tree and handed the gun to Zach. "You run hard as you can. I'll be behind you. Just make sure she's safe. Help her if she's not. We don't have the time for me."

Zach nodded once. "I'll see what I can do." Then he was off.

It about killed Ty to watch Zach run off, knowing Jen's fate was in his hands. No. Her own hands and Zach's hands and all the help they had coming.

He didn't even consider waiting. He braced himself, then took off after Zach in the fastest limping job he could manage. Maybe he wouldn't save the day, but he wasn't going to take the chance that he wouldn't need to.

He'd do whatever he could, fight through any pain, suffer any consequences to be sure Jen was safe.

IT WAS FREEZING in the cabin, even with the fire crackling in the hearth. The windows were open since he had to air out all that carbon monoxide he'd poured inside. He'd gotten a bit of a headache himself when he put the straitjacket on Jen.

And everyone said his odd collection of things would be a waste.

He laughed, pleased all over again at the genius. He wished he'd thought of the carbon dioxide sooner. It would have saved him some trouble.

But he'd been able to use his bear trap. Ty's blood was on it now. Worth it. Everything was worth blood.

Jen moaned, moving weakly against the straitjacket that tied her arms behind her and her body to the couch. He watched her slowly drift to consciousness from his position by the window, breathing in fresh air.

He wanted to watch the fear creep into her. Wanted to see the panic on her face when she realized where she was. When she realized he'd immobilized her completely. When she realized no one could or would help her now because he was the only one here.

He laughed again, and her eyes flew open. Pretty eyes. Such a shame to squeeze until they popped right out.

Would that be bloody? Hmm.

He thought for a second about focus, about goals, about what Dr. Michaels had always told him.

But she'd been wrong. Leaning into the black was so much better. Hadn't everything gotten better since he'd stabbed the good doctor? Once he was done with Ty, he'd go back and finish the job.

Revenge. It wasn't just for Oscar anymore, and though a part of him felt guilty, a part of him was too excited about what was to come.

Blood. Blood. Blood. Ty's suffering would be for Oscar. Jen's blood would be for him.

Her eyes darted around the room as she swallowed and moved, trying to escape the straitjacket. She wouldn't be able to, but it'd be fun to watch her try. Fun to watch her scream and beg.

He'd watch for as long as that thrilled him, then he'd kill her. Just like Dr. Michaels, but he'd finish the job. Leave her ripped apart and bloody for Ty to find.

He frowned a little. It would be possible someone else would find her first, and that wouldn't do. No, Ty had to be the one who stepped into all the glorious blood he'd soon shed.

He still had some work to do to perfect his plan.

He watched her struggle against the bonds he'd put on her, and smiled. He'd have the perfect view to do just that.

Chapter Seventeen

Jen pretended to slip back into unconsciousness so she could think. She tried to remember what had happened or how she'd ended up immobile on the couch.

Her arms were wrapped uncomfortably around her body, but she couldn't move out of the position. It was like she was tied together, fastened to the couch.

Panic came, though she tried to fight it. She wanted to pretend like she was still unconscious but she just… she couldn't. She writhed and tried to free her hands, move her arms only a little, but she couldn't.

She sobbed out a breath, was afraid she wouldn't be able to suck in another. She opened her eyes as she desperately tried to move her limbs. What had he done to her? Why couldn't she move even her arms?

She blinked once, then twice, thought maybe she was hallucinating before she came to the conclusion that her eyes were not deceiving her.

He'd put her in an honest-to-goodness straitjacket.

"Worked out that it fit almost perfectly."

She jerked at his voice, even though she knew he'd been there. It wasn't that he spoke that gave her a start, it was how…conversational he sounded.

"One of my foster mothers used to put me in it. I kept it. A token of the time."

"That's horrible," Jen replied. Talking helped ease some of her panic. If she could focus on Braxton, on talking, she could take her mind off the fact that she couldn't move.

"It was horrible. And now it's horrible for you."

"Th-that doesn't seem very f-fair," Jen managed. She tried to ignore the fact she couldn't move. Because she had to be able to get out of this, or at least stall…whatever he was going to do to her. The longer she could keep him from hurting her, the better shot she had of someone coming to save her. Them.

God. Ty. Zach. They were all tied up in some fashion or another now. She didn't understand how one lone, crazy man had been able to best all three of them.

Except no. He hadn't bested them yet. She had to believe there was a way out of this. As long as she believed, there was a chance.

"Fair?" He laughed, and there was no edge or bitterness to the sound. He seemed genuinely amused. "You don't actually think life is *fair*, do you?"

She wouldn't answer that—not with the awful joyful gleam in his ice-blue eyes. "I-it's Braxton, right? You're Braxton."

He tilted his head and studied her. "Are we going to be friends now, Jen? You were nice enough to give me a candy bar, right? You're going to be nice enough to talk to me. Soften me up and maybe I'll let you go."

She closed her eyes and breathed. She thought about Ty. If he were in her place, he wouldn't panic. He wouldn't cry. Sure, he had military training she didn't, but she could be as tough as him when push came to shove. When she had to be.

"I know you're going to hurt me because you think it'll hurt Ty, but—"

He laughed again, louder, but it had an edge to it now that had her swallowing at the lump in her throat.

"Now you're going to lie to me?" he demanded, still standing over by the window. "You're going to lie there, in a *straitjacket*, and tell me Ty doesn't care about you. Oh, Jen, you're stupider than I gave you credit for. You think I don't know you let him touch you? You think I don't know everything that went on in that room last night?"

Horror waved through her, a crawling sensation of disgust crept along her skin as he pointed to the bedroom she'd shared with Ty.

"You…"

"Amazing what you can learn from watching people on video. Your third wheel friend knows that, doesn't he? Don't worry. It was dark. I couldn't really see anything, but I know what you did. I know what you said. Love is such a powerful motivator, don't you think? When you love someone, you want to hurt the people who hurt them."

"No. You want to heal the hurt in them, not punish the person who hurt them."

Braxton laughed bitterly. "Oh, aren't you full of it."

"No, I'm not." Was she really arguing with a homicidal maniac? It was probably pointless and stupid, but it kept her attention off the horrible sensation of forced immobility. "If someone hurt Ty, I would want to help Ty, not worry about stupid, selfish revenge."

"Stupid?" he repeated in a low, dangerous tone. "Selfish?"

"Yes, stupid. And selfish on both parts. I would want

him okay, not someone else hurt. And Ty would never want me to hurt people *for* him. If he had a problem, he'd deal with it himself. I know you're trying to… You think this means you cared about your brother—"

"Cared?" He almost screamed the word but then he seemed to shake himself. He turned away from her, muttering something she couldn't hear. Then he repeated her words, till he was just muttering the word *himself* over and over again. As if he was working out a math problem, but every word he uttered was simply *himself*.

"You've given me an idea, Jen." He turned back to her, affable and pleasant again. "An interesting idea. Do you think Ty would sacrifice his own life for yours? Or would he hurt you to save his own skin? Which one's love?"

Without knowing what Braxton was planning, thinking, she didn't want to give him any answer. So she simply swallowed.

Braxton finally moved away from the window, but he moved toward her and that was when she realized he had a very large knife in his hand.

"Do knives make you nervous, Jen?" he asked, sounding almost concerned, almost human. He twisted the knife one way and then another. When he knelt next to the couch, she whimpered no matter how she tried not to make a noise.

Braxton smiled, brandishing the knife above her head. "You're terrified. My, my. I quite like them. Anything sharp really. Blood is so…interesting. So soothing. Would Ty shed his own to save you yours?"

A tear slipped over. She could feel it trail down her cheek. Braxton pointed the sharp tip of the knife at it. She squeezed her eyes shut as the tip of the knife touched the teardrop and pierced her skin. It hurt, but she couldn't move. She was stuck, the tip of the blade cutting into her skin.

"Blood and tears." He made a considering noise, but the knife eased off her cheek. She felt something trickle down her chin—tears or blood or both—and tried to believe she would survive this.

But she didn't have any idea how.

THE CABIN CAME into view, and with it, Zach standing behind the stables. Ty's body was becoming slowly numb. He welcomed it, as long as it didn't interfere with his ability to move forward.

"He's got the windows open," Zach said by way of greeting.

Ty glared at Zach when he finally reached him. "Then get in there and—"

"I scoped it out. We need to work this together. I go in guns blazing, not only do I end up dead, but she might, too. We'll have to find a way to draw him out."

"The concussed and the mangled foot?"

"If it's all we got. I'd like to wait for the cops."

Fury, fear and sheer frustration welled up inside Ty like a tidal wave destroying all the numb. "Wait for... Are you—"

"I said I'd like to, not that I would." Zach scanned the trees, calm and sure. Ty might have been reassured if he wasn't so scared. "What's taking them so long?"

Ty tried not to think about all the worst-case scenarios. The wind having knocked down trees to block the road, Braxton having men working for him, happily picking off cops as they came.

He couldn't think about it now. He had to get to Jen. "What's the situation inside?"

Zach eyed him and Ty knew in a moment it was terrible, but before he could start forward, Zach spoke in clear, concise military tones.

"She's tied up. I need you to be prepared for that. He's got the door booby-trapped, but the windows are open. I don't see any traps, but I've got to believe he's got something going on there. He's bested us once, so we can't let him do it again. We have to be more careful than we were. Smarter."

"Tied up where? How?"

Zach scrubbed a hand over his face, smearing some of the blood across his cheek accidentally. "On the couch. I can't be sure, but I think he's got her in a straitjacket."

Ty swore and moved forward, but Zach grabbed his arm again, this time giving it a good yank.

"You're not new to this," he snapped, his voice firm. "You know dangerous situations, and people who would do anything to prove their point. You know the dangers and everything that could go wrong. You have to forget it's Jen for right now."

"That's bull. Why did I do all those things in the army? Because they were supposed to keep the people I loved here safe. Why'd you get kicked out of the FBI, Zach? Because you cared about your family more than you cared about procedure. So, don't give me that crap right now."

"I'm not talking about arbitrary procedure. I'm talking about a plan that prioritizes getting Jen out of there without getting anyone hurt."

"I'll get hurt. Ten times over." He'd go to hell and back and enjoy the ride.

"You think she'd want that?"

"I think I don't care." But it poked at some of his certainty. She wouldn't want that. It'd hurt her, and that was the last thing Ty wanted. She was already being hurt, far too much. His fault, and his guilt was talking. She wouldn't want that either. "What kind of booby traps?"

"The door's got some kind of trip wire. My instinct is explosives. Potentially enough to blow this whole clearing to hell."

Ty fought the fatigue and pain going on inside his body to think. *Think.* Jen had tried to understand Braxton, tried to understand his emotions. She'd been right, and he needed to think like she had.

"He incapacitated us, but didn't kill us," Ty said. "He could have. Easily."

"Yeah."

"He wants to torture Jen, but he wants me alive to see it. Whatever trap he's got going on in there isn't big scale because that'd ruin it. End it. He wants me to suffer—if we all die, I don't suffer."

"Okay. Okay. I'll give you that. But two things we have to keep in mind. First, I don't think he cares if *he* gets hurt as long as he gets revenge, so that's not a threat to him. Second, if you go in there, he hurts Jen. The closer you are to her with him the more likely he is to do something to her."

Zach was right. It burned, but Zach was right. The minute Ty stepped foot in that cabin, Jen was in at least twice as much danger. Which meant he had to do something that went against every fiber of his being.

He had to trust someone else with Jen's safety. He

had to put it all in someone else's hands. He had to trust, and he had to believe, in someone aside from himself—not just Zach, but Jen, too.

Guilt told him this was all his fault and he should take responsibility for it. Guilt told him he couldn't let Zach get even more hurt when this was Ty's own fight.

But Jen... Here, in that cabin, she'd forgiven him everything—his faults, his choices, the things he'd done or not done. Everything he'd hated himself for, she'd washed away with forgiveness. And she always had.

She'd told him to let it go, to forgive himself, and he had tried, or had believed he might someday. But in this moment, he had to. Because if he didn't, Jen would more than likely die.

"You'll go in," Ty said, having no trouble snapping into army ranger mode. "There's a secret passageway on the opposite side of the cabin, but it's been sealed. Still, with the right timing, the right tools, you can either unseal it or create enough noise he comes out."

Zach nodded.

"If I situate myself in the hayloft, I've got the perfect position to pick him off if he comes out the door."

Zach rose an eyebrow and nodded toward Ty's foot. "How you going to get up there?"

"Carefully," Ty replied. Zach held out the gun Ty had given him and Ty took it. "You'll be unarmed."

"You're better off with the gun. You can pick him off through a window, we end this. Besides, he took my gun and my phone, but I've still got my knife." Zach motioned to his boot. "Vanessa gave me that idea."

"Thank God for Vanessa and her arsenal. Let's go." He motioned Zach to follow him back into the woods. Zach offered an arm, but Ty shook his head. Walking hurt like nothing he'd ever experienced, but Jen's life hung in the balance. He'd deal.

They moved through the cover of the trees to the opposite side of the cabin. Braxton couldn't know he was out here and free, or Jen and Zach were in even more danger.

Ty moved up the side of the cabin and showed Zach the secret passage and where it had been sealed.

Zach pulled out the knife. "This should do the trick. If not, I'll start banging away, try to lure him out."

Ty nodded. "I doubt he knows who you are, so hurting Jen to get to you won't matter to him, hopefully. He might think you're of some emotional connection to me, though. He might even know you're my cousin, my blood. So he could hurt you again, to get to me. We can't discount that."

"Yeah, I haven't let a man best me twice in this lifetime. I don't plan to start now."

"That's the Carson spirit." Ty studied the clearing, the cabin. "I'll be in the hayloft, out of sight, but if you get him out the front door, I can take him out. Jen's the priority."

Zach nodded, already prying at the seal on the door. "You should get out of sight now. I'll see what I can do here, but no matter what, I'll get her out. That's a promise."

Like Jen had chosen to forgive him, love him, Ty chose to believe Zach. He clapped him on the shoulder. "Take care of yourself, cousin." And then he limped for the stables, gun at the ready.

BLOOD AND TEARS, but Ty wasn't here. Should he kill her and then bring Ty to the aftermath? Better for him to watch. He'd get the blood, and the revenge. Oscar wanted the revenge. He wanted the blood.

But she was right there and all it would take was a few minutes. He could cut her to ribbons and it would be done. Right now. No more waiting.

Why did he have to wait?

"Braxton, I know you want to hurt me…"

Her voice was so sweet he wished she'd stop talking. It wasn't like the doctor's voice. The doctor had always been so cold. So condescending. Jen sounded afraid of him.

He liked that.

"Could you let me out of this thing? I don't care if you tie me up again. I just can't lie like this."

He walked back over to her. She wanted out, and maybe that would suit his purposes. Maybe a little fight would make this all sit right. He'd had to fight the doctor. Element of surprise, yes, but she'd tried to push him off.

He'd liked that. The way she'd hit and begged and still he'd plunged the knife into her skin.

His stomach jumped with anticipation, even more so when Jen's fear shone in her eyes like tears.

"You want out?"

She swallowed visibly. "Just a little? I know you have to keep me tied up, but if I could just move a little. My circulation and I… I…"

Desperation. He liked it on her. Fear and desperation. It was what he wanted from Ty, but maybe he'd practice on sweet Jen. He held the knife over her head again, watched as she squeezed her eyes shut and braced herself for another cut.

The one from before was just a little dot now, a little smear of blood and tears down her cheek and chin.

Pleasure spurted through him, dark and wonderful. If only this moment could last.

"Cut yourself," he said.

"What?"

He liked the way she paled. Fear. He liked her fear so much. It was better than a shot of whiskey. Better than the drugs Oscar had liked so much that Braxton had never understood.

Why do drugs when you could make someone afraid? When the power of that could stir everything inside you?

"I'll free one arm. If you take the knife and cut yourself. More than I did on your face." He wondered if it would be more or less satisfying to watch her cause herself pain, or if it would be better for him to do it. Her hurting herself would cause Ty more pain, he thought, but the blood on her face made him wonder if he cared. "Maybe your wrist. It'd take a while for one wrist to bleed out."

"But…"

"One wrist. Then I decide if I do the rest, or you do. One wrist. Then we get Ty. I'd like to get a better look at Ty's blood, too. Maybe so would you."

"Braxton—"

He laid the flat of the blade against her cheek. "Sweet Jen didn't do anything to deserve this, but you love a monster. Maybe you're a monster, too. Monsters need to bleed, Jen. Isn't that what all the fairy tales tell us?"

But she didn't answer. She only cried.

Chapter Eighteen

Jen would scold herself for crying later. For now, it was the release of fear she'd needed to center herself. "Okay, Braxton," she said, opening her eyes and making sure to look at him, to try to be a person to him. "I'll cut my wrist if you let me have one arm."

One arm would be all she'd need. There was a pistol in the cushion of the couch, unless he'd found it when she'd been unconscious. But she'd take the chance—had to.

Zach and Ty were stuck and she had to be able to save herself, and them.

Braxton could hurt her, *would* hurt her, but as long as he didn't kill her she had a shot. And he wouldn't kill her as long as Ty was somewhere else, so there was some bright side to his being stuck.

She just needed to get to that gun, and she just needed it to be there. One arm. All she needed was one arm. Didn't matter if she had to cut herself to do it.

She breathed in and out, trying to accept the fact she would have to do it. She'd have to cut her own flesh and…

She had to convince him to free her arm first. She

had to actually get him to do it before she worried about pressing a sharp blade to her wrist.

An involuntary shudder moved through her, but she forced herself to look at Braxton and tried to treat him like a human being even though whatever made someone humane was clearly missing in him.

"I've killed before, Jen, you know," he said, so simply, so *conversationally* the way you'd tell someone you didn't care for pizza. He stared at her intently, looking for a reaction.

She didn't know what kind he wanted. If she did, she'd act it out and give it to him. She'd go along with whatever he wanted. "I'm sorry," she whispered.

"Sorry?"

It wasn't the answer he wanted, but what was? What could she say to just make him untie her?

No time for panic. Breathe in. Breathe out. As long as Ty isn't here, you have time.

But did Ty have time? Did Zach?

She couldn't think about them.

"Are you going to let me go? Please? I'm going to have a panic attack."

He laid the flat of his blade against her cheek like he'd done before, and again she couldn't hide her response. A shudder, a wince and more tears welling behind her eyelids.

She opened her eyes when he did nothing. He was grinning. Finally, it started to make sense. He wanted her to be afraid. He wanted her to shudder and wince at the idea of his killing people, over the idea and possibility he could kill her.

"Panic attack. I might like to watch that."

He was never going to let her go. He was going to torture her until… When?

"But I'd like to see your blood more," he continued. He pressed the knife against her cheek until she hissed out a breath when it lightly scored her chin.

He leaned in closer, his face so close to hers she could feel his breath against the blood dripping down her neck.

"Please let me out," she whispered, letting her fear and her tears run free, since that's what he wanted from her anyway. Fear and tears and blood. "Please. I just need to sit up or move my arm. Please. Anything."

He didn't lean away, though he did pull the knife off her skin. But then he replaced it with something much worse.

His tongue.

A groan mixed with a scream tore from her throat as she struggled to move her face, her body, her entire being away from him as he licked the blood off her face.

But he only made a considering noise, as if he was mulling over the taste of her blood.

Shudders racked her body and true fear crept through everything. She didn't know how to fight insanity. She didn't know how to escape. A tiny part of her wondered if death wouldn't just be easier.

The thought passed. Ty was out there, trapped. Zach was trapped and probably hurt. Her entire family was trying to solve the mystery of Braxton Lynn. Someone would make it here eventually and help her.

Ty was counting on her. He'd left her alone thinking she could handle anything that came her way, so she would. She *would*.

If she believed that, she could endure anything.

Anything.

"Please, Braxton. Just a break from the straitjacket. Besides, if you take all this fabric off you'll be able to cut me wherever you want."

"I want to watch you cut yourself, Jen. A test. Which do I like better? Inflicting pain? Or making you inflict pain on yourself? I get blood either way."

"Then just free my arms. Please. *Please.*"

He sighed heavily. "Fine. But only because I want the experiment. It's important to find out what makes you feel the best, isn't it?" He undid some strap, then rolled her to the side so her back was to him. "I thought I liked revenge. Doing something for my brother. Ty was supposed to be Oscar's brother, but he ratted him out. Did you know that about the man you let touch you? That he's no better than a cowardly tattletale?"

She bit her tongue against the need to defend Ty. He wanted her fear and her desperation, but she doubted he'd care for her anger.

There were sounds, the gradual loosening of the fabric holding her arms around her. She nearly wept with relief, but then Braxton paused.

"If you try anything, this is my plan. Cut you to ribbons. Bathe this room in your blood. Then bring Ty in to see your mangled corpse that he should have been brave enough and smart enough to save. One attempt at escape, one look at the door, one wrong move—you're dead, and he sees it *all.*"

She didn't suppress this shudder since she knew he liked it. If she gave him everything he liked, maybe he'd make a mistake—get too excited. No matter what, as long as she did what he said, he'd keep her alive. She wouldn't be the sacrifice he made to hurt Ty.

Braxton pushed her up into a sitting position. He held the strap of one arm tight around his fist. He tugged the other sleeve off. "I'm going to give you the knife. You're going to slice your wrist. If you do all that, I won't put the straitjacket back on."

Jen nodded, and her arm that was now free shook. Even if she could muster up the guts or strength to cut herself, she wasn't sure her limbs would cooperate. Still, Braxton slowly pressed the handle of the knife into her palm—holding her other arm still by the straps on the jacket.

With his hand now free, he pulled a gun out of his pocket. Everything inside her sank. It was the gun she'd hidden in the couch.

"Hope you weren't planning on using this." He smiled indulgently.

She shook her head even though that's exactly what her plan had been. Still, he'd given her a knife. Maybe he had the gun pointed at her, but she had a weapon, too. If he let go of her other arm, she could knock him down.

She just needed the right moment.

But he just kept smiling, like he knew every move she'd make and had a counterplan for it. He didn't take the straitjacket off her completely. Instead, he pushed the sleeve still on her arm up, revealing her wrist and adjusting his hold onto her forearm.

"Cut yourself. And don't wimp out. A real cut. I want to see blood *gush*. I like knives better, but if I have to shoot you to get blood, I'll do it. So, pick your poison."

Jen briefly considered letting him shoot her. It might be better for her in the long run. But she had a knife now. He'd untied her. Her feet were still fastened together, but she had a weapon and she wasn't tethered to the couch any longer.

"Go on now."

She nodded, arms still shaking as she slowly brought the knife to where he held her wrist out for her. She'd only have to lunge forward, right in the gut. He'd shoot her, but he'd be hurt, too. Wouldn't it be worth it?

"Do it now," Braxton ordered, jerking her wrist toward the knife. "Or I'll put you back in. I'll carve that pretty face of yours all up while your arms are tied around you. Would you prefer that, Jen?"

No, she wouldn't, but she was afraid he was going to do it anyway. But first, she'd cut herself. It excited him, and if he leaned down to lick her wrist like he'd done with her face, she'd have the best chance to stab him where it would do the most damage.

She closed her eyes and pressed the blade to her wrist, inhaling sharply to give herself one last second before she inflicted pain.

But then she heard something. Like a door being opened somewhere. She kept her eyes closed, even as hope soared through her. She had to cut herself and keep Braxton's attention.

"What the hell was that?" Braxton demanded as she opened her eyes.

He not only looked away, he turned, which gave her the opportunity to strike.

A SCREAM TORE through the air. Ty immediately jumped from the hayloft. He saw stars, the pain in his foot so bright and burning he nearly lost consciousness.

When a gunshot sounded, Ty didn't care about the pain. He ran.

He stopped for a moment at the window, but he couldn't see anything. It'd have to be the door—regardless of booby traps.

Zach was reaching the door just as Ty rounded the corner.

"Was just about in when I heard it. I'll kick in the door. Stay to the side. We'll give it a minute, me in first since I've got two good feet, then you follow and shoot."

Ty nodded.

Zach reared back and kicked. It didn't open the door, but it jarred it, so Zach kicked again. This time it splintered, and opened weakly.

Almost immediately there was another gunshot.

They both swore, but there was no time to consider the ramifications of Braxton's shooting at them. Zach went in first, a low roll that hopefully got him some cover. Ty moved in, weapon drawn.

Braxton stood behind the couch, his arm wrapped around Jen's throat. She was limp and lifeless, blood smeared all over her face. Braxton held the barrel of the gun to her head and grinned.

Jen was too close for comfort, but they simply didn't have another option. Ty aimed and fired.

Braxton jerked back and Jen fell to the floor. Zach and Ty moved forward as a unit. Red bloomed on Braxton's shirt and he touched the wound and smiled. "Look at all that blood," he murmured, transfixed by the sight of his own fingers drenched in his own blood.

Then his eyes rolled back and he collapsed in a heap. Ty didn't think he was dead—he'd probably just passed out.

"I'll tie him up," Zach said.

Ty tossed him his phone. "Call Laurel again and find

out what the damn holdup is. We need that ambulance."
He looked down at Jen. Her face was covered in blood
and she was so pale and lifeless everything inside him
went cold. He fell to his knees next to her and nearly
wept when her eyes fluttered open.

"You're okay," she murmured.

"Where are you bleeding, darling?" She tried to
move, but he stopped her, afraid she'd hurt herself more.
"I don't see where you're bleeding from."

"He smeared it all over me. He…" She shuddered,
closing her eyes again. "S'okay, though. Have to."

"Have to *what*?"

"Get shot. It's like… It's like. Laurel and Cam and
Dylan, they all did."

"Baby, shh. Just tell me where—"

"But then it'll be okay, right? Because they did, but
now it's good. We'll be good, because I got shot. It's
the answer to the curse. It'll be okay."

She wasn't making any sense, but he didn't care.
"Yeah, it'll be okay. It has to be." It had to be. With
shaking hands, he moved his fingers over her, trying
to find the wound. It had to be on her back, but he was
loath to turn her over. But there was bleeding that had
to be stopped.

"My arm," she mumbled. "Hurts. Under my arm."

He didn't know which one she was talking about, so
gently he lifted the one closest to him, but she shook
her head sluggishly.

He lifted the other one, found the bleeding, gaping
wound right under her armpit. Not fatal, thank God, but
they needed to stop the bleeding. Get her safe.

"Stabbed him, but he shot me."

Ty nearly wept right there, but he held it together and took the first aid kit Zach handed him.

"We have to get her to a hospital," he said, opening the case and pulling out all the bandages inside. He handed half to Zach to start unwrapping.

"How? On your bike?"

Ty shook his head, pressing the first pad of gauze to her wound. She hissed out a breath, but her eyes remained closed and her breathing was getting too shallow for his comfort. "What did Laurel say?"

"Trees down everywhere. Their cars were tampered with. The ambulance is trying to get up here, but without a road—"

"We'll carry her to it, then." Ty wrapped more bandages, as many as he could manage, as tight as he could manage, around her arm.

"I don't know if you recall the fact your foot is torn to hell."

"You'll carry, then. We have to get her to that ambulance. We'll bandage her up and get her out of here."

"What about him?"

Ty didn't even glance back at Braxton's body. "He can rot in hell."

Chapter Nineteen

"I convinced him to let my arms free."

"How did you do that?" Thomas asked gently.

Jen sat in the hospital bed, tired and a little off from the drugs they'd given her, but she'd felt up to giving her statement to the police. She wanted to get it all out and over with, before the nurses let her family back in, before she saw Ty.

She wanted to get rid of all the ugliness so it could be behind her. "He told me he'd let my arms loose if I cut myself for him."

Thomas raised an eyebrow as he wrote that down on his notepad.

"He was obsessed with blood. He seemed to lose his grasp on reality or humanity with every passing moment. The need for revenge against Ty sort of faded into…bloodlust I guess." She shuddered again, was pretty sure she'd flash back to Braxton whenever she saw blood.

But she was alive and Braxton… "Thomas, is Braxton…"

"He made it to the hospital, but he'd lost too much blood."

"Braxton said…" She swallowed against the wave of

nausea—didn't know if it had to do with the drugs or everything else. "He said he'd killed people."

Thomas nodded solemnly. "Laurel's been in touch with the authorities in Arizona. They've been able to connect him to an attack on his therapist, along with a murder of one of Oscar Villanueva's victims."

She slumped in her bed, far too aware that she could have easily been another of his murder victims.

"Do you want to stop for now? I can come back—"

"No. I want it over with."

"All right. So, he untied you?"

"Yes, and then there was this noise and I took the moment of distraction to stab him, but he had a gun and he shot me. I'm not sure he meant to, it was more of an impulse response. I mean, he wanted to hurt me, but I don't think he wanted to kill me yet. But things get fuzzy from there."

"You don't remember Zach and Ty coming in?"

"No. No, it just kind of goes blank. I remember talking to Ty in the cabin. He was trying to figure out how I was hurt. Will Ty be in trouble, since I can't remember?"

"No. We have Zach's statement, cut-and-dried self-defense. Ty will be fine."

Jen nodded, closing her eyes against the fatigue.

"You should rest, Jen. I've got enough to build the case and file everything. I may need to ask you a few more questions in the future, depending on how everything goes, but we're mostly done."

Jen grimaced but she nodded. "All right." She tried to smile. "Thank you."

Thomas paused on his way out of the hospital room. "I'm... I wish we could have done more."

Jen shook her head and sighed. "You did what you could. We all did. And now it's over."

Thomas nodded and slipped out the door. Jen allowed herself a moment of quiet, of release. They'd all done the best they could, and now it was over. Everyone she loved was safe, and she'd survived.

Everything was going to be okay.

It was an emotional acceptance because there had been a moment there, before she'd managed to convince him to take the straitjacket off, and for a second there after he'd shot her, where she'd been certain she was going to die.

But she was alive.

She heard the door swish open, and opened her eyes to see Ty. He had a crutch under one arm, and a medical boot on the foot.

She hadn't seen him since the ambulance, and she'd been in and out at that point. But he'd held her hand the whole way to the hospital.

"You should've told Hart to scram."

She held out her good arm to him. "I wanted it over. Did you sneak back here or are you allowed?"

He managed a smile. "Which do you think?" He moved over to her, relying on the crutch. She scooted to the side of the bed so he could slide onto it next to her.

They didn't say anything else. He just wrapped his arms around her and she leaned into the strong wall of his chest.

She thought she might cry, but she didn't. Instead, she just breathed. It was over, and she had this. Everything was okay.

She hadn't realized she'd said it out loud until Ty spoke.

"Yeah it is," he said before kissing her temple. "You know when they'll spring you?"

"Tomorrow they said. They didn't let you out already?"

"Discharged and all." He fidgeted irritably. "I'll have to have some surgery later, but they want some of the wounds to heal first."

"Not everyone can say they have a limp because of a bear trap."

"Making jokes already? I'm impressed, darling." He kissed her again, and his grip on her never loosened.

"I don't want to think about horrible things, or be angry or sad or scared for at least a month."

"Let's shoot for a year."

"Maybe two."

He laughed, but then he just held her, so she held him back. "It really is okay," she whispered. "And there's a lot of okay left to get."

"I know. It's going to take me a little while to... Hell, I thought you were dead, Jen."

She pressed her forehead into his neck. "But I'm not. Which means we have a lot of plans to make. So, you think on that."

The door opened again, and her whole family poured in. A nurse started mounting objections, but Grady easily sweet-talked her out of the room.

Hilly rushed over and gave her a hug, while Dylan insisted Vanessa take a seat. Zach hovered in the background, but Jen motioned him over.

"Glad you're okay, Jen," he offered.

She gently touched the bandage on his temple. "Thank you for everything."

He shrugged, clearly uncomfortable, and then he quickly moved away as her father came over and gave her a hug. Laurel perched herself on the little sliver of bed at the end.

"Well, here we are again," Jen said, opting for cheerful. "But you know, it's over now. We all got shot, and we'll all get our happily-ever-afters."

"Oh, for heaven's sake," Laurel muttered. "There's *no curse.*"

"Not anymore," Jen agreed, grinning when Laurel rolled her eyes.

"What about Zach?" Hilly asked. "He's a Carson."

"I'm a Simmons," Zach replied firmly.

"No, Hilly's right. Zach's one of us," Grady replied. "But we're out of Delaneys for him to pair up with."

"Eh, you never know when one will pop out of the woodwork," Vanessa returned with a grin. "Watch your back, Zach."

He scoffed, but Jen rather liked the idea. And she liked having everyone around, talking as if things were normal. As if she wasn't hooked up to a hospital bed, as if nothing had terrorized any of them over the course of the past year.

It was nice. It was…perfect really. A cleansing moment to put everything about yesterday behind her.

She tried to hide the yawns, the exhaustion, but pretty soon Laurel was shooing everyone out, assuring Jen they'd all be back tomorrow.

Ty didn't budge.

When her family was gone, she snuggled into him, ready for a nice long sleep.

"They'll make you leave," she murmured into his chest.

Ty only held on tighter. "Like hell, darling."

Epilogue

Ty cursed the crutch that had been a part of his life for too many months now. The surgery had been successful, but healing was annoying.

"You're pushing yourself too hard," Jen insisted as they walked across a stretch of rocky land at the edge of Carson property.

They'd been staying out at the Carson Ranch, where there weren't as many stairs to navigate as there were at his apartment above Rightful Claim and hers above the store.

Still, he was antsy to have a space of his own, to be done with healing and get on with living.

So, they'd start living. "What do you think?" he asked, waving a hand to encompass the stretch of field in front of them, the mountains sparkling in the blue-sky distance.

She smiled up at him, confusion written in her expression. She was the most beautiful woman he'd ever known, and she was all his. His faults and errors were no longer the black marks that held down his soul. Because in Jen he always had a place to find his salvation, and love.

"It's a pretty view," she offered.

"How'd you like a kitchen window looking out over that view?"

The confusion left her features, and something else he couldn't quite name replaced it. A certainty—the sure sign of a Jen Delaney plan in the works.

He found he quite liked going along with Jen Delaney's plans.

"I don't think I'd like it, I think I'd love it. But before you go getting ideas, there's one thing you're going to have to do first."

He dug around in his pocket, pulled out the velvet box and popped it open. Pleased that he'd managed to surprise her, he pulled the ring out and held it in the light so it sparkled. "This what you had in mind?"

She nodded wordlessly, tears already falling over her cheeks. He wiped one away, then took her hand.

"So, what do you say, Jen Delaney. Ready to promise your life to a Carson?"

"I always have been," she whispered, grinning at him, urging him to put the ring on her finger.

He slid it on easily, but kept her hand in his. "Anything else before we break ground?"

She took a deep, shaky breath. "I want lots of babies," she said, and though her voice wavered, her smile didn't. "Babies and forever. That should do it."

"We can start working on the babies thing right now if you're up to it."

She laughed, the sound carrying on the wind as it filled up his soul, because that was what his second chance with Jen had done—filled the empty places inside him, washed away the guilt he'd carried for so long.

Love and trust were that powerful, and he'd never let himself forget it.

He kissed her hands, looked into her eyes, and gave her the one thing he knew she'd never expect. The words. "I love you. I can't remember a time I didn't. I don't want to ever remember a time I didn't."

More tears spilled over, and she lightly wrapped her arms around his neck, careful not to move him so he had to put undue pressure on his foot. "I love you with everything I am," she whispered. "I always will. We can survive anything, so we will."

"Yeah, we will."

Always.

* * * * *

WITHIN RANGE

JANICE KAY JOHNSON

Chapter One

"Birdie!"

Helen Boyd glanced in the rearview mirror first to her two-year-old son, then out the side window to the row of crows sitting on the electrical wire.

"Lots of birds," she agreed. "Those are crows. Crows are always black." Helen had the passing thought that in some cultures, they were considered bad luck. Or was that ravens?

Jacob tried to shape the word, which came out sounding more like "cow."

"Crow," she repeated. "Like 'row, row, row your boat,' only it's *c-row*."

He giggled. "K-k-krow."

"Yes." She laughed. "And we're home!" Thank heavens; her feet were killing her, and she was starved. The day had been so busy, she'd never had a chance to stop for lunch. And, ugh, this was only Tuesday.

Home was a small rental house with an even smaller detached garage that held the lawn mower, a rolling tool chest belonging to the landlord, and some boxes and furniture that might have been left by previous tenants. There was no room for a car, so she parked in the driveway.

Helen climbed out stiffly, her attention caught for a brief moment by bright sails on the Columbia River. Her view was barely a sliver, but that was better than nothing. This was June, but the day seemed way too chilly for anyone to want to go windsailing. Whoever was out there was sure dedicated to the sport, she'd learned. The winds channeled through the Columbia Gorge were one of the biggest draws of the small towns strung along the banks of the river east of Portland.

She circled around to release Jacob from his car seat and swing him up in her arms, using her hip to bump the door closed. "Hamburgers for dinner tonight," she told him.

"Hot dogs!" he shouted.

She planted a big kiss on top of his head. "Hamburgers."

He loved to argue. "Hot dogs."

"Hamburgers." After letting them in the front door, she set him down, staying crouched beside him for a minute. "Do you have to go potty?" He still wore a diaper at night but was doing pretty well using the toilet during the day.

"Uh-*uh*," he declared.

"Hmm." Tempted to kick off her heels right now, Helen decided to make it to the bedroom first. Set a good example. Or maybe she should dump them straight in the trash. There was a good reason they'd been on clearance. Knowing Jacob would follow her, she started for the hall—and came to an abrupt stop, staring into the kitchen.

What on earth was that?

Her heart thudded hard. Jacob, fortunately, was clambering up onto the sofa. She took a tentative step, then another, disbelief and fear clawing inside her chest.

It was a high-heeled shoe sitting all by itself that had first puzzled her. She had *on* the only pair of black pumps she owned. But then...then she saw the woman who lay sprawled on the kitchen floor.

Fingers pressed to her mouth, Helen tiptoed closer. Dark hair fanned over the lifeless face, but Helen could see enough...including the hideous dent in the woman's head.

"Oh, no, oh, no." Helen backed away.

From just behind her, Jacob said, "Mommy?"

Whirling, Helen snatched him up and pressed his face to her shoulder. Then she ran for the front door, pausing only to grab her purse on the way.

"THAT THE HOMEOWNER?" Detective Seth Renner glanced toward the car parked somewhat crookedly at the curb in front of the house.

The uniformed officer followed his gaze. "Don't know if she owns it or rents, but that's her. Name's Helen Boyd. She's got a two-year-old in the car."

Easy to imagine how quickly she'd fled the house when she discovered a dead woman on her kitchen floor. Unless, of course, she'd had something to do with the death, but he wasn't ready to speculate yet.

Instead, he signed the log the responding officer had started, bent to put on disposable shoe covers and stepped into the house. Scanning the living room, he saw evidence that a toddler lived here: a small plastic wagon piled with building blocks, a tidy pile of simple wooden puzzles on the fireplace hearth and a crib-size comforter crumpled at one end of the sofa. Built-in shelving to each side of the fireplace held books, including a good-size collection of children's picture books. Coffee table with rounded edges. Foam had been fitted to cover the sharp edges of the brick hearth. TV. If not for the books, the room would have been stark.

Because there was no art, he realized. Maybe this was a rental, and the woman didn't feel like she could put holes in the walls. Although, he'd have expected to see framed photos or something decorative on the mantel.

He shook his head slightly and moved on to the kitchen, pausing in the doorway to study the body and then work outward to the surroundings.

No indication of a struggle. His first guess was that the victim had been in the kitchen, heard something and started to turn, only to be stunned by the single blow. Dead from that moment, she'd dropped to the floor. Finally going forward to crouch beside her, he did note a dirty mark on her white blouse. It didn't go with her businesslike attire: fitted blouse, blazer, black pencil skirt, heels and hose. A shiny black handbag sat on the small kitchen table, a smartphone beside it. Had the killer kicked her once she was down?

He snapped on latex gloves and gingerly reached in the handbag for a wallet, opening it to see the license in a clear plastic sleeve. Photo looked like a match to him. Seth studied it. Andrea Sloan, brown hair, brown eyes, five foot six, thirty-six years old, organ donor.

Too late for that.

He let the wallet fall back into the purse, looking instead at the woman's face, slack in death.

Why had Andrea Sloan been killed? And why *here*, in another woman's house? Unless she was a close friend, sister, something like that to the owner-renter who'd discovered her?

Still gazing down at the body, he called for a crime scene unit from the Oregon State Police, then walked through the rest of the house. It was immaculately clean and uncluttered. Apparently, the kid didn't go to bed without putting away his toys, and Mom or Dad— was there a dad?—didn't toss dirty clothes over the single chair in the slightly larger bedroom that held a full-size bed, bedside table with a lamp and clock, and a dresser. No art here, either, no photos. Curious, he nudged open the sliding closet door to find it less than a third full. Several pairs of shoes lined up in a neat row on the floor, some unexciting dresses, blazers, skirts and slacks on hangers. Nothing that appeared to belong to a man.

The bathroom was shared with the kid. Nothing suggested a man lived here, either. A toothbrush holder and two toothbrushes sat alone on an otherwise pristine counter.

Pretty clearly, the residents consisted of a single mother and child.

Time to talk to the woman.

Going back outside, he shed the shoe covers and followed the narrow concrete walkway to the sidewalk and the car, a Ford Focus he guessed to be at least ten years old, possibly a lot more than that. He opened the front passenger-side door and bent to look in.

"Ms. Boyd? I'm Detective Seth Renner. I need to talk to you. Is there someplace—" A small boy poked his head between the seats.

"Boo!"

Seth pretended to jump, suppressing a grin. "And who are you?"

"I'm Jacob," the boy declared. He had an impish face, a scattering of freckles across his nose and russet-red hair.

"It's good to meet you, Jake."

"Jacob."

"Ah." Seth focused on the woman again, taking in her appearance and noticing she had more than a passing resemblance to the dead woman. Although if they were related, wouldn't Ms. Boyd have said so?

"Is there someone who can watch Jacob for a few minutes?"

"I… Yes. If she's home, my neighbor is usually willing. Let me—" She jumped out, slammed her door and hurried around to his side, letting him see that she was five foot six or seven, long-legged, thinner than he suspected she was meant to be. When he backed away from the opening, she took his place.

"Jacob, honey, let's go see Iris."

"I like Iris," he stated in apparent delight.

Seth had noted the movement behind the front window of the house next door. In fact, he intended to interview whoever lived there next. He strolled behind Ms. Boyd, who carried the boy on her hip. The front door opened even before they reached the small porch, revealing an elderly woman with deep wrinkles and a warm smile for the little boy.

Ms. Boyd explained briefly that she'd arrived at home and somebody had gotten into her house. She needed to talk to the detective. "Could you…?"

"Of course I can!" Iris cast a worried look at Ms.

Boyd but beamed at Jacob. "I just baked chocolate chip cookies. Would you like one, Jacob?"

He held up his hand with all five fingers splayed. Iris laughed and took the boy's hand. The door closed.

Surely at his age the kid couldn't count. He obviously got the concept that more fingers represented more cookies, though.

For just a minute, Ms. Boyd stayed where she was, looking as if she'd give almost anything to follow her son inside. But finally her shoulders squared and she turned.

"Do we have to go in my house?"

"No," he said. "Why don't we sit in your car?"

Relief seemed to loosen some of the fear he'd seen on her face. Her teeth closed on her lower lip and she nodded. "Yes. Okay."

He let her get into the driver's seat again, guessing she'd feel more comfortable there, more in control. He had to move the passenger seat way back to accommodate his long legs, which meant she had to twist a little to look directly at him.

"Detective…? I'm sorry, I know you introduced yourself, but—" Her voice trembled.

"Renner."

Her eyes fastened on his. "I'm sorry. It's just—"

"You're understandably upset." He watched her closely while trying to appear relaxed and even friendly. "Tell me about your day. Anything out of the ordinary?"

"Not until I got home. The rest of the day… Do you care?"

"I'd like to hear about it."

"I commute to Portland every day. I work as an executive assistant."

He took a notebook from an inside pocket and jotted down the name of the company, her boss and the phone number.

"I left at 5:30. I'm pretty insistent on that, since I have to pick up Jacob from day care by 6:00."

That sounded standard to him. He made a note about the day care, too, an in-home one.

"I parked in the driveway, like I always do."

He left the question of why she didn't use the garage for another time. She sounded steady enough now to make him curious. Anxiety wouldn't have surprised him; her poise did.

"I carried Jacob in," she continued, "set him down and started toward the bedroom."

"Just like that?"

She stared at Seth. "I told him we were having hamburgers, and he insisted he wanted hot dogs. Oh, and that he didn't need to use the potty. Is any of that relevant?"

He smiled. "No, you sound like you were rushing."

"Well, I was, because my feet hurt." She glanced down. "They still hurt."

He saw that she wore black pumps. "They look similar to the shoes the victim was wearing."

No, her outfit didn't match, but color-wise…yeah. Almost. A cream-colored, finely knit cardigan over a sleeveless top, and black dress pants. If someone had seen her go out the door, then caught sight of this Andrea Sloan in the kitchen, a mistake might be possible.

Seth reminded himself not to jump to conclusions.

Ms. Boyd swallowed. "I know. There was a weird minute—"

A weird moment?

Shaking her head, she said, "I just thought, did I leave my shoes in the middle of the kitchen floor? But they were still on my feet, so that didn't make sense, and I'd already seen the…her legs. But…my mind wasn't making the connection right."

"That's often the case when you see something completely unexpected," he said gently.

She shuddered. "Yes. I took a step closer, and then realized Jacob was coming into the kitchen after me, so I grabbed him and my purse and raced outside. My hand was shaking so much I had trouble getting the key in the ignition, but I locked all the doors, backed out of the driveway and kept backing halfway up the block. I didn't come closer until the police car arrived."

"That was smart. You couldn't be sure there wasn't somebody still in the house."

Her steadiness must have been a facade, because her fingers twisted together and he saw fear on her face. "Do you think he was?" she asked.

"He?" Seth repeated.

"I just assumed it would have to be a man… I mean, could a woman have enough strength to bludgeon someone to death like that?"

Not likely for a woman, but he wouldn't rule one out. "I doubt the killer was still in the house when you arrived home." Seth's guess that the murder had happened within the last half hour or so suggested the killer hadn't been gone long, though.

He asked her what cars she noticed parked on the street. She turned her head, telling him she recognized the pickup truck near the corner as belonging to the man who lived in that house. Otherwise…

"That almost has to be her car, doesn't it?" He followed her gaze to the sedan right in front of her car.

"I'll find out," he said, and continued to ask questions.

No, Ms. Boyd hadn't seen anyone outside or even looking through their windows when she turned onto the block and then into her own driveway, although she really hadn't paid attention. "Less than usual," she admitted. "Because my feet hurt."

"New shoes?"

"Yes, and I'm going to throw them away."

He smiled faintly, then asked, "Does anybody else have a key to your house?"

The way her hands continued to writhe, he was surprised he hadn't heard the snap of her knuckles cracking.

"The landlord must." She frowned. "And… I suppose Andrea might have had one. I guess she must have, or she couldn't have gotten in, could she?"

He didn't even try to hide the spike of anger. "You know the victim?"

Her gaze slid away from his.

"Any reason why she might have been in the house?"

"But there isn't any reason for her to be here. I mean, the real estate firm she works for also manages the property, but I haven't needed any repairs, and I can't imagine anyone complained that I was doing damage to the house. Why else would she have let herself in?" Alternating between determined poise and vulnerability, Ms. Boyd was now all but vibrating with indignation that spilled over. "I can't believe she's allowed to just do that. If I'd thought anyone could just poke through our stuff, I wouldn't have rented a house through that firm."

"I'll be talking to her boss, but I seriously doubt she was supposed to let herself into rentals when the tenants weren't there. That makes me wonder why she did. Have you heard from her in the recent past?"

Ms. Boyd shook her head. "Not a word. She showed me the house, I filled out the application, went into the real estate office to sign some paperwork and pay first and last months' rent. They gave me the key and that was it."

She and her son had lived here for eleven months, she said. And yes, she'd run into Andrea a few times since at the grocery store or pharmacy, so she must live here in town. They'd been friendly, in a casual way. "She'd ask how the house was working out, we might talk about some event here in town or the weather. Nothing really personal. I think she was only being polite."

"Is she married? Does she have children?"

Her forehead creased. "She's married, I'm pretty sure, but I don't know about kids. I don't remember her saying anything."

His phone rang just then. He was relieved by the interruption, as he was undecided about how much more he wanted to ask her right now versus later. Particularly whether he should, bluntly or subtly, mention the physical resemblance between the two women.

After the brief conversation, he turned to her and said, "You won't be able to get back in your house for at least twenty-four hours, probably longer. Do you have a friend you can stay with?"

"But... I need some of Jacob's things. And mine!"

Her feet hurt, he remembered. "Give me a list of the most important things, and I'll see what I can do."

THE DETECTIVE'S EXPRESSION was completely uncompromising. He wasn't going to let them back in the house at all. The idea of going back in made Helen feel sick, anyway. She couldn't until the body was gone, and even then…how would she feel cooking in that kitchen? Walking right across the vinyl where Andrea had died, even when the blood had been washed away?

Not letting herself look at the man who seemed to take up more space than he should, she pressed a hand to her stomach. "I don't know if I can keep living there."

He had unnervingly blue eyes, which she knew were intent on her face right now. Somehow, that intensity compelled her to turn her head and meet those eyes.

"Death doesn't have to contaminate a home," he said calmly.

"But murder?" Helen asked around the lump in her throat.

"You knew Andrea Sloan. Would she want to haunt you?"

All she felt was revulsion. "I don't know. How can I tell, when I have no idea why she was in my house?"

Detective Renner kept studying her for long enough to make her want to squirm. He must be a whiz at interrogations. Finally, he inclined his head. "Give yourself time. Tonight, it's probably best if you stay at a hotel."

Since he had that notebook handy, anyway, she dictated a list of essentials to him. "I can go buy some of the stuff if I have to, but I really need the blue stuffed bunny on Jacob's bed, and his blankie. It's probably on the sofa."

"Yellow?"

"Yes, that's it. The clothes and diapers and whatnot aren't as important. Oh, it would be good if you could grab his potty seat from the bathroom."

"Okay. I doubt it's a significant part of the crime scene." He smiled, got out and walked up to her rental, disappearing inside.

She rubbed her breastbone, as if to ease a strange pressure beneath it. Detective Renner had a nice smile, one that encouraged her to trust him, that crinkled the skin beside his eyes and softened the hard lines of an angular face she'd first thought looked dangerous. He wasn't handsome, exactly, not like Richard. God knew she'd never trust a smooth, well-dressed, handsome man again. But trusting this detective wasn't an option, either, even if he was a decent man.

Helen Boyd couldn't trust anyone, a cop least of all.

In fact, the smart thing for her to do was bolt, before this cop had a chance to look into her background and discover she didn't have one.

Her mind worked furiously, forming arguments on both sides. Running without changing identities wouldn't do any good. Unless she reverted to her previous one temporarily…? But what if Richard was watching for Megan Cobb? At least here in Lookout, she couldn't imagine that he'd make a move while the police were actively investigating a murder and keeping an eye on her, too.

Conclusion: she and Jacob were safest here for the moment.

She sagged, with no one to see her. She didn't have a lot of stuff, but hated the idea of taking off with only what they were wearing. They'd done that last time, and it had been hard to start completely over. This time around, she *couldn't* go without Jacob's blankie and his bunny.

She did keep a couple of packed bags ready, in case they had to bolt. She'd put family photos and other mementos in them, so she didn't have to carry them around in her purse all the time. Cash, too, and the birth certificate and driver's license that would turn her back into Megan Cobb. Plus changes of clothes for both of them.

Tomorrow, she'd decide what to do. Andrea Sloan's murder might not have anything to do with her.

And to think, she didn't usually allow herself any illusions.

At last, she pulled herself together enough to get out of the car again and go up to her neighbor's door. If only a chocolate chip cookie and milk could make her feel better. If it turned out Andrea had been killed in her place, Helen didn't know how she could go on. Except, of course, she had to. Jacob needed her.

Allie needed her, too, but she couldn't think about that, or crushing guilt might leave her unable to protect Jacob—and he had to come first.

Chapter Two

Seth was the sole detective on a police force that had only twelve sworn officers altogether, including the chief. If absolutely necessary, he could borrow an officer or two to help in an investigation. So far, beyond keeping the responding officer on the doorstep until the CSI team and morgue van arrived, Seth didn't want help. He preferred to talk to neighbors and then the husband himself.

He put off speaking to Ms. Boyd's boss until morning, but did call the day-care operator, who confirmed that Jacob's mother had picked him up about five minutes before the six o'clock deadline. Until the ME gave him a more informed time of death than he had so far, Seth couldn't rule out Ms. Boyd. She'd have had to go home to meet the victim, kill her and then pick up her little boy while appearing completely unperturbed. Hard to see her as that cold-blooded…but it was conceivable. It meant she was a hell of an actor, though. He really believed the seesawing emotions he'd seen were genuine.

That said, his instincts were sending up some flares. He suspected that Helen Boyd had secrets.

For now, he wanted to keep her cooperative, so after

making his phone calls, he located a suitcase in the hall
closet and filled it with the kid's clothes and toys first,
including a blue stuffed rabbit, before invading her bedroom. He tossed sneakers into the suitcase first, took a
pair of jeans off a pile in a bottom drawer, a T-shirt and
zip-up sweatshirt from the middle drawer, then made
himself open the top drawer. It was astonishingly neat,
by his standards. He took out an oversize Eeyore T-shirt
he presumed she wore as a nightgown, a plain beige cotton bra and two pairs of panties, then closed the drawer
before thinking, *Wait.* Socks. He tossed two pairs in the
suitcase, then went to the bathroom.

The crime scene investigators might not be happy
with him, but he couldn't see what they'd learn from
Ms. Boyd's clean clothes or her or her son's toothbrushes. He did peek in the medicine cabinet, which
could often be revealing. In this case…nope. No
prescription drugs. Only ibuprofen for her, cherry-
flavored painkillers for Jacob, bath powder, floss and
hair spray and gel. Stick deodorant, which he tossed into
the suitcase along with the toothbrushes and toothpaste.

A minute later, he carried the suitcase and plastic
potty seat out to her living room, where he paused to
pick up the thin, tattered blanket before going out to
her now-empty car. He was taking advantage of unlocked doors to set everything on the back seat next to
the boy's car seat when Ms. Boyd came hurrying out
of the neighbor's house carrying her son.

She told him she'd go to the Lookout Inn, a pricey
place to stay, but without driving a distance she
didn't have a lot of choice. The bed-and-breakfast
inns in town probably weren't any cheaper, and wouldn't
afford as much privacy.

"All right," he said. "One more thing. Would you allow me to look in the trunk of your car without a warrant?"

She recoiled. "You think I— Of course you can look." Cheeks flushed, she handed over her car keys, then stayed where she was.

The trunk was as tidy as the floorboards of her car and the house. He did lift the cover to be sure no bloody pipe lurked beneath with the spare tire and jack. Nope.

After slamming the trunk lid, he gave her back the keys. "I may check on you later."

She looked less than happy at the idea, but dipped her head in apparent resignation and leaned into the car to fasten her drowsy son into his seat. A minute later, she drove off.

Left standing on the sidewalk, Seth watched the car proceed cautiously down the street until it turned out of sight. He swore under his breath and rolled his shoulders.

She left him unsettled. And he didn't think it was just the uncomfortable fact that she was an attractive woman.

After some thought, he decided part of the problem was that her responses had veered from the norm. Which led him back to where he'd started: Helen Boyd wasn't telling him all she was thinking, by a long shot. But what was she hiding?

HELEN JUMPED SIX inches at the soft knock on the door of the hotel room even though she'd expected it. She had horribly mixed feelings about seeing Detective Renner again tonight. She wanted to know what he'd learned, of course. How could she make decisions otherwise?

But he made her nervous; he watched her with those penetrating blue eyes until she felt as if he was reading her mind.

He also wasn't the only one who could find her here. She approached the door cautiously.

"Who is it?"

The detective's voice both reassured her and didn't. Like she had a choice about whether to let him in.

He dominated the room from the moment he stepped into it. She couldn't quite figure it out, since she had the feeling he was trying to be unassuming. Some of it was size; he certainly topped six feet, which made him a whole lot taller than she was. Broader, too, with impressive shoulders and a rangy, athletic build.

As she backed away, she decided unhappily that the quality was innate. The strength of his control and purpose, his determination, were impossible to miss. She wondered if his police chief or whoever was his direct boss ever dared to give him an order.

Of course, he started by assessing her with those sharp eyes before sweeping the room in search of…who knew? Enemies crouching behind the bed or peering from the closet? At last, his gaze settled on Jacob, sound asleep on one side of the queen-size bed. He looked so small in the big bed, so defenseless.

In a low voice, the detective asked, "Will we wake him if we talk?"

Helen shook her head, knowing her voice softened because of his concern. "An earthquake wouldn't wake him once he's really conked out. He's a very early riser, though."

His laugh was quiet and a little gravelly. It sent a shiver of reaction over her skin. "I won't keep you long."

He still eyed Jacob as she led him to the pair of small upholstered club chairs by the window. "He's past needing a crib?"

"Oh, yes. He was only fifteen months old the first time he climbed out of his crib." She grimaced at the memory. "He fell, of course, screamed bloody murder—" She pressed her hands to her cheeks, feeling the heat. "That was a poor choice of words."

Another rumble of a laugh settled her nervousness a bit.

"Fortunately, he wasn't hurt, but we transitioned to a mattress on the floor pretty quick. Which turned me into the world's lightest sleeper. Every night, I imagine him wandering around the house while I sleep, completely unaware." Why was she babbling? "I may not get a good night's sleep again until he leaves home for college."

His smile was a little crooked. "According to my mother, that's no guarantee."

Helen gave a choked laugh. "Thank you for that thought." She looked down at the table, clasped her hands together on her lap and struggled for calm before she lifted her chin again. "Have you found out anything?"

"Nothing to explain her death yet, I'm sorry to say. I was able to talk to her husband. You were right. The car at the curb was hers."

"What about children?" That possibility bothered her terribly.

"Two stepkids," he said. "Thirteen and fifteen. Her husband is ten years older than Ms. Sloan. The kids weren't home, so I can't say how they'll take her death."

With a huge lump in her throat, Helen only managed a nod.

"None of the neighbors saw anything helpful, unfortunately. Most weren't home until five thirty or later. Your Iris naps late every afternoon."

She closed her eyes momentarily. "I knew that."

He was silent until she looked at him again, when he said, "So now I have a problem." All traces of humor or sympathy had vanished from his face. The shadow of his evening stubble only made him appear more threatening. "I have to understand the connection between you and Ms. Sloan. It wasn't chance she was killed in your kitchen."

"I don't know!" Helen cried. "I don't *have* a relationship with the woman."

"After seeing the two of you, I might have guessed you were sisters," he said slowly.

"That's ridiculous," she protested, stiffening when she realized that hadn't come out as forcefully as she'd hoped. "Even in a town this size, there must be a lot of women with dark hair and brown eyes. And…and about the same height."

"Close enough in age to be twins." He sounded both thoughtful and inexorable. "And it's more than coloring. You have similar bone structure, noses. Straight on, I wouldn't mistake you for her, but at a quick glance…" Renner shrugged.

Light-headed, Helen could feel the speed of her pulse in her throat. Dear Lord, she should have run. Before this man got too curious about her.

"I don't understand." Her voice came out little more than a croak, but that was surely natural, given what he'd just suggested. "I'm a single mother. New in town.

I haven't been on a date since my divorce. The only man at work who ever asked me out just got engaged to someone else. I do my job, and the rest of the time Jacob is my whole life. How could I have an enemy?"

"Ex-boyfriend. Ex-husband." Seemingly relaxed, he never looked away.

She could tell him. She could say, *I think my ex-husband murdered Andrea, thinking she was me.* But then what? Richard was sure to have an indisputable alibi—he'd have been in a meeting with someone like the Seattle city mayor or a congressman. Anyway, admitting to that much would mean revealing her real name—and Detective Renner would soon find a warrant for her arrest. If she'd killed a man in Seattle, why not a woman here in Lookout? Richard was smart enough not to have left so much as a fingerprint behind, she thought bitterly.

Fingerprints. Oh, dear God, if this detective submitted hers, a match would pop up immediately.

Panic pushed her to her feet. She grabbed the chair back for support. Voice shaking, she said, "I don't appreciate you scaring me this way. Maybe Andrea has been stealing from renters in every house she has keys to. She could have a partner that…that she betrayed somehow. Or a lover. What if they met in other people's homes during the day? Do you know *anything* about this woman?" She put everything she had into this scathing speech. "Or did you decide right away that I must be some kind of… I don't know, ex-CIA agent on the run, or a femme fatale with cast-off lovers hunting for me?"

Standing stiffly, she defied the detective's continued contemplation.

Seemingly unmoved by her defiance, he said, "I really hadn't gotten that far in my thinking. And of course my first assumption is that Ms. Sloan was the intended victim, not you. My hope was to get you thinking, in case there's something you're not telling me."

She pretended that wasn't a question. "This has been an upsetting day. I'd like you to go now."

His eyebrows flickered, but he bent his head in acknowledgment and rose to his feet as casually as if he'd made the decision himself. As he strolled to the door, he said, "I assumed you were already asking yourself these same questions, Ms. Boyd. You're smart enough to have been scared. It wasn't my intention to make it worse."

Helen didn't hold back a snort.

Almost to the door, Renner turned, expression inquiring.

"Of course you meant to scare me! Congratulations, you did a great job." At least that wasn't a lie.

"You're wrong," he said quietly. "Lock the door behind me." He wasn't all the way out into the hall when he added in a much harder voice, "I'll expect you not to leave the area. Do you understand?"

"Yes!" She felt herself vibrating with tension. No chance he wouldn't be able to see that.

"As long as you're not her killer, I'm on your side, you know." He nodded and closed the door behind him.

Helen leaped forward and, with shaking hands, turned the dead bolt and hooked on the probably useless chain. Then she stood still and strained to hear any sound from the hall, with no idea whether he still stood there or was walking away.

In listening to that silence, she had a horrifying thought. If Richard had killed Andrea, where was he now? Had he been somewhere he could watch when she arrived home and the police responded? If he had, he'd know where she was—and he'd have seen Jacob. And that was assuming the private investigator who'd trailed her in Southern California hadn't seen Jacob.

A dry sob escaped her. Who was she kidding? To know she had a child, Richard had only had to step inside her house. The high chair at the table alone would tell him.

Most of her desperation to escape him had been to ensure he never knew she was pregnant. There was no possibility that he was capable of being any kind of parent. He was the kind of man who lashed out without warning, both verbally and physically. He could smile, wish their dinner guests good-night, close the door and knock her to the floor because she'd done or said something earlier that had displeased him. Even with his housekeeper and a nanny as a buffer, an active boy would try his nonexistent patience. He'd search for her qualities in Jacob and determine to eradicate them, along with Jacob's every memory of her.

This kind of terror was like being shaken by a vicious earthquake. Even though she'd been sure he had found them once before, she'd let herself get complacent since she moved to Lookout. She liked her job, and Jacob was a happy boy. Their little house had felt safe.

They would *never* be safe. She couldn't forget again. He wouldn't give up; she knew that. Monsters didn't. The best she could do was stay a step ahead. Which meant leaving, as soon as she could figure out how.

Oh, dear God. What if Richard, too, was staying at the Lookout Inn.

With a muffled cry, she darted across the room to test the lock on the slider that led out onto a balcony.

SETH LAY AWAKE for long stretches that night. Every time he dozed off, he'd find himself starting awake, adrenaline firing through his body like an electrical shock.

Gritting his teeth and punching his pillow into a new shape, he had to convince himself repeatedly that there wasn't anything else he could have done before morning.

Except, maybe, sleep in the hall outside Helen Boyd's room at the inn to make sure she didn't disappear—and that a killer didn't get to her and that cute kid of hers.

He groaned and rested his forearm over his eyes. Damn it, the woman was right; his initial focus *should* be on the actual victim's life, her character, her husband, friends and acquaintances. And it was—he'd talked to her husband for the first time this evening, but he'd go back as many times as he had to. Tomorrow, he'd talk to her boss and coworkers, get the names of friends. Find out if there was even a whisper suggesting she had a lover or might be up to something illicit.

But he'd always paid attention to his gut, and while Helen was trying hard to play the outraged innocent, she wasn't a good liar. And she *was* lying; he had no doubt about that. All he had to do was look at the turmoil in her eyes that should be transparent instead of clouded with a darkness he didn't think was entirely caused by her discovery today of a dead body in her house.

He couldn't see her as a killer, but he had to be damn sure he was thinking like a cop, not a man drawn to a woman. He couldn't afford to let himself have even a momentary thought about her as an attractive woman.

Damn. Seth sat up in bed and swung his feet to the floor. He remained there for a minute, head hanging.

If he fell asleep with that picture in his head, he risked having an erotic dream involving a woman he would almost certainly interview again in a murder investigation. A woman who'd looked like she hated him by the time she insisted he leave her hotel room.

Not happening.

Even though he wasn't hungry, he scrambled eggs and ate breakfast to fill the last dark hour before dawn. Then he showered and drove to Hood River to attend the autopsy.

The medical examiner didn't come up with any surprises. Andrea Sloan was in good health generally. She had been killed by a blow to the head. The ME thought the weapon used was a short length of pipe, considerably fatter than the tire iron in the trunk of Ms. Boyd's car. The victim had also taken a blow to her side that had broken ribs, probably postmortem. A kick, the ME suggested.

Seth would walk through the house again today now that he had a warrant, but felt sure he wouldn't find the weapon. The garage was his best possibility, but he'd looked in the window and guessed Ms. Boyd, at least, went in there only to retrieve the lawn mower and return it when she was finished cutting the grass.

He was at the real estate office when it opened, where he started with the victim's coworkers, all horrified by the news of Andrea's death. He was assured that she was likable, charming, energetic, with the best sales record in the office. He also learned that she didn't work on the property management side of the business.

The owner of the office, a woman in her fifties, explained that Andrea had sold a couple of properties for a man named Dean Ziegler, as well as a house to him, and as a favor had agreed to manage his rentals. At Seth's request, Tina Daley dug in the records, reporting that Ziegler owned an apartment house with ten units and three rental homes.

The only key to any of those units missing was the one Seth had collected as evidence.

Andrea's assistant, a young woman in her twenties named Brooke Perry, insisted she'd have known if Andrea had received a phone call about a problem at one of the rental homes.

"The only reason I can imagine she'd have been there was if the renter had asked to see her." Her forehead creased. "Or if Mr. Ziegler wanted to meet her, or insisted she inspect the house, I suppose. But I really think she'd have said if he'd called." She hesitated. "I was surprised when she left at five thirty. That was early for her."

"Did she say anything about where she was going?"

Brooke bit her lip. "She said something like, 'I don't have any appointments, and anything else can wait for tomorrow.'"

A tomorrow that would never come for her.

Seth asked for Ziegler's number and address. The man was evidently retired as a vice president with a local bank. Seth called, found he was home and drove to a spectacular Tuscan-style mansion on a bluff above the river. Turning, he saw Mount Hood seemingly hovering almost near enough to touch, too. Hell of a view all around.

Ziegler turned out to be a slim, silver-haired man who was well-preserved for the seventy-three years old the DMV records said he was.

"I'm shocked," he repeated several times. "Why

would anyone want to hurt Andrea? She's good at her job because people like her."

Once they were seated in an enormous living room with gleaming wood floors and a wall of windows looking out at the river, he spread his hands and said, "Tell me how I can help you."

Seth couldn't decide how genuine that was, but explained that, at this point, he was trying to get to know the victim, in a manner of speaking. "Hobbies, friends, any problems in her life, of course."

"Problems? I really don't think she had any. Well, maybe two." Ziegler smiled wryly. "Both teenagers."

"The stepkids."

"Defiant fifteen-year-old boy, sulky thirteen-year-old girl." He shrugged. "My sense is that she actually had an okay relationship with them. She'd laugh telling me about them. They're just at difficult ages."

Fifteen-year-old boys had been known to kill before…but to follow a stepmother to a house where she wasn't supposed to be, then take her down with a single, powerful blow? Seth didn't believe it.

"I've met her husband a few times," Ziegler continued. "Nice guy. Did you know he's in banking, too? Manages a branch here in town."

Seth did know that. It had crossed his mind that a real estate agent and a banker could be up to something questionable together, but again…why was Andrea at the rental? In fact, trespassing in it?

"Andrea did have a certain reserve," Ziegler commented. "I sometimes thought she had to work at being as outgoing as she appeared to her clients." He frowned. "I do believe her warmth was genuine, and she and Russ had a connection those of us who've been divorced three times can only envy."

Seth left a card and asked the guy to call if he thought of anything that might be helpful in uncovering the reason she'd been targeted.

If she was, he thought again, as he drove down the winding, paved lane from the house.

Next on Seth's agenda was to stop at the craft brewery where Andrea Sloan's husband, Russell, had supposedly met two friends right after the bank closed at five o'clock. According to him, he'd left his car in the bank parking lot and walked to the brewery. Andrea had let him know not to expect her before six thirty or seven.

When Seth asked if she had said why she'd be late, he'd answered dully, "She didn't work conventional hours. Weekends, evenings…" He shrugged. "When somebody looking to buy is free, she made herself available. We didn't eat dinner most nights until seven thirty or eight."

There wasn't any chance Ziegler had intended to sell Helen's rental, was there? Seth asked himself belatedly. That nobody had told her yet?

Sitting outside the brewery, situated in a handsome old brick building in the oldest part of town, Seth called the man and asked.

"No, as long as I can keep a tenant in it, a little house like that makes more money for me than I'd get from selling it."

"She hadn't recommended you sell?"

"She never said a word about it, and I didn't, either."

Seth went into the brewery and asked to speak to the manager. A man with a billiard-ball bare and shiny head came out. Prematurely balding, Seth guessed, since the guy didn't appear much older than he was.

"Sure, I know Russ Sloan," he said readily. "He's one of a group of other professionals and downtown merchants who gather here often. He was in yesterday afternoon, in fact."

At Seth's request, he reran security footage that showed Sloan walking in with a second man at 5:11, both laughing, and leaving just before 6:30. Unless he'd hired a killer, that let him off the hook. Especially since finding a hit man wasn't as easy as many people thought.

Seth thanked him and went back out to his car.

It would take a big slice of his day, but he wanted to talk to Ms. Boyd's boss in person. He could grab some lunch on the way.

Chapter Three

Two days had passed since Andrea was murdered, and Helen sat on the edge of the bed watching Jacob fitting pieces into one of his simple puzzles. He'd been really good, considering his routine had been turned on end. *She* was the one on the verge of a breakdown. All her mind did was spin with thoughts and fears interspersed with pictures, starting with that single high-heeled shoe lying on her kitchen floor and ending up with Detective Renner's narrowed eyes as he asked questions that told her he thought *she* might have killed Andrea.

Mixed in were fleeting memories of the moment she realized she was pregnant. The surge of love when her newborn son was placed in her arms.

To top it all off, both mornings when she'd gotten dressed, she was reminded that Detective Renner had handled all these clothes, including her underwear. Did he notice the practicality of everything she wore? Helen hated that thought.

Having the phone ring was a welcome novelty.

But who else? It was Detective Renner, letting her know she could return to her rental house. "I've taken the tape down," he said tersely.

She wanted to ask about the blood but didn't. She

could clean it up. She could. Living there with the constant awareness a woman had been killed in the kitchen, a woman who had likely died in her place…that was something else altogether.

The weight of guilt clashed with the ever-burning determination to keep Jacob away from Richard. If he'd found her there instead of Andrea…he'd have Jacob right now. Her family might not even know for ages, and unless he was convicted of murder, they'd lose if they took her ex-husband to court to contest custody. Her whole reason for being was to keep her son safe, give him a chance to grow up knowing he was loved.

"Thank you for letting me know," she said politely.

"I'd suggest having the locks changed and consider installing a security system."

No matter what she did, she wouldn't feel safe in that house, but the reality was that she couldn't afford to keep staying at a hotel. Conserving her money was especially important now.

"Your landlord might agree to bear the cost," the detective continued. "Especially since it was his employee killed in your place."

That gave her a tiny lift of hope. He was right. But no matter what, she'd pay to have the locks changed. Now, today, even if that cost extra.

A security system would be reassuring if she intended to stay any length of time…but she didn't. Of course, she couldn't tell the detective she planned to disappear as soon as she could.

"Yes, all right," she said, realizing Renner was probably waiting for a response. "Do you know any more?"

"I haven't made an arrest, if that's what you're asking." He spoke curtly, betraying frustration. "Which means I'd like to sit down with you again, Ms. Boyd."

Her throat constricted. Could she hold him off long enough to make preparations for starting over again?

Did she have a choice?

"I suppose you'll find me there. If I pack up and check out right away, I won't have to pay for another night here."

"Then I'll meet you at the house."

Just to make her day better.

Setting down the phone, she bent to kiss Jacob. "We're going home, kiddo. You finish putting your puzzle together while I pack."

He lifted his head. "Hot dog?"

"You're hungry?"

He nodded vigorously. Hot dogs were his current favorite food, although mac and cheese was right up there, too. While staying here, they'd eaten makeshift breakfasts in the room, gone out to lunch each day and used room service for dinner. Darkness felt too dangerous; they were safer staying behind locked doors.

Fortunately, she was pretty sure there were hot dogs in the freezer at home. "We'll have lunch. *Maybe* a hot dog."

It didn't take her ten minutes to throw everything into the suitcase. Jacob was fascinated by the lobby attendant who insisted on taking both the suitcase and potty seat out to her car.

In the past year, he'd gone through a stage of being painfully shy with everyone for no discernible reason, just recently becoming more curious and ready to grin at complete strangers. Maybe earlier she'd infected him with her tension, and as she felt safer his confidence returned. Kids undoubtedly reacted to their parents' subtlest cues.

She locked the car even before she started it, as she always did. As she drove out of the lot, she craned her neck trying to see if anyone was paying attention to them. Disconcerted, she saw that Jacob, too, was turning to look around.

With this being a working day, there wasn't much activity. From what she'd been told, tourist season didn't really boom for another week or two, once schools let out. You wouldn't know that looking at the windsurfing business next door, though. She knew vaguely that they rented small boats as well as windsurfing equipment. Like much of the rest of June, today was sunny but still chilly, and she could see multicolored sails swelling with the wind out on the choppy water. If someone over there was keeping an eye out for her, she'd never be able to pick him out.

She was quite sure nobody followed her home—but then, Richard or anyone he hired wouldn't have to follow her to know where she was going. Leaving their stuff in the car, she carried Jacob inside, setting him down on the sofa with his blue bunny.

"Wait right there for me," she said sternly.

He bounced on his butt. "Hurry, Mommy."

Battling extreme reluctance, she steeled herself to look in the kitchen. She couldn't let Jacob see the blood…

But the vinyl floor was spotless. No dead body, no blood.

Well, she'd known the body would be taken away, but she didn't think police officers would clean up crime scenes.

Helen stared. Squeezed her eyes shut and opened them again. Still clean. She'd scrub the floor herself once Jacob was napping, just to be sure, but somebody had done this for her.

Thinking of the man who managed to be both unrelenting and occasionally thoughtful, she had a good idea who'd done it. The kindness weakened her, even if he'd been thinking about Jacob and not her at all.

"I want hot dog," her son reminded her.

Helen laughed. "Okay, okay!"

She raced through the house, looking in closets and pushing the shower curtain aside before dashing out to get their bags. She didn't see a soul. Everyone must be at work, and even Iris's car was missing.

Fortunately, Helen found buns in the freezer as well as an unopened package of hot dogs. If she heated a can of baked beans and peeled some carrots, the meal would be perfectly adequate.

Jacob hadn't gotten through half of his hot dog and one carrot stick when the doorbell rang. He started wriggling like an eel to slither out of his high chair.

"No way," she told him, but had to lift him out to go to the front door. Escape artist that he was, she couldn't leave him alone for a second when he was high enough to take a fall. He'd figure out how to unsnap the belt anytime now, she felt sure.

Hand on the dead bolt, she raised her voice. "Who is it?"

"Detective Renner."

With the usual mixed feelings he inspired, she unlocked and opened the door. Jacob bounced in her arms. As soon as he saw the detective, he grinned and exclaimed, "Boo!"

Renner laughed. "Boo to you, too."

Just as well that no two-year-old could grasp the concept of a police officer, or wonder why he kept wanting to talk to mommy.

"We're finishing lunch," she said.

"No problem."

When they got to the kitchen and she lifted Jacob to put him in his high chair, he struggled.

"No!"

The debate was short. He was done with lunch, or just refused to be confined again, she wasn't sure. She had to find one of those plastic seats that would boost him to table height. He'd be a lot happier. It amazed her that her thoughts could seamlessly shift to ordinary mommy mode under the circumstances.

Helen didn't let Jacob watch much TV but decided to make an exception. He climbed up onto the sofa, grabbing his blankie, while she pulled up a video.

She turned to see that Renner waited in the doorway to the kitchen, watching. Of course he was; she might be hiding a cache of diamonds in the cushions of the couch along with all the crumbs.

Her shoulder brushed his arm when she hurried into the kitchen. Finding she'd lost her own appetite, she cleared the table, then decided grudgingly that she ought to at least offer him a cup of coffee.

"Instant," she warned.

"That's fine." His mouth quirked. "I'm not picky."

Dumping a spoonful of grounds in her own mug, she said, "A cappuccino would taste really good right now. Unfortunately, having one regularly is not in my budget."

"You can dump a lot of money really fast at those

coffee drive-throughs," he agreed. "Although—" He stopped so fast, she almost heard the brakes screeching.

"Although what?" She eyed him suspiciously.

He gave his head a shake. "I was going to say something completely inappropriate. Can we forget about it?"

Inappropriate? What could he have been thinking? Her cheeks felt warm, but she needed to know. Still hovering at the stove, she asked, "If I absolve you in advance, will you tell me?"

"You can afford the calories. That's what I was thinking."

Oh, good, nice to know he thought she was too skinny. Stress had a way of doing that to her, and she lived with a steady dose. Even pregnant, she'd had trouble gaining enough weight.

He wouldn't have been thinking any such thing unless he'd noticed her body in a way that had nothing to do with any crime committed. The recognition he might be attracted to her was only momentary. Yes, he was undeniably sexy. But if all went well, she wouldn't see him again, because she and Jacob would be as far away as she could manage, as soon as possible.

Emotions flat again, she poured water into the mugs and carried them to the table. Renner declined her offer of milk and sugar, both of which she dumped generously in her mug.

"I should be fat," she said lightly. "Hot dogs, cheeseburgers, macaroni and cheese. We don't eat the way I did before I had Jacob."

The detective laughed. "I'm sure." He was nice enough not to mention that the foods she'd named also happened to be cheap, not just appealing to a toddler's taste buds.

Helen stirred her coffee. Procrastination had its appeal, but she wasn't a fan. "I don't understand what it is you think I can tell you," she said.

His expression changed. More accurately, vanished. He had a flat, guarded look that might be normal for a cop on the job.

"When is the last time you saw Andrea Sloan?"

She shook her head. "You're looking for some connection that doesn't exist. But let me think…" Grocery store? No, there'd been once since then. "I was jogging. Mostly, I take Jacob in his stroller, but that day Iris kept him. Andrea runs, too. I'd forgotten that. We came face-to-face, jogged in place for a minute to exchange pleasantries, then went our separate ways. It was… I don't know, six weeks ago? Two months?"

"Did you know she jogged?"

Helen shook her head. "Not until then."

"Were you dressed alike?"

She didn't like the way he'd fixated on their resemblance. "No, she wore a brand name, formfitting running set and, I'm sure, top-of-the-line running shoes. Me, I wear a T-shirt and sweats or shorts depending on the season and weather." She remembered inwardly cringing that day at what Andrea probably thought of her outfit.

"Pleasantries?" he asked.

"Chilly, but at least it's not raining. House is still working out great. Nice to see you."

A smile showed in his eyes, she'd swear it did.

"No calls since then?"

"No."

"Can you think of any reason at all she would have wanted to speak to you?"

"No! It doesn't make sense. If this weren't such a small town, I'd have probably never run into her again after I signed the rental agreement. You can see yourself that I haven't trashed the place—"

As if she'd crashed into a plate-glass window, a horrifying thought struck her. What if Richard had called or stopped by the real estate office, asking questions about her? Could Andrea have come by to warn her? If Richard or his hired hand had made her nervous enough, she might have let herself into the house to be less visible.

Yes, but if he'd actually seen Andrea, how could he have made the mistake?

But he might not have, Helen reminded herself. Andrea's assistant might have told her that a man was hunting for Helen, or Richard might have called rather than showing up in person.

Helen jumped up. "I have to check on Jacob." She found him asleep, thumb slipping out of his mouth.

With the remote, she turned off the movie and TV, then gently picked him up. She straightened, to see that, once again, Renner had followed. "Naptime," she murmured.

He nodded.

At least he didn't follow her. Jacob never opened his eyes as she laid him down and tucked him in, then pulled his door almost closed.

Renner didn't return to his seat at the kitchen table until she did.

"You thought of something, didn't you?"

Her heart picked up tempo. "Something?"

"About Ms. Sloan."

"I don't know what you're talking about," she said flatly.

He studied her speculatively. "Oh, I think you do."

"I had nothing to do with a woman I hardly know getting murdered in my kitchen." That sounded almost panicky. What did it matter? But she had to get rid of him. "I don't want to talk to you anymore without a lawyer."

WHATEVER SHE'D THOUGHT had scared the life out of her, and, man, Seth wanted to know what it was. Almost forty-eight hours had passed since Andrea Sloan had died, and he had no more idea why she'd been killed now than he had at the beginning. The one and only person he'd spoken to during this investigation who was acting squirrely was this woman. And he wanted to know why.

"I haven't accused you of anything," he said mildly. "I don't believe you killed Ms. Sloan." Which was true. But she knew something, he'd bet on it.

She crossed her arms, as if holding herself together. "Is your name Seth?"

"What?"

"I'm sorry—" Hot spots of color appeared on her cheekbones.

"Don't be sorry."

"It's not like I'd use—I mean, I'll still call you Detective—I just…" She shook her head, unable or unwilling to explain.

He could hope she would be less intimidated if she thought of him by his first name—except that he needed her running a little scared of him.

And, yeah, he hated that.

"Where did you live before you rented this place?" he asked abruptly.

Any color had drained from her face. "Los Angeles. North Hollywood, to be exact."

Truth, he thought. "Why did you move?"

"I wanted to raise Jacob someplace where we could get to know our neighbors, where he could safely ride a bike when he gets old enough. I spotted a listing for my current job online, researched the area and applied."

That sounded reasonable, although he wondered. "Does Jacob's father see him?"

Her back stiffened. "He didn't want children and has no interest in Jacob."

Now there, Seth thought, was a lie. "Where does he live?"

"LA."

"His name?"

"Richard—" Anger flared in her eyes. "It's none of your business. You can't contact him!"

Her alarm was very real, but Seth reminded himself that there could be a lot of reasons for her sensitivity with the subject that had absolutely nothing to do with the murder he was investigating. If she'd been an abused woman, for example, he didn't want to draw the abuser's attention to her, or the boy. On the other hand, what if she didn't have legal custody? That would explain some of what he was seeing, and it wasn't something he could ignore as an officer of the law. One thing he did know: Jacob was her son. Their resemblance was unmistakable.

Right now, he'd lose her if he kept pushing.

"You color your hair," he heard himself say.

She jerked back and lifted a hand to her head. "What makes you say that?" Her lips thinned as she realized she'd given herself away. "That *really* isn't any of your business."

No, it wasn't, but he'd been intrigued by her creamy skin from their first meeting. She had a redhead's complexion, freckles and a redheaded son.

"That was intrusive," he agreed. "I apologize. You have beautiful skin, and it made me think—" Damn, he was stepping in it here.

Helen Boyd studied him from those gold-flecked caramel eyes that were every bit as pretty as her skin. Then she sighed. "Yes, I color my hair. I always hated being a redhead."

"What about your eyebrows?" His mouth was running away from him.

"I...sometimes touch them up." She blushed, something she must do easily with that skin.

For a minute that stretched too long, they stared at each other. He drank in the rare sight of her sitting absolutely still, her lips parted as if she'd been on the verge of speaking. Her chin, he couldn't help noticing, was a little on the square, stubborn side.

She was the first to wrench her gaze away. "Are you done with your questions?"

"Yes." Seth had to clear his throat. "For now."

What had he been *thinking*? Coming on to a person of interest, if not a suspect, in an investigation was inexcusable. He had to get out of here, now, before he couldn't resist touching her.

Helen didn't even stand when he did, although when he reached the front door he realized she had followed, still keeping her distance. Seth opened the door and turned to face her.

"Let me repeat that I'm here to help, if you need

it. You're worried about something. I wish you'd tell me what."

He might as well not have bothered to speak. She'd shuttered her expression and only waited. He'd go, but needed to be sure she'd taken seriously his concern about her security.

"Have you spoken to your landlord?"

"I left a message at the property management company, but I also called a locksmith. He's supposed to be here at four to change the locks."

"Good," Seth said softly. He nodded and left.

HELEN LOCKED THE door then slumped against it, feeling so much she couldn't identify.

Had any man ever looked at her like that?

Yes, the last time she was attracted to one. Richard.

His burning gaze had convinced her he wanted her desperately, loved her. She'd been such a fool, let herself be manipulated, controlled. Never again, she'd vowed. Not a vow she could afford to forget. So why was she getting weak in the knees because Seth Renner had implied he thought she was beautiful, had claimed she could depend on him?

Oh, the answer was simple enough. She had needs, but unlike women who allowed themselves to be deluded over and over again, Helen wouldn't dare succumb to temptation. Her fierce need to protect Jacob would keep her from being that dumb. Even if she met a wonderful man who truly was everything he seemed to be, she'd have to lie to him, and what kind of relationship would that be? Lies corroded. Lies kept her from making friends, even.

For Jacob, she'd do anything.

While he napped, she'd make a plan instead of letting her thoughts run in panicked circles.

Helen went back to the kitchen, dumped out both mugs of barely touched coffee, and fetched a pen, notepad and her last bank statement. She had never done online banking. That took another kind of trust.

Would Seth… No, no, no. Would *Detective Renner* think to flag her bank account? Ask the bank, maybe, to inform him if she closed out the account, or withdrew a substantial amount of the balance? *Could* he do that legally?

Sure he could. All he'd have to do was get a warrant.

Well then, she'd assume he had. If she dared take at least a few days, even a week, she could stop by an ATM daily. She had to believe that Richard wouldn't be an immediate threat. Even he might have been shaken to discover he'd killed the wrong woman.

What if he thought he'd been *pursuing* the wrong woman? That Andrea lived in this house—she'd had a key, after all—that there'd been a mistake made and his ex-wife wasn't actually in the vicinity? Hope shimmered briefly as Helen wondered if Richard had gone back to Seattle to berate his private detective for being wrong?

The hope was shortlived. He would have checked the ID in Andrea's purse. The license plate on her car. Neither would match the name of the woman who rented this house, the one the private detective had identified as her.

Still, he'd back off, surely, until the investigation petered out and a cop wasn't coming by the house daily.

She hadn't checked him out online in at least a week,

and obviously that had been a mistake. Helen opened her laptop and entered his name.

He popped up immediately in a *Seattle Times* article about a political event held yesterday evening. She kept searching, found mention of a dinner he was to host this coming Saturday to raise money for a congressional candidate launching a primary assault on an incumbent who had probably infuriated Richard by ignoring his advice.

Helen sat thinking. Saturday was two days away. Portland wasn't that long a drive from Seattle. Still, he'd want to be careful. When he first began hitting her, she'd thought he was losing his temper, that he lacked self-control but was genuinely shocked and sorry. Over months she came to understand that he was never careless in a way that might come back to reflect on *him*. No, his sense of self-preservation was finely tuned.

She'd have until Sunday or even Monday, she decided. She could mostly empty her bank account with three-to five-hundred-dollar withdrawals, followed by a bigger one on her way out of town. And, of course, she had the emergency cash she kept stashed in the to-go bags tucked behind some junk in the garage.

That would give her time this weekend to prowl a cemetery or two in Portland—or better yet, across the river in Vancouver, Washington. Surely, she could find the grave of a girl child who, if she'd lived, would be close to Helen's age. Once she and Jacob were a safe distance away, she'd request a birth certificate.

Tomorrow, she'd better go back to work. She needed to live as unremarkably as possible until she was ready to go.

Chapter Four

"Mommy! Don't go!" Tears pouring down his face, Jacob clung with all his strength to Helen's neck.

Close to crying herself, she continued to kneel just inside the front door of the day care, holding him. Jenna Fischer, the young woman who operated the home day care, crouched, too.

"Jacob," she coaxed, "Neil's been waiting for you to play trucks with him."

He wailed.

What else could she do but leave him? If she didn't go to work, she'd draw unwanted attention. Anyway, succumbing to his pleas would set a precedent that would come back to bite her. She'd never had to wrench his hands off her, but this morning might be a first.

"Jacob." She did her best to sound firm and hide how distraught she felt at his misery. "Honey." She gave him a small shake. "You like spending your day with Jenna and Neil and Evan. And even Courtney," she teased.

He shook his head hard. She thought his tears had slowed.

"Okay, maybe not Courtney. But she's not so bad, is she?"

Jacob didn't yet care whether his friends were girls

or boys. But Courtney, almost four years old, was bossy. According to Jenna, most of the time the three boys did what Courtney ordered them to do, because she was good at organizing games. Helen could tell that Jacob, at least, felt a glimmer of resentment.

"We're having macaroni and cheese for lunch today," Jenna said, smiling. "*And* ice-cream sandwiches."

Sniffling, he wiped his wet cheeks on Helen's blouse. Oh, well. She was a mother. It was a rare day she made it to work unwrinkled and completely stain free.

At last, he reluctantly let Helen go and took Jenna's hand. Walking out, she suspected that he'd quickly forget he hadn't wanted her to go and start playing with his friends. If only it was so easy for her.

The last sight of his woeful expression and puffy, red eyes was sure to stick with her all day.

And that wasn't even the worst of it, she thought tensely as she waited in a short line at the bank drive-up ATM. If Richard now knew about Jacob's existence, everything had changed. Was he safe at the home day care? Most of the time Jenna kept the doors locked, but toward the end of the day, the door was open for the pickups.

Would Jenna not want to keep Jacob if Helen talked to her about being extra careful because she was concerned about her ex-husband?

She withdrew three hundred dollars and pulled out of the bank parking lot, only to immediately get stuck at a red light. Her gaze flicked to the dashboard clock. She should have waited to do her errand after work.

As if the inside of her head was a pinball machine, her thoughts bounced back to Jacob. If she intended to stay in town, she could move him to a larger day care.

Except he would always be vulnerable while she was at work.

Plus, if he didn't want to be left at Jenna's, imagine if she tried to drop him off mornings at a strange place full of adults and kids he didn't know! No, she couldn't do that to him. But, oh God, what if…?

Don't think about it.

By the time she reached her office, stowed her purse in a drawer and responded to an instant message from her boss, her facade of calm felt paper-thin.

BY MIDMORNING, SETH had completed background searches on Andrea's husband and several of her co-workers. He'd made good progress looking at her closest friends, too, as well as their husbands. Dean Ziegler; the fact that he and Andrea were both married to other people didn't mean they hadn't hooked up. Maybe she was trying to break it off and Ziegler didn't like that. Seth had to seriously consider him, given that he owned Helen's rental house and presumably had kept a key.

But so far, the only search that had raised red flags for Seth was the one he'd done on Helen Marie Boyd.

To all appearances, she'd emerged naked from the sea, as in Botticelli's painting, *The Birth of Venus*.

Damn it, he had to quit thinking about her that way.

Supposedly, she'd lived and worked last in California. If so, she had had still been using her married name. That was assuming Boyd was her maiden name. That would explain the giant blank where her history ought to be.

Seth just didn't believe in either possibility, in part because he had failed to find a divorce including that name in any Southern California county.

He also couldn't forget the turmoil he saw in her eyes. The darkness he guessed was fear. There could be a lot of reasons for that, especially after she found the dead woman in her kitchen. Even before he pointed out Andrea's resemblance to Helen, she'd thought about the possibility another woman had died in her place. He'd put money on it.

Why did he suspect she was as afraid of him because of the badge he wore as she was of whatever trouble followed her?

Irritated at himself, Seth shook his head. The fact that he was a cop might not have anything to do with her lack of trust. She didn't know him. It was equally possible that she'd been living in a gray area legally.

He brooded for a good ten minutes before deciding all he could do was show up on her doorstep over and over and over again, until she *did* know him.

HE RANG HER doorbell at six forty, figuring she and her boy would have eaten by now.

Her car was there in the driveway, but he didn't hear a sound until the door abruptly opened and she appeared, arms crossed, looking less than happy. "I told you I wouldn't talk to you again without my lawyer being present."

He lifted the bag he carried in his left hand. "I come bearing gifts this time."

She didn't so much as glance at the bag. "You've asked me a million questions already."

"I have," he agreed. "Fair warning—you won't get rid of me until I figure out who killed Andrea Sloan."

"Because you think I did it."

He frowned. She hadn't believed his previous reassurances. "No, I actually don't, but I do believe you're part of the answer."

Her eyes flickered, shadows falling where they hadn't been an instant before. After a moment, she opened the door wider and stepped back.

He hid his relief. She was well within her rights to insist on that lawyer, but was apparently relenting. It was also possible she couldn't afford to hire any attorney worth having, but had thought the threat would be enough.

"You shouldn't open the door without knowing who wants in," he said as he walked in.

"I peeked out the window."

"You might want to get a peephole installed. The better ones give you a good view of your porch while you're standing several feet back from the door."

Helen gave a wry look over her shoulder as she led him to the kitchen. "While I'm at it, why not have surround the house with barbed-wire fencing?"

Seth cleared his throat. "That might be a little extreme."

"Mommy?" Wearing denim overalls and a miniature, bright red cowboy hat, her son popped out of his room down the hall. Seeing Seth, he grinned and raced toward them, skidding to a stop at the last minute to grip his mom's leg.

"Jacob." Seth smiled down at him. "I like the hat."

The boy swept it off and held it out to Seth.

"I don't think it would fit me." Seth took it and settled it back on Jacob's head. Then he tipped up the brim with one finger. "There. Get along, partner."

"Giddyup!" The kid galloped down the hall, then back, giggling by the time he reached them.

"Have you eaten yet?" Seth asked.

Her brown eyes widened. "I'm afraid so. That's not what—" She nodded at the bag.

"No, but I'm hoping you haven't had *d-e-s-s-e-r-t*."

"You're trying to bribe me."

"You'd be doing me a favor to take this off my hands," he lied.

Helen rolled her eyes. "Let's see what you have."

"Actually," he said, taking the lidded plastic container out of the bag and setting it on the counter, "this is courtesy of my father. A couple of ladies in his neighborhood are constantly baking goodies for him. He grumbled that he had to let out his belt a notch just last week." Seth peeled off the lid. "Tiramisu cheesecake and oatmeal raisin cookies."

She peered in at the cheesecake, already sliced, and the dozen or so cookies. "I accept."

A minute later, Jacob sat in his high chair to eat his cookie and drink milk from his sippy cup. Helen poured coffee for herself and Seth, and served the cheesecake on plates.

She slipped a first bite into her mouth and made a humming sound, obviously savoring the sugary treat before she finally swallowed. "Have you *tasted* this?"

He shifted uncomfortably. "No," he said, a little hoarsely.

"If I were your father, I'd marry the woman who made this."

Seth gave a rough chuckle. "She drives Dad crazy. Anyway, as far as I can tell, he's not interested in remarrying."

"Really?" Her forehead furrowed. "Are your parents divorced?" Helen made a sound that was too sharp to be a laugh. "Wow. Listen to me, pretending you're not here to interrogate me. And eating your food." She pushed her plate away.

"Please." Without thinking, he covered her hand with his. "I didn't want to take all this home. I thought you and Jacob could enjoy it. Please," he repeated, looking from her face to his hand, still resting on hers. He felt quivering tension and the fineness of the bones beneath his fingertips and palm.

Damn.

He pulled his hand back. What kind of idiot was he? That she, too, slipped occasionally into thinking of him as a man rather than a detective didn't help, only heightening his awareness of her.

This moment, he absolutely could not tell what she was thinking. She did pull the plate back toward her and, after a tiny hesitation, resume eating.

Breaking the tension, Jacob demanded, and got, another cookie. Seth asked what he'd done today, then tried to piece the answer together from an indignant insistence that Neil had hit him, but Jenna told a story with puppets and they ate mac cheese and he didn't *want* to go to Jenna's today, he wanted to stay with Mommy. At least, that's what Seth thought he'd said. Some of his words were clear, some incomprehensible, although Seth could tell the boy's mother understood every one.

At last Helen lifted him to the floor. While she was still bent over, he whispered something.

She ran her hand gently over his head and smiled, her face softening. "Yes, you may play with your animals for a few minutes, but then it will be bedtime."

He scampered away, her gaze following him. The tenderness changed to worry.

"Usually, he loves his day care, but today he cried and refused to let me go. It was…really hard."

Before Seth could offer sympathy, she set down her fork and lifted her chin. "Can we get this over with? I have to get Jacob ready for bed, and fold laundry, and—"

"I get it," he said gruffly. *We are not friends.* "You said you lived in Hollywood."

"North Hollywood," she corrected.

"Okay." He leaned back. "Were you still married then?"

She became very still, only her eyes vividly alive. Before he could prod her, though, she exclaimed, "What difference does it make?"

"I need to know you if I'm to find out what connects you and Andrea."

"But… I didn't meet her until I arrived here in Look-out." Helen's bewilderment appeared genuine. "If she ever lived in California, she didn't say so to me."

They went back and forth. She didn't want to tell him any specifics. Not her former employer, sure as hell not her ex-husband's name, although she did imply the move here came on the heels of the split from her spouse.

"I don't want any contact with him," she repeated stubbornly.

"Because he might try to take Jacob from you?"

"No!" She tried to sear him with her eyes, but mostly Seth thought she was afraid. "I've already told you all this! He never wanted children. It's me—"

"He didn't want to let you go," he said slowly, his pro-tective instincts firing up at the very idea of her being terrorized by any man.

"No," she whispered. "At the end, he said he'd kill

me if I tried to leave him. I had to get away and hide before I could get legal help to divorce him."

Seth forced himself to take a mental step back. He still couldn't be sure there was a brutal, possessive ex-husband at all. The possibility existed that she was really afraid of *him*, the detective who wouldn't take no for an answer.

"How did you escape him?" he asked.

"I went to a battered women's shelter," she said with such dignity, he felt chastened.

Or was *manipulated* a better word?

Damn, it was hard to hold on to his usual detachment.

"I can check out this man's whereabouts without drawing attention to you. I promise," he said. "All I need is a name."

Helen pressed her lips together and glared at him.

"It doesn't make you even a little nervous that a woman who looks a lot like you was murdered a few days ago here in your kitchen?" He turned in his chair, zeroing in on a stretch of the vinyl floor. "Right about there, if I remember right."

Her gaze followed his, her expression suddenly stricken.

Feeling like a ruthless bastard, Seth waited.

"You don't understand," she said softly.

He kept his own voice quiet. "But I want to."

Her eyes met his, so much hurt in them he dreaded seeing.

"I can't take a chance. I just can't."

The flat finality of her statement had him studying her. What was really going on here? The battered-woman scenario worked in some ways, but not in others. It took a strong woman to tell a detective to his face that she wasn't going to cooperate in his investigation. She had no trouble ordering him to get out when she'd had enough.

And yet, he did believe she was genuinely afraid. Of something.

After a minute, he nodded. "I'll leave you in peace, then." He paused. "For tonight."

Her eyes dilated.

"Helen, you *can't* keep your secrets from me. You might as well resign yourself. I'll find out what I need to know, one way or another."

Pale as a ghost, eyes huge and dark, she stared at him as he turned and then left.

When he got outside to his vehicle, he planted his hands on the roof, let his head fall forward and swore, long and viciously.

He hated the terrified look in her eyes and couldn't help wondering why he had gone into law enforcement.

ON TIPTOE, ROBIN stretched to reach for a box on the shelf closet, the one that held her few precious mementos. It was stupid to risk so much for them, she knew that, but recovering even this little bit would feel like a victory, a step toward regaining her dignity. She wasn't the pathetic creature who'd numbly put up with Richard's vicious treatment.

I'm not her. Not anymore.

She managed to get her fingertips to each side of the box and tug gently so that it inched forward.

Two minutes, and she'd be out of here.

The softest of sounds came from behind her, and the hair rose on the back of her neck.

Before she could whirl, hard hands gripped her from behind.

"Here you are, right on time," a man growled. Not Richard. Thank God, not Richard.

She wrenched free but fell to her knees. Furious, scared. *So stupid.* She managed to crawl, throw herself toward the bedroom doorway, but he grabbed her hair and wrenched her head back. A knee in the middle of her back drove Robin to the hardwood floor. She was screaming, still fighting. She twisted enough to sink her teeth into the fleshy part of his hand.

Yelling, he hit her. Momentarily, her vision dimmed, but then she realized the blow had sent her flying toward the bed. Robin kicked behind her, felt her foot connect with some part of her assailant's body. She scrambled almost upright and grabbed the lamp on the bedside table. Not one of the pair *she'd* chosen, of course; Richard had smashed those and replaced them with obscenely expensive art deco metal-and-stained-glass monstrosities.

Heavy. She had barely a second to get a good grip. To spin, applying all the force she could muster. To see the lamp base smash into the man's head. To see the shock on his face, to watch the life leave his eyes, to stand stunned as he crumpled.

Only now did she see that the bloody face *was* her ex-husband's. She shook as she stared down at him. *I killed him.*

But then she heard a creak in the hall outside the bedroom. Someone else was here. With her hands trembling, she could hardly hold on to the lamp, yet somehow she lifted it again as if she were a baseball player stepping up to the plate.

Another creak.

"MOMMY?"

Muddled, Helen shot up in bed. It wasn't Richard there that night. It wasn't. So why did she always see his dead face?

Shaking off the sticky web of sleep, she focused on the small shape hovering beside the bed. *Jacob.*

She couldn't let her little boy see her crying. Oh, God. She pulled up her covers and wiped her cheeks, although she still tasted the salt of tears.

"Jacob? What's wrong?"

"I heard scary sounds." His voice sounded...soggy. As if he was crying, too.

"Oh, honey! I'm sorry." She must have cried out in her nightmare. *Please don't let me have actually screamed.* Helen sat up, but didn't turn on the lamp as she usually would have. Instead, she bent to scoop him up and snuggled them both beneath the covers, where it was warm and felt safe, if only she never slept again, never dreamed. "Better?" she murmured against his head.

"My room is scary," he mumbled.

"Just for tonight, you can sleep with Mommy," she murmured. "Okay?"

His head bobbed and he burrowed into her, his knees digging into her stomach. Helen felt another sting of tears at the joy of holding his small, compact body tight. She hadn't known it was possible to love another person so much. The scariest thing in her world was the idea of losing him.

"Sleep tight," she whispered, softly stroking his back until his breathing slowed and his muscles went lax.

Her recurring nightmare was always so vivid, so real...except for the twist at the end. A shameful part of her wished it *was* Richard she'd killed, instead of his butler-bodyguard. He was a monster. Instead, she was haunted by the slack face of a man she hardly knew.

She stiffened. If Detective Renner had entered her fingerprints in that FBI database, he'd know who she was, that she was a person of interest in a previous murder. Why hadn't he? Or had he?

Her teeth wanted to chatter, but she clenched them. She had to take off soon, before it was too late.

Chapter Five

Helen awakened to the peculiar sensation of bobbing as if she were in a small boat riding the wake of a bigger one. With a groan, she pried open her eyes to see Jacob jumping up and down on her bed. His diaper had overflowed, which explained the strong smell of urine. He hadn't yet noticed she'd opened her eyes.

If she felt dazed, it was with surprise because she'd slept, after all. And hadn't had another nightmare, or at least didn't remember one.

Her brain began to resume functioning. This was Saturday. Usually she welcomed the weekends. Even though she had to do errands, she also had time to do fun things with Jacob. Today, she felt weighed down by dread.

Detective Renner would be back to ask more questions. She had to pack without a curious two-year-old *or* a nosy detective noticing. Knowing how much she'd have to leave behind didn't help her mood. Not counting when she first left home for college, this was her third experience of starting entirely over, Jacob's second— but since he'd only been seventeen months old last time, he'd been oblivious to the disruption of sneaking away in the night. This time would be different. It was just as well that he wouldn't understand he'd never see Iris again, or Jenna or bossy Courtney.

Wanting to give him one last day of normalcy, Helen tackled Jacob, but even as she tickled him and laughed along with his giggles, she plotted her day.

Grocery shopping had become a necessity. They'd make it through breakfast, barely, with what remained in the refrigerator and cupboards. Plus she'd need to take some food with them—snacks for Jacob, a small cooler with drinks, breakfasts and probably lunches she could prepare their first days in cheap motel rooms, so they didn't have to waste money eating out, or stop at stores too soon. The less he and she were noticed, the safer they'd be.

Helen hated that she couldn't let Jenna know Jacob wouldn't be coming back, and that they didn't dare say goodbye to her or Iris. Her mother would describe it as stealing away into the night like thieves.

With sadness that might even be grief, she was dismayed to see Seth Renner's face in her mind's eye, too, as if he were part of what she hated to leave behind. Given the way he'd been questioning her, that made zero sense. Even so, she didn't like knowing that he'd probably think she'd fled because she *had* killed Andrea and feared his investigation.

The disconcerting part was a suspicion he'd also be at least a little hurt because she'd disappointed him, hadn't trusted him. Because he'd never know what had become of her and Jacob.

He'd let her see something she'd never have. As she put together breakfast and then showered quickly, she kept remembering not only the relentless questioning but also the detective's patience and occasional kindness. His smiles for Jacob, the oddly tender note she heard a few times in his voice—the heat in his eyes when he let down his formidable guard. He'd reminded her of what some people were lucky enough to find.

Except, it couldn't possibly be Seth himself she would miss. What she felt was a foolish wish not to be so entirely on her own, that's all.

She'd forget him in no time, except as one more threat, another person who might be tracking her.

THE DAY FELT like summer when Helen ushered Jacob out the front door for the grocery expedition. He immediately cried, "Iris!"

Helen turned to see her neighbor returning from the curb with her newspaper.

Iris waved enthusiastically. "Where are the two of you off to?"

With Jacob, Helen crossed her own somewhat scruffy lawn onto Iris's manicured one. She wrinkled her nose. "Grocery shopping, what else? But since I have to go, is there anything I can pick up for you?"

"Oh, if you wouldn't mind, I forgot eggs when I went to the store yesterday." She smiled at Jacob. "Perhaps this young man would like to stay with me while you do whatever you need to. I thought I'd do a little weeding out back, and I have a plastic bucket and shovel, you know. He can help me."

When she chuckled, Helen had to join her even as her heart ached. Oh, she'd miss Iris. "You're a saint," she declared. She'd have had to say no if Iris had intended to work on her front flower beds, but in back... that ought to be safe enough.

One more thing to hate: how often she used that word in her thoughts. *Safe.*

It was a relief to be able to set off on her own to make another ATM withdrawal and do her shopping. She took her time, calculating what meals would be most practical to make on the run. At last, she went to Walgreen's and bought several modestly priced new toys that should entertain Jacob during days of driving. She'd leave those in the trunk so they'd be a surprise.

She parked, took the groceries into the house and put away everything that had to go in the refrigerator, then slipped out her back door carrying the carton of eggs for Iris. No fence separated their yards.

Iris and Jacob must be inside, leaving the bright blue plastic bucket and yellow shovel on the grass, and a real shovel left standing in what would be a small vegetable garden.

She had started across the yard, when the screen door slammed open, bouncing against the side of the house. A dark figure burst out. In a shocked instant, Helen realized the man wore a ski mask, and had Jacob slung over his shoulder.

With a scream of rage, she dropped the eggs, grabbed the shovel and tore across the lawn to intercept the man who held her sobbing, struggling child. His head swung toward her at the last minute. In a horrible replay of her nightmare, she swung the shovel with all her strength. This time she went for his shins.

He tried to dodge. The blow was glancing, but enough to send him staggering. In that moment, Helen threw herself at him, closing her hand around Jacob's kicking leg even as her shoulder connected with the man's chest or side. Jacob tumbled from his shoulder and she caught him, staggering back.

She retreated a step, her eyes locked on the furious, slitted eyes not hidden by the mask. Heart thundering, Helen knew he'd overpower her easily. She should have held on to the shovel.

She took another step back. He advanced…and they both heard the wail of an approaching siren no more than a few blocks away.

He broke away and ran, disappearing around Iris's detached garage and down the alley, the slap, slap of his footsteps receding.

With a dry sob, Helen sank to the grass, cradling Jacob. She had him. *Thank you, God.*

THE SECOND HE heard Iris Wilbanks's address over the police radio, Seth switched on his lights and siren and accelerated away from the curb. Yeah, this was a small town, but he didn't believe in coincidences.

A patrol officer indicated that he was responding. Seth chimed in to say he was on his way, too.

Since he'd been less than half a mile away, he pulled up in front of Iris's house only seconds behind Officer Todd. He leaped out. His gaze went to Helen's house, but the drawn blinds didn't even twitch.

"I'll go around back," he said tersely, and Todd nodded. As Seth rounded the house, he heard a solid knock on the front door and the young officer calling, "This is the police! I'm coming in."

He felt a torrent of anger and relief and probably more at the sight of Helen sitting in the middle of the yard clutching her sobbing boy. Her fear hit him hard. He'd seen the same expression on the faces of parents who'd had a child go missing, or be hit by a car after running into the street. The knowledge that the unimaginable loss might have happened.

He wasn't even aware of crossing the lawn, only that he crouched beside Helen. However much he wanted to take her and Jacob in his arms, he had to do his job. "Was somebody here?"

"He went that way." She pointed past the garage. "I heard him running down the alley."

"How long ago?"

"Only...only a minute or two."

Seth sprinted, despite knowing he'd be too late. Gun in hand, he reached the side street, where he saw no movement at all...but heard the receding engine of a car.

He ran to the closest house. No one home. The one across the street, the kids were watching cartoons and nobody had seen anything.

Ten minutes later, he walked back to Iris Wilbanks's house to find the backyard empty. He opened the screen door and followed the voices inside.

A pair of paramedics had the woman on a stretcher and were obviously ready to transport her. She was conscious but looked bad, tiny and fragile. Bandages were wrapped her head, and an oxygen mask covered her face.

A distraught Helen stood at her side, Jacob on her hip. "You saved him. I'll never forget. Thank you."

"Ma'am, we need to go," one of the EMTs said.

"Yes." Helen squeezed the older woman's hand and stepped back. Then she saw Seth and came to him, as if it was the most natural thing in the world.

"Hey, buddy," he murmured.

Jacob kept blubbering, and who could blame him?

Even if the piece of scum hadn't actually gotten a hand on the boy, he must have seen unfamiliar violence.

"I need to sit down," Helen said suddenly.

He allowed himself to wrap a supportive arm around her as he steered her to the sofa. She sank down as if her knees had given way. Seth excused himself, and he and Dave Todd stepped onto the front porch, both watching as the ambulance pulled away.

"Were you able to talk to the victim?"

"She kept saying, 'Jacob, Jacob,' over and over again."

"That's the boy's name," Seth said. "Okay, let's get the story from Ms. Boyd. She lives next door." He nodded toward her house. "Last week's murder happened in her rental. She tells me she left behind an abusive ex. I'm thinking the two crimes have to be related."

Todd nodded, and the two men went back into the living room. Seth sat on the coffee table facing Helen, while Todd chose a wing chair a little farther away. Fortunately, Jacob's sobs had dwindled to rhythmic snuffling.

"All right," Seth said, "can you tell us what happened?"

"Iris offered to watch Jacob while I grocery shopped. She said he could help her work on her vegetable garden." She almost sounded steady. "I came home, took my groceries into the house and went out the back door with a carton of eggs for Iris."

Seth could just imagine how much help a two-year-old would have been.

"They weren't outside, though," she continued. "I was partway across the yard when the screen door slammed open and a man wearing a ski mask ran out.

He—" her voice broke "—he had Jacob over his shoulder." Her desperate gaze met Seth's. "If I'd been twenty seconds later—"

He couldn't help himself. He reached out and took her hand in his, not surprised to find her fingers were icy. "You weren't."

After a minute, she nodded.

"How did you get Jacob away from him?"

She told them about having noticed the shovel, snatching it up and swinging at the kidnapper's legs. The stumble, her tackle.

"He took off because he heard the approaching siren." Helen shivered. "Iris must have called 9-1-1."

"She did," Todd confirmed.

"She saved Jacob. And she got hurt so badly doing it. I should never have left him with her. Never!"

Out of the corner of his eye, Seth saw the other officer's brows rise, not only at what she'd said, but also the passion in her voice.

His fingers tightened on her hand. "Helen." He waited until he had her full attention. "Was this your ex-husband?"

She shook her head slowly, some bewilderment showing. "No. He was bulkier than Richard. Anyway, I saw his eyes. They were light colored. Gray, I think. Richard's are brown."

"Is your ex-husband the kind of man who'd send someone else to snatch his son for him?"

She didn't hesitate. "Yes."

So he either had scumbag friends or money to hire some muscle.

"All right," he said. "Give me a minute, and then I'll walk you and Jacob home."

Dave Todd followed him outside.

"File a report with what you know," Seth said. "I'll head over to the hospital to talk to Mrs. Wilbanks. With a little luck, she got a better look at the guy."

"You're thinking Ms. Boyd's ex-husband is behind this?"

"If somebody had grabbed the boy when he was momentarily alone, I'd be more likely to consider other possibilities. But to attack openly like this? Assault a woman to get at the kid? Yeah, I think Jacob's father has to be behind it."

"And the murder." Gravity aged Dave Todd's boyish face.

"That, too."

They exchanged a few more words before Todd got back in his patrol car. Going back into the house, Seth asked, "Ready?"

"Yes, of course, but you don't need to—"

He cut her off. "I do."

Helen bit her lip, nodded and started to push herself up. With reaction setting in, she collapsed back onto the cushion. Seth reached for the boy. "I'll carry him."

"If you'll just help me up…"

He waggled his fingers. Jacob looked at him shyly from red, puffy eyes, then took his thumb from his mouth and held up his arms. Seth lifted him, holding him close. "Good boy. Mommy had a tough day."

Helen stood, expression mulish. "And yet, somehow I've always managed fine before."

"Today you don't have to."

She got all the way to the front door before stopping suddenly. "Wait. Iris won't have her insurance card or her keys."

"Good thought. Can you find them? I'll lock the back door while you're looking."

He bent over so Jacob could push the button on the doorknob. That wouldn't keep an eight-year-old kid out. Dismayed, Seth decided to pick up a dead-bolt lock and install it himself before the home owner was released from the hospital.

Helen handed over both the key and the Medicare Advantage card, waiting on the porch while he locked the door. They'd started along the sidewalk when she exclaimed, "Oh, no! I dropped her eggs. I should go—"

Seth put his free hand on her lower back and gently propelled her forward. "There's no urgency. I feel sure Iris will be admitted to the hospital for the night, at least."

Helen seemed to stumble over her pride when he offered to go get them all hamburgers and fries, but reluctantly accepted.

"Let me walk through your house first," he suggested.

"Please," she said simply.

He hadn't expected that the creep would have circled around and let himself into her place to wait, but had to be sure, checking under her bed and in their closets before feeling satisfied enough to leave.

A local burger restaurant had no drive-through but better quality food, so he went there. As he waited for the order, an uneasy feeling crept over him. He didn't like Helen and Jacob being unprotected even for half an hour, although he honestly didn't expect a repetition of the attack so quickly. And maybe that wasn't even what worried him right now. Helen had to know her ex wasn't going to give up, so what would she do?

He had a suspicion he knew.

IT HADN'T BEEN easy getting rid of Seth, but he did finally leave.

Even on the front porch, he'd turned to give her one last piercing look. "You have to tell me who this guy is. You know that, don't you?"

Knowing she was lucky he'd been patient this long, she said in a small, cracked voice, "Tomorrow."

"All right," he said, sounding astonishingly gentle. "Get some rest, Helen. I'll have patrols drive by regularly this afternoon and during the night. Keep your phone handy. Do you still have my card?"

She nodded.

"Put my number in your phone. If something happens, call 9-1-1 first, then me. Okay?"

"Yes." She felt her smile wobble. "You've been…really nice. Thank you."

He smiled ruefully, not moving. All he did was study her face for longer than was comfortable. Finally, he gave his usual clipped nod and walked down her concrete walkway toward his car. A lump in her throat, Helen watched him go, thinking that even when he appeared relaxed, he wasn't; his head kept turning so he could take in his surroundings, and she suspected he could hit a dead run in about one stride.

And if all went well, she'd never see him again.

When she put Jacob down for his nap, he conked out instantly. Helen hoped all the excitement today had worn him out enough so he'd sleep longer than usual. In case he didn't, she had to hustle.

She'd wait until dark before she went out to the garage to get the two bags she always kept packed. For now, she'd have to revert to her previous identity and pray it wouldn't occur to Richard that she might do that.

Selecting carefully what they could take, she packed everything in a couple of black plastic garbage bags. She openly carried those out to the car under the theory that anyone watching would think she planned to drop them off at the thrift store or maybe the waste disposal site. Nonperishable food went into a cardboard box and grocery bags that she wouldn't take out until after dark.

Midafternoon, Jacob still not having stirred, she called the hospital, where she was told Mrs. Wilbanks would be spending the night but was responsive and talking. The receptionist put the call through to Iris's room, but nobody answered.

When she tried again after dinner, she was able to talk to Iris, whose first words were "Oh, my dear! Jacob must have been so scared. I didn't do a very good job taking care of him, did I?"

"You did a fabulous job," Helen said firmly. "We saved him because you slowed that awful man down and called 9-1-1 immediately. I got home in the nick of time, but what made him take off was the approaching sirens. I am…so grateful to you, Iris. Losing Jacob—" For a moment she couldn't speak, but knew she didn't have to tell Iris, of all people, what she felt.

The older woman had two adult children, both male, one living in Boston, the other in a Portland suburb, but she'd once confided that her daughter had died from childhood leukemia when she was ten. She and Helen had sat side by side holding hands for several minutes.

Iris was the closest thing Jacob had ever had to a grandmother.

After calming her now, Helen asked how she was feeling, and was unsurprised to hear about a headache. "A concussion, the doctor said," Iris concluded. "I'll look ghastly for a while, too. My left eye is almost entirely swollen shut, and I'm going to have a whopper of a black eye. My jaw hurts, too. I might have lost some teeth, so it's lucky I don't have any." She sounded almost cheerful. "My dentures are intact, thank goodness."

"You're a brave woman, and I'm luckier than I deserve to have you for a neighbor."

Usually Iris would have demurred, but this time she said with satisfaction, "I'll have to call both boys tonight and tell them all about it."

Helen said tentatively, "Did you get a good look at your attacker?"

"I'm afraid not. The detective came to see me earlier, you know. He was so nice. I'm sorry I couldn't help. I heard footsteps—he came in the back door, you see—but I had only started to turn when something slammed into my head. It might have just been his arm, or fist."

"Just?"

Iris chuckled, then moaned. "Oh, I shouldn't do that!"

"I'm sorry—"

"Don't be silly. Jacob ran, you know. I crawled for the phone, and had already dialed 9-1-1 before he got his hands on Jacob and tore out."

Helen hated the image of Jacob trying to run away.

She thanked Iris several more times.

After setting down the phone, Helen stayed where she was at the kitchen table, wrestling again with her conscience. But in the end, what choice did she really have?

None. If she told Seth everything, she risked going to prison and leaving Jacob to Richard's mercy. No. She had to do this.

With a sigh, she took out her checkbook to verify that she'd paid all of her bills, and tucked the latest bank statement into her purse. She'd stop at an ATM wherever she found herself after midnight and take out more money. From that point on, she wouldn't dare use her debit card again. She'd be leaving close to five hundred dollars in the account, but that couldn't be helped. Worse come to worst, she could call her mother and beg for a loan—although she hated doing that.

No, she had enough to take care of them for a few weeks, until she could stop long enough to put together a new identity. Goodbye, Helen, hello… Who knew? Whoever that woman was, she'd have light brown hair, Helen had already decided. Blond was too memorable. Her natural color was out.

Once Jacob had gotten up from his nap, Helen did her absolute best to keep him from guessing that anything was about to change. She played a game with him, helped him build with his plastic blocks, even watched a Disney movie with him after dinner. Tucked him in, set her alarm and went to bed herself, hoping she could sleep but failing.

At midnight, she got up, packed the last few things—including the connecting blocks—and slipped out to the garage with a flashlight. Shuddering, she had to shake a big spider off one of the duffel bags before she could lift them from hiding and carry them out to stow in the trunk of her car. The remaining packaged food in the kitchen went in the trunk, too. She closed it as quietly as she possibly could, and looked around for any movement in the darkness. Her skin prickled with her nerves, and her chest ached with regret she tried to shake off.

Last was the ice chest, which would ride on the back seat next to Jacob.

She hadn't turned on her porch light, of course. Her eyes had adjusted some to the darkness, but she still had to watch her feet carefully so she didn't trip on the front steps. That was why she'd almost reached the car before she saw the tall man leaning against the back fender, arms crossed.

He shook his head. "Not happening."

Chapter Six

Seth straightened, took the ice chest from her and inclined his head toward the house. Without a word, Helen turned and retraced her steps.

Inside, he set the ice chest down on the kitchen counter. Face pinched, she'd gotten only as far as the doorway.

"You've been spying on me."

"I have."

"How did you know...?"

There was no easy answer to that. "You only had a few alternatives. I could tell you weren't going to open up to me." He shrugged. "There was something about the way you thanked me." As if she was really saying goodbye.

She wrung her hands together and pleaded, "Please let me go. Richard won't give up. He'll keep coming after me."

"You?" He cocked an eyebrow. "Or his son?"

He lost sight of her shocked stare when she gave an anguished cry and spun to present her back to him.

"Helen." Seth went to stand right behind her. He hesitated before setting his hands on her shoulders and gently squeezing. "Let me help you."

He had no idea whether she saw him as anything but the detective who'd become a major obstacle. Until her secrets were laid bare, he couldn't let himself feel more. She sparked something powerful in him, though. His one certainty was that he needed to keep her close where he could protect her and her son.

With his hands still on her, Seth felt the shuddery breath she drew. "I didn't want to go," she said, so quietly he just heard her. "But I'm scared to stay."

"You have to talk to me, Helen."

The quivering tension in her body relented, and her shoulders sagged. Finally she nodded and, as his hands fell away, faced him. "You haven't left me any choice."

No, he hadn't.

Once she sat at the kitchen table, he pulled out a chair and did the same. "Jacob asleep?"

"I was going to wake him last thing." Her eyes looked more like bitter chocolate than caramel right now.

He couldn't afford much sympathy. "Where did you live before you came to Lookout? You must know I haven't found any background on you before you moved here."

"We did live in Southern California. I told you the truth about that. The thing is…" She looked away, then back to his face, the jut of her chin defiant. "I changed my name."

"I didn't find a divorce decree."

"It wasn't in this state, and… I mean, I did legally go back to my maiden name after the divorce, but later when I had to run, I took on a new identity. When he found me in LA, I did it again. I wasn't Helen Boyd until the day I left."

Well, damn. He'd suspected as much, but taking

on new identities wasn't easy these days. "Who were you before?"

"Um… I was Megan Cobb. She… I found her in a cemetery in Seattle. She died before her first birthday." Once again Helen averted her face. "I felt like I'd stolen something." She swallowed. "I did."

"And Helen?"

"Her grave is in Bakersfield, California. She was eight when she died."

Her voice held pity for children who hadn't had a chance to grow up, for their parents, too, but also sharp regret because stealing those identities hadn't kept her and Jacob safe, after all.

"How long had you been in Southern California?" he asked.

"A year and a half. Jacob was born there."

"How did you know your ex-husband had found you?" Seth wondered if she realized she was clutching herself.

"Over several days, I kept seeing the same man. Just glimpses. At the grocery store, near the bus stop I rode to work. The one that wasn't far from Jacob's day care. That time—" she rocked slightly "—he was pointing a camera at me. One with a huge lens."

"What did you do?" Seth couldn't help hearing the growl in his voice.

She seemed calmed by his anger. "I got off the bus at my office, went in like I always do but slipped out through the parking garage. Took a couple of different buses until I got home. I threw a few things in a suitcase, picked up Jacob and just started driving."

"To Bakersfield."

"Yes. I'd decided to stay off major freeways."

"And then you headed toward home."

She chewed on her bottom lip for a minute before her desperate gaze met his. "That might have been stupid, I don't know. I thought it was the last thing Richard would expect."

"The question is how he found you in the first place. And whether he did."

"Why would anyone else be watching me? Or hire an investigator?"

Seth shrugged his concession then grilled her. Had she maintained any hobbies from when she was married?

No. She looked at him like he was nuts. How was a single, working mother of a baby supposed to have *time* for hobbies?

What about work? Was she doing the same kind of jobs she'd had when married, or before her marriage?

Richard hadn't let her work outside the home. His insistence was her first clue that a trap was closing on her. And no, she'd worked in community development with a specific focus on Seattle's problem with a growing homeless population.

"That's how I met him." Her fingernails appeared to be biting into her upper arms. "He— I spoke to the city council. He talked to me afterward."

It was all Seth could do to tamp down his reaction. "Tell me about your family."

"My father died over five years ago, from a heart attack. It's just Mom, me and my sister, Allie."

"How much contact do you have?"

"Very little. I don't know what can be traced, and

what can't. Once in a while, I buy one of those cheap phones, call and then throw it away. That's it."

"Do you always call your mother? Your sister?"

"No. I alternate, and Mom still has a landline, too, so sometimes I use that one."

"Okay." He rolled his shoulders to stretch tight muscles. Here was the part he was really going to hate. "Tell me about your marriage."

THE FIRST WORDS that came out of Helen's mouth were "I was stupid." Even before Seth shook his head, she wished them unsaid. She knew better. She was a smart, educated woman who'd read about abusive relationships and how manipulative, power-mad men wrapped their coils slowly around their prey. Like dipping a toe in cold water, then going ankle-deep, thigh-deep—at which point she'd known she was in trouble—but getting out wasn't so easy once she plunged into the icy depths.

"What happened is on *him*," he said.

"Yes. Yes, it is," Helen agreed fiercely. The counseling she'd received while in the women's shelter had helped her recover her confidence. For her, it happened fast, because she'd escaped her marriage quickly. It hadn't lasted even two years.

"Why did you fall for him?"

She gazed at a bare stretch of wall so that she didn't have to see what Seth was thinking.

Voice tight, she said, "He's handsome, maybe the most intelligent person I'd ever met, seemingly committed to a lot of good causes. He…has this sort of force field. I guess it's charisma, but once people are sucked in, they want him to like them. They tend to do what he suggests, too."

"Sounds like a warlock."

"Yes. I never figured out if he really is well-intentioned in his stances on issues. Maybe I satisfied his need for control while he had me." She hated feeling shame, didn't deserve to feel it, but that was a battle she hadn't entirely won yet. "It was classic. He didn't want me to work, always thought of something the two of us could do when I planned to get together with a friend or Mom or Allie. His intensity kept me from noticing. I thought this sort of passionate closeness was normal in the first year of marriage." She meant to laugh, but the sound was discordant. "Then he started giving me the silent treatment if I displeased him, which was awful since half the time I had no idea what I'd done or said. The first time he hit me, I almost left him, but he groveled, and I was sure I'd provoked his temper, and…" Her muscles rigid, she hadn't moved since she'd started talking. "Only then it happened again. And again. I made up my mind to leave him. Unfortunately, the housekeeper called to let him know I was packing to go, and he came home. He beat me so badly, he had to take me to the ER. I think the doctor there suspected, but I made up some story because Richard was sitting there holding my hand, so loving and solicitous. After that, he told me no woman left him, and if I tried, he'd kill me. That made me wonder—" She hesitated.

"About?"

"He'd been married before, to a woman he met when he was a graduate student at the University of Michigan. She'd died in some kind of accident, supposedly."

Seth said something she was just as glad not to hear.

"I was essentially a prisoner from then on. The housekeeper lived in, and a man started work as sort of a butler but really more of a bodyguard—and prison guard. After that, no matter how careful I was, I couldn't please Richard. I made visits to half the emergency rooms in the city. He kept entertaining with me as his hostess, but made sure I never had a chance to be alone with any of the guests." She let out a long breath. "I'm not sure I'd have had the nerve to latch onto someone I didn't know very well and beg for rescue, anyway."

"But you did escape." Seth's voice was guttural.

"Yes. I waited for a chance when no one was watching. I'd been stealing a little bit of money at a time from Richard. He'd drop his coins or a few dollars on the dresser at night. You know." Her shrug had to look as stiff as it felt. "I didn't need much. When I saw my chance, I walked out. No coat, I couldn't take anything. I…had bruises on my face. I walked quite a way before I saw a taxi. When I got in, the taxi driver took one look at me, then drove me to a hospital. A social worker called a women's shelter for me. Someone came to get me." She stopped.

"You were pregnant."

Helen turned her head slowly to look at him. His face remained impassive, but his eyes glittered with what she knew was fury. Seeing that let her relax a little. It comforted her.

"I had been feeling tired and nauseated for several weeks, but I thought it was stress. Thank God I left when I did." The alternative still horrified her. "He had no idea I was pregnant."

Seth leaned forward. "Do you have scars?"

"I… Only a couple. He…mostly broke bones."

Muscles in the detective's jaw clenched. His blue eyes burned into hers. "Will you show me?"

Startled, she shrank back. "Show you?"

"Your scars."

He needed proof, she supposed. After a moment, she nodded.

His chair scraped back. Bending her head, she tugged the collar of her sweatshirt aside so he could see the spot low on her neck.

"He sometimes smoked cigars. Expensive Cuban ones, of course. He sort of stabbed me with the burning tip of one."

Her fingers could have unerringly found the scar, even though the skin there no longer felt any sensation. Still, she'd swear she felt Seth lightly touch it with the tip of his finger.

"I have a couple of other places, but I'd have to take clothes off, and I…" Her cheeks felt hot. She didn't want to strip in front of him, for a whole lot of reasons.

"Okay." He gently tugged the neckline of her shirt back up. She could hear him breathing behind her. What was he doing? But then he returned to his place at the table, his expression grim. Helen knew what was coming.

"What's his name, Helen?" He frowned. "What's *your* name?"

Panic skittered over her. "You can't—"

"I can't what?"

"I don't know!" she exclaimed. It was obvious Richard already knew where she was. "I just—"

He waited.

Was there any chance at all he could ask questions about Richard without learning about the bodyguard's murder?

She closed her eyes in resignation. What could she do but tell him? At least for now, running wasn't an option. The knowledge gave her a claustrophobic feeling.

Possibly because she was, once again, trapped? Another man had seized control over her life? Yes. Dear God, *yes*.

And yet…relief was part of what she felt, too. She hadn't wanted to leave this life and people she'd come to care about behind. Surrendering the burden of responsibility, if only briefly, that was a relief, too.

Unless, of course, she ended up being arrested.

Unreadable, Seth kept watching her.

"Richard Winstead. He's…a corporate attorney in Seattle. He sits on several advisory committees appointed by the mayor and city council members." Bitterness etched her voice when she added, "If you ask around about him, all you'll hear are glowing compliments."

"He's not the first successful man to abuse his wife. Domestic violence covers every social class."

She swallowed and nodded. "I'm Robin Hollis."

Seth's smile reached his eyes. It was warm and a little crooked. "Thank you, Robin." He resumed his cop mask. "Here's what we're going to do first. If you'll give me permission, I think we should compile your medical records."

Stung, she said, "You don't believe me." Except… Confused, she realized he'd said "we." Twice. As if *they* were taking action, not just him.

"I do," he said calmly. "It would help to show undeniable proof to a judge that you suffered not just one incident but ongoing abuse at the hands of your then-husband. The dates of your visits to the various ERs are important. I won't be surprised if doctors or nurses noted some suspicion of abuse, too."

She'd thought of requesting her records herself, but had been afraid to give a mailing address to the various hospitals. To have them sent to her mother might have drawn attention to her. One of her fears had always been what Richard might do to Mom and Allie to punish her.

"Yes. I'll sign a permission form."

"Good. We'll start with that." He tapped the ice chest. "Might be a good idea to put everything in here back in the fridge."

Suddenly exhausted, she pushed herself to her feet while she still could and lifted off the lid. "I need to get some things from the car, too. My toothbrush is out there."

"Do you have to brush your teeth?"

She blinked at him. Did she really care? No. "I suppose not."

Shaking his head, he stood. "You need to get to bed. I'll put the food away."

"But…"

"I'm sleeping on your couch tonight, Robin."

"To keep me from taking off once you're gone."

He smiled. "I admit the thought crossed my mind that you might try, but I want you to get a good night's sleep, too, and I know you won't if you're listening for a break-in."

He was right. A part of her had been dreading his departure. She felt guilty, though. This had to be above and beyond the call. Could he get in trouble for staying in her house?

"If I promise—" she began.

Seth shook his head. "Go to bed, Robin."

"It's weird hearing my name."

He put his hands on her shoulders, turned her toward the living room and gave her a nudge. "Sleep tight."

She almost smiled at hearing that. Mom always said the same when she'd tucked her daughters into bed. "There's an extra pillow and some blankets in the linen closet."

"I'll be fine."

She went, afraid she'd still lie awake wondering about the consequences of her telling him so much. She peeked in at Jacob, as she always did before going to bed herself, closed her own door while she shed her clothes, then cracked it open again to allow her to hear Jacob. Bedside light off, she crawled into bed and conked out.

SETH LAY ON the couch, one shoeless foot on the floor, the other extending beyond the padded arm. Considering that it looked as if she'd bought it at a garage sale, the couch wasn't half bad as a makeshift bed. Just not long enough. That wasn't all keeping him awake, though.

Every time he pictured her buckling Jacob into his car seat and driving away, his guts knotted. If he hadn't listened to his instincts, Helen—no, Robin—would be gone, no question. He wouldn't have gotten her out of his head for a long time.

Mentally replaying her story didn't help, either. It wasn't as if he hadn't seen plenty of domestic abuse during his career; brutality at home was a staple in any patrol officer's job, small town or big city. He'd never been sure how he'd controlled his anger in those situations. He'd never get why a man would want to hurt any woman or child, far less the ones he loved. This time, he already felt more than he should for Helen Boyd aka Robin Hollis. Seeing the scar had fired his temper. Now, when he closed his eyes in search of sleep, he saw her face with lopsided swelling, purple bruises, a swollen eye like Iris Wilbanks's.

Yeah, he sounded capable of being that cold-blooded.

Seth's thoughts kept veering to the woman down the hall. Better not to wonder if she slept on her back or curled on her side, if she'd gravitate toward the warmth of a man sharing her bed. Hard to stop himself, though. Hard not to wish he'd seen more than glimpses of the woman she'd been before she got sucked into the orbit of a monster.

Her choice of profession before her marriage suggested that compassion was a big part of her makeup. That hadn't changed; all he had to do was remember her kneeling beside her injured neighbor, holding her hand.

He tried to push away the memory of her saying she'd been tired and nauseated for only a few weeks before she escaped. She had to have hated the SOB by the time she got pregnant. Had she been cooperating, trying in self-defense to please him, or had he outright raped her whenever he felt like it?

Make sure there really is a Richard Winstead who'd been married to Robin Hollis, Seth cautioned himself. He believed in the anguish he'd seen on her face, but call him a cynic. He still needed to see those doctors' reports and X-rays.

It was a long night despite getting a late start. He got

up to use the bathroom once, pausing in the hall after turning out the light to look in the narrow slot of darkness that was her bedroom. He wished he could see her, know whether she'd actually been able to sleep.

He did finally drop off, but the sleep was light. He jerked awake at regular intervals, thinking he'd heard something, lying still listening until he was sure he hadn't. The deepest sleep must have come toward morning, because he opened his eyes to find a short person staring at him from less than a foot away. He had to blink to bring the caramel-brown eyes, disheveled red hair and freckles into focus. His nostrils flared at the distinct smell of pee.

"Hi," the little boy said engagingly.

"Good morning." Seth had to clear his throat. "Do you need a bath?"

Jacob's head bobbed.

"How about a shower?"

His eyes widened in alarm, and he shook his head hard.

Okay, Seth remembered a time when he'd been terrified of getting water in his eyes or mouth, too.

"Mommy awake?" he tried.

Another headshake.

Well, this would be a first for him, but why not?

Chapter Seven

Waking to the sounding of water running and a huge *splat*, Helen shot upright in bed. Dear God, Jacob hadn't turned the tub faucet on himself, had he?

She sprang out of bed and raced toward the bathroom, but before she reached it, she heard the low rumble of a man's voice, then Jacob's giggle. She stopped dead in the hall, gaping at the open bathroom door. Seth Renner—*Detective* Renner—was giving her son a bath? Had he tried to wake her up and failed? What time was it anyway?

She retreated to her bedroom and sat on the edge of the bed so she could see her clock: 8:56. Since Jacob was usually awake by 6:30, she couldn't remember the last time she'd slept this late.

She threw on her robe—terry cloth and not a thing of beauty—and padded across the hall to the bathroom.

"Mommy!" Jacob cried joyously. He started to scramble to his feet, but Seth laid a hand on his skinny shoulder and shook his head.

"Sit, buddy. You don't want to slip and fall." Then he turned his head and smiled at Helen. Sitting on a plastic stool she'd bought for the express purpose of supervising baths, he wore the same khaki trousers, and a white T-shirt he must have had under the button-up she remembered from last night.

What riveted her attention was his bare feet.

Big feet, to suit his height, a few dark hairs curling on his toes. Solid feet, she thought, for no good reason except she liked them better than Richard's, which had been narrow and fish-white. Not that she had any business liking Seth's feet, or even staring at them.

"My socks got wet," he said. "I didn't realize what a messy business this is."

"Why…?"

"I woke up to find somebody staring at me. He said when he tried to wake up Mommy, she grumbled and rolled over."

"He did not!"

This smile crinkled the skin beside his eyes. "He was happy to discover a second-stringer snoozing on the couch."

She laughed even as she shook her head. "I can't believe I didn't wake up! What would he have done if you hadn't been here?"

"Well, I don't think he's tall enough to unlock the front door yet, but he might have gotten into the refrigerator."

"I'm hungry," her son declared.

"Me, too." Seth's eyebrows rose.

Jacob bounced. "I want waffles."

Didn't Seth plan to go home today? Imagining him leaving, she felt a spike of anxiety. Yesterday, Richard's minion had tried to steal Jacob in broad daylight. What was to stop him once she and Jacob were alone?

"Waffles it is," she agreed, not quite as lightly as she'd intended. "Except I'd really like to have a shower first."

"I think it's time for Jacob to get out, anyway." Seth grinned at the two-year-old. "You're getting crinkled fingers and toes."

He was, which made her wonder how long he'd been happily splashing and playing in the tub while she slept, oblivious.

"Okay, kiddo." She grabbed his towel from the rack and handed it to Seth. Her hand brushed his, but she pretended she hadn't noticed. "Mommy's turn."

"Mommy's turn," Jacob said obediently. When Seth held out the small plastic bucket that still held a few toys, Jacob put the ones he'd been playing with into it.

Packing yesterday, she hadn't included of bath toys, Helen thought, suddenly stricken. Jacob especially loved his bright red boat and the purple shark.

Seth was watching her, she realized, reading her emotions. She forced a smile. "If you two can handle this, I need to find myself some clean clothes." Some that weren't in the trunk of her car.

Even as she thought that, Seth said, "Do you need me to go out and get something from the car?"

"No, I'm fine. I didn't try to— You know." *Take everything.*

His expression changed, the warmth disappearing, but Seth gave a curt nod.

Helen fled for her bedroom.

SHE'D MADE WAFFLES from scratch. Seth couldn't remember the last time he'd had any that good. She even made him a second waffle. While he ate it, Helen—no, damn it, Robin!—took Jacob down the hall to use his potty chair. The boy didn't seem to need a diaper during the day. Nights must be different.

"He sleeps too soundly," she said with a fond smile for the boy. After rinsing off his plate, Seth found her keys in an outside pocket of her purse and went out to grab the first load from the trunk. Two duffel bags, looking pretty scroungy.

Coming down the hall, she saw what he was carrying. "Oh, those are—" She eyed him warily. "I keep them packed. You know."

"Go bags."

"Something like that," she admitted.

He shook his head. "Should I bring in just the boxes?"

"No, I need the bags, too, but I can help."

"Won't take me a minute." He went back outside before he had to get mad at her again for planning to run out on him.

Once everything was inside, he went into the kitchen, where she was rinsing dishes. "I'm going out to get my laptop," he told her.

"Where are you parked?"

"Alley behind Mrs. Wilbanks's house."

She narrowed her eyes. "Sneaky."

He just smiled. Once he'd returned, he pulled up a list of hospitals and urgent care facilities in King County and when he read it aloud, she identified six places where she'd been treated.

Six. Seth wasn't smiling anymore.

Since this was Sunday, it wouldn't do any good to send off the requests before morning, especially since he'd need her to come into the station to sign a permission form he could scan.

In the meantime, he had no intention of going anywhere. Which was fine today as long as he didn't get called out, a possibility even on his days off. If that happened, he'd have to figure out what to do with Robin and Jacob. He wouldn't leave them unguarded.

Speaking of which… He closed his laptop and said what he was sure were her favorite words: "Let's talk." Seeing her anxiety, he shook his head. "Nothing bad."

"Then what?"

"I don't want you staying here," he said bluntly.

Her mouth tightened. "Then you should have let me go, shouldn't you?"

"I need to know where you are." He hoped she didn't understand how sincerely he meant that.

She only frowned. "I guess I could go back to the Lookout Inn. The security there is probably decent. Better than a bed-and-breakfast."

"But not good enough. You'd be easy to find. It'll be best if you just disappear. We'll leave your car here, slip out the back door during the night."

Now she looked wary. "Where would we go?"

He wished he could take them home—and the force of that desire was good reason to nix the idea. Along with the fact that, unless he took some vacation, she and Jacob would be unprotected while he worked.

"To stay with my father," he said. Although maybe he should have called Dad before proposing this, Seth realized belatedly. "He's a retired cop, has lots of room."

"You're kidding."

"No."

Helen—damn it, he didn't like being so confused—

Robin shook her head. "We can't descend on your father. I've never even met him! And with a two-year-old…? Have you asked him?" she queried with spot-on suspicion.

"I'll call him right now."

Robin jumped up. "There's got to be someplace else we can go. I've gotten to be friends with one of my co-workers—"

He leaned back in his chair and crossed his arms. "Can she protect you? Does she have family you'd be endangering?"

"Oh, God." She plunked back down onto the chair, looking dazed.

Seth said gently, "I'm sorry, Robin."

Her eyes truly focused then. "Maybe you shouldn't call me that."

"Why not? It's safe to say your ex knows what name you've been living under."

Her mouth tightened.

Seth took out his phone and tapped his father's number. Robin leaped up and said hastily, "I'd better check on Jacob. And let you talk to your dad without me listening in."

"It's okay—"

But she was gone. She was probably right, he thought, just as his father said, "Son?"

"Hey, Dad. Ah, listen, I need to ask a favor of you."

There was a pause. "What is it?"

"I'm looking for someplace for a woman and her toddler son to stay for a few days. She's in a tough spot."

"This somebody you're seeing?"

"No, nothing like that." Did he sound as falsely hearty as he thought he did? "We talked about the Realtor who was murdered. She was killed in a rental house. This woman is the renter. I think Ms. Sloan was killed by mistake. She looked a lot like Ms. Boyd." He caught himself. "Hollis. Crap. She's living here under a false identity to escape an ex-husband."

Silence. He'd worried before about women mixed up in his investigations, but Seth had never put one under his father's protection. Dad was waiting to hear what this was really about.

"Yesterday, somebody tried to snatch her son. She'd left him for a couple of hours with her next-door neighbor, an older woman named Iris Wilbanks."

"I know Iris," his father put in. "Did she get hurt?"

"The creep knocked her down, so she has a concussion and a black eye. Doctor kept her overnight, but she's coming home today. How'd you meet her?"

"She worked at the library. Nice lady."

"Yeah, she is." Seth sighed and told him how Robin had fearlessly rushed the abductor and gotten her son back. He outlined the rest of her history—the abusive ex, the changed identities, even her attempt to take off again.

"You getting involved with this woman?"

Seth winced. His father knew him too well. "I'm trying not to," he said.

"Why?"

He glanced at the doorway, glad to hear her talking down the hall. Even so, he lowered his voice. "You have to ask? She's involved in my investigation. I can't a hundred percent swear she's telling the truth yet."

"Uh-huh."

"Dad."

"Of course she's welcome." There was a smile in his

father's voice. "Won't mind having a kid around the house, either. It's been a long time."

"You had your grandkids for two weeks at Christmas." Seth's sister, Grace, tried to get home with her girls at least twice a year, sometimes with her husband, sometimes not. The bedroom with two single beds Dad kept for the girls would do nicely for Robin and Jacob.

"Why Grace had to marry a man based in Chicago, I don't know."

"Maybe because she went to the University of Chicago," Seth suggested, smiling at his father's oft-heard grumbles.

Robin appeared in the doorway, hesitating when she saw he was still on the phone. He waved her in.

"I want to sneak Robin and Jacob out in the early hours tonight. You don't have to get up. I'll let us in and put them in Ivy and Sara's bedroom."

His father snorted. "You know I won't sleep through that. I'll at least say hello."

"Okay, Dad. Thanks."

He harrumphed. "Maybe I'll see more of you while they're with me."

"I'm sure you will."

Putting his phone down on the table, Seth said, "Dad's glad to have you." He told her about his two nieces, the bedroom she'd share with Jacob, and the wealth of toys and kids' DVDs his father kept around. "He's a good guy."

Her smile was crooked. "So is his son." Pause. "Most of the time."

Seth laughed.

HAVING SETH HANGING around all day was unnerving. Of course, if he hadn't been here, she'd have been so tense she wouldn't have been able to do anything but listen for every tiny creak, or peer through blinds when cars passed in the street or alley. Instead, a big, sexy man had inserted himself calmly into her home, interacting comfortably with Jacob and talking to her as if they were longtime friends. Or lovers.

He did take his laptop out off and on, mostly seeming engaged in doing searches. That made her nervous. He'd find plenty about her under her real name, first because of the work she'd done, then because of her marriage to a prominent man. Was he reading about her parents? And what about her sister? He wouldn't have any reason to track down information about Allie's health problems, would he? *Please, no.*

Of course, Seth would be researching Richard. Robin wished she knew what he was thinking. He looked up frequently, his gaze going straight to her. Clearly, even while he appeared immersed in whatever he was reading or doing, he remained aware of her.

Well, she was aware of him, too. Painfully so. He looked good slouching, feet stacked on the coffee table, or sitting up bent over the laptop. His long fingers, the sinews and veins in his hands mesmerized her, as did the thickness of his wrists, the strength in tanned forearms below rolled shirtsleeves. No matter what she did, she'd find her gaze straying to him—and, most often, his eyes would already be on her.

She gave herself lectures. She couldn't forget that friendship wasn't what had him spending his Sunday here with her and Jacob. He was keeping an eye on her so she wouldn't take off. Yes, and guarding them, too; she couldn't deny that.

What disturbed her most was that by the time she

escaped from Richard, she hadn't been able to imagine ever letting a man close enough to hurt her again, emotionally or physically. Her several-month stay in the battered-women's shelter had reinforced her determination. Every woman there was running from a man who'd once promised to love and cherish her but chose instead to use his fists on her—or systematically destroy her confidence. Most had been in damaging relationships much longer than Robin had been, in part because she'd had more confidence to start with and been lucky enough to grow up with parents who were happily married. Her father was often laughing in her memories. He'd had a special glint in his eyes for her mother until the day he died.

Robin felt ashamed, thinking about her father. With him as an example, how could she not have seen beneath Richard's charming surface before she married him?

But she also knew what Dad would say. *You got out of it as quick as you could. You'll for damn sure make sure he never has a chance to hurt your baby.* If Dad had still been alive, she suspected she'd have left Richard much sooner—and gone home instead of hiding out in a shelter.

But Allie hadn't been sick then; in fact, they hadn't known that she had only one kidney. Mom hadn't become worn with worry for both her daughters, the sick one and the one who could so rarely be bothered to call or take time to stop by the house, who invited her mother and sister to dinner at her elegant home only on rare occasions. When, of course, Richard had seen to it that they didn't have time for private conversation. When he'd been at his warmest, funniest, and they, too, had fallen into that force field.

Until Robin had called from the shelter to tell them what her marriage had really been like, they'd undoubtedly thought she was glad to leave them behind for a more glamorous life with a wealthy, politically influential man.

She shook off memories of him when it came time to tuck Jacob in for his nap.

"I like Seth," he said sleepily.

She kissed his still-round cheek and murmured, "I do, too."

She eased the door almost closed and stayed facing it for a minute. Why Seth? Why did he feel…trustworthy? Why was her body all too responsive to him, when she hadn't thought about a man in a sexual way since a year into her marriage?

With a sigh, she returned to the living room.

Wouldn't you know, he looked up immediately, his blue eyes piercing her.

"Come sit down." He patted the cushion next to him.

Her feet quit moving. "Is this going to be another interrogation?"

His mouth curved. "No."

She approached reluctantly, finally sitting beside him. He turned his laptop slightly to allow her to see a photo of Richard engaged in intense conversation with the previous mayor.

"Handsome man," Seth said, tone neutral.

Taken by surprise, Robin couldn't tear her eyes from that face. Lean, his strength wiry, his face thin with perfect bones, a sensual mouth and extremely dark eyes beneath a slash of dark brows.

A shudder racked her. "Looking at him makes my skin crawl."

Seth slapped the laptop closed. "I'm sorry. God! What was I thinking?"

"You…you wanted to know more about him." With each hand, she gripped the opposite forearm, kneading hard.

"Robin." Seth took her hands, prying them away from her arms. "Don't. Please."

She shook her head. "I've been following him on social media and in the news. I wanted to be sure he was in Seattle where he belongs. I've seen pictures before. Tonight… I don't know why it hit me that way."

But she did. It was because of what she'd been thinking, comparing Richard to Seth. Richard's touch, his cold rebukes, had been cast in sharp relief. She hadn't known she could act until that last year, but she'd hated every minute.

She shivered.

With an exclamation, Seth dropped her hands and pulled her into his arms. Without a second thought, she all but burrowed into him, wrapping her arms around his hard torso.

"I'm sorry," he said roughly. "I think I wanted—" He swallowed.

Robin tried to lift her head. "You wanted?"

"I was being an idiot. Reading about him and thinking—"

He kept doing that. There was something he'd rather not admit.

She struggled back and Seth released her. They were left staring at each other.

"What?" Suddenly mad, she demanded, "What did you think?"

His mouth twisted. "I feel like a country hick in

comparison, that's what. I know I'm being illogical. I despise every breath the son of a bitch takes, but I didn't like knowing—" Looking appalled, he closed his mouth and seemed to retreat without seemingly moving a muscle.

Knowing what? She couldn't imagine.

"I can see why he impressed you." Seth was good at the expressionless thing, except when he almost slipped.

"No. You don't understand." She laid a hand on his arm, which became even more rigid. "I wasn't attracted to his wealth, or the fact that he seemed to have so much influence on a lot of important people. I detested the entertaining he took for granted we'd do, and his house—" She barely controlled another shiver. "We seemed to have so much in common. He listened to me, acted as if he respected my opinions." If the curve of her mouth looked bitter, that was because it was. "Until he suddenly didn't want me working, got mad at any suggestion *he* wasn't enough to satisfy me. Oh, and how dare I counter his brilliant ideas? By then I'd started to wonder if political expedience wasn't his main consideration when he took sides on issues."

Seth didn't say a word, but lines gathered on his forehead.

"I know you're just doing your job." She gestured vaguely, encompassing the sofa where he'd slept last night, the fact that he was still here. "Considering that you must still doubt everything I've told you, you've been kind and protective. Jacob doesn't know many men, but he trusted you immediately. And you're, well…" No way she could finish *that* sentence.

One eyebrow flickered. "Trustworthy. Kind. Sounds like a nice dog you adopted at the local shelter."

"It's not like that." Seeing his disbelief, she blurted, "He can't measure up to you in any way."

His eyes narrowed slightly. Then he rolled his shoulders and said drily, "At least I don't beat women."

Cheeks warm, Robin mumbled, "You know that's not what I meant."

His eyes had never been so blue. Her heartbeat did some gymnastics while they looked at each other. He wouldn't touch her, she knew he wouldn't, but Robin was shaken to realize how sure she was that he wanted to.

And that she was extraordinarily tempted to take the decision out of his hands.

Chapter Eight

Seth rose abruptly from his place on the couch. "I'm going to take a look around outside."

Sitting in a rocker, Robin had been reading—or pretending to read, just as he'd pretended to be absorbed in the news on his computer. He'd noticed she hurriedly turned a page whenever he glanced her way, and rarely in between. Now she only nodded.

He stalked through the kitchen and utility room. Neither room was lit, and Robin hadn't turned on the porch light, either. It was a very dark night he let himself out into. Clouds had moved in earlier; now, a wind gusted through the alley and backyard. He stepped to one side of the door and waited for his eyes to adjust to the relative darkness.

In town, it was never entirely dark, of course. Halfway down the alley, light poured out of an open garage. Streetlamps stood at corners throughout the neighborhood. But the houses to each side of Robin's were dark. Seth had sent a patrol officer to bring Iris home from the hospital earlier. She must have already gone to bed.

He walked up the alley, then back until he reached the cross street, careful not to let his booted feet crunch on the occasional gravel. Once, movement seen out of the corner of his eye had him tensing, until he saw a cat leap over a six-foot fence. His unmarked department car remained inconspicuously tucked up close to Iris's small, detached garage.

Moving silently, he circled Iris's house, then Robin's rental. Nothing. At nearly nine o'clock, everybody in the neighborhood seemed to be tucked in to stay. He hadn't heard a car engine since he'd come outside, only a few clangs of metal inside that open garage.

Still restless, glad for the cool night air and the distance from a woman he hungered for but couldn't allow himself to touch, Seth wasn't eager to go back inside. Robin might start to worry if he didn't reappear, however. He hoped she'd go to bed soon and get some sleep before their planned getaway. Four a.m. There shouldn't be so much as a mouse astir, and no hint of dawn yet, either.

He'd quietly let himself in and locked the new dead bolt on the back door when he heard a phone ring. Had to be Robin's. Strange, when nobody had called all day. The only time she'd been on her phone was to talk to Iris once she was home.

Not wanting to scare her, he called, "It's me," and stopped to pour a glass of cold water from the pitcher in the refrigerator.

"Seth?" She was suddenly there, clutching her phone. "It's a strange number."

This was probably innocent: a sales call, a family member using a burner. But threats...those might be next. He set the glass down on the counter. "Answer."

Eyes locked on his, Robin answered after the fifth ring. "Hello?"

All Seth could hear was a man's voice, but her outraged expression told him who this caller was.

"How did you get my phone number? And what do you want?"

The man talked. Seth thought she might crack the phone case, the way her hand had tightened. He had to fight the desire to snatch it out of her grip and tell the son of a bitch what he thought about men who terrorized women.

But she was already talking again. "You're crazy," she said scathingly, stunned disbelief showing, too. "Oh, why am I surprised? Of course you are." The man's voice cut like a whip, but over the top of it, Robin talked right over him, gaining volume as she went. "The answer is no. I already know you don't keep promises. More to the point—" she was almost yelling now "—I would *never* give up my child to anyone, and especially not *you.*"

Seth didn't think he'd ever heard so much loathing in anyone's voice.

Apparently having cut the creep off, she dropped the phone onto the table and paced the length of the kitchen and back. "How *dare* he call me? Did he think for a minute that I'd just hand over Jacob? Or was he only goading me?"

When she started past him again, he stopped her with a hand on her arm. "Tell me what he said."

"That he'd let me go if I gave him his son. Signed a note conceding custody to him."

"That's brazen."

"He thinks he's untouchable. Who would believe me if I told them what he'd done to me? What he's really like?"

"I do," Seth said simply.

Her lips parted. She blinked. "I… How can you?"

A little shocked to have said that—no, to believe in her so absolutely—he shook his head. "Doesn't matter. I wish I could have recorded that call, though. He all but admitted he was responsible for the attempted abduction."

"Yes." Her shoulders slumped. "I hate him."

"Yeah." He sounded hoarse to his ears. He wanted to gather her into his arms, as he had for those brief moments on the couch, but knew he needed to keep his distance. She'd passed the point of being a suspect in his eyes, but starting anything with her was highly inappropriate. No matter what, he couldn't put her in a position of feeling coerced, not when she needed to be able to depend on him. As for him, whatever his gut insisted was truth, he'd be smart to see some proof before he gave Robin Hollis–Helen Boyd–Megan Cobb his entire faith—and maybe the something more that formed a tight knot under his breastbone.

ROBIN'S HEAD KEPT TURNING, although she couldn't make much out in the dark. Beside her in the alley, Seth carried Jacob, who was still half-asleep. A duffel hung over his opposite shoulder, while she carried a box and one of the big black plastic sacks full of clothes.

They'd reached his car when she gasped. "His car seat," she whispered.

"I got it." He eased open the back door and gently placed Jacob in the seat, buckling him in with a deftness that told her he'd done this before. "Slipped out earlier," he murmured. "Brought the potty seat, too. Lucky he didn't need it."

Her lips formed a "thank you." She didn't know if he heard it. The bags all went on the seat and floor by Jacob. Seth urged her into the front passenger seat. "Lock. I'll get the rest."

She did as he asked, watching the side mirror as he melted back into the darkness. With her awareness that they were alone, prickles of apprehension crawled up her spine. What if somebody lunged out of the darkness right now? That man in the mask could break the car window with one smash of a hammer, unlock the back door and have Jacob out before she could do much. A bullet could come out of nowhere and she'd be dead. Richard had sworn more than once that he would kill her if she fled. After she'd rejected the "deal" he proffered today, what was to stop him? For all his liberal stances, he owned a sizable collection of guns, from 9 mm handguns to rifles and worse.

She should have told Seth about Richard's guns, and that he was an expert marksman. Was Seth armed tonight?

Nothing moved in the darkness. She swiveled to see that Jacob had sagged sideways in deep sleep again. He'd be up bright and early, but she could probably vacuum around his bed in the middle of the night without waking him.

Where was Seth? *Please hurry.*

As if she'd conjured him, a dark shape materialized behind the car. The trunk lid rose without a sound. Seth set his current load inside and eased the lid back down with barely a click that she felt more than heard. She unlocked the doors to let him in.

The minute he was behind the wheel, he locked them in again and started the engine.

"I'll bet he's watching," she said.

Driving slowly down the alley, Seth glanced at her. "Round the clock surveillance is expensive."

"He's rich."

"And conspicuous in a small town like this. You don't think any of your neighbors wouldn't call the police if they saw a guy sitting for hours on end in a car? Or lurking in the alley? Crossing backyards?"

"Yes, but…"

A warm hand covered hers where she clutched the seat belt. "Quit worrying."

"I forgot to tell you that Richard owns guns. He target shoots a couple of times a week."

In a different tone, Seth said, "Does he, now? Did he teach you to shoot?"

"He tried. It didn't go well."

"Why not?" He sounded genuinely interested. They'd exited the alley and were driving down a deserted street.

"It freaked me out. The way the gun leaped in my hand."

"What kind of gun?"

"It was a Beretta M9, he said. Kind of tan colored."

Seth grunted. "Pricey, which figures. Too big for you. If he'd really wanted to teach you, he'd have started with something with less punch and sized for smaller hands."

Had Richard really wanted her to share his hobby? Funny, Robin thought, that she'd never asked herself that question, but in retrospect she thought his goal had been for her to see how deadly *he* was with a weapon in his hands. Precautionary intimidation. If only she'd guessed as much. She'd have become a crack shot if it killed her, scared *him* a little.

Seth drove several blocks before he added, "If some-body were to take a shot at you right about now, he'd be my number one suspect."

"He may not know I've told you about him. He might think I'm hanging on to my Helen Boyd identity."

"If this works, he won't be able to find you either way. Seems likely he'll assume you've taken off again."

"I have."

He chuckled quietly. "Less than a mile between Dad's house and yours."

They did some zigzagging along the way, Seth keeping an eye on the rearview mirror. Robin compulsively did the same using the passenger-side mirror. They had left town before the car slowed and he turned into a long dirt driveway. There seemed to be an orchard to one side and a pasture to the other.

"Is this where you grew up?"

His hands flexed once on the steering wheel. "Yep. I had a lot of fun here as a kid."

What should pop out of her mouth but "You're... You seemed to know your way around a car seat."

"Is that a question?" He was clearly teasing. "I have two nieces. Sara is seven now, Ivy four. My sister brings them out here a couple of times a year, and Dad and I go to Chicago alternate years for Christmas."

"Oh. That's nice."

"Which part?"

"All of it," she said honestly. Not being able to see her mother and sister created a constant ache in her chest, made worse by Allie's illness. Neither of them had even seen Jacob. She didn't think he really understood the concept of grandmothers or aunts. Childbirth would have been so different if Mom and Allie both had been with her, had counted fingers and toes, held Jacob when he was tiny and bundled in a blanket so that only his head emerged.

"You miss your family," Seth said in a husky voice, even as he parked beside a farmhouse nestled in some big old trees. She'd given away more than she intended.

Finding out how much of a family man he was made her pray anew that he never learned she had it in her power to heal her sister, and hadn't done it.

A side door to the house opened, spilling light across the lawn. The man coming out was close to Seth's size with strong shoulders and a confident stride. His hair seemed to be white.

Seth opened his door and went to meet his father. They half hugged, in that guy way. Feeling shy, Robin got out, too.

Seth made quiet introductions before saying, "Let's get inside. Bed ready for Jacob?"

"Sure is. He doesn't need a crib?"

"No." For no good reason, she spoke barely above a whisper, as if there had to be listening ears out there. "At home, I have his mattress on the floor, but he'll be okay on a regular bed."

Michael Renner nodded. "What can I carry?"

As before, Seth carried Jacob inside and disappeared deeper into the house. Even a few days ago, she would have felt an anxious need to trot after him. It was too easy to trust this man.

"The bedroom is upstairs," his father said. "I already have gates out for the top and bottom of the stairs. Had 'em for my nieces, and held on to 'em in case my daughter had another one."

Robin let one of the duffels slide off her shoulder onto

a stool drawn up to a breakfast bar on a big, granite-topped island. The kitchen was gorgeous, with Shaker-style maple cabinets, double ovens and a wrought-iron rack for pans hung over the stove top. The room was warm and welcoming, unlike Richard's kitchen.

"This is beautiful," Robin said, looking around. "Perfect."

His smile looked a lot like one of Seth's, except Michael's skin had more crinkles. He was still a good-looking man, and his hair wasn't white the way it had appeared outside but instead blond. Or, well, probably a mix. Seth had gotten his blue eyes from his father, but maybe his darker hair from his mother.

"I had it redone a few years ago." His tone was elaborately casual, but Robin suspected he knew to the day when the work had been done. He cleared his throat. "My wife—Seth's mother—had cancer. She'd dreamed of redoing the kitchen, and I wanted to make sure it happened." He looked around. "I just wish I'd gotten to it sooner."

Startled, Robin saw that she'd rested her hand on his forearm, and he was looking down at it. Embarrassed, she snatched back her hand.

He only smiled and said, "Thank you. Let me show you to your bedroom. I'm guessing you didn't get a lot of sleep earlier."

She wrinkled her nose. "I tried."

A low, rough chuckle charmed her.

"This is so nice of you," she hurried to say. "I mean, taking us in this way. Seth insisted you would before he'd even asked you. I guess you didn't have a lot of choice."

"Nonsense." His kindness was tangible. "Seth

wouldn't have brought you here if you weren't in some serious trouble. I may be retired from the job, but I'm not incapable."

"Did Seth tell you about the man who tried to take my son?"

"He did."

"I've never been so scared in my life." And that included the two times she'd been certain Richard would kill her, when he'd lost even a semblance of restraint. "If anything happens, please save Jacob first. No matter what."

Eyes keen, he studied her face. Then he nodded.

At the same moment, she realized Seth was hovering in the kitchen doorway and had undoubtedly heard her request. Well, she would have asked the same of him when she got a chance, anyway. She tipped up her chin, saw his eyebrows twitch. Finally, he inclined his head in acknowledgment. And agreement, if she wasn't mistaken.

Then he came into the kitchen as if nothing had happened. "What do you need upstairs right now?"

Robin picked out the bag that held her toiletries and pajamas as well as clean clothes she could put on in the morning. Which was all of about two hours away, thanks to Jacob's early-rising habit.

Seth had wrapped Jacob in his blankie after lifting him out of the car, so she knew he had that. Blue bunny was...in that bag, she thought, along with a bunch of Jacob's clothes and toys. She picked it up, too, before being hit with an inexplicable feeling of abandonment.

"I suppose you're going home."

Seth shook his head. "No, I'll sack out here. Dad

keeps my bedroom for me, except when my sister and her family are home and need it."

"Oh." Feeling uncharacteristically shy again, Robin said, "Well, good night, then."

"To you, too."

As usual, she hadn't a clue what he was thinking as he watched her follow his father toward the staircase.

HOLLOW-EYED FROM lack of sleep, pain throbbing in his temples, Seth poured himself his third cup of coffee for the morning and got on the phone as soon as he reached his desk.

It didn't take him long to connect with a sergeant at Seattle PD who proved willing to look for any domestic violence calls to Richard Winstead's address.

"Not a one," he said at last. "You know who Winstead is, don't you?"

"Better than you do, I suspect. I suppose the house is on a big piece of property."

"I'd call it an estate. Waterfront. That part of Magnolia—" He broke off. "You're suggesting neighbors wouldn't have been able to hear crashes or someone screaming."

"I'm asking."

"It's a butt-ugly house," the sergeant said thoughtfully. "I've heard it's like Bill Gates's, wired so lights turn on when someone walks into the room and off when they leave it. That kind of thing. Heat and appliances can be controlled from a distance by an app. I guess it was on the cover of a magazine for architects, but when I drove by I thought the really nice older brick mansions on each side were doing their best to lean away."

"I know the kind of place you mean," Seth said, kneading the back of his neck with the hand not holding the phone.

"I thought Winstead was divorced," Sergeant Hammond said thoughtfully.

"He is. Unless he's remarried, that I don't know about."

"Ah, let me check." The clatter of fingers on a keyboard came through the phone. "Nope." He paused. "The divorce wasn't contested. Is there something I should know about this?"

"His ex-wife is here in Lookout. I'm investigating the murder of a woman in the ex-wife's kitchen. Victim looked a lot like the ex. I think she was the intended victim."

"Robin Winstead."

"Robin Hollis now. She went back to her maiden name. And yes. She says Winstead swore if she ever tried to leave him, he'd kill her."

"You got any proof?"

"I'm working on it. Okay if I get back to you in a few days?"

"Looking forward to it."

Seth modified a template for requesting medical records and printed a couple of copies, then drove back to his father's house hoping Robin would be awake. She'd been deep under when he left, although Jacob was wide-awake and cheerful. Seth had disposed of the sodden diaper, cleaned up and dressed the little boy, and escorted him downstairs. He'd been happily settled in front of a short stack of pancakes when Seth left. Dad liked making pancakes.

Wan and sporting purple bruises beneath her eyes,

Robin sat on one of the stools in the kitchen nursing a cup of coffee when he walked into the house.

He raised his eyebrows. "Where's Jacob?"

"Your dad took him outside. Apparently there's a tire swing out there?"

"Hey, yeah." His headache relented briefly. He half sat on the stool beside her, laying the manila folder on the granite surface of the island. "Ivy and Sara love it. Dad will watch out for him, don't worry."

Her freckles stood out more than usual, he saw, probably because the only other color in her face were those circles under her eyes. He wanted to smooth some of that stress away, massage her neck and shoulders until she moaned.

Instead, he kept his hands to himself as she smiled, looking as exhausted as he felt.

"I know. Your father's being really sweet. You, too. Jacob said you gave him another bath."

"We boys have to stick together." Man, he needed to get out of here. Seth flipped open the file and took a pen from his shirt pocket. "I need your signature."

She stared blankly at the permission form. Eventually, he thought she actually started taking it in, finally signing both copies and pushing them back to him. He gently removed the pen from her hand.

"Take a nap when Jacob does this afternoon, Robin. I'll bet you didn't get three hours of sleep last night."

She searched his face. "You look tired, too."

"I'll cut the day short if I can," he said gruffly. There was plenty he wanted to say and do, but he restrained himself, leaving with her a distantly polite "Thank you," grating as though he'd lost a layer of skin.

Chapter Nine

The next day, Robin came to the conclusion that Seth intended to stay at his father's house as long as she and Jacob were there.

His presence both relieved and unsettled her. Robin would have felt horribly guilty if his poor father had been left alone to deal with the awkwardness and extra work of guests he hadn't even invited. But when Seth was home, she became self-conscious, aware every second of where he was, whether he was watching her or they might touch in passing, how she looked…and of all the darkness in her past that he didn't know about.

When he came in the door on Tuesday, his expression was grim enough to alarm her. His face was harder than usual, the angles sharper.

To give herself a minute, she turned on the burner beneath the water that needed to boil for the pasta. "Something's wrong."

He shook his head, but the deeper lines in his forehead and beside his mouth didn't smooth out. "Smells good."

She was making spaghetti, which Michael said was a favorite of his and was also a meal a two-year-old would eat. Robin asked fiercely, "Then why do you look like that?"

"Look like—" He scrubbed a hand over his face without having any effect, then glanced around. "Where's Dad?"

She grimaced. "Where do you think? He created a fiend when he put Jacob on that swing."

A faint smile rewarded her. It vanished almost immediately. "I got some of your medical records today."

"Oh." She couldn't meet his eyes.

"Several of the hospitals emailed records and X-rays. They were hard to look at."

"Surely you've handled domestic abuse cases before."

"I have. But damn, Robin. I didn't know any of the women as well as I do you. I didn't—" Seth shook off whatever he'd been about to say. "There were a couple of notes expressing doubt at how you were injured. I'm having trouble understanding why the doctors who saw you didn't call the police."

She clasped her hands together so he wouldn't see the tremor. "Richard, that's why. He'd probably met most of the doctors at fund-raising events. He's that well-known. Slick, too. Along with always having a believable explanation, he was really good at seeming scared for me, loving. Looking back, I don't understand why I didn't speak up. Maybe I thought—"

Seth cut her off. "It's not on you, Robin. Abused women rarely ask for help in that situation. You have to know that. Maybe you didn't think you'd be believed, and you knew what the consequences would be once he got you home. Maybe you still loved him, had hope he really was sorry."

"No. Not that." She was glad of an excuse to turn away from his troubled gaze to stir the sauce and dump the spaghetti into the now-boiling water. "I was afraid of him. And yes, he's a lot more compelling than I am. I *didn't* think anybody would believe me."

"Even your family?"

"If Dad had still been alive, I would have gone to them." She thought. "But if I'd put Mom and Allie in the position of having to defend me, I don't know what Richard would have done. He had a temper, but mostly he was so cold." Hard not to shudder. "He could be smiling one second, knocking me to the floor the next. No warning. I didn't want him even remembering I *had* family."

Seth swore again. "How are you talking about this so calmly? Working on dinner as if it all happened to someone else?"

She huffed in disbelief. "You think I'm *calm*? I'm refusing to crumple up in a sobbing heap, that's all. Your people-reading skills need some fine-tuning."

He moved so fast, she didn't have a chance to retreat. He was suddenly right there in front of her, inches away, his fingers flexing as if he wanted to reach for her. His visible regret, even anguish, brought a lump to her throat. "I'm sorry," he said roughly. "I know better."

"No." Damn it, her eyes stung. Refusing to let herself cry, she took an angry swipe at her cheeks with the back of her hand. "Oh, crud. I'm a mess."

"Robin." Now his hands did close on her shoulders. "I swore I wouldn't do this, but I think I need…" He didn't have to finish the sentence. His hard embrace said it all.

She responded the way she had last time, taking

comfort from him she didn't deserve but couldn't resist. Laying her cheek against his shoulder, she wrapped her arms around him and let herself lean against that solid body and soak in his strength. It could be for only a moment; she didn't want his father to walk in on them, and she couldn't let herself weaken for too long.

His heart vibrated against her breast, and she felt him rub his cheek against her hair. Or had he kissed her on the head? That lump in her throat had swelled to monumental proportions.

"Robin," he murmured. "You really get to me. You know that, don't you?"

She straightened enough to be able to see his face, eyes that had never been so blue. "Because you feel sorry for me?"

"Angry for you," he corrected. "You're a strong woman." His jaw flexed. "A beautiful woman. And I shouldn't have even said that."

"Why not?"

"As much as I want to kiss you, I need you to be able to trust me more." He made a sound in his throat. "Which means I should get my hands off you."

His arms tightened instead, for only an instant. Feeling his arousal, heat settled low in her belly.

"I like your hands on me," she admitted.

He groaned. "I'm trying to behave myself."

She ached to feel his mouth on hers, but how could she initiate anything when she still had secrets? Still, she gripped his shirt in both hands, unable to look away from him.

His head bent slowly, so slowly she knew he was giving her time to retreat. Instead, she pushed herself up on tiptoe to meet him.

APPARENTLY HIS RESOLVE was tissue thin, because Seth did exactly what he'd sworn he wouldn't: he kissed the woman who depended on him to protect her son and keep her safe.

The woman who'd drawn him since first sight.

He might want to devour her, but he did keep enough of a grip on himself to make the first contact gentle. A brush of his lips over hers. Back again. He lifted his head and saw the stunned pleasure on her face, her eyes melting caramel, her lips parted. That's all it took for him to lose it. He groaned, cradled the back of her head so he could angle it for the best fit, and deepened the kiss. His awareness of his surroundings blurred. All he knew was her, the soft press of her breasts against his chest, the taut arch of her back, her taste and breath and small, involuntary sounds. He gripped her butt to lift her, and somehow pulled out the elastic in her hair to free the silky mass to fall over his hand and her shoulders. He turned her, wanting to boost her onto the counter so he could get between her legs.

But…damn, there was a voice. Not *a* voice—his father's. And it was close.

"Shoot," he growled, bumping his forehead against hers. "Dad's coming."

With a gasp, Robin tore herself away. "Jacob!"

Her son. A boy who'd probably never seen his mommy being kissed by a man before. Even as Seth understood her alarm, he didn't like her obvious shock. She'd kissed him as much as he'd kissed her.

Her back to him, she mumbled, "I almost forgot the vegetable."

"Okay by me." He might have tried for lightness,

but that came out husky. And, *hell*, he couldn't let his father see him like this.

Robin had found a chiding expression for him by the time Dad and Jacob came in the door from outside. Seth had almost hustled out of the kitchen when Jacob rushed to her.

"Mommy! I swinged *high*!"

She laughed and scooped him up for a hug. "I'll bet you did."

Seth kept going. "Gotta wash up."

He used the hall bathroom to wash his hands and wait for his body to accept defeat. Nothing more was going to happen tonight. With the door open, he heard his father say, "Smells good."

"Like father, like son."

God, he loved even her voice, irresistibly warm.

This wasn't helping. Seth reached over to close the bathroom door and stared at himself in the mirror. Mostly, he saw the same bony face as always. He ran a hand over his jaw. Yeah, he could use a shave. And maybe his lips were a little swollen. He'd never seen himself as a handsome man, not like—

Disgusted with himself, he splashed some cold water on his face. Looks didn't make the man. And she'd welcomed his kiss, which he hoped wasn't a mistake.

When he returned to the kitchen, Jacob rushed to Seth, who hoisted him high over his head. The boy squealed in excitement and laughed. Seth lowered him to his feet and said, "I think it's time for dinner, buddy. What do you say we set you up at the table?"

"Thank you," Robin said distractedly.

He had to wonder whether her cheeks were pink from the heat of the stove or self-consciousness with him.

"Michael," she said, "will you get the garlic bread out of the oven?"

The house had a rarely used formal dining room. The family had always gathered in the kitchen, where the table easily seated six. Like the stair gates, Michael had kept a high chair, which Seth now strapped Jacob into. The kid immediately grabbed his spoon and began banging it on the tray. He chanted, "Sghetti! Sghetti! Sghetti!" until Michael distracted him with a piece of bread.

Seth caught an odd, possibly wistful expression from Robin, who'd paused to watch her son. He strolled over to her and, in a low voice, asked, "What are you thinking?"

"What? Oh! Just about dinner."

"Not just about dinner."

He thought she was concentrating on draining the spaghetti, but she said suddenly, although also quietly, "Just how much Jacob is enjoying attention from you and your dad. He's never really known a man very well. When his day-care operator's husband comes home, Jacob is really shy with him."

She poured the spaghetti into a large ceramic bowl and handed it to him. "Sauce is already on the table. I'll get the peas…" She glanced around, as if sure she'd forgotten something.

"Parmesan?" he suggested.

A minute later, they sat down around the table. Seth thought of how empty his own house was, and didn't like knowing that Robin and Jacob wouldn't stay forever. In fact…was that what she'd been worrying about, too?

His father and he had been giving Jacob something

important. Clearly, Robin didn't have any men in her life to replace them. Seth switched his gaze to the boy, who had cheerfully splattered his cheeks in red sauce as he switched between a fork and his hands to shovel in the pasta.

"Sghet-ti," he sang around a bite.

Seth laughed. "Let me wipe your face."

Jacob submitted to the cleaning, then grinned at Seth and deliberately smeared his hands over his face.

Laughing again, Seth said, "Okay, we'll wait to clean you up until you're done eating."

"This is an especially perilous meal," Robin said with amusement. "You notice I used a *giant* bib."

"I did. Although I think he's got some sauce on his sleeves."

She rolled her eyes humorously. He liked that she didn't stress over messes.

Aware his father's gaze rested on him, Seth concentrated for a minute on eating. What he'd just discovered was that he didn't want any other man in Robin's life, or to fill Jacob's need for a father.

The realization felt like a tiny lurch in the fabric of reality. Man, he was getting *way* ahead of himself. Yes, he knew now that she hadn't exaggerated her abuse at the hands of Richard Winstead. At least that much she'd told him was the truth. He remained uneasy, in part because she must have known that she could have gone to the cops in Seattle. Whatever Winstead's reputation, her medical records were overwhelmingly persuasive, and Seth hadn't yet received them all.

Was Robin truly still so terrified of the man, she wore blinders, thinking she had to live her entire life on the run? Or was there more?

As if she were a child again, Robin wound the tire swing around and around before she climbed into it. Spinning until she couldn't tell up from down was fun then. So why wouldn't it be now?

Because she already knew how it felt to have her life spin out of control?

To heck with it. She was going to do this.

She put one leg at a time through the tire, worn bald before it found a new life. Firmly gripping the rope right above the knot, Robin took a deep breath and lifted her foot from the ground.

The tire spun once, twice, three times, gaining speed. She leaned back and looked up at the tree branches and the sky. Her eyes couldn't focus anymore, so fast did everything tear by. Oh, Lord—bile rose into her throat. She was going to be sick. She had to stop… With a bounce and a countertwirl, the tire slowed and she hung there for an endless moment.

"Fun?" Seth asked.

She clapped her hand over her mouth and squirmed out of the tire, falling to her knees on the grass. She was humiliatingly aware that he'd crouched beside her and was gently rubbing her back while she dry-heaved.

Thank God, she didn't quite puke, but her mouth tasted awful and she felt as if she was still in motion.

With a hint of humor, he said, "You wouldn't catch me dead doing that anymore."

"Ugh." Robin let her head sag. "It used to be fun."

"Stinks to get older."

Her stomach muscles hurt and her head still swam. "Just what I needed to hear."

He chuckled. "Lie down. You'll feel better."

Since she wasn't capable of doing much else, she

sprawled onto the grass on her back, arms and legs splayed. There were the tree branches above her again, still moving—no, only the leaves danced in a breeze—against the blue backdrop. Seth had risen effortlessly to his feet and looked down at her. At the moment, he was the quintessential detective, wearing dark slacks, a white button-down shirt, a badge clipped to his thin black belt and a big black gun holstered at his hip.

"Why are you home?" she asked.

"Decided to take the afternoon off. Hey, let me get you something to drink." He disappeared from her limited range of vision.

Something to drink? To rinse her mouth out, he meant. Robin ran her tongue over her teeth and made a horrible face. He was right, though; she did feel better with her body, head to heels, in contact with the nice, solid earth.

Seth walked into sight with a can of lemon-lime soda in his hand. Her gaze zeroed in on it.

He laughed, crouched again and helped her sit up, then popped the top off the can and handed it to her. Then he sat, too, his back to the thick bole of the maple tree.

Robin sipped cautiously at the drink.

"I've been thinking," he said in a casual tone that instantly made her wary. "Why don't you use my phone and call your mom and sister? It should be safe." He shifted his weight to dig his smartphone out of a pocket.

She gave her head a hard, almost frantic shake. Not the reaction he'd expected, she saw from his narrowed eyes.

Or maybe it was. Was he just being nice to suggest

she call home, or did he have another motive? Could his phone be set up to record everything she said?

Sure it could, although she felt guilty. If he was just being nice…

"Why not?" he said softly.

And she knew. This was a setup.

"All I'd do is scare them if I told them what's been happening. I'll wait until, well, things are resolved." Like Richard behind bars? Uh-huh, and how long would he stay there? He'd have no problem paying bail, or hiring the sharpest, most amoral attorney in Portland or Seattle to represent him.

If she stayed in hiding, how would Richard ever be caught doing anything to *get* arrested? Did Seth, a small-town detective, have a chance in hell of finding proof Richard had hired the unknown stranger who had tried to steal Jacob?

Of course not.

Sitting cross-legged, she asked somberly, "What are we doing here, Seth? Jacob and I can't become the guests who never go away. Your father doesn't deserve that. It's not that I'm eager to go home—" would the rental even feel like home? "—but if I don't become bait, there's no way to nail Richard. And how's that going to work, when I refuse to put Jacob at risk?"

"I wouldn't ask you—" He sounded offended.

"Then what?" Robin jumped to her feet. "You should have let me go." She left him and hurried toward the house.

The tension was getting to her. That was the only explanation. It was ironic, since she was certain she hadn't been safer in years. Here she was with a police detective and a retired cop guarding her and her child.

If only Seth didn't inspire feelings in her she'd believed to be dead. After that last year with Richard, how could she have melted in Seth's arms the way she had? If they'd really been alone, she doubted she'd have stopped him if he had hauled her off to his bedroom.

So, okay, he was attracted to her, but even assuming there actually was a resolution—whatever that might be—and she stayed in Lookout instead of returning to Seattle, why would he go for a woman with such a turbulent background, a woman who was also an emotional disaster? Tall, athletic, sexy and with those startlingly blue eyes, he surely had women coming onto him wherever he went.

And all that was assuming she didn't end up back in Seattle not by choice, but because she had to fight a murder charge.

Face it, she shouldn't be thinking about a man at all, when she ought to be praying she could go home to Seattle so that she could give Allie one of her kidneys.

Looking through the window over the sink, she saw Seth walking slowly toward the house, lines of perturbation showing on his forehead, his gaze somehow turned inward.

Sure, she thought desperately. Just put him out of her head. Nothing to it.

If only he wasn't so ever-present…and so sexy.

Chapter Ten

Seth was already getting to know Sergeant Gordon Hammond of the Seattle PD well enough to be comfortable talking out possible strategies. Robin was right; they'd never catch this SOB red-handed unless they opened an apparent window to tempt him into making a move.

With her permission, this morning Seth had forwarded her medical records to Hammond, who'd sounded as grim as Seth felt when they talked this morning.

Hammond had been finding it harder than he'd expected to keep an eye on Richard Winstead's whereabouts.

"He has a private plane, I've learned. If we had a warrant, I could be informed when or if he flies in and out of Boeing Field, but as it is, I don't have a good contact there. Some of his activities are well-publicized, but there are enough gaps, I'd have to have someone on him twenty-four seven to keep track of his whereabouts."

"What about this week?"

"Well, in theory the man works full-time. He's a partner in a major law firm, after all. In practice, he attends every city council meeting, and he's on at least two subcommittees. In the next couple of weeks, all those meetings are during the day."

"Committees?"

"Housing, Health, Energy and Workers' Rights is one, and isn't that a mishmash, and then there's Governance, Equity and Technology." Hammond was clearly reading off a website or his notes. "Both committees can meet up to a couple of times a week."

"A man of dependable judgment," Seth said drily.

The sergeant snorted. "I suppose his civic activism is good for the law firm."

"Oh, I imagine his partners consider it part of his contribution to the firm's profits."

More thoughtfully, Hammond said, "I'm assuming there'd be some record if he *didn't* attend a meeting he was supposed to be at."

"I'd rather know in advance when he's out of town." Seth rested his elbows on his desk. "And then there's the problem of his hired help."

"Since you can't be sure Winstead has ever been in Lookout, that's the bigger problem, I'd say."

"Ms. Hollis hinted at the possibility of offering herself as bait. I don't like it, but I might find a way to make it appear she's back home at the rental." His department didn't have any female officers, but the county and a neighboring town or two did. He might be able to borrow a stand-in.

He frowned. What were the odds he'd find one who bore any resemblance to the woman who was currently giving him sleepless nights?

"If she's willing to testify," the sergeant said hesitantly, "we could bring him up on the abuse."

"Even if he were convicted, he'd be out of jail in the blink of an eye and mad as hell."

"How did he find her? Twice?"

Seth pinched the bridge of his nose between his thumb and forefinger. "It's harder to disappear than it used to be. We both know that. Doesn't sound like she had any professional help, either."

"And he can afford to write a blank check to a PI."

Seth gritted his teeth. "If I can find out who that is, I'd like to have some words with him."

Hammond agreed, and promised to let Seth know what he learned about Winstead's plans in advance.

A report half an hour later that shots had been fired at the high school pulled Seth away from his desk. Over the next hours, he interviewed dozens of students and the baseball coaching staff before finally arresting a young idiot who appeared shocked at the official response and insisted, "If I'd really wanted to shoot someone, I would have! All I did was…"

Get himself in some serious trouble. But at least there were no victims. Thank God.

Of course, writing reports killed the rest of Seth's working day. He didn't know when he'd been so glad to leave work. If that's what he was actually doing, he mused. Cops had been known to blur the relationship line between professional and personal, but not him. With Robin and Jacob, though, he'd crossed right on over. In fact, he wasn't sure he could find the line again, unless and until they walked out of his life.

Halfway to his father's house, Seth was still brooding. That was also the moment when he realized he hadn't been paying any attention to the traffic around him. Usually it was instinct. Given that he could lead someone right to Robin and Jacob, he'd been even more careful than usual in the past few days.

A silver sedan and a black crossover were behind him. He took an abrupt turn at the next intersection. The crossover kept going, the sedan stuck behind him. Both roads were well-used, so that didn't necessarily mean anything. Two more turns, and he'd lost the sedan, too. Still, he zigzagged the rest of the way to his father's, and remained uneasy when he got there, watching for any traffic passing on the quiet country road at the foot of the driveway.

He went in and said hello to everyone, changed into old clothes he kept here for the times he helped his father with yard work or maintenance and went back out. He knew where to find the crawler for sliding under cars, and used it and a flashlight to examine the underside of his Ford F-150 pickup truck. He slid his fingers inside the bumper and beneath the license plates, failing to find anything.

When he sat up, his father and Robin both stood over him.

"Car problem?" his father asked.

"Where's Jacob?" He turned his head.

"Watching TV."

"Nothing wrong with the truck. I just got to thinking how easy it would be to plant a tracker." It was Robin he looked at when he said, "I'd be bound to lead someone to you eventually."

"What a wonderful thought." She whirled and hurried back into the house.

His father nodded at his pickup. "You sure you would have found it?"

"Not a hundred percent, no. I need to take a look inside, too, even though I kept the doors locked."

Michael shrugged. They both knew how easy it was to pop a window and unlock a car or truck. Patrol officers carried a tool to help them do exactly that for citizens who'd locked their keys inside their own cars. Seth, for one, could do it in twenty seconds or less.

"Robin cooking again?"

His father scowled. "I offered to grill, but she insisted. Seems to think she owes me something for letting her and the boy stay here. As if they're any kind of burden."

Seth grinned. "When the truth is, you're enjoying the company."

"Nice lady who cooks, great kid. Of course I am." His father smiled. "Remember how whiny Ivy was? And that stretch when I swear the only word Sara knew was *no*?"

Laughing now, Seth said, "Yeah, I think that's why Grace brought the girls out here that time. She was ready to tear her hair out. Huh. Jacob is bound to learn the power of 'no.'"

They were both chuckling when they returned to the house, where spaghetti was once again on the menu.

Robin apologized. "I made way too much sauce. I don't know what I was thinking. Usually at home I freeze it in small batches, and I could have done that, but I thought why not have it another night?"

"Sghetti," her son said happily.

Jacob was less enthusiastic about the broccoli until Seth held up a clump and said, "Look, a tree," and gobbled it like a monster. Jacob gleefully followed suit.

Robin shook her head. "Why didn't I ever think of that?"

They all laughed.

His dad said, "So what's this I heard about a shooting today?"

Robin's alarmed gaze swung to him.

"A stupid teenager, what else? He was mad because the baseball coach suspended him after he was arrested at a kegger. He just wanted to scare him a little in payback. Apparently the kid hunts, and insists he made sure he didn't hurt anybody."

"I hope he wasn't eighteen," Michael said.

"Had his birthday in January. Boy's in trouble. I don't think he gets it."

Seth saw Robin eyeing Jacob with some wariness, clearly concerned for him.

His father declared that he'd take KP duty tonight, and Seth sat Robin down to talk. They went outside onto the deck so Jacob could run around on the lawn and she could keep an eye on him.

"Do you know whether Richard kept an investigator on retainer?" Seth asked.

"Like a firm, you mean? Why would he?" She made a face. "Before he set out to find me, I mean."

"He may have other ongoing problems. You can't be the only person who has seen behind his facade."

She seemed to be thinking about that, but shook her head in the end. "I don't know about that. Anyway, wouldn't his law firm employ investigators?"

Not ones Winstead would dare use for sleazy work. "Did he ever receive threats?" Seth asked.

"Not that I know of, although he did—"

She covered the alarm quickly enough to make Seth doubt what he'd seen. "Did what?" he prodded.

"Well, I was going to say that the house is well-staffed. That would provide protection when he was home."

"It might. Did he drive himself, or have a driver?"

"Sometimes he'd have someone drive him," she said slowly. "Mostly not."

Seth made a mental note to have Hammond look into Winstead's employees.

"Did he have any employees you'd classify as body-guards?"

Robin jumped to her feet. "Jacob?"

Seth had been keeping an eye on the kid, too, and had seen him go behind the big cedar tree. Before he could tell her, the boy peeked around the trunk. "I hid," he told her proudly.

"No more hiding," she said firmly. "Stay where I can see you."

Seth said, "Hey, I saw a soccer ball in the garage. Let me go get it."

Once he brought it out, he spent a few minutes showing Jacob how to kick the ball and move with it. It was a kid-size one, another leftover from his nieces' visits.

Shaking his head as he returned to the deck, Seth said, "I think it'll be a few years before he's ready to join a team."

"His coordination isn't quite there, is it?"

"Nope." Where had they left off? "Bodyguard," he said, remembering.

"Yes, he did," she said, sounding composed. "The man was his occasional driver. I wondered, though, because he looked like a bodybuilder, you know?"

"What was his name?"

"Oh, boy. I didn't see much of him. McCoy? Mc-Cormack? Mc-something. He was there only about the last year of our marriage. He probably got axed after I made my getaway."

There was something a little too casual about her speech. Seth studied her. "You think his real role was prison guard?"

"Probably. It seemed like every time I went outside, he was *there*. Stepping out of the garage or whatever, eyes on me. You know Richard wouldn't have tolerated incompetence."

"No, I don't suppose he would have," Seth said thoughtfully. He couldn't guess what she wasn't telling him, but he'd lay money there was something. Had she had a relationship with the man? Had he helped her, or at least turned a blind eye, when she escaped? No, if that were the case, why wouldn't Robin say?

This was only one reason why he should have kept his hands off her.

"Could this guy have been the one who grabbed Jacob?"

"No." Not so coincidentally, she chose then to turn her head and focus on Jacob, who had given up on the soccer ball and was rolling down a slight incline.

"You sound sure."

"The guy in the mask wasn't bulky enough."

"But he was too big to be Richard."

"There's…a lot of ground in between, you know."

"Like me, say."

She stole a look at him, her gaze sliding from his shoulders down his torso and along his outstretched legs. Flushing, she said, "You're at least as tall as the bodyguard. You're just not…not muscle-bound."

He had to shift his weight to accommodate his body's response to her lingering inspection, and the betraying warmth in her cheeks. The temptation was there to tease, but Seth hadn't forgotten his earlier thought. *Stick to business.*

"Does your mother know you found a body in your house?"

"No!" She stared at him in outrage. "I told you!"

"You said you didn't want to call now. You might have let her know when it first happened. Say, when you were staying at the inn."

"Well, I didn't."

HE STILL THOUGHT she was lying to him, and he was right. Robin knew she'd never been a very good liar, which was an irony for someone who'd spent two and a half years lying about something as basic as her name.

Even when she wasn't looking at him, his sharp, assessing gaze made her want to squirm…and tell him everything. She had to get away.

Acid burning her stomach, she asked, "Are we done?"

"We can be." Seth raised his eyebrows. "Doesn't mean we have to rush inside."

"I'm lucky Jacob has entertained himself this long."

"You're right. I'm on the job."

With easy athleticism, he bounced to his feet. In no time he had a giggling Jacob chasing him around the yard. When he let himself be caught, Seth turned the tables and lumbered after her son. He scooped up Jacob,

powerful biceps flexing, tucked him under one arm like
a football and raced around the yard.

Breath catching, Robin started to rise to her feet.
Jacob would be scared… But he wasn't, she saw in as-
tonishment. They both ended up sprawled on the grass,
laughing.

She'd swear Seth was enjoying himself as much as
Jacob was. In that moment, she felt something entirely
unfamiliar. *Yearning* was the word she came up with.
Why couldn't Jacob have a father like this, instead of
the one she prayed he never meet? What couldn't *she*
have a man like this?

Seth embodied such contradictions: ruthlessness and
a capacity for protection, with kindness and a powerful
defensive instinct. The guardedness that she guessed
was typical of cops with an ability to live in the moment with a little boy.

He did want her, but Robin couldn't imagine he
wouldn't despise her once he knew she'd been tested
three years ago and been found a match to give her sister
a kidney, but hadn't done it. Endless rounds of dialysis
kept Allie from having any kind of a life. She couldn't
hold a job or even live alone. If she had a boyfriend,
she'd never said so during any of her brief conversa-
tions with Robin. Allie must hate her, Robin thought
with familiar self-loathing. When she screwed up her
life, she'd damaged Mom's and Allie's lives plenty, too.

Maybe she should give up and tell Seth everything.
Get it over with. Why put off the inevitable?

Because he was a cop. He couldn't let her confes-
sion that she'd killed a man slide. She could claim
self-defense, but since she'd been trespassing at the

time, Robin suspected law enforcement wouldn't see it that way.

She discovered suddenly that he'd gone completely still, and she was the object of his unnervingly intent gaze. For charged seconds, Robin couldn't look away. If he could see right through her...well, let him.

In the end, she took the coward's way out and fled into the house.

SETH MADE SOME calls to neighboring jurisdictions on Friday, and determined that Hood River County Sheriff's Department employed a female deputy who might pass as Robin to a distant watcher who saw her moving past a lighted window in the house. She wouldn't fool anyone who got a good look at her, though.

There was a lot Seth didn't like about the idea of setting a trap, however. Starting with the possibility that if Winstead was as good a shot as Robin thought, he could fire from across the street, put a bullet through Deputy Jennifer Hadleigh's head and vanish in seconds. Of course, he'd discover in no time that he'd killed the wrong woman—again—and they'd be back where they started.

Since Seth hadn't worked with the deputy, he had no idea how competent she was, either. Or whether she'd agree to this scheme.

What he did know was that Robin would balk if he suggested putting another woman at risk in her place. That needn't stop them, of course, but while he wouldn't describe himself as sensitive, he knew what Robin desperately needed was to feel in control of her life, not in even less control.

Sometimes, how you made something happen was as important as the result.

The wistful, maybe sad expression on her face when she watched him play with Jacob out on the lawn kept coming back to him. Ignoring his father's curiosity, Seth had followed her last night after she announced her intention of going to bed at a ridiculously early hour. With a hand on her arm, he'd stopped her at the foot of the stairs.

"You don't have to run away from me," he'd said in a low voice.

She'd huffed out a breath. "I have no idea what you're talking about. I'm tired. Jacob's an early riser."

"You have no idea how much I want to barrel right through the walls you've built to keep everyone out."

Her breath hitched. "Please don't," she'd said so softly he'd had to lean forward to hear her. "I need them."

And then she'd jerked away and dashed upstairs, never glancing back.

He'd had to go back to the living room and face his father, who knew him well enough to have a good idea how mixed up he was where Robin was concerned. Fortunately, Dad was also smart enough not to push too hard.

Forcing himself to concentrate on work, Seth sent an email request to Sergeant Hammond inquiring about Winstead's current and former employees. After that, he turned his attention to other investigations that had gone on the back burner. The most significant was a recent series of burglaries, car prowls and mail theft. He'd begun to wonder if they were all being committed by the same person or persons.

He'd started his career with Portland Police Bureau until his mother got sick and he took the job here in town so he could count on being free to help both his parents. Once Mom was gone and his father was past the worst of his grief, Seth could have gone back to the much larger law-enforcement agency, but had discovered by then that he liked the pace of small-town policing and the independence of being the only detective on the Lookout police force. Four years later, he didn't have any regrets.

The kind of crime spree occurring here now was far more common in a city. While patrolling as a rookie, he'd broken up a ring of thieves by sheer luck. Turning a corner in a residential neighborhood, he saw a man leave a panel truck in a driveway, scan for anyone watching and stroll around the side of the house. Seth had parked where his marked unit would be hidden behind the larger panel truck and waited. He hadn't been surprised when the guy reappeared with his arms full. When he saw Seth, he leaped into the truck and tried to take off. Seth had taken the precaution of blocking the tires.

Turned out the electronics and jewelry he'd just stolen was nothing compared to what was already in the back of the truck. Once a responding detective identified the guy, they found his garage full of stolen household goods. Fingerprints nailed two of his friends, who were holding more stolen goods. A lot of people were really happy to come into the police station to identify their stolen items.

Seth had already talked to the patrol officers here in Lookout as well as the county patrol sergeant, and urged everyone to keep an eye out for something as simple as a car moving from one mailbox to another—particularly if the driver was removing mail from the boxes rather than tossing fliers in newspaper boxes, say.

Sooner or later, a sharp-eyed cop would be in the right place at the right time.

Listening with half an ear to the police radio, he checked email. Oh, good—a response from Hammond already.

HEARING THE TV, Robin stepped into the living room. There was a lot of laughter from a talk show that didn't look like anything she could imagine interesting Michael. But gosh, who knew? He was in his recliner with his feet up, apparently watching. Maybe he usually spent all day glued to the television. Maybe he loved soap operas and out of self-consciousness had been depriving himself. It was none of her business.

But seemingly still unaware of her scrutiny, he grabbed the remote and irritably flicked through several stations.

"Hi," she said. "Sorry to interrupt. I'm making soup and sandwiches for Jacob and me, and I thought I'd see if you're ready for lunch."

"You don't have to wait on me." The TV went dark, and he dropped the remote onto the end table. After a minute he said, "I'm fighting some heartburn, but maybe eating something mild will help."

"Are you sure it's heartburn? It might be worth getting checked out at a walk-in clinic."

He smiled at her and lowered the footrest. "I've seen my doctor, and I'm on prescription meds for this. It comes and goes."

"Is my cooking too spicy? I could—"

Michael looked and sounded a lot like his son when he laughed. "It's probably that damn beef jerky I decided to gnaw on earlier."

She laughed. "That does sound like a good possibility. Well, lunch will be ready in ten minutes."

In the kitchen, she heated soup and grilled cheese sandwiches. Which might be a little fatty for someone suffering from heartburn, but Michael could decide that for himself.

Jacob, who'd been playing with his blocks, decided he needed to use the bathroom. She was leading him down the hall when she heard a rattling sound from behind her. The back door handle turning? Had Seth come home early again for some reason?

She glanced back to see the reappearance of a nightmare.

A masked man just outside lifted a gun to slam the butt into the glass pane in the door. Glass shattered, and he reached inside for the lock.

Robin screamed.

Chapter Eleven

Scream still ringing in her ears, she backed out of sight. Michael was at her side instantly. To her shock, he held a big handgun that he must have been carrying all along without her noticing.

"Get Jacob upstairs," he ordered her in a low voice. "Find something to defend yourself with if you can. Don't argue. Now *run*."

She lifted Jacob into her arms, bent over to make a smaller target and ran.

The intruder had started across the kitchen. "Stop!" he yelled.

But she was out of sight, leaping up the stairs. Terrified for Michael down below, but Jacob had to come first.

A bullet smacked into the wallboard just behind her. Three more steps, two. Panting, she debated. Which room? Which room?

Another bark of a gun firing, then a second shot. *Please, God, don't let Michael be killed.*

She lunged into the bathroom, shoved the door shut with her hip and set Jacob down in the cast-iron tub. "Lie down, honey. Don't get up until I tell you to." After whirling back to lock the door, she saw Jacob struggling to stand. "Down! Do you hear me?" She'd never spoken to him so sharply before. She couldn't let herself care that tears ran down his cheeks.

Shouts. More gunshots.

"Mommy?" he whispered but curled up in a ball in the tub.

"Don't move," she snapped. Weapon. Had to find a weapon.

She yanked open the medicine cabinet, but it was nearly empty. She'd brought shampoo and gel in here, but no hairspray. Roll-on deodorant wouldn't hurt a flea.

Her eye fell on the toilet, and she snatched up the porcelain lid. Then she positioned herself by the door, listening hard. A couple of the stairs squeaked, this being an old house. She'd hear anyone coming.

Unless he'd already gunned down Michael and taken the stairs while she was talking to Jacob.

More scared than she'd been even during the earlier abduction attempt, Robin held her breath and waited.

Seth was wadding up the wrappings from the sandwich he'd just finished when his radio crackled.

The dispatcher sounded typically calm as she gave the code for shots fired. "The caller can't see the gunman but thinks he or she must be on the neighbor's property. Any available units respond."

The address was Dad's.

Feeling as if he'd just been gut-punched, Seth accelerated from the curb, lights already flashing. He reported his current location and intention of responding with ETA. Two other officers chimed in, as did one county deputy who seemed to be the nearest of all of them. Then Seth hit the siren, too, and wove his way through the streets toward his father's house.

He decided not to call either his father or Robin, in case they were hiding. Seth reminded himself that Dad wouldn't be easy to take by surprise. He was carrying, and hadn't lost any of his reflexes or skills.

Dad would do anything to protect Robin and Jacob.

Five minutes.

If any of them died, if that bastard took Jacob… Seth's jaw ached and fear swelled in his chest.

The deputy reported on the radio that he was turning into the driveway. He saw no vehicles, didn't hear gunshots.

Seth was close, flying down the narrow, two-lane country road. He got on the radio. "I'm two minutes out. Wait for backup."

The deputy agreed.

Seth took the turn into the driveway at high speed, leaving on his siren and lights as he bumped up the driveway.

He braked right beside the sheriff's department car. The deputy was crouched behind an open door. Didn't look young enough to be a rookie, thank God. Seth was glad to see he, too, wore a vest. After Seth had been shot while with Portland PB, he'd never slacked off wearing his on the job, uncomfortable as they sometimes were.

"This is my father's house," he explained. "There was an attempt to abduct a toddler in town a few days ago—"

"I heard about it."

"He and his mother are holed up here with Dad, who is a retired cop."

They agreed to split up, the deputy going to the front

door, Seth slipping around to the side door. He held his Glock in a two-fisted grip, the barrel pointed down. The quiet didn't reassure him; Dad and Robin would have heard the sirens and come out.

Then he saw the door standing open, glass pane shattered, and he knew real terror.

ROBIN FINALLY REALIZED she was going to pass out if she didn't breathe. What was *happening*?

From the tub came quiet, hiccuping sobs, but Jacob stayed put.

Did she dare open the door and take a look out?

No. If it was safe, Michael would tell her. If he was dead…it wasn't safe.

Her hands shook. She rested the toilet lid on the vanity top but kept her grip on it.

She had to believe Richard wouldn't shoot through the door, risking the bullet hitting the son his ego demanded he claim. Because this was an old house, the bathroom door was a solid slab of wood, not flimsy like the one in her rental house.

Wait, she told herself. *Wait*.

If only she had her phone.

With no clock or watch, she couldn't see the minutes as they passed. Time felt compressed, or maybe stretched; either way, she had no sense of how long it had been since she heard anything but Jacob.

Except suddenly there were voices downstairs, loud commanding ones. Richard, insisting she come out and hand over Jacob? No, that was an exclamation of alarm. It couldn't be Seth, could it? How would he have known to come?

In the act of fumbling to undo the old-fashioned lock,

her fingers froze. Michael wouldn't have had a chance to call 9-1-1 until after the shooting stopped. If he was alive.

No, she didn't dare assume this was a police response.

SETH SWORE VICIOUSLY at the sight of his father on the floor, leaning against the wall but listing to one side. His left hand was clamped to his bloody shoulder. His right hand held a gun that rested on his thighs. Blood matted his hair, and his eyes were glassy.

"Dad!" Seth crouched beside him and gently pried the weapon from his hand.

"I hit the bastard. He must have been wearing a vest."

"But you aren't." Should have provided one, he thought—except he'd convinced himself nobody would find Robin here.

"Robin and the boy, upstairs," his father grunted.

"Gunman?"

"Gone."

The deputy was suddenly there. "Ambulance is en route."

Seth swiveled on his heels. "Will you stay with him?"

"Yeah, let me grab something to stop the bleeding." He returned in seconds with a pile of kitchen towels.

Seth didn't holster his Glock as he moved silently up the stairs. If his father had hit his head, he could have briefly lost consciousness and not know it. If he had…

Seth called, "Robin?"

"Seth?"

Relief at hearing her voice poured through him. "Jacob with you?"

"He's… We were in the bathroom."

Once he reached the hall above and saw her waiting, he wanted desperately to take her in his arms. Instead, he ordered her to go back into the bathroom while he cleared this floor. That didn't take long. Through his own bedroom window, he saw the circus outside: four police vehicles all with flashing lights, and an ambulance coming up the driveway.

How had the intruder made his getaway? The roads had been empty for the past half a mile or more.

Once he had holstered his handgun and returned to the bathroom, he couldn't stop himself from gathering woman and boy into an embrace that was probably too tight.

ROBIN SAT IN a chair holding Jacob on her lap, and watched Seth pace the waiting room. He hadn't wanted to let her come to the hospital, but she'd pointed out that hiding was currently hopeless. Richard knew where she was.

Besides, if she and Jacob hadn't accompanied him, Seth would have had to post at least one officer to guard her at his father's house. That seemed wasteful.

Guilt balled in her stomach like a too-big serving of potato salad that had gone bad. Twice someone had offered to get her a soda, but Robin had shaken her head both times. She was already queasy.

She should never have let Seth take her and Jacob to his father's house. Now Michael was in surgery to have a bullet removed. He'd been shot because of her, just as it was her fault that a perfectly nice woman had been brutally murdered and her family left to grieve. She felt like a Jonah, endangering everyone around her. Sooner or later, Seth would notice that her life was a train wreck and get smart enough to jump out of the way.

On his circle around the room, he paused in front of her. "You okay?"

Robin nodded, even though she wasn't.

"Let me take him." Seth bent to reach for the small boy she held.

Sound asleep, Jacob became deadweight. Her arm had gone numb twenty minutes ago. Still, she made an automatic protest. "I'm fine."

"No, you're not," Seth growled, and pried the boy out of her arms. Jacob's eyelids didn't even flicker during the transfer. Holding Jacob snugly against one shoulder, Seth went back to pacing. The sight was incongruous given that he still wore a Kevlar vest and a handgun at his hip. A man simultaneously capable of violence and tenderness.

She had the sudden imagine of him walking the floor with his own child someday. No gun, pajama pants hanging low on lean hips, powerful torso bare as he comforted his baby by skin-to-skin contact. Patient, strong, affectionate.

Her distress rose like floodwaters behind a dike.

He'd be an amazing father.

Robin had to move. Rising stiffly to her feet, she said, "I need the restroom."

"I'll walk you."

"It's just around—"

The blue eyes skewered her. "You don't go anywhere without me. Remember?"

She nodded and let him usher her around the corner to an unoccupied restroom.

He opened the door and verified that it was empty before he let her go in.

She didn't dawdle the way she might have if he hadn't been hovering outside. Instead, they marched back to the waiting room.

Robin perched on the same chair she'd occupied before. "You still haven't heard from Sergeant Hammond?"

"It hasn't been that long."

It felt like forever. Her sense of passing time was definitely skewed today.

She wasn't certain that it was Richard who'd shot Michael, but she thought so. It was true she had barely caught a glimpse of the intruder, but mostly she was going on his voice. She *knew* his voice.

Seth hadn't argued. In fact, even before his father was put in the back of the ambulance, he'd called the Seattle PD sergeant, asking him to locate her ex-husband.

The surgeon walked into the small waiting room, his mask dangling around his neck. "Detective Renner?"

Robin was on her feet without conscious thought. Seth faced him.

He smiled. "Your father came through the surgery fine. We'll keep him overnight mostly because of the potential for concussion."

A bullet had grazed his head. Michael, of course, had said it wasn't more than a scratch.

"Good," Seth said hoarsely. "When can I see him?"

Probably another forty-five minutes. A nurse would come out to get him.

After the surgeon left as quickly as he'd appeared, Seth sank onto a chair. For once, his vulnerability showed. "*God.* To think Dad had to retire to get shot."

Robin's guilt increased. She made herself sit down, too, but felt her whole body vibrating. "You mean, he had to meet *me* to get shot!" she exclaimed.

Seth frowned at her. "He wanted to help."

"And look what happened," she challenged him. "Will you let me leave?"

"Hell, no!" he snapped, anger flaring. "Is that what you think? You're too much trouble?"

"I know I am!" Seeing Jacob squirm, she pressed her lips together.

Seth jiggled her son with easy competence until he settled back down in what was obviously a comfortable embrace. "No, Robin." His voice was a rumble, bass to Richard's tenor, suddenly soft with compassion in contrast to the frustration of a minute ago. "We'll find a way out for you, and we'll do it together."

Looking down at her clasped hands, she nodded because that's what he'd expect. He hadn't said where she and Jacob would go next, who else would be at risk to try to keep them safe. When she found out, then she'd have to make a decision.

Seth's phone vibrated on his hip. He picked it up, said, "It's Hammond," and answered with a terse, "Renner."

When she reached for Jacob, he let her take him.

MORE TO KEEP from waking Jacob than because he expected to say anything he didn't want Robin to hear, Seth walked out into the hall to take the call.

Hammond asked first about Michael.

"He's out of surgery, no permanent damage. No thanks to Winstead. Did you have any luck finding him?"

"No." The sergeant did not sound happy about it. "I'm

getting the runaround from the law firm and his house-keeper. A senior partner claims Winstead is conducting confidential business this afternoon. Housekeeper says Mr. Winstead will be entertaining guests this evening for dinner. No, she didn't see him this morning, but she rarely does. He is an early riser and has usually eaten and left the house by the time she arrives."

"She doesn't live in."

"She says no one does. She did admit that there is an apartment over the garage, however, and another apartment in the house built for servant quarters. She just claims neither are currently occupied."

He'd ask Robin about that.

"Airplane is gone, no flight plan filed." Hammond paused. "Anything on your end?"

"An officer called rental car companies. Richard Winstead hasn't popped up anywhere."

"So he either borrowed a car or has ID in an alternate name."

"I'd guess the second. He wouldn't want to trust even a friend to keep his mouth shut."

"No." Hammond sighed. "I have a patrol officer down at Boeing Field. I can't guarantee he won't get called away, though."

"Understood."

"Your father doesn't think he wounded the guy?"

"Dad says he went for chest shots. One knocked the intruder backward into the kitchen island, but he rebounded quickly, fired a couple more shots and fled. Had to be wearing a vest."

"Hmm. I guess he didn't expect to face an armed opponent."

"That's my take. He'd have killed Dad, but when he

failed with the first flurry of shots, he wasn't confident enough to continue the attack."

"Hard to explain a GSW to his distinguished guests tonight," Hammond said drily.

Seth felt a smile tug at his lips. "Yeah, a gunshot wound might be socially awkward."

Hammond sighed. "So what's the plan?"

"I haven't had a chance to plan," he admitted. "For tonight, we'll go back to Dad's house. If this was Winstead versus hired muscle, we should be safe tonight."

"What's your gut feeling?"

"He only said a word or two, but Robin seems sure that this time it was him. Hiring someone to grab the boy is one thing. You could claim the mother has gone on the run with him, and you're concerned for your son's safety. Hiring a killer is another story. From what she's said, Richard Winstead has a major ego problem. He'll need to kill her himself, not have it done second-hand."

"Can't argue," Hammond said, sounding weary.

After promising to keep each other updated, they left it at that. Seth returned to the waiting room, pausing in the doorway before Robin saw him. She looked exhausted, drained, although he knew the minute she saw him she'd go back to pretending she was fine.

His heart muscle cramped. She was beautiful to him even now, without makeup, with her hair unbrushed, without the spirit that had sparked his interest at that first meeting. He ached to see her truly relaxed and happy, teasing…or flushed and dazed with passion. The punch in his belly reminded him of how very vulnerable she was right now. He couldn't push.

He walked over to her, irritated when she straightened in the chair despite the sleeping weight of the boy and smoothed out the lines on her face.

"Sergeant Hammond hasn't found Winstead," Seth reported, lowering himself into a chair beside her. "Seems as if he's getting the runaround from staff and the senior partner in the law firm. He's determined that the small plane Winstead owns is not in the hangar, though. If he rented a car when he got down here, he did it under another name."

"That's sort of ironic," she said.

He smiled crookedly. "Yeah, it is. He could have asked for advice from you on how best to do it."

"Except I didn't do it well enough."

Seth let that go. Would he ever have met her if her latest identity had stood up to scrutiny? "According to the housekeeper, your ex is entertaining tonight at home," he said. "If that's true, he can't linger here in Oregon."

"Will we know?"

"Hammond is going to call the house, insist on speaking to him."

"Oh." Some of her tension slid away. "Then…then we don't have to worry tonight."

He laid a hand briefly over hers, balled on the arm of the chair. "I can't forget that he *wasn't* the one who tried to abduct Jacob. If you're sure?"

"Positive."

"Okay. That means we can't totally relax. Once I see Dad, though, we'll go back to the house. With some precautions, we should be fine."

What he'd really like was some backup, Seth thought. He wondered how soon he could get a security system installed, and whether he had to ask his father's permission first. *Probably*, he decided reluctantly.

"Tomorrow is Saturday. I can take the weekend off and then work from the house for a few days," he told Robin. "I'll make sure we have regular patrol drive-bys, too. I wish I knew how he got away so fast. The neighbor who heard the shots and called 9-1-1 didn't see or hear a vehicle. Unfortunately, nobody was at home in the house to the north of Dad's. Best guess, Winstead parked there."

"I know I'd have heard a car arriving. I was in the kitchen putting together some lunch. Except when I was out in back, I've always heard yours when you come home."

He captured her hand again. "Bet you never got that lunch, did you?"

Robin wrinkled her nose. "I've been feeling so sick about what happened, I'm just as glad I didn't eat. But when Jacob wakes up, he's going to be miserable."

"Just as well Dad hadn't eaten," Seth commented, "considering he had to be put under."

Worry darkened her eyes. "I didn't tell you he was having an attack of heartburn. I wanted to have him checked out at the ER, but he insists he's seen the doctor about it and is on medication. Did you know about it?"

"Hell, no!" Seth said, exasperated. "That's Dad for you. He doesn't want to admit any weakness. You must have caught him at a really bad moment, or he wouldn't have told you."

A tiny smile lit her face. "It could be a father-son thing, you know. Here you are, the young bull in the herd…"

He growled his opinion of that, although he suspected she saw his amusement. Yeah, she could be right. That sounded like Dad, too.

He heard his name just then, and insisted Robin bring Jacob through the swinging doors so that they weren't left exposed in the waiting room. The nurse found a chair for Robin, who told him to take his time.

He didn't need long, though. His father was surly about having to stay the night when he'd be perfectly fine at home. "What are you hanging around for?" he grumbled. "Where are Robin and Jacob?"

"Out in the hall."

"For God's sake, take them home!." He glared at Seth. "I don't need you hovering over me like a damn vulture."

Seth laughed. "I love you, too, Dad." He sobered. "Thank you for what you did today. For protecting those two when I couldn't."

"You know me better than that."

"I do." Seth gripped his father's hand. "I wanted to say it, anyway. If Robin had been killed, Jacob snatched—" Throat clogged, he couldn't finish, wasn't ready to say, *I'd have never gotten over it*. Ridiculous considering what a short time he'd known them…but still true.

Never comfortable with talking about emotions, Dad snorted and said, "Get out of here."

Seth was reassured enough to do just that.

Chapter Twelve

A stop at a Dairy Queen after leaving the hospital improved Jacob's mood, and even Seth's, Robin thought. Maybe hers, too. French fries and ice cream fixed everything.

It was astonishing how quickly Michael's house had started to feel like home. Robin sighed with relief walking in—until she saw the torn wall in the hall just beyond the kitchen. These weren't just bullet holes, Seth explained, because a crime scene investigator had dug the bullets out of the wall. More blasé about it than she could be, he experimentally poked his fingers in one hole. His father had fired fewer shots, and had been more accurate, so presumably a couple were embedded in the intruder's Kevlar vest, while only one shot had nicked a corner of the kitchen island.

She stood looking around. "A shoot-out *here*." If she hadn't lived through it, she'd have thought it inconceivable—but then, she'd never expected to find a dead body in any place she lived, either.

Seth glanced at her. "It can happen anywhere."

"Apparently. When I moved here, Lookout seemed so peaceful."

"Relatively speaking, it is. That's why the department needs only one detective. But we have burglaries, domestic abuse, assaults, drunkenness and ugly traffic accidents just like anyplace else."

And the occasional murder.

Seth had mentioned buying some Play-Doh, and now he said, "I need to cover that broken glass. Once I've done that, let's be artists."

Jacob liked watching Seth tack a piece of plywood he'd found in the barn over the upper half of the door. Robin tried to let Seth off the hook on the artist part—him buying the stuff in the first place was contribution enough—but he shook his head. "I need an excuse to play."

Lacking any artistic ability, Robin was intrigued to see how deftly he created a variety of animals before squishing them out of existence to form the next. Jacob concentrated hard and made a creature he called a "doggie" that was semirecognizable and not a whole lot cruder than her own efforts, which Seth eyed with amusement.

Jacob settled down then with his Tobbles, a toy that he seemed to find endlessly fascinating. He could make towers, nest the individual pieces, spin them and laugh uproariously when he knocked the whole thing down.

Seth made coffee for himself and Robin, calling to check on his father while it brewed.

"Asleep," he reported.

"During his whole career, he was never shot?" she asked, her guilt stirred again.

Seth shook his head, smiling. "Most cops aren't. A lot never fire their own gun, either. Some of it has to do with where you work, some with how good you are at de-escalating tense situations, but luck plays a big part, too."

"You wear one of those vests."

"I do, in part because I have been shot. Didn't feel good," he added.

Robin hated the image of a bullet penetrating his flesh, him falling back, bloody and stunned like his father had been. Still, she was curious. "Were you, I don't know, more nervous about doing your job afterward?"

He hesitated. "Nervous? No. More cautious? Yeah. It was a burglary in progress, and I'd left myself more exposed than I should have." He shrugged. "Live and learn."

Here she'd spent years with fear an ever-present companion, and Seth, who did a dangerous job, seemed blithe about the risks. Go figure.

He asked about her childhood, and she found herself sharing good times and bad. He opened up a little about losing his mother, probably because she'd just talked about her father's death and how hard it had been to accept.

"When she was first diagnosed, I was still at an age to have some swagger," Seth admitted. "On the job, I thought I could change the world. And why not? I'd never had big worries at home. Mom and Dad had a solid marriage, there were never any serious financial problems. I won't say Grace and I were spoiled, but maybe close. As a kid, I thought my dad was a real hero, invincible."

And he was, until *she* had come along, Robin couldn't help thinking.

She said quietly, "Today he really was a hero. I'll always see him that way."

"Yeah." Seth cleared his throat. "Yeah." After a minute, he said, "Seeing him break down after Mom's diagnosis, that really shook me. Of course she'd get better! My family was golden, right? Why wouldn't he have faith?"

"He knew more than you did."

His rueful gaze met hers. "Probably. To Grace and me, my parents tried to sound upbeat. Mom's chemotherapy was going great. Sure, she lost her hair, but that summer was hot, and she bragged about how cool it was. Not having to wash, dry, style hair was a bonus. Maybe she'd stick to wigs and not bother growing her hair out again. She admitted to occasional nausea, but nowhere near as bad as she'd expected." Seth gazed at the front window, seeing the past instead of the present, Robin guessed. "I was still living in Portland," he continued. "Never occurred to me to wonder if I was getting the whole story. Until *wham*. Dad told me he was taking retirement. Mom had decided to refuse any more treatments. They weren't working, and all they did was make her miserable."

Robin reached across the sofa cushion separating them and took his hand. He grabbed on hard, sinews standing out on his forearm.

"I hadn't been home in weeks." His mouth twisted. "Too busy, you know."

"Because your parents didn't *want* you to feel that they needed you," she pointed out.

"God forbid they be a burden on me."

"Seth." She waited until he was looking at her. "It's also possible they needed that time with just the two of them. If you'd insisted on coming home to help sooner, you might have robbed them of a chance to appreciate each other and…say goodbye."

He stared at her, unblinking. Finally, his shoulders loosened and he let out a heavy sigh. "Maybe."

"And you came when they did need you," she said gently.

"Yeah." One corner of his mouth curled. "Thank you." And he lifted her hand to his mouth.

The lingering kiss on her knuckles sent tingles up her arm. She hadn't known how sensitive the skin there was.

Or maybe Seth made her whole body sensitive.

Jacob came over for a cuddle and wanted a snack. Robin peeled and cut up carrots and celery, setting out peanut butter and cream cheese for dips. She discovered that Seth liked peanut butter as much as her two-year-old did, but at least *he* didn't smear it all over his face.

He had to take several phone calls that she gathered had to do with other investigations. Robin decided the late-afternoon DQ meal wouldn't hold them until bed-time, and put potatoes and eggs on to boil for a potato salad.

Jacob was getting whiny and tired by the time the salad was ready to eat. She plopped him into the high chair with a toddler-size serving while she also made a fruit salad.

Seth had gone outside to talk, and she heard his phone ring one more time before he came in.

"That was Hammond. Your ex is definitely home. He claims to have flown to Spokane today. Of course he refused to name the client he supposedly met with. Attorney-client privilege." He shook his head. "I'll bet he has some whopping bruises on his chest."

She stopped halfway between the refrigerator and the table. "Really?"

"Oh, yeah. Bullets don't penetrate the vest, but that doesn't mean the impact isn't tremendous. You can end up with broken ribs or collarbone, too."

"I can only hope," Robin said acidly.

He smiled faintly. "I was thinking the same thing."

After cleaning up Jacob's face, she gave him a piece of cantaloupe to gnaw on and squish. She and Seth sat down to eat. Jacob started squirming long before Robin finished her meal, so she washed his hands and face again and set him down. Seth put on a video of cartoons for him and came back to the table.

"He's winding down."

"Yes. I'm glad he didn't see more today, and didn't understand what was happening."

"Me, too. How are *you* holding up?"

Of course she was fine.

Seth snorted. "I don't buy that. *I'm* not fine. I came home to find my father bleeding on the floor. I saw that bullet hole above the stairs. How close did that come to you?"

She swallowed. "Too close. If not for your father—" The knuckles of her hand holding the fork gleamed white.

"Then quit pretending with me, okay?" He shouldn't snap at her, but he'd been all over the emotional map today. The least she could give him was honesty.

Her temper sparked. "That's not really fair. I'm a single mother. For Jacob, I can't let myself surrender to emotion or the flu or anything else. I'm not in the habit of whining, anyway."

Had she stayed with a vicious man longer than she had to because she couldn't bring herself to ask for help? Seth was smart enough not to say that out loud. She was right, anyway; he wasn't being fair. He thought his problem was that he wanted to know she trusted him. Did he want her to throw herself in his arms so he could feel manly?

Probably, although he might not respect her as much if she weren't a woman who pulled herself up after every near-disaster and did what she had to do. Even if that was, occasionally, trying to take off in the middle of the night to go it alone.

"You're right," he said gruffly. "I'm sorry."

"Why do you suppose Richard called me?" she asked abruptly. "He couldn't have really believed I'd just hand over Jacob."

Seth forced himself to shift gears, to consider her question logically. "You so sure about that? He may be incapable of understanding maternal love. Or any love, for that matter."

"I suppose that's true." She pushed back from the table. "I need to put Jacob to bed. If you're not done eating—"

"I'll put the leftovers away." Would she come back down, or go to bed herself, however ridiculously early the hour? He didn't ask. It might be best if he didn't see her again this evening. His control felt shaky.

She nodded and left the kitchen. He heard her soft voice and then footsteps on the stairs.

Seth had another helping of potato salad, called to check on his father again and started clearing the table. The whole time, he pictured Robin upstairs. Kissing her son good-night. Brushing her teeth, washing her face… getting ready to take a shower?

He listened, but didn't hear water running. Changing into pajamas, then.

He closed the dishwasher door and stiffened at the sound of footsteps on the stairs again. She appeared in the doorway.

"I don't know if I can actually sleep yet. I keep thinking…you know."

Seth knew.

"I thought I might watch TV or find a book."

"You don't have to ask permission." He dried his hands. "Why don't you pick out a download of a show if you see anything that appeals to you? I wouldn't mind watching a movie."

"Okay." She vanished into the living room.

Seth squeezed the tight muscles in his neck. A quiet evening with only the two of them could tempt him into doing something he shouldn't. After the brutality of her marriage, Robin might not be ready for a physical relationship with a man. Disturbed by the reminder, he turned off the overhead light in the kitchen and followed her.

She sat cross-legged on the floor in front of the television with the remote, flipping through the options. Hearing him, she looked over her shoulder. "It's been years since I've watched many movies. Richard—" She shook off that memory. "Since then I haven't had the energy."

"I can see why, with your living 6:30 a.m. alarm."

She smiled. "Is there something you want to watch?" *You.*

"Maybe something on TV if you'd rather." He hesitated. "Or we can talk, or sit here in dead silence. Whatever you'd prefer."

After a minute she nodded, rose gracefully to her feet and approached the couch as warily as an antelope nearing a watering hole shared with a pride of lions.

He made a move to stand. "Would you rather be alone?"

"No. I mean, if there's something else you'd rather be doing…"

Seth smiled gently. "There's nothing." He relaxed at one end of the couch and lifted his arm. "Come here."

She came, melting into him as naturally as if they spent every evening like this—which he'd like to do. Seth cuddled her close and bent to rub his cheek against her hair. With his jaw bristly, strands of her hair clung to his face.

"Hey," he said, lifting his head. "Your hair is growing out."

"Out?" Robin sat up, clapping a hand to the top of her head. "You mean the color?"

"Yep. Let me see." He waited until she dropped her hand and scrutinized the quarter of an inch—if that—of auburn roots. "You'll let it grow out, won't you?"

"No!" She twisted toward him in alarm, before blinking. "Well… I guess I can. You know, I was planning to go with light brown next."

He tapped a forefinger on the freckles scattered over the bridge of her nose. "You're a redhead, whether you like it or not." Damn, the huskiness in his voice would tell her what he was thinking.

If she couldn't already.

"Seth?" she whispered.

He cupped her jaw and cheek both, tracing her lips with his thumb. "Yeah?"

"Would you kiss me?"

He made a hoarse sound and obliged. The instant she parted her lips, his tongue drove inside. If hers hadn't stroked his, twined around it, he might have retreated. As it was, the kiss quickly became deep and passionate. He kneaded the back of her neck, slid his other hand up her rib cage until it rested just beneath her breast.

When he lifted his mouth from hers for a quick breath, she scrambled onto his lap. Seth caught one glimpse of her face, cheeks flushed, eyes dreamy. Body surging, he repositioned her so that she straddled him. The tight clasp of her thighs drove him wild.

As the kiss became hungrier, he heard a low moan that had to have come from her throat. The sound ratcheted up his arousal. His evening beard must be scratching her skin, but if so she couldn't mind too much.

She squirmed on him and his hips rocked involuntarily. He slid a hand beneath the hem of her shirt and stroked her back, finding the sharp edges of her shoulder blades, the delicate string of vertebrae. He squeezed her waist, wanting to get his hand between them but unwilling to give up the pleasure of feeling the soft pressure of her breasts against his chest.

Damn, he wished she wasn't wearing pants. He kneaded her butt, nipped her lower lip. Desperation drove him to tear his mouth from hers.

"Robin, let me—"

Her stare held no comprehension.

"I want you."

"Yes," she whispered, and rocked forward and back until he was in acute pain.

A harsh groan escaped him. "No, we need to—"

What? Have sex right here on the sofa? With him distracted, they'd be vulnerable if someone shattered glass again and entered the house fast. He realized he'd quit paying attention to sounds from outside.

At least upstairs he'd have a warning.

"My bedroom," he said.

Her lashes fluttered. Was that uncertainty he saw on her face? Having to ask that question forced him to recall his own reservations. He made himself lift her off his thighs and set her beside him on the couch.

"Robin," he said again, gruffly. "I told myself I wouldn't put you in this position."

"This...*position*?"

Seth swore and lifted a shaky hand to scrub over his face. "You're depending on me to keep you safe. If you have any mixed feelings..."

Her spine stiffened and her chin jutted. "You think I'd go to bed with you if I really had reservations?"

Her tone told him he'd insulted her without intending to.

"That's not—"

"It is." Anger and hurt blazed in her eyes. "*I* asked you to kiss me."

He glared at her.

Robin jumped up.

Seth stood, too, and reached for one of her hands. "I just didn't want you to feel compromised."

There was surprise on her face, but hurt was still there, too.

"What I said is about me. Cops have to be extra careful. I thought you were under enough pressure. That...

what I feel for you could wait." He grimaced. "Except, once I kiss you, I forget about doing the right thing."

Shoulders still stiff, she said, "I'm an adult, Seth. I don't know what will happen with Richard. Tonight feels like we're in the eye of the hurricane. Everything is still swirling around, but here, now, we're safe. I'm attracted to you. This...feels new to me. I was afraid I'd lose my chance if I let the moment pass by."

"I'm sorry." He leaned forward to rest his forehead on hers.

"Let's not look for excuses," she said softly, nuzzling him. "Maybe this isn't the right time."

He jerked his head up. "Don't say that. I was trying to be...scrupulous. But the truth is I've been aching for you, Robin."

She took long enough to search his face that he was afraid she would back off. A nerve jerked in his cheek. Yeah, he wanted her desperately, but he didn't know why he felt so much was riding on her decision now. There'd be a later.

But a tight, uncomfortable knot in his chest made him remember what happened to his father today. Half an inch to the right, and the shot that grazed Dad's head would have killed him. The bullet hole above the staircase told him how easily Robin might have been wounded if not killed, too. He could have lost either or both today.

I was afraid I'd lose my chance if I let the moment pass by.

She was right. Tomorrow, anything could happen. He needed tonight.

THERE REALLY WASN'T any decision at all. Robin understood why Seth had worried that she might feel pressured. It was right for a man with his sense of integrity. She'd gotten mad, but really he'd been trying to protect her. Again.

She stepped forward, smile tremulous. "Good."

His arms came around her hard. She held on tightly, too.

"Will you go up to my bedroom?" he asked, voice rough. "Let me do a last check down here."

"Okay." She let go, feeling his equal reluctance as he released her. "Hurry."

Robin dashed upstairs, pausing only to release the spring-loaded gate at the top and reattach it when she was on the other side. Along with corralling Jacob, it would slow down an intruder.

She rushed to the bathroom to brush her teeth before tiptoeing into her bedroom to check on Jacob. Sometimes he curled into a tight ball to sleep; other times, like now, he sprawled in a careless way that made it easy to picture the future when her little boy would be taller than her, with a deep voice and whiskers.

She cocked her head. Had she heard a bell tinkling? That was strange. Robin tugged Jacob's covers higher and then stepped out of the bedroom to find Seth coming down the hall toward her, his eyes locked in on hers.

Her mouth dried. Just like that, she was a woman, not a mother. His purposeful stride was pure male, predatory in a good way.

He glanced past her into the guest room. "Asleep?" he murmured.

She nodded. "I heard something."

He nudged her a few steps down the hall and into his

bedroom, dominated by a king-size bed. "I tied bells to doorknobs downstairs and to both child gates."

"You set up the one at the bottom, too?"

"I did." His voice was as intense as his eyes. "I want you to feel safe."

"To be able to think about nothing but you."

"Yes."

"I can do that," she whispered, and he kissed her, possessive, greedy…and tender.

Chapter Thirteen

Seth steered her to his bed, where he turned on a lamp. Robin was briefly jarred from the mood when he reached behind his back and produced a handgun that he set on the bedside stand.

Then, instead of kissing her, he began slowly undressing her. After pulling her shirt off over her head, he unhooked her bra. Robin wriggled her shoulders so the straps slid off and the bra dropped to her feet. He stopped for a long moment, his eyes heated as he looked. Matching desire lit coals low in her belly.

She wanted to see him, too. He stood still while she unbuttoned his shirt, but took over to shrug out of it and toss it away. He was beautiful with those wide shoulders and powerful chest, defined muscles that tightened and jerked when she splayed her hands on him and explored. Finding the circle of puckered skin on his side below his ribs, she paused for a brief moment of combined fear and thankfulness that he'd survived. He lasted a whole minute or two, then said, "I want you naked."

They stripped in record time, her able to kick off her slip-ons, Seth having to kneel to untie his boots. She heard a thud when one hit a wall. While he was unbuttoning his trousers, Robin pulled back the covers and crawled onto the bed.

In seconds, he was with her, over her. Kissing her with such tenderness, her bones seemed to dissolve. At last he kissed his way down her throat, rubbed a scratchy cheek on her chest and then reared up to take her nipple into his mouth. She cried out, whimpering when she felt the rhythmic pull all the way to her toes. She kneaded what she could reach of his back. Weight on his elbow, he switched to the other breast.

By the time he returned to her mouth, Robin was desperate. Her fingers dug into those strong muscles as she tried to pull him closer. She wanted him inside her with unfamiliar urgency, but if anything he slowed down, stroking her body and finding every sensitive spot, until finally his fingers slid between her legs.

Her back spasmed into an arch as she felt herself tightening, tightening. "Please," she heard herself say. "Now."

He was there, pressing against her, when suddenly he lurched away.

She heard a ripping sound and within seconds, he was back, seating himself deep with a long thrust. And then he did it again, and again, and her body instinctively matched his pace.

This felt glorious, and yet she was frantic, too. She didn't have to chase an orgasm; it slammed into her. Even as she spasmed, he made a guttural sound and went rigid.

When he sagged down on her, he rolled, taking her with him. Robin ended up with her head on his shoulder, where she could both feel and hear his racing heartbeat. She laid her hand right atop his heart, where it seemed to belong.

And then a chill trickled through her bloodstream. She'd been afraid he wouldn't trust her if she told him all her secrets, but her silence suddenly felt wrong.

She had to tell him everything…but not now. It wouldn't be so terrible if she waited, would it?

He planned to work from home for a few days, so she could talk to him in the morning. Give herself the rest of the night. Soak up all the memories she could, in case his reaction to her confessions was what she expected. Of course he wouldn't be able to ignore the things she'd done…and not done.

But he was hers for tonight.

HOLDING ROBIN CLOSE, stunned, Seth knew he should say something but had no idea what. The thoughts he was having were wildly premature.

"That was amazing," he said after a moment.

Robin murmured something indecipherable.

Apparently she hadn't taken offense, because they made love twice more during the night, and, having awakened to the gray light of dawn, Seth had just cupped his hands around her breasts when a perplexed "Mommy?" came from the hall.

"Damn," he muttered.

Robin shot up, disheveled and disoriented, clutching the covers. "What? Where—Jacob?"

"Bright-eyed and bushy-tailed."

"Jacob?" Robin breathed. "Seth, I don't suppose you can reach any of my clothes."

"Uh…" Seth leaned over the edge of the bed and

was able to snag her panties and jeans. And, stretching, his shirt.

"I'm in here," she called.

"Mommy?" Jacob appeared, wafting the smell of urine. "The bed is wet."

"I can handle this," Seth suggested. Beneath the covers, he yanked on his knit boxers, then swung his feet to the floor and stood. "How about I start you a bath while Mommy gets dressed?"

"Yeah!" Jacob snagged his hand.

Seth grinned over his shoulder at Robin, who still looked discombobulated.

An hour later, the sense of happiness and optimism he'd started the day with had waned. He'd known that sleeping with Robin would change their relationship. How could it not? What he hadn't expected was her to shut him out.

Her smiles were polite and didn't reach her eyes. She jumped up and left the table when Jacob finished eating. Seth was left to finish alone. When he wandered after them to the living room, she concentrated her attention on Jacob. Tiny worry lines scored her forehead. She kept her distance, pretending not to notice when he held out a hand to her.

She did focus on him after he called the hospital. "Will they let your dad come home today?"

"He needs to wait to see the doctor around eleven. He says the nurse thinks he'll be released."

"Oh. Oh, that's good."

Jacob tugged at her shirt. "Mommy, look!"

She admired the tower he'd built and clapped when he toppled it.

Feeling invisible, Seth went back to the kitchen and poured another cup of coffee.

What was going on? He'd swear the night had been as good for her as it was for him, so why would she regret anything about it?

Brooding wouldn't help, so Seth opened his laptop and went online to check his email. He scanned the list. Nothing new from Hammond. Had the sergeant been able to leave an officer watching Winstead's house? Likely not, given the usual budgetary restraints.

His phone rang, a county deputy letting him know that two houses on the outskirts of town had been broken into during the night and the usual electronics, wallets and jewelry taken.

"Fits the profile," the frustrated deputy reported. "One couple was out of town. It was a neighbor who saw the back door open and called. The other family slept through the intrusion."

Frowning, Seth tipped his chair back on two legs. "They've been careful so far *not* to enter homes when people are there."

"Method of entry was the same."

Mostly flimsy back-door locks had been jimmied. Why did people bother with dead bolts on the front if they were going to make it so easy to break into their houses through other doors or windows? Seth particularly disliked exterior doors that had glass panes. Witness yesterday's break-in here. He had so far been unable to persuade his father to replace the damn door, although he'd already made up his mind to do it without asking permission.

"You going to try for fingerprints?" he asked now.

"Captain says yes. He's ticked."

"I am, too. Haven't heard yet, but I'll let you know if anyplace in town got hit last night."

As he set down the phone, he saw Robin hesitating just inside the kitchen. Jacob was settled in watching a movie.

"Are you busy?" she asked.

"No." He nodded at the chair across the table. "Coffee?"

"I think I'll pour myself some water."

She did so and sat down. He could only call her expression bleak. "There are…things I haven't told you."

No kidding. He raised his eyebrows while keeping his mouth shut.

Her gaze slid away. "I should have told you before we…" She stole a look at his face.

"I'm listening."

She shifted in place, moistened her lips and blurted, "I killed a man."

The front legs of his chair crashed back to the floor. *"What?"*

"I think I killed him," Robin said more softly.

"You think."

"I didn't hang around to be sure, okay?"

Seth stared at her. "Start at the beginning."

Hot spots of color on her cheeks and tightly clasped hands betrayed how artificial her calm was. "It was after the divorce. When I saw the chance to sneak out of Richard's house, there wasn't time to go back for anything. I didn't care about clothes or… But I kept some things that were important to me in a box on the shelf in the closet."

He didn't like where this was going.

"I read online that Richard would be away for a few

days, on some kind of conference in San Francisco. I chose a day the housekeeper would be off. I'd have been out of luck if he'd changed the gate code and lock, but he hadn't, so I let myself in. The house was completely silent." Her throat worked. "I hurried upstairs and felt so lucky to find the box where I'd left it. I grabbed it, but when I turned around, *he* was there."

"The bodyguard," Seth guessed. Dread filled his stomach.

"Yes. I'm sorry, I do know his name. It's—it was—Brad McCormick. He gave me this nasty smile and said, 'The boss knew what he was talking about. Here you are, right on time.' And then he grabbed me and started dragging me toward the door." Her voice wobbled.

"Robin."

Naked anguish in her eyes, she said, "Let me finish."

He managed a nod.

"I dropped the box on the bed. I was fixated on not letting anything get broken, which sounds stupid, but—" She hunched her shoulders. "I fought. He… seemed to enjoy it. I thought he might rape me."

He wasn't sure he was capable of speech.

"I managed to scramble away enough to get my hands on the lamp. The base was wrought iron and stained glass, and it was really heavy. I hit him in the head and he just…fell over. I picked up my box because if I didn't anyone would know I'd been there, and I left. Waiting for the bus, I was shaking and my teeth were chattering and I knew I should call 9-1-1 in case he *wasn't* dead, but how could I? So I didn't do anything, which is one more thing to feel guilty about."

"He assaulted you." He didn't recognize his own voice.

"But I was trespassing. With the divorce final, I didn't have any right to be there."

Seth shook his head. "You should have been able to pack the things that were important to you when you told your husband that the marriage was over."

She let out a shuddery breath that might have been a sob. "I did have a social worker call and ask him for the small things that were important to me. She offered to meet him. He laughed and hung up on her."

"So you tried doing it the civilized way." Was he making excuses for her? Seth discovered he didn't care.

Robin squeezed her hands together so hard it had to be painful. "I watched the newspaper. I kept expecting to get arrested. But the police never came, and I never saw anything about the death in the paper or online."

"I can't believe Winstead wouldn't have accused you if he found his employee dead in the master bedroom." He hesitated. "Were there surveillance cameras?"

Shock slowly altered her face. "I...don't know."

"You might have only knocked him out, you know."

"I hoped, but I hit him hard. There was a lot of blood." She closed her eyes. "I've been so afraid ever since then that I'd be arrested and convicted and *he'd* get Jacob."

Unable to sit still any longer, Seth shoved his chair back. "I swear that won't happen." His commitment to the letter of the law had just been supplanted by something more important.

"How can you promise that?"

"Unless he has time-and-date-stamped footage showing you entering the house, how can he prove you were there? That you hit this Brad McCormick over the head? There could have been burglars in the house. He could have been in his boss's bedroom because he was in league with them, only there was a falling out." Seth stalked toward the patio door.

She protested, "But my fingerprints would be on the lamp!"

He swung around. "Sure they were. You shared that bedroom for two years. The surprise would be if your prints *weren't* on the thing."

"The housekeeper…"

"Dusting doesn't remove fingerprints."

Robin's headshake looked dazed. "If I hadn't already known I was pregnant, I would have gone to the police. I hope you believe that."

He went to her and crouched beside her. "You have to know I do," he said roughly.

Her eyes shimmered. "There's something else you need to know." She became fascinated with the the tabletop.

Seth stood, looking down at her. In this light, he could see the auburn roots of her hair better. It made her look vulnerable, as if she'd quit protecting herself from him.

"Will you sit down?" she asked timidly.

Was she *afraid* of his reaction? Hating to think that, he confined himself to a nod. He walked to the doorway first to reassure himself that Jacob was okay. The boy seemed engrossed by the Disney movie.

Then he forced himself to sit across the table from Robin again. Her face was as colorless as he'd ever seen it. Against that backdrop, her eyes were dark and bruised.

"I've mentioned my sister."

He braced himself.

"A FEW YEARS AGO, Allie—short for Allison—was diagnosed with a kidney disease called glomerulonephritis. Doctors don't know what caused it. A lot of the common triggers don't apply to her. It turned out she had only one kidney." Keeping her gaze deliberately unfocused so she didn't have to see Seth's reaction, Robin kept to a near-monotone. "She had to move home. At first she kept working, but she couldn't when she started dialysis. I was still married when her doctor started talking about a transplant. I got tested and was a match."

Of course, Seth had seen her torso and knew she had no scar from surgery.

"When Richard found out I'd been tested, he flipped out. His wife wasn't giving away a body part. He seemed repulsed by the idea that I'd be left with a scar." She took a deep breath. "I had already made up my mind to leave him, and Allie wasn't desperate."

"But by the time you were free, you knew you were pregnant."

"Yes." When the pregnancy test came up positive, she felt so conflicted that it was like the shocking aftermath of a car accident. She had to be sure she could love this baby, Richard's child. Feeling in her heart that she could came as a huge relief. Guilt was in the mix, because Allie was counting on her, ebullient with hope, and now Robin wouldn't be accepted as a kidney donor for nearly a year.

She went on, "Her kidney has continued to fail. They've searched for another donor, but have not found anyone." She made herself meet Seth's eyes. "I could have done it, but I was afraid to go back to Seattle. Afraid Richard would find out. My mother wouldn't be able to stand up to him to keep Jacob safe." She made herself look at him, see a hard gaze out of eyes gone a turbulent blue. Focusing on her hands, she finished in a voice barely above a whisper. "I'm the only person who can save her, and I won't. Allie must hate me. It's…one reason I don't call home more often."

There. Now he knew, and would despise her.

Only… Seth had circled the table and picked her up as effortlessly as if she were a child. He sat down, Robin on his lap, cradled within the solid strength of his arms. She buried her face against his chest so he couldn't see it.

"I do not believe your sister hates you."

He sounded so gentle, Robin felt a tremble deep inside, as if a fault line was shifting.

"We know that Richard has hunted long and hard for you. He has to have spent a fortune paying investigators. Do you think for a *minute* that he wouldn't be watching your mother and sister? That if she were to go in for surgery, he wouldn't know?"

No. She didn't think that. He wasn't just abusive. It had become increasingly obvious that beneath the surface he was an obsessive, crazy man.

"Would Allie be happy to have a new kidney if you died giving it to her?"

"But I wouldn't necessarily—"

"If Winstead had a shot at you, I think you would," he said. "Is your sister still eligible for a kidney?"

Robin bobbed her head.

"Then there's time for you to give her one. I'd rather bring that creep down first, but if this drags on, we'll go to Seattle and I'll make damn sure nothing goes wrong, for you, your sister or Jacob. Do you hear me?"

It took her a minute to regain enough composure to raise her head. He meant it, every word.

That movement inside, the fault line, cracked wide open. Robin had always known she *could* love him. She just hadn't imagined it could happen from one second to the next and be so painful. Remembering what he'd said about his younger self, she thought, *He still has that swagger.* She believed he'd try to keep his promise, but how would she live with herself if he died?

HE'D LIKE TO THINK he had gotten good at reading what Robin was thinking, but there'd been the one moment, an expression Seth didn't understand. Hope, disbelief, fear. Taken together, what did it mean?

He shook the worry off and concentrated on his search, eliminating the Brad or Bradley McCormicks not the right age, who'd never lived in the Seattle area, who didn't meet the description Robin gave him. Why didn't anyone of that name appear on the list of Winstead's former and current employees that Hammond had forwarded to Seth?

An alternative name caught his eye: Braedon McCormick. Seth tugged at the string. This McCormick had been in the army, deployed twice to Iraq, then went to work as a deputy in Lewis County south of Seattle. Didn't last long there, although Seth couldn't determine whether he'd been fired or quit. Following his brief stint in law enforcement, he became an investigator with a somewhat sketchy-seeming PI firm. His name popped up a couple more times...and that was it. Seth tried every option he could think of, concluding at last that only two likely reasons for the disappearance existed. Number one, Braedon had moved out of state; it could be tedious trying to pull up a driver's license or PI license application in another state. Number two, he was dead, albeit with no fanfare. No investigation into his death, no obituary, no funeral.

Seth listened to the clatter from the kitchen where Robin was putting together lunch. Dad would be showing up any minute; one of his buddies from his cop days was giving him a ride home.

Seth stretched as he debated calling Hammond to talk about this McCormick guy. There was a lot he didn't want to say, but a Seattle PD officer might be able to find something Seth couldn't.

While he was still waffling, his phone rang. Hammond.

"Renner here," he answered.

"Thought I'd let you know Winstead is staying put for the moment," the sergeant said. "Real conspicuously. Went out for a fancy breakfast this morning with a female tech executive, then stopped by city hall where he somehow corralled a journalist to give a statement about a proposed referendum. Last report, he went to Palisade for a waterfront lunch with one of the mayor's assistants."

"Pricey?"

"Very," Hammond said drily. "Gotta wonder what his plans are for dinner."

"Listen, Ms. Hollis remembers a man who worked for Richard who isn't on your list. Last name McCormick. He went by Brad, but I think his legal first name is Braedon." He shared what he'd learned about the man.

"He might technically still have been working for the PI outfit," Hammond said. "Does Ms. Hollis think he could have been the one who grabbed her kid?"

No, she thinks the guy is dead wasn't something Seth was prepared to share.

"That's a possibility. He was a sometime-driver for Winstead, but she thought he was more of a bodyguard." He hesitated. "During the months while she was trying to find an opportunity to leave the bastard, this McCormick was always there, watching her."

"All right," Hammond said readily. "I'll start digging."

Question was: Would he unearth a body?

Chapter Fourteen

Robin shut the bathroom door in Michael's face, wishing it had more than one of those useless little push-button locks that could be opened with a bobby pin. *Jacob* could probably pop it.

Not that Michael would try. No, he'd just linger where he'd be sure to see her when she came out.

That seemed to be the Renner men's plan: keep an eye on her at all times. Since Jacob also tended to trail her, she was about ready to go seriously crazy.

She closed the toilet seat and sat down, digging her fingers into her hair and tugging. What would they do if she didn't come out?

Fiddle that stupid lock to open the door, that's what. In Michael's case, he'd act solicitous, be anxious to know why she felt compelled to hide. Seth would just give her a smoldering look that said he was as frustrated as she was. And yes, sexual frustration definitely contributed to her mood. There was no way that she and Seth could make love again in this house with his father home. And where would they go that they couldn't be followed? Outside, where anyone could walk right up to them? Head to his house, leaving Jacob vulnerable with only an injured man to guard him?

She and Seth hadn't talked about it. The closest they came was the first night after Michael was released from the hospital, when Seth walked her to her bedroom door and murmured, "Damn, I want to haul you off to my bed."

She'd squeezed her thighs together in a futile effort to stifle the powerful bolt of need.

Yesterday, during Jacob's naptime, Seth all but dragged her outside and around the corner of the house where he could kiss her until she was limp. Then he'd escorted her back to the deck where he gave her updates from his contact at Seattle PD.

He'd probably wanted to kiss her before giving her the bad news. Braedon McCormick had vanished within a time frame that fit with her having caved in his head.

"There's a lot that's hinky about it, though," Seth had added. "Why wouldn't Winstead have reported the death, if in fact he came home to find this guy dead? If your ex suspected you, he could have gotten you in trouble, which I'd expect him to enjoy. If he'd called 9-1-1 without mentioning you, SPD would have investigated the death under the assumption there'd been an intruder. I doubt they'd have considered him a suspect. Instead, it's looking as if he buried the body or dumped it in the Sound."

She didn't get it, either, although she repeatedly mulled over something else Seth had thrown out. What if she *hadn't* killed Brad McCormick? Furious because his trusted employee had screwed up, her ex-husband could have finished the job, but realized he'd likely left forensic evidence that would give him away.

She'd seen Richard's icy rage when an employee hadn't jumped high enough when he snapped his fingers. Yes, he was capable of murder in a temper as well as killing in cold blood—or, as the law put it, with malice aforethought. Say, an ex-wife who'd had no business leaving him.

With a sigh, she finally gave up and left her bathroom refuge to find Seth and Michael engaged in what appeared to be an intense conversation in the kitchen. Seth broke off midsentence, and both their heads turned the instant she appeared.

"You okay?" Seth asked.

"I'm fine." She'd chosen his least favorite words in the world.

His jaw muscles knotted.

She crossed her arms. "What were you two talking about?"

"Making plans," he said shortly.

"While I was safely out of earshot?"

His mouth tightened.

"You know the smartest thing would be for Jacob and I to go somewhere Richard couldn't find us. You could help me."

"Not an option," he said curtly.

"Why?"

"You need to be free to live when and where you choose. To use your real name." He glanced at his father then back to her. "To get medical care, visit your mother and sister."

She thought he was done. He wasn't.

"Get married."

Robin gaped at him. Was he implying...? Her heart felt as if it was playing hopscotch.

Had she imagined that slight nod?

After a moment, she said in a low voice, "I know

you're right. But your dad was hurt because of us, and if it happened again, to either of you—" She couldn't finish, couldn't say, *If either of you died*. She couldn't forgive herself for that, either.

"Hey." Seth stepped forward and tipped her chin up. "Don't worry so much." He bent his head and kissed her lightly.

It was the first time he'd done anything like that in front of his father, who had been a silent spectator to the scene. Had Michael already figured out that something was going on between them? Or had Seth told him?

She backed away. "I'd better...um..." Spend some time with her son. That was it. She said so, and fled.

SETH COULDN'T HELP wondering why Winstead was so obviously keeping the world apprised of what he was doing and where he was doing it. He might as well be buying billboard space up and down I-5 between Seattle and Portland.

Now, if Robin was wrong in believing that the guy's ego would demand he kill her himself, his current public busyness made sense. With him so easy to track, he might think Robin and the police would relax. A hired gun could stroll right in and take care of her. With Winstead's alibi well-established, he could go straight to court demanding custody of his son.

As things stood, he'd get it, a truth that burned like acid in Seth's gut. He had seriously considered suggesting a quick marriage to Robin so he'd have some legal claim on Jacob, but that wouldn't give him any certainty of winning a custody battle, even with Robin's medical records to show the judge. Didn't matter that Winstead had never met Jacob, when he had the argument that the child's mother had never given him the chance.

He heard the rumble of an engine before he saw a large panel truck coming up his father's driveway. Right on time. Seth went out to meet the lumberyard driver and help unload the door he had ordered. Installing it would give him something to do this afternoon.

Given the thump the door made when he leaned it against the clapboard wall, he wasn't surprised to let himself in to find Robin hovering.

"I'm replacing the door," he said.

A smile played at the corners of her mouth and lit eyes that had been shadowed too often since he'd met her. "I don't know if I want to stick around to hear the fireworks or not."

He turned on hearing the thunder of small, sock-clad feet. Jacob, coming to find out what was up. Seth squatted and the boy threw himself into his arms, allowing Seth to rise easily and swing him in the air. He chortled and held out his arms as if he was flying. He'd taken to galloping to find Seth half a dozen times a day so he could "fly."

Laughing with him, Seth felt a clutch beneath the breastbone. It was a credit to Robin that the boy had such an open, winning personality despite the ongoing fear she'd lived with. Seeing her in his freckled face didn't hurt, either. Seth wouldn't at all mind this kid calling him "Daddy."

Yeah, he was a goner, and twice over.

"Gotta do some work, buddy," he said, when he set Jacob down.

Robin took the boy's hand. "Do you need to go potty?"

"No!" Jacob insisted. "No, no, no, no!"

"Uh-oh." Seth grinned at her. "The terrible twos may be upon us. Ah...where's Dad?"

"While you were outside, he took a pain pill. He said he thought he'd lie down for a while."

Seth grunted. "Why does everybody say, 'I'm fine' when it's a lie?"

"Gee, I don't know. Maybe as an alternative to whining?"

Laughing, he caught her close for a kiss.

Robin laughed and blushed, too.

Seth was able to remove the old door without a lot of racket. He was tapping a shim in place while installing the new one when Dad stomped into the kitchen.

"Did you forget this is *my* house?" he demanded.

"Nope." Seth tested the swing of the door and decided he could go ahead and replace the molding and install the new dead bolt. "What? You wanted me to put in a new pane of glass as an invitation to break in?"

His father glowered. "I keep my weapon close."

Seth narrowed his eyes. "Sure, but normally in a gun safe. You need the house to be secure enough that you have time to dial the combination and get the damn gun out. And I've decided I'd had enough of this argument."

With a snort that sounded like a bull about to charge, his dad stalked out.

"He's mad at you," Robin said after a minute.

Seth smiled. "Not really. It's all bluster and fury."

"Butting heads is more like it."

ROBIN HEARD THE shower running in the master bedroom bath when she slipped out into the hall after tucking in Jacob. Michael must be getting ready for an early bedtime. He'd tried to hide how much he was hurting today, but she'd been able to tell. The physical therapist he'd seen yesterday wanted him doing a set of exercises twice a day. Robin tried to stay out of sight when he did them so he didn't feel as if he had to stifle all the pained sounds. She'd noticed Seth doing the same.

Tonight, when she started downstairs, Seth was waiting for her at the foot. His eyes never left her. He might as well have been touching her, given the way her body activated in response.

"Thought Jacob would never go to sleep," he mumbled, and kissed her.

That's all it took for Robin to forget about her son upstairs, never mind Seth's father. She flung her arms around Seth's neck and rose on tiptoe so he didn't have to bend over so far.

He solved that problem by lifting her until she could wrap her legs around his waist and ride his erection. Groaning, he carried her to the kitchen, where he lowered her to the granite top on the island. His hands were free to rove, and she could still clasp her ankles behind his back and rub against him.

Seth raised his head once and seemed to be listening before he dived back in with a kiss that was all raw need. Within seconds, Robin quit thinking. Here and now was good. Who needed to breathe?

She managed to squeeze a hand between them to unbutton his jeans and fumble for the zipper tab.

Seth wrenched his mouth away from hers and reached down to grab her hand. "Not here." Dark color burnished his cheekbones. "Bathroom. We can lock the door."

Robin was far enough gone to think that was a great idea. To heck with what his father would think if he came downstairs with perfect timing to see the two of them stepping out of the bathroom with wild hair, swollen lips and clothing not quite fastened right.

Seth carried her again. She squirmed against him until he was swearing under his breath. He had her pants off within about five seconds of them reaching the tiny half bath.

"Lock," she mumbled.

"What?" The blue of his eyes was molten. "Oh. Yeah."

He pushed the little button, picked her up and planted her butt on the edge of the vanity top. It didn't even cross her mind that the edge of the sink didn't make for comfortable seating. She was too busy easing down the zipper to free him.

He backed away long enough to sheath himself and then without any preamble drove inside her. When she cried out, Seth stifled the sound by covering her mouth with his. He moved fast and hard, giving her exactly what she seemed to need. Tender and slow was for another time.

Her body imploded. Seth followed, the throbbing almost setting her off again.

Finally, his head dropped forward to rest on her shoulder. He was shaking.

It took them a few minutes to get dressed, but once they had they went to the living room and cuddled on the sofa.

"Sorry," he murmured. "It's awkward sharing the house with a parent. I've been trying to keep my distance from you. I haven't been doing so well with it, though."

"No." Robin rubbed her cheek on his shirt. "Me, either."

They lapsed into a contented silence. It had to be five

minutes before Seth said, "Earlier, when you asked, Dad and I were talking about my idea of putting a woman cop in your house."

Robin pulled away, incredulous. "You think Richard's stupid? He'll know I'd never go back there."

"No, I don't think he'd fall for that, but if I can sneak you away again and the woman cop moves in *here*..."

"What, you're going to abandon your father to face another attack?"

"I intend to send him with you. I'll stay here."

No wonder they'd been arguing. Hadn't Seth known how insulted his father would be?

"I hate that idea," she said fiercely.

His arm tightened around her. "I know."

"He found us here." The certainty had the weight of dread. "He may be back in Seattle, but somebody has to be watching. Richard will find us wherever we go."

"I'd suspect his PI saw my name linked to the investigation and took a look at my house and then my father's, except..."

She had no trouble finishing his sentence. "Detectives don't take their work home with them." Thinking about that, she scooted far enough away to let her really study him. "Why did you?"

"You know why."

"Because you were attracted to me?"

She'd swear she saw a smile in his eyes that hadn't touched his mouth.

"Because I knew you were going to take off. Because with Jacob you were especially vulnerable. Because you looked too much like a dead woman." Now the smile reached his lips. "Because I felt a lot more than lust from the beginning."

Robin made herself ask. "Are you sorry?"

"No." His big hand closed gently over hers. "Never. I'd have been haunted by you for a long time if you'd succeeded in disappearing."

"I...wouldn't have forgotten you, either." She looked away for a moment. "I knew you'd be hurt when you found we were gone," she admitted.

"You were right," he said quietly, eyes intent on her face. "I would have been."

She would always feel guilt about Andrea, but she knew how lucky she and Jacob were that Seth had been the detective in charge of the investigation. He seemed willing to take any risk for them. Robin thought he'd risk a whole lot for any vulnerable woman or child. But...if his dad was right, he'd never brought one home before.

It still boggled her mind that she was able to trust him so absolutely. She could probably thank her father for that. Even at the worst with Richard, she hadn't forgotten that steady, kind men did exist.

"Do you think Richard has given up? That...he's hoping you'll decide it wasn't him who broke in here and shot your dad?"

His face hardened. "No." He hesitated as if not sure he wanted to say this, but chose to go on. "I think he's setting us up."

"I can't imagine he'd be satisfied by killing me secondhand," she argued again. And yet... She tried to get into her ex-husband's head. "I don't know," she finally admitted. "I can also picture how smug he'd feel if the police came to talk to him. He could be laughing inside." She formed an expression of dismay and concern. "'Detective, I was dining with the mayor last night. A

dozen people can vouch that I was there. I don't understand what you think I can tell you.'"

"He'd be home free, except for one little problem."

"The man he'd paid to do his dirty work."

Sounding grim, Seth said, "But Brad McCormick's
disappearance suggests your ex-husband knows how to
solve that kind of problem."

Robin couldn't believe she was having this kind of
conversation about her own, hypothetical murder. Seth
didn't seem to be taking it in stride, either, thank goodness; he looked more disturbed than she felt.

"The thing is," she said slowly, "I still think he'd get
a big charge out of killing me himself. I could never tell
if he actually *enjoyed* hurting me, but…"

Seth's big body jerked.

She swallowed and finished, "There'd be something
in his attitude afterward."

His face set with cold determination. "Let me just
say that if I'm going to have a shoot-out with anyone,
I'd just as soon it was him."

A miniflashback rattled her. "One shoot-out was
enough, thank you. If only we could prove he was here
and you could get a warrant for his guns."

"We've flashed photos at rental-car companies. Cops
in half a dozen jurisdictions have helped. We've even
tried ones in Vancouver." The city was across the Columbia River from Portland, which put it in Washington State. "Unfortunately, given that he owns a small
plane, your ex can land at a private field anywhere.
Now, after all his effort to assure us he's an extremely
busy man who couldn't possibly get away, he'll have a
plan to make the round-trip as fast as possible."

"Lovely thought." She was hugging herself again.

Seth noticed, too. He lifted his arm, and she all but dived into his embrace.

"Damn, I wish I could sleep with you tonight."

Robin thought that this time he wasn't even thinking about sex. She pressed a kiss to his throat. "Me, too," she whispered.

NOT LONG AFTER breakfast the next morning, Robin turned to Seth. "Can you do a grocery run? We really need some basics."

He frowned but gave a grudging nod. He obviously didn't want to leave, but the couple of local grocery stores didn't deliver. "Make a list and I'll go."

"I already have a list. Just give me a minute to make sure I haven't forgotten anything."

Two minutes later, he was gone after a few quiet words with his father.

Michael had a holster on his belt now to carry his gun. Most of the time, Seth wore a long-sleeve shirt with the tails loose to hide his service pistol. Michael wasn't bothering. Robin knew that by now she ought to be used to seeing men openly carrying lethal weapons even to the bathroom or to get a snack out of the refrigerator, but she hadn't totally adjusted. Every time Richard had opened his huge gun safe and insisted she admire his collection, she'd felt queasy. There was a reason why she'd closed her eyes when he made her try target shooting.

And yet here she was now, being guarded by armed men. And glad of them, if a little unsettled.

Michael currently sat at the kitchen table, the newspaper open in front of him. He appeared to be glaring at the new exterior door.

"Damn kid thinks he can tell his old man what to do," he growled.

"He's scared for us," Robin reminded him.

"Mommy?" Jacob had been sitting on the floor playing with his simple wood puzzles, but now he got up and tugged at her pant leg. "Potty."

"Then let's go." Since his kiddy seat was upstairs, she bent to pick him up.

A dark shadow slid across one of the kitchen windows covered by a sheer roller shade.

Chapter Fifteen

Seth's foot kept easing from the accelerator. Apprehension rode him. He shouldn't have left the house. Left Robin, Jacob and his dad.

If he hustled, he could get to town, do the shopping and be back in not much over half an hour. That wasn't very long to be away. They had to eat.

He watched his rearview mirror, checked his phone. If anything went wrong, Dad or Robin would call.

He was lucky this road was so little traveled. If it carried much traffic at all, cars would be piling up behind him.

When his phone rang, Seth pulled to the shoulder. Sergeant Hammond, he saw as he answered.

"We've lost him," Hammond said without preamble. "Winstead is scheduled to be a speaker at a Rotary Club dinner tonight, but that gives him plenty of time to get down there and back. I just called Boeing Field. He didn't file a flight plan—rarely does, according to the woman I spoke to—but he did fly out several hours ago."

"He could already be here." *And I just left my family unprotected.*

"Where are *you*?" the sergeant asked.

"Not where I should be," Seth said, panic making it hard to get the words out. He ended the call, dropped his phone on the seat and wrenched the steering wheel to make a U-turn. Then he slammed his foot down on the accelerator.

ROBIN FROZE, HANDS outstretched but not yet touching Jacob. Could she have imagined what she thought she saw?

No.

Mouth dry, she whispered, "Michael."

He swiveled toward her, going to alert just from what he'd heard in her voice.

"Someone's outside."

He rose soundlessly, pulled his gun and held it in a two-handed grip with the barrel pointing down. He reached her in a couple of strides. "You two upstairs."

She picked up her son and made sure he was looking at her when she touched her finger to her lips. "Shh."

He let out a kind of squeak and burrowed into her.

"Come with us," she whispered.

Michael nodded.

Robin placed each foot as carefully as she could. The hall felt like a refuge until she saw the raw holes in the wallboard they hadn't yet repaired.

She looked back to see Michael with his back to her, his gaze sweeping the house. She crept up the stairs rather than racing the way she wanted to. *Get Jacob in the bathtub. Call Seth and then 9-1-1.*

Or the other way around?

He might not have gotten all the way to town. Robin's thoughts had fragmented, leaving her with no idea how long it had been since he left.

She was shaking by the time she bent over to lay Jacob down in the cast-iron tub.

"No!" he cried. "Don't go, Mommy! Stay!"

She clamped a hand over his mouth. "Shh, shh, shh."

His teeth chattered under her palm. Freckles stood out on his face like dots made by a permanent marker. The terrible fear in his eyes undid her.

Hearing the squeak of a floorboard, she spun, almost falling over. It was Michael, right outside the bathroom.

"Got your phone?" he asked quietly.

Her head bobbed as she slid it from her pocket. "I'll call. But…what if there's nobody here?"

"Better safe."

Than sorry. Of course he was right.

Seth answered after one ring, his voice tense. "Robin?"

"We think… *I* think I saw someone right outside. We…we're upstairs."

"Dad with you?"

"Yes."

"I'm on my way back. I'll be there in about two minutes."

From town?

"Hammond called. Winstead took off in his plane hours ago."

Oh.

Glass shattered downstairs. Jacob let out a cry and Robin jumped.

"He just broke a window."

"Lock yourself in the bathroom again," Seth demanded.

"But I can't leave your dad—"

"Do it." That implacable note in his voice demanded obedience. "I'm almost there."

She knew the call had been dropped, but said, "Seth?" anyway.

Silence.

SETH GOT ON the radio to demand backup. He'd have asked for SWAT except the team wouldn't make it out here in time to do any good. If he was lucky, another unit might be nearby.

That piece of scum had already been on the property watching the house, waiting until the inhabitants gave him an opening. This time, by God, he wouldn't be driving away so he could take the podium in front of a bunch of businessmen to impress them with his ideas, passion for the underdogs, sharp sense of humor and make it seem impossible he was a predator with blood on his hands.

Seth's truck crested the hill on the two-lane country road at an unsafe speed, but he didn't so much as tap the brakes.

"CLOSE THE DOOR," Michael snapped. Bending slowly as if his joints hurt, he lowered himself to the floor. As Robin watched, he stretched out on his belly in the hall. That put him in a good position to see anyone coming up those stairs before they saw him. Only then he groaned and his face twisted as he tried to stretch his arms out in front of him with the gun pointed straight ahead.

Robin's stomach cramped painfully. He'd been wounded in his right shoulder. She'd known his mobility was hampered. *Could* he squeeze the trigger?

She crawled out. "Let me—"

He shot her an angry glance. "Get back in there. I can do this."

"Do you have another gun?" she whispered.

He stared fixedly at the empty space above the stair-case. "Gun safe in my closet. There's a backup." He reeled off a combination.

She looked back at the bathtub, unable to see Jacob without standing all the way up. This was how it would feel to be ripped in half. Go. Stay.

No. She couldn't crouch helpless in the bathroom while a wounded man in his sixties died to defend her.

Still bent over, she ran for the master bedroom.

A sudden, furious barrage of gunfire deafened her. Crying out, she dropped to the carpeted floor. That sounded like half a dozen guns. Richard hadn't come alone this time.

In the sudden silence, she crawled the rest of the way into the closet, twirled the dial with a shaking hand and took out the pistol she recognized right away as a revolver.

She pushed herself to her feet and hurried to the doorway, setting her back to the door as she'd seen actors do in action shows on TV, edging over to see the hall.

Michael hadn't moved. The wallboard and ceiling above him were shredded, but from the back he appeared unhurt and alert. With a moan, Robin got down and crawled fast toward him and her terrified son.

HALF A MILE. Quarter of a mile. Seth's truck rocked and swerved as he made the turn into the driveway.

He swore at the sudden realization that he wasn't wearing his vest.

God, had Dad been wearing the one Seth had borrowed for him?

That's when he heard a volley of gunfire. So many shots, it was like approaching an outdoor gun range.

He wouldn't accept that he was too late.

Sunlight glinted off windows that appeared unbroken across the front of the house. Hoping to draw the gunman or gunmen out of the house, he skidded to a stop in his usual parking place. At a fleeting glance, he saw neither movement nor any damage here, either.

Even as he shut down the engine, Seth bent over to get out, intent on shielding behind the door he'd just opened. He hadn't quite made it when the windows in the truck exploded simultaneously and he fell the rest of the way to the packed gravel.

Teeth clenched, he scrambled behind the rear bumper, forcing himself to regroup. It had been a while since he'd heard or seen what a semiautomatic assault rifle could do.

Crouching behind the truck, he lifted the hatch and grabbed his Kevlar vest.

In the act of reaching for a tab on the vest, he saw something that made him pause. Dark splotches on the gravel. Oh, hell. Blood soaked his shirtsleeve and dripped from his hand. One of those bullets had found him, and he hadn't even felt it. Still didn't feel it. He wiped blood off his hand on his jeans and finished closing the Velcro.

Judging from the earlier blast, Winstead had shot his way into the house. Did he already have Jacob? Seth shook his head. The only possible way that bastard could have gotten his hands on the boy they all loved was by killing the two adults in the house. They'd made it upstairs, he knew that. He wouldn't believe they were dead.

He knew from experience that the pain would hit suddenly. He hoped it held off and didn't blindside him. His Glock held in firing position, he crept along the passenger side of his truck, careful not to give away his position with a crunch of gravel. Being up against an assault rifle didn't intimidate him. He needed only one shot—the right shot.

ROBIN HAD REACHED Michael and the bathroom door when a second explosion of gunfire began. She dropped to the floor again, and saw Michael try to pancake himself. Since shreds of wallboard didn't fly, she worked out that the shots weren't here in the house.

"Damn it," Michael ground out. "I'll bet Seth just got here."

Suddenly sick, she felt sure Seth had driven up openly in an attempt to draw Richard's attention. If he'd died in the hail of bullets—

Robin wiped a wet cheek. "It sounds like Richard brought an army. Why would he do that?"

Michael took his gaze off the head of the stairs for a fleeting instant. "I don't think he did. Sounds like an assault rifle to me."

Feeling even sicker, Robin could only think, *Of course.* After reading about school shootings where teenagers had gotten their hands on an AR-15 or the like, Robin had been horrified when she first saw the two Richard owned. She asked why he had them and he'd said, *Because I can.* Imagine what the members of the Seattle city council would think if they knew he owned guns at all, far less the most lethal of them. That was Richard in a nutshell: the facade of being a compassionate man, an activist, that he wore like the too-thin crust of cooling lava over the deadly red-hot flow beneath.

"What can we do?" she whispered.

Michael shook his head. "Nothing."

So she crouched in the doorway to the bathroom, sweaty hands gripping the gun. And waited.

SETH FLATTENED HIMSELF on the ground beside the front fender of the truck. He'd see legs and feet if that piece of scum appeared around the corner of the house. Winstead might be a crack shot, but he hadn't served in the military or had police training and experience. From the way Seth had barreled up to the house, Winstead must know other cops would be on the way. His window of opportunity was closing. He'd want to be sure Seth was dead before he resumed the attack indoors. Even if he was capable of patience, he couldn't afford it.

Unless he assumed Seth was down.

Or unless he really did already have Jacob and was even now fleeing through the woods to wherever he'd left his car. That ugly possibility and the complete silence felt like an itch Seth couldn't scratch.

His gut said he was doing the right thing. But a single glance told him he was bleeding like a stuck pig.

Another burst of gunfire came from inside the house. Seth jumped to his feet and ran.

MICHAEL ROLLED, GROANING. Blood. New blood.

"If you want the kid to survive," Richard called up

the stairs, arrogance in his voice, "you won't shoot.
You'll let me come up and take my son. Too late for
yours. He's dead, and you're outgunned."

No!

In horror, Robin saw that during the fusillade, Michael had dropped his pistol. He fumbled to pick it up,
but he couldn't seem to close his fingers. In desperation, he reached for it with his left hand.

The devastation of knowing that Seth was dead felt
like hearing the bone-rattling crack of thunder right
above her when she was utterly exposed in the open,
waiting for the lightning bolt. What Richard couldn't
know was that her unacknowledged grief served as fuel
to make her hate burn even hotter.

Robin rose to her feet slowly, still unable to see Richard. She braced her feet the way he had taught her.
Gripped the gun with both hands, finger resting on the
trigger. *Aim low*, she told herself, almost coldly, *assume
there'll be some kick*.

There was the top of a blue baseball cap.

One more step, she begged him silently.

He took it, their eyes met…and from the foot of the
stairs came a harsh command.

"Drop the gun! Now!"

Richard whirled, rifle still held in firing position.

She pulled the trigger, heard the *crack* of other shots,
and saw Richard fall forward and disappear. Three loud
thuds had to be his body bouncing down the stairs.

"Robin?" Seth called, sounding frantic. "Dad? I'm
coming up."

Her arms lost all strength and sagged so that the
gun pointed at the floor. "We're here," she managed to

say. "We're okay." And she crouched to set the handgun down.

Just as Seth appeared, his face hard and expressing the terror he had felt, she heard a siren in the distance.

ABOUT READY TO abandon Michael's old pickup in the middle of one of the rows of parked cars at the hospital, and who cared if it got towed, Robin finally spotted an open slot. She pulled in, jumped out and ran for the emergency room entrance.

They hadn't let her go to the hospital with Seth and Michael. "They" being responding law enforcement that included a couple of different uniforms and ranks from chief to deputy. She wasn't injured, so they expected her to walk them all through what happened. Anyway, they told her she wouldn't be allowed to take a child Jacob's age into a recovery room or to visit either man if they were put in intensive care or even moved to a room to spend the night.

Hanging on to her sanity by a fragile thread, she had told the whole story from beginning to end twice, and today's events half a dozen times. Interviewed in the living room, she'd still been aware of the flashes going off as a crime scene investigator photographed her ex-husband's body, sprawled over the bottom steps, booted feet up, head down.

She would never forget the sight of the man she'd once married dead from multiple bullet holes. Although thank goodness for Seth, who had carried Jacob downstairs, making sure he didn't see even a blood splatter. Except, maybe, the blood dripping from Seth himself.

She still didn't know if her shot had killed Richard or hit the body armor he'd worn. Hers hadn't been the only shots fired, though. Seth had fired multiple times, she thought, and Michael at least once. Whichever of them had killed him, she didn't feel the teeniest bit of regret.

Iris had been glad to take Jacob once Robin had been allowed to leave. Now she hurried up to the receptionist.

"Seth Renner? The detective?"

"And you are?"

"Robin Hollis. I'm living with him and his father," she said simply. "The investigators held me up to take my account of what happened."

"Let me check."

Two minutes later, she returned. "Mr. Renner senior is still here in the ER, but Detective Renner was taken to surgery. I show him as being in recovery now."

Robin asked if she could see Michael, and was ushered through the double doors. She found a frantic man wearing his own pants and a hospital gown who insisted no one would tell him anything. They'd had to remove a large splinter—the four inches long kind—but felt most of his "discomfort" came from the previous wound. He'd been to X-ray and was now waiting to be taken for an MRI when all he wanted was to know how his son was.

With his blessings, she rushed to the surgical suite, where she had to wait for a maddening fifteen minutes before she was permitted to see Seth.

Half-sitting up in bed, he was crunching on ice chips. He looked both wonderful and awful, woozy, his skin pasty and his hair lank—but alive. Awake. His expression lightened the minute he saw her, and he reached out his good hand.

Robin latched onto it. "They removed a bullet?"

"No, just had to do some repair work," he said

grumpily. "They didn't even have to use full anesthesia. I'm not in a daze, and I want out of here."

She leaned over and kissed his scratchy cheek. "Your father is just as crabby."

He demanded to know what had been happening, so she told him about the questioning, about taking Jacob to Iris's and what she knew about his father's condition.

Then he focused on her in that way he had. "Are you all right, Robin?"

Her smile turned tremulous, but she said, "Yes. It was horrible and scary, but…"

"It's all over."

"My knees keep wobbling, but at the same time I feel as if I can take a full breath for the first time in years. If you hadn't stopped me from taking off…"

"I did a lousy job protecting you." His voice was bleak, his eyes unflinching. "If Hammond hadn't called, I don't know whether I'd have turned around and gotten back in time."

"I thought you were dead." The memory was so vivid, for a fleeting moment he *was* dead. The memory of her shock and horror was that real. "I thought…" Her throat clogged.

"You believed him?" For all his postsurgery state and self-imposed guilt trip, Seth pulled a grin from somewhere. "No faith in me at all."

Cheeks wet, she leaned over to press her face to the white blanket over his chest. His heart beat strongly, his chest rose and fell. "I hope I killed him," she mumbled.

"No." He stroked her hair, his voice a rumble that was somehow also soft. "You saw plenty to give yourself years of nightmares. You don't need more on your conscience."

Impatient with herself, she wiped away tears and

reared up. "Why would it be on my conscience? He intended to kill *us*, and then steal Jacob. Abuse him, hit him—" Robin choked on the rest. What would Richard have turned her sunny-natured child into? It didn't bear thinking about.

"Okay." Seth ran his knuckles over her jaw, his expression so tender her eyes burned again. "Have you called home yet?"

She stared at him. "What?"

"Bet your mother would like to hear from you. Your sister, too. They'll get to meet Jacob at last." Then he smiled crookedly, his eyes clearer than they'd been. "They can let the doctors know to schedule that surgery."

"I had to see you." Actually, the thought of calling home hadn't even crossed her mind yet. But if it had... she would still have raced right to the hospital.

Seth captured her hand again. Suddenly he looked uncertain. "You'll stay in Lookout, won't you? I mean, after you visit your family. You have to know I'm in love with you."

"I'm in love with you, too." Her vision was annoyingly blurry. "Damn it, you're turning me to mush."

"Good." This smile blazed with happiness. "C'mere." He tugged, and she went.

Normally Robin would have wondered how he could kiss like this with a cocktail of drugs still in his bloodstream and a heavily bandaged arm. As it was, all she could do was kiss him back. Starting gentle, they took the leap into passion. If he'd been in a private room, they might have gotten really serious, or as serious as his blood loss allowed. As it was... Robin broke away to rest her head against his shoulder.

His hand played in her hair, and his chest rose and

fell with each breath. Robin felt impossibly young. No, that wasn't quite it, she decided, finally identifying a long unfamiliar emotion.

Hope.

Epilogue

On a sunny July afternoon, Robin's small family bar-becued and celebrated in her mother's backyard. The sun shone, Mom's treasured roses bloomed brilliantly, Seth flipped burgers on the ancient Weber grill set up on the patio and Jacob had just collapsed in the shade after running in circles until he was too dizzy to stand.

Having refused help beyond Seth's contribution, Mom bustled in and out of the house carrying food and dishes. Her cheeks looked a little pinker than the warm day justified, possibly because Michael smiled every time he saw her.

Robin and Allie lay back comfortably in match-ing chaise lounges. Sunlight and shade flickered over them when the breeze moved the leaves of the flower-ing cherry tree. Robin wore a strapless sundress, Allie shorts and a polo shirt that hid her dialysis catheter and port, but let Robin see how frail her sister had become.

"You know I'm going to lose my best reading time," Allie commented lazily.

Robin turned her head to grin at her. "Dialysis was so relaxing?"

Allie laughed. "I just figure I should add a cloud so the silver lining isn't too dazzling."

The surgery was scheduled for tomorrow. By the end of the day, Robin would be short one kidney, and Allie would finally have a healthy, functioning one. Sometimes Robin still had trouble believing they'd gotten this far. And as she did every time she had that thought, she looked toward Seth. Her savior, her lover, her fiancé.

He'd asked to adopt Jacob, who would soon have a grandfather as well as a grandmother.

The smile he gave her was warm, sexy…and a promise.

He set down the plate of burgers on the table and raised his voice. "Come and get it."

Jacob leaped and ran straight to him. Seth scooped him up, gave him an exceptionally gentle airplane ride and plopped him into his booster seat.

Feeling as if she could float to the table like dandelion fluff, she instead rose to her feet and held out her hand for her sister's. "Enjoy this. I think you're about to find out if hospital food stinks as much as I hear it does."

Allie smiled with simple delight. "Small price to pay."

"You're right." They hugged, found their places at the picnic table and started to dish up.

* * * * *

COMING SOON!

We really hope you enjoyed reading this book. If you're looking for more romance, be sure to head to the shops when new books are available on

Thursday 13th June

To see which titles are coming soon, please visit

millsandboon.co.uk/nextmonth

MILLS & BOON

Want even more
ROMANCE?

Join our bookclub today!

'Mills & Boon books, the perfect way to escape for an hour or so.'

Miss W. Dyer

'Excellent service, promptly delivered and very good subscription choices.'

Miss A. Pearson

'You get fantastic special offers and the chance to get books before they hit the shops'

Mrs V. Hall

**Visit millsandbook.co.uk/Bookclub
and save on brand new books.**

MILLS & BOON